What Re

Acknowledgement to my wife Alice Windus-Ansaldi
my advisor through my writing.

A Run to the Dark Side weaves a story of a young Bronx boy through his challenging childhood, the Vietnam War and the aftershock. The delicate threads illustrate a compelling tale of love, loss and resiliency that will surprise the reader with unexpected ironic twists until the last page.

A sequel is essential to satisfy the question of what happens next!

—Patricia Petillo Whyte,
Greenwich Village, New York

A captivating teary-eyed story about a lonely Bronx boy turned hero. This Bronx saga will draw the reader in and beckon them to flip the pages.

—Marian Bendoni,
a Bronx native

This story is an emotional cardiogram of a broken heart and the tenacious aftermath.

—John Michael, Editor-retired,
Da Bronx, New York

Politically incorrect in many spots this book actually projects a realism that was part of Bronx life in the 50's and 60's. Be prepared to clean out your tear ducts.

—Michael Paul, Millbrook,
New York

A RUN TO THE
DARK SIDE

A RUN TO THE DARK SIDE

VINCE ANSALDI

gatekeeper press

Columbus, Ohio

This book is a work of fiction. The names, characters and events in this book are the products of the author's imagination or are used fictitiously. Any similarity to real persons living or dead is coincidental and not intended by the author.

A Run to the Dark Side

Published by Gatekeeper Press
2167 Stringtown Rd, Suite 109
Columbus, OH 43123-2989
www.GatekeeperPress.com

The cover design, interior formatting, typesetting, and editorial work for this book are entirely the product of the author. Gatekeeper Press did not participate in and is not responsible for any aspect of these elements.

ISBN (paperback): 9781642379464
eISBN: 9781642379471

FOR
MY BROTHER JOE

A

simplistically

written

complicated

story

FORWARD

Now York City is home to the largest population of Italian Americans in the United States. The largest influx of Italian immigrants started in the late 19th and early 20th centuries.

East Harlem in Manhattan would become the first New York City neighborhood to be settled by large numbers of Italian immigrants and was appropriately dubbed "Little Italy." The population of the Lower East Side's Mulberry Street soon followed and another "Little Italy" was born.

In the 1930s, East Harlem was over-crowded with Italian-American immigrants living in run-down tenements and apartment buildings in poor ethnic neighborhoods. These immigrants were employed as semi-skilled and unskilled laborers. Most worked with a pick and shovel, loading wheelbarrows or as brick and stone laying masons. Others toiled in the kitchens of swanky restaurants.

Prohibition had a great influence on the rise of organized crime in the Italian communities. The traditional old-fashioned Italian criminals known as "Mustache Pete's" way of doing business soon gave way to the rising young Sicilian-Americans known as the "Young Turks." The older Mustache Pete's primarily extorted money and goods from other Italians in return for protection. The protection was from them and a well-bribed police department. The younger members desired to work with the already established Jewish and Irish gangs. This presented a much better opportunity to earn large sums of money without fleecing their own heritage.

They made huge profits from the distribution and sale of illegal alcohol enabling them to buy the protection they sought. The Mafioso, as they were called, made up less than one tenth of one percent of the Italian-American population. They became known for their boldness and bravado. Although small in numbers, the Mafioso was a malignant cell to the reputation of law-abiding Italian-Americans. During that time Americans saw Italians as a poor fit for democratic citizenship. The actions of the Mafioso had most Americans believing that all Italians were prone to violence. In the early 1900s, it was not uncommon for employers to boldly tell Italian immigrants seeking work, "We don't hire Italians."

World War II created a strong feeling of nationalism in the United States. Italian immigrants who were not yet U.S. citizens were viewed as "enemy aliens." President Franklin D. Roosevelt wisely sought Italian American support for the war effort and lifted that designation on Columbus Day 1942. Astonishingly, a half-million Italian Americans served in the U.S. military during World War II. Many had to fight on the same soil where their parents were born.

When the war ended, many Italian-Americans developed their own businesses. Construction, restaurants, paving and carting companies were owned by Italian-Americans. Many of these businesses prospered by creating jobs for other

Italians. Sadly, the veil of the malignant cell known as the Mafia often overshadowed the legitimacy of their success. If an Italian owned a small but successful business of any venture. he was considered suspect, someone to watch closely. If the business grew in size, the owner was deemed to be "connected." They would fall under the constant scrutiny of the FBI and the IRS. Simply put, if you made a good living and your last name ended in a vowel, you were suspected of being a Mafia-connected criminal.

Successful Italian-American businessmen and professionals moved to good solid neighborhoods. They socialized and befriended their American neighbors. Their children were sent to prominent colleges where they earned degrees in law and medicine. They married outside their Italian heritage. Yet the malignant cell was ever so present in the shadows of their refinement. If an Italian girl married an Irishman at an expensive venue, the father of the bride had to be "connected." An expensive honeymoon? Someone's "connected." The christening of a child was held at a fine Italian restaurant? They're "connected." The stigma had developed an untiring stamina.

During the 1960s and 70s Italian-Americans slowly assimilated into the fabric of the great American society. Well-to-do Italians moved to the suburbs where they were more influenced by American culture. The stigma of the "Mafia-connection" on everyday blue-collar Italians was finally beginning to fade. Unfortunately, high profile Italian-American businessmen who legitimately amassed great sums of money continued to be suspected of the "Mafia-connection."

In the early 1980s the malignant cell of the Italian-American reputation was cast into remission when a diverse ethnic group of New York voters overwhelmingly elected an Italian-American to the highest office of the Empire State.

PART 1

It ain't a crime if you don't get caught.
—*The House of Pain*

CHAPTER 1

In July, 1933 New York City mobsters were entrenched in a savage power struggle to gain territorial control of East Harlem. As the Great Depression worsened, nickel and dime gambling in the daily numbers racket became the only hope for the downtrodden. The morbid streets of East Harlem were painted red by the Sicilian Mafia with the blood of their enemies. The popular penny ante number game once owned by the black hoodlums of Harlem was now in their control.

Ten-year-old Francis DeRosa was awakened by the sound of gunshots echoing off the brick courtyard walls behind his East Harlem tenement. He rolled his body out of bed and on to the safe- haven of the wooden floor where a stray bullet couldn't find him. Slowly he made a serpentine crawl as his boney elbows dragged him to the rear window. He knelt, nervously peeking out through the corner of the yellowed cigarette-stained lace curtains searching for the shooter.

The silhouette of a man suddenly appeared from the shadows of the courtyard made barely visible by the dim luster of the quarter-moon. Two victims lay motionless on the concrete walkway exiting the courtyard. The shooter moved hurriedly toward them, making his escape. He stopped by the bodies. Mindlessly he shot four more times, two shots in each of their heads. Death was certain. Young Frank watched as the gunman ran. He knew his build, the shape of his head, the bushy hair and his familiar gait. Mostly he recognized the blue shirt he had given him for his birthday. It was his older brother Nick.

In a few brief seconds two men had forfeited their existence to the life-style they had chosen. Frank's bedroom door burst open as his panic-stricken parents checked on their son. They embraced his shaken body, inquiring if he was okay. Carefully, his father peeled back the side of the curtains to view the courtyard from his fifth floor apartment. He could plainly see the lifeless bodies saturated in their own blood. "Frankie, did you see anything?" he asked in a demanding voice.

Frank loved his brother Nick, a high-school drop-out. In his junior year, Nick had beat up a teacher so badly he had to be hospitalized. The wild teenager was imprisoned for eighteen months. While in prison, his fearless fighting skills gained him favor with the older, Mob-connected inmates. He was offered a good paying job doing what he was good at, beating people up who didn't make their loan payments.

Frank was a different kind of child, passive and kind. After a few seconds of silent bewilderment Frankie calmly answered, "No Dad, just the two guys lying on the ground."

It was an awful lot for the ten-year-old kid to absorb in a few seconds. He was now certain that his nineteen-year-old brother was more than just a rumored number runner. He was a mobster hit man, a murderer. That night, the young innocent child tossed and turned, knowing he'd lied to his parents. This would be the first of many sleepless nights. Going to confession was eminent. He hoped the Priest wouldn't ask him what he'd lied about. If asked, he would be forced to lie again. He could never rat on his older brother.

The sleeplessness induced panic and a renewed search into the future. His young heart nervously fluttered as he thought about the dismal future the mean streets of East Harlem offered. The youngster possessed a very common juvenile admiration for his older brother, but one thing became certain. He would never seek the life his brother had chosen. At ten, he'd already become a skilled swimmer, unmatched by his peers. Swimming cleansed his mind of troublesome thoughts, and like a prescribed narcotic, momentarily erased his fears. That night, young Frank's hope conquered his fears as he set his sights on becoming an Olympic swimmer. He was old enough to know that, without hard work, dreams could fade into regret.

Frank had learned to swim at age four while on vacation in Putnam Lake, New York. At six he became the youngest member of the East Harlem Boys' Club. His first swimsuit was purchased at the second-hand store on 125th street. The moth-eaten second-hand Kelly green swimsuit displayed a large shamrock on the front. If that didn't discourage an Italian kid from swimming in public, nothing would.

Frightened by his brother's destiny, Frank mapped out a training plan the very next day. In spite of his young age, he'd already mastered swimming the length of the pool. His confidence overshadowed any fear about the ten foot depth at the far end of the pool. By age ten, he developed a lust for dare-devilish dives as he courageously pushed himself to the limit.

Rod Tobin, an Olympic silver medalist, was the senior swimming instructor of the touted East Harlem Boy's Club. Rod tutored the young over-zealous boy, and massaged his raw, unorthodox movements into Olympian perfection. Slowly and with great determination, the young dare-devil improved at every stroke. By age ten, he was recognized as the club's premium diver.

Francis rapidly learned the benefits of aerobic exercise on the heart. Convinced that running would improve his stamina and the ability to swim under water, he became an obsessive runner. Only a brief childhood illness could prevent the youngster from swimming and running; he became an addict for physical fitness. He started running one mile before swimming and two miles thereafter. People from every venue of the Boys Club rallied to poolside to marvel at the dare-devil youngster. By age twelve, he had developed a pattern of running ten miles a day, which allowed him to hold his breath for two minutes.

In 1936, Frank celebrated his thirteenth birthday just as the Great Depression made life harder and harder for the low-income tenement dwellers of East Harlem. His father worked two menial jobs and gladly drove a limo for a funeral company to make extra money. Frank's parents quietly endured many nights of self-denial but never failed to provide for their children, Maria and Frank. After serving his prison sentence, Nick moved into a furnished-room above the bar his mobster boss owned. He visited his parents rarely but always had a rubber-band-bound roll of cash for his mother. Grateful for his much-needed generosity, she refused to see the path her oldest son had chosen. Surviving the Great Depression required individual sacrifice, but Frank never gave up on his dream of becoming an Olympic swimmer.

In the early summer of that year, Rod Tobin invited Doctor Jacobs, the principal of the Columbia Prep School for Boys, and his Athletic Director, Mr. Thompson, to observe the unique dare-devilish swimming skills of the young Frank Derosa. Accustomed to being the center of attraction, the boy paid little attention to the two well-dressed men who seemed impressed by his every move.

The lauded 94th Street Columbia Prep School for Boys educated the children of Manhattan's elite. Parallel to the school's scholastic achievements was its highly reputable swimming team. A school's current student population often mandated the success of any athletic endeavor. Mr. Thompson was a high-spirited, encouraging, swimming coach but was unable to find a star swimmer, someone who could rally his team past the semi-finals. The reputation of the school would be exalted if he could bring home a National Championship.

Dr. Jacobs, a Harvard graduate, was pragmatic and straight-forward. He said to Rod Tobin, "I have to have this kid enroll in Columbia. I've been around the block more than once and I've never seen anyone like him. I want to speak to him."

Tobin's face became expressionless as he coldly remarked, "Just so you know, he's an unrefined street kid, so be prepared. Don't become dismayed if he doesn't tell you exactly what you want to hear."

The tall, slim doctor's grin grew wider as he touted, "And that lack of refinement is another reason the boy has to come to Columbia."

Tobin made the introduction as Doctor Jacobs and Mr. Thompson shook the young boy's hand. Doctor Jacob's face was rapturous with enthusiasm as he said, "We observed you swimming and diving for less than ten minutes, and Mr. Thompson, my swimming coach and I have come to an immediate agreement. We want to offer you a scholarship to our prep school. It's one of the finest in the country. You would get a great education, but more importantly, we believe that you could lead our swimming team to a National Championship."

The words didn't register until Frank's young brain processed the words swimming and championship. Where else could he go to school and swim every day? But the youngster was prone to distrust. His father and his eldest brother Nick constantly preached, "Non fidarti di nessuno," "Never trust anyone."

Frank's deep dark Italian eye's darted between Jacobs and Thompson, occasionally resting on Tobin's face as to seek some instant advice. As Tobin remained silent he shrugged and said, "I'll think about it. I'll let Rod know in a day or two."

When Frank arrived home, it was dinnertime. It was a Wednesday; dinner was an English muffin pizzas made from day-old muffins, left over tomato sauce, and a small amount of the precious dried Romano cheese. Frank told his parents about meeting Dr. Jacobs and Mr. Thompson from the prestigious Columbia Prep School for Boys. His parents listened dutifully as Frank filled them in on all he recalled. His Dad said bluntly, "It sounds like a great chance for you, son, but we don't have that kind of money." Disappointed, Frank lowered his head as his voice became a shallow whisper and he said, "Papa it's a scholarship; we don't have to pay anything."

His father responded, "But Frank how will you dress? I pass that school all the time and those kids are dressed like dignitaries. They ride home in limousines, for Christ's sake."

Unwilling to yield to defeat, the resolute young Derosa kid lugged his shoeshine box fourteen blocks to the 125th street train station the next Saturday morning. The busy station had a heavy flow of well-dressed businessmen who prided themselves on displaying a pair of glossy shined shoes below their finely tailored suits. It was the ideal venue for amateur shoeshine boys. With unwavering determination he sacrificed training at the Boys Club for a few Saturdays to amass enough money to purchase suitable school clothes.

His home-made shoe box contained polish, brushes to apply, brushes to shine, rags, and plastic coated playing cards. He learned customers became upset if the shine boy got polish on their socks. Frank brought a deck of cards and slid the cards between the shoe and the socks; any polish that accidentally missed the shoe ended up on the card, avoiding the customer's sock. He was often complimented on his innovative trick; sometimes that earned a hefty five cent tip.

After a long day of shining shoes a tired Frank Derosa painstakingly climbed the ninety stairs to his parent's fifth-floor apartment. He made his way down the long narrow corridor to the kitchen. As his empty stomach growled for nourishment, his senses welcomed the aroma of the fried garlic and onions. He embraced his Mom and suddenly found himself suspended in the air, spun in circles like a tornado-stricken weather vane. His over-powering brother, Nick, had stopped by for a visit.

The boys sat with their Mother at the oval metal kitchen table. Nick was well dressed, his hair neatly groomed and his face closely shaven. He looked more like a movie star than a gangster. His voice muted to a soft low register as he said, "So I hear my baby brother is being offered a scholarship to that fancy prep school down on 94th Street. Is that right, Frankie?"

Tired and hungry, Franky shrugged, saying, "That's what the principal told me, so I guess it's true."

Nicky's voice grew louder, more deliberate as he asked, "Is that what you want to do?"

Young Frank became nervous at the sudden outburst but nodded affirmatively.

Nicky glanced at his wide-eyed Mother as he said, "Then it's done. Someone in this family is going to make it big, and that someone is you, little brother." Nick struggled to conceal an erupting grin. Choking on his laughter, he said, "I have a good steady job. I'm going to buy you decent clothes so you can fit in with all those elite aristocrats. I don't want you to ever be ashamed of your Italian last name." Suddenly he thrust his grinning face closer to his mother's and said loudly, "You don't think there's a lot of WOP'S in that school, do you, Mom?" His mother blushed in embarrassment but remained unresponsive. Nick sarcastically commanded, "You put that shoeshine box in the garbage. Those days are over. You're a Derosa."

On the first day of school, Frank was given a home-made meatball sandwich and a piece of fruit. He was greeted by Doctor Jacobs, who provided him with a sketch of the school layout delineating his assigned classrooms. The doctor accompanied him to the first class, homeroom, where he was given his other classes and a schedule that indicated he had swimming class every day.

When lunch time came Frank became anxious. The cafeteria was adorned with upholstered chairs; fine linen tablecloths were draped over the bold dining tables and plush rugs graced the floor. He'd never been in such a fancy room. The hyper youngster sat next to Joe Collins, a familiar face from his homeroom. They exchanged names and began to eat. Joe was eating from a high-priced tray of cafeteria food. Frank was embarrassed to open his common man's brown paper bag. Other kids started to fill up the empty seats; it seemed everyone had purchased the expensive cafeteria food.

Joe Collins asked, "So where did you get your lunch, Frank?"

A street savvy boy annoyed by his lack of wealth, Frank replied, "My father has a master chef from Italy and part of his job is to make my lunch. He's old-fashioned and doesn't want me eating cafeteria food." Joe kept staring at the sandwich. Frank asked humorously, "Want to try it?"

Joe replied, "Sure, I'll try a little piece." Frank borrowed Joe's sharpened cafeteria knife and cut him a two-inch piece from the heel of the seeded Italian bread. Joe's American palate was tantalized by the flavorful Italian cuisine. This encounter gave birth to Frank's first attempt at becoming an entrepreneur. Every Friday, he collected money for Monday's lunch order. On Sunday night, he purchased meatball sandwiches from the neighborhood pizzeria, cut them in half and sold them for twice the price.

The swimming instructor spoke at the end of the school day, giving the boys instructions and rules of behavior for his class. Finally, the class was dismissed. When Frank walked out to 94th street, he saw a long line of cabs and private limos picking up his fellow students.

When he arrived home, his proud mother jokingly asked, "So how was your first day of school, Professor?"

Dryly he answered, "Well, they're all rich. I don't think any of them even know how hard people have it right now; they live in their own world. I don't even think they know there's a Depression going on in this country."

The following day Frank attended a special class attended only by the swimming squad. Mr. Thompson's face glowed with amusement as he studied the expression of the older students as they observed the young dare-devil dive.

In an attempt to become socially compatible with the elite of New York, Frank's Dad maneuvered to pick him up from school every Friday with the funeral parlor limo. Frank sat in the back seat and posed like the son of royalty, waving to his classmates.

At the end of sophomore year, Frank led his team to the New York State Championship. He was now accepted with great admiration by his fellow students. In junior year, he was voted team captain. Captain Derosa led the Columbia Prep School for Boys to a National Championship. His popularity with his fellow students became unmeasurable. Harvard,

Rutgers, and Notre Dame offered scholarships to the fearless daredevil.

His desire to become an Olympic swimmer never faded but fate had other plans for Frank Derosa. Unlike his brother Nick, he viewed himself as an American first, and then an Italian. On December 7, 1941, the Japanese bombed the U.S. naval fleet in Pearl Harbor. During the Christmas break, Frank joined the Navy. His parents were proud but frightened about their eighteen year old boy going off to war.

Nick Derosa was now part of a world created by ambitious powerful men, knaves of fearless demeanor. The organization had its own rules of governance. They refused to be governed by Ivy League college scholars who so craftily managed to sweet-talk and manipulate a block of voters to gain positions of importance. Most politicians were the sons of wealthy, dishonest businessmen who could steal more with a pen and a phone than ten men with machine-guns. They believed the U.S. legal system was rigged against them. Their world demanded respect. They were men of honor. Silence was their way of life. Dishonor and disrespect resulted in the forfeiture of life.

By age twenty-seven, Nick had proven himself a worthy member of organized crime. He prospered in loan sharking and gambling. His fierce reputation as an enforcer proved to be an asset to his growing loan sharking business. No one risked borrowing money from Nick Derosa unless they were certain they had the ability to pay. He was a rising star in the underworld of New York.

Nick was displeased that his kid brother joined the Navy. An ex-convict and two-time felon, he was unconcerned about being drafted. Unexpectedly he arrived at his parent's apartment to talk to Frank. He coaxed his kid brother to accompany him to the neighborhood bar that he now controlled.

Nick sat at a table in the rear of the bar, hidden from the eyes and ears of inquisitive patrons. He ordered the waiter to bring a champagne bucket of ice and six beers. They toasted each other and began to drink. Nick said sourly, "You're a big boy but you know t I don't approve of you joining up. You should have at least finished high school. I gave you plenty of money, didn't I?"

Frank's face became a purplish red as he nodded affirmatively. Nick continued, "No more sermons, you're my kid brother and I love you. I think the Navy is probably the safest branch to be in during an all-out war. Just be careful and look out for yourself. Capisce?"

Frank was indeed a big boy now, a man. He had a lot bottled up inside him, causing an aching need to vent. The time to speak his mind had arrived, as no man could be guaranteed to safely return home from war. This could be the last time they ever spoke. Frank's eyes squinted defiantly as he said, "You love me and want me to be careful. Thanks Nick, but what about you? Are you ever careful, or do you think money makes you immortal? When I was ten years old, I could have told Mama and Poppa what I saw you do, but I didn't. You were my brother and I couldn't rat you out. I looked up to you and loved you."

The comment startled the cool gangster. His face became bleached of color as he asked inquisitively, "Rat me out about what?"

Frank was still angry, but restrained his voice to a low whisper. He said, "I saw you kill those two men in the courtyard. They were probably already dead after you shot them the first time but you shot both of them two more times in the head. I don't want to come home from a war and find out my big-wig brother was assassinated. You can believe that taking numbers and lending money makes you an accountant, but you're a gangster, so don't preach to me."

Nick was unresponsive for a great length of time. Frank became anxious as he could read the twisted anger in his brother's face. Finally, Nick smirked and bitterly answered, "We're brothers but we're polar opposites. I hated school with all their bull-shit rules, but you loved it. Like a trained dog, you complied with their every demand. You're right, little brother, I am a gangster. But I don't think I had too many choices. Maybe I'll be dead by the time you get home but remember this; if it wasn't for me our family would be living on the street eating out of garbage cans. Papa is a good man and works two jobs but what you don't know is those jobs are part-time. I pay the rent and the electric bills and I don't even live there. Most times it's me that puts food on the table. Mama did a good job of sheltering you and Maria from the truth but now you have it.

One more thing, remember the guy who took Maria out and punched her in the face because she wouldn't fuck him? If you come home from the war and I'm still alive, I'll tell you what happened to that little faggot. It will make what I did to those two guys in the courtyard seem like a chocolate marsh-mallow sundae."

Listening to his brother's tirade, Frank was embarrassed that his youth and innocence had prevented him from recognizing his brother's devotion to the family.

The always respectful Frank Derosa bid Dr. Jacobs and his team farewell before leaving New York. On January 2, 1942 Frank Derosa boarded a train to Pensacola, Florida for his basic training. Impressed by Frank's courage and determination, Dr. Jacobs reached out to a Harvard classmate, a commissioned Admiral in the Navy. He briefed the Admiral about the boy's incredible swimming ability and asked him to be a mentor. After basic training, Frank was made a Naval swimming instructor in Pensacola. There he was safe and never found out about the influence of Dr. Jacobs until the war ended in 1945.

Earning a stellar reputation as an instructor, Frank was promoted to Lieutenant in 1944. He never pushed his men; he inspired them through example. His squad was required to run ten miles daily and hold their breath for two minutes.

Frank was a deep-thinker. He recalled learning how to swim in upstate New York when he was four. The frightening experience of learning how to put your head under water remained clear in his memory. He started to ponder; when we are in our mother's womb, we're surrounded by water. "Could it be that the earlier a kid learns how to swim the easier it will be?" Obsessed with this sudden realization, he jotted down drills a parent could do with their infant in preparation for swimming.

Getting the parents involved was a necessary ingredient to make his theory workable. When a parent took a bath, they brought the tot in the tub with them. Placing the child in front of them, they could pull the child forward and push them rearward. A game, he thought, you have to make it a fun game. In the absence of soap in the water, the child should have the head placed under water for short intervals. The parent could then stand holding the baby in one arm and turn on the shower ever so gently, letting the baby's face get accustomed to the constant barrage of water. Water would indicate fun and the infant would not become traumatized by its presence. His prepared thoughts went from tub drills to pool drills. Parent and child putting their heads under the water for brief moments were paramount in teaching the child how to swim.

In early 1944, the Lieutenant began working with Henry Armstrong, the six-month-old son of his Captain. Mrs. Armstrong was a dutiful co-instructor. Henry Armstrong astonishingly completed his first solo swim at ten months old. The magnitude of this feat was viewed as New Age thinking and earned Derosa a place on the front page of *Life Magazine*. When the war ended in 1945, the demand for his services became nationwide. He chose the colleges based on their geographic location to New York City where he lived. His success at enabling an infant to swim was the beginning of a life's work for Lieutenant DeRosa.

The young Lieutenant arrived home on Saturday, September 8, 1945, six days after the official end of World War II. He lugged his duffle bag from the 125th Street train station to his parent's tenement on 108th Street. There he was welcomed home by his overjoyed but sobbing parents. His sister Maria introduced Frank to her fiancée, Carmine Cioffi, aka "Meatballs." Cioffi was the son of "Rocco the Ice Man." He and his father delivered ice to private homes and small business owners in East Harlem. Their business thrived as they were the only ice dealers permitted to operate in that overly-crowded business oriented section of East Harlem. All of Manhattan's ice distributors were fearful to encroach on the Cioffi territory. The Cioffi's business was protected by East Harlem's newly ordained crime boss, Nick Derosa.

A homecoming party was planned for that evening at the 111th Street Bar and Restaurant, a building and business recently acquired by his brother, Nick. Informed that the entire family had travelled great distances, the young Lieutenant agreed to attend. Frank refreshed himself from the long ride home and wore his Lieutenant's uniform to gratify the wishes of his proud parents.

All the furniture in his parent's apartment was brand new. The once shoddy exterior and tired interior of the 111th Street Bar had received an expensive facelift. The young Lieutenant didn't have to speculate about how this all happened—he knew. Nick made his bones when he was nineteen years old. He was a good earner, a strong enforcer, and now an untouchable "made man."

Nick looked well. He didn't carry the appearance of an overindulging crime boss, a fat Mafioso. Frank was seated at the center table of the newly-refurbished dining hall as his relatives arrived from the five boroughs. He became fatigued from their sincere, slobbering gestures of love. They were a proud family of Italian immigrants who loved America. None of them could envision a Naval Lieutenant in the family.

Nick, the maestro of the party, also had to respectfully greet the guest. Finally he made his way to the center table. Frank rose to greet his brother. Four years ago, when Frank left for the War, his brother looked like a gangster. Now he was one. He had the swagger of a leader, a powerful man of authority. The brothers traded an appraising stare before erupting into laughter. They embraced and exchanged a customary European kiss on the cheek. Nick said enthusiastically, "Welcome home, little brother. I was really proud when your face made it to the front page of *Life Magazine*."

Frank concealed his dissatisfaction for his brother's newly acclaimed power but answered sarcastically, "I was really proud when your face didn't make it to the Post Office wall."

Unamused, Nick returned an icy stare as he softly bit the knuckles of his closed fist, gesturing his displeasure.

This was truly a once-in-a-life-time celebration. The most destructive and damaging war in the history of the world had ended. Thankfully, all of the drafted Derosa cousins made it home without injury. Nick hired a small local band to play Italian classics. The guests ate traditional Italian food and drank from an unlimited supply of expensive imported wine. The more they drank, the more they danced.

Nick firmly held his little brother's bicep and ushered him into the quiet solitude of his office. The office held a dozen small tables, each equipped with a telephone. It was unmistakable that this was the main policy room the street runners, "bookies," called to register their bets. The rules were simple and straight-forward. If a bookie accepted a bet and didn't register it, he would become responsible for payment. If he reneged on a winning bet, the house would make payment and the bookie would end up an unemployed cripple or dead.

The two brothers sat in the far corner of the room. As Frank outlined his plans for the future, he could read approval on his brother's face. Frank timidly asked, "Nick, if you don't mind me asking. How do you get away with this shit? Except for Sunday, all these phones have to be answered. That's a lot of people. It's amazing you don't get raided by the cops."

Nick smiled, exposing his lady-killer dimples and said emphatically, "Frank the average cop in New York City makes two hundred and fifty dollars a month. I pay the precinct Captain twenty-five hundred a month—Tax free. In return, I become a protected, hands-off operation."

Nick suggested the two of them return to the dining hall and join their guests. But Frank reminded his brother of the conversation they had prior to him leaving for the Navy. He bluntly asked, "What happened to Johnny DeMarco? You said you would tell me if I returned home from the war and you were still alive. So, big brother here we are. What happened to DeMarco?"

Nick returned to his chair and sat down. He was annoyed that his kid brother asked such a question like a nagging vulturine. He composed himself from the initial discomfort of the question and said, "I didn't want you going off to war in a ravaged state of mind so I sugar-coated what happened to Maria. The truth is, she did refuse to have sex with him, but he was over-powering and violated her. He was inside her. She became pregnant and I had to arrange for an abortion. Mama and Poppa were never told about the abortion, so don't let it slip. Now, before I tell you what happened to Mr. DeMarco, you tell me what I should have done. Remember, you were young and two thousand miles away."

Frank's eyes smoldered with anger as he digested the choking words his brother had told him. He cried out, "I think you should have killed him and I wish I was here to help you."

Nick was pleased with his answer and repeatedly kissed him on the head of closely cropped hair. Very softly he said, "I did, but before I beat him to death, I shoved a stickball bat up his fat ass. I told him it was a present from Maria. He cried like a faggot. I beat him unconscious with my bare hands and with the help of some spiked brass knuckles. I put him in a fifty five gallon drum with holes in it and dumped his ass into the Long Island Sound. Sometimes in a weak moment of contrition I think about how horrible it may have been if he was still alive. Then I think about what he put our sister through and I feel absolved from my deed. My soul is cleansed."

In October of 1952, Sam Corvo read an article in the *Daily Mirror* praising Lieutenant Derosa's success as a Naval swimming instructor. Sam and Frank had known each other from East Harlem and had both since moved to the Bronx. Sam contacted his old neighborhood friend and set up a private swimming lesson for his five-year-old son. They met at Evander Child's High School in the Northeast Bronx where Frank taught neighborhood children on the first and third Saturday of each month. Sam's youngest son, Daniello, was getting a one-on-one private lesson with the renowned Lieutenant, an extreme and unusual favor.

Sam Corvo married his childhood sweetheart Annabel Jantz, a German-American girl from Yorkville, in Manhattan, New York City. They resided in a two-family Victorian owned by Sam's parents in the Van Nest section of the Bronx. The home had a double lot, a four car detached garage and a garden, cherished by Sam's Sicilian father, Joe. A dead end street devoid of traffic and the cacophony of the city made it more rural than other Bronx neighborhoods.

The Corvos had three living children, Joe, Rosemarie, and Daniello, the youngest. Daniello's twin brother Sammy died at age three from brain fever, a commonly used laymen's term for spinal meningitis. It was a strand of life that was hard for the young couple to handle. Sam had endured the loss of his brother Marines during the war but was not prepared for the loss of a child. Annabel maintained a deep faith in God and was resolved to be a good wife and mother, dedicating her life to her family.

Daniello was an unusually athletic child, but he became morose after the death of his brother. The twins were always together and the child could sense something was different; he was alone. Annabel started reading her son stories to fill the emptiness. He loved listening to his mother's voice and he was able to read by age three.

Sam had to work overtime on the next scheduled Saturday so Annabel drove to the lesson. The Lieutenant approached the attractive mother and said, "You must be Mrs. Corvo, I'm Lieutenant Francis Derosa. My pleasure to meet you."

Annabel warmly smiled and replied, "Sam had to work today. Please call me Annabel. The Mrs. Corvo greeting makes me feel old." The Lieutenant laughed at the humor in her comment and complimented her youthful beauty in a gentlemanly fashion.

The Lieutenant sat Daniello by the side of the pool, instructing him to observe his head movements. He took the child by the hands to gain his full attention. He said," I want you to watch me swim but most importantly I want you to watch me turn by head so I can stay on the top and breathe." A quiet child, the boy didn't respond but nodded his head, indicating that he understood. The Lieutenant put him back in the water with the floating board. Daniello was floating on his stomach as he turned his head, but still required the Lieutenant's guiding hand under his stomach to stay afloat. The lesson was over and both the Lieutenant and Annabel were pleased. By the first Saturday in November, lesson four, the extraordinary five-year-old swam the length of the pool.

On the Wednesday before Thanksgiving, Sam Corvo and some of his fellow Operating Engineers agreed to stop for a few drinks at the Astor bar on Eastchester Road, a centrally located venue. John Chan, the oiler, was a key component in keeping the machinery and the job up and running. He was a pure professional. He was Chinese-American but the stigma of the war often caused strangers to erroneously mistake him for Japanese. John Chan was a proud veteran of the U.S. Army who fought on various fronts as a trained sniper, a skill he never spoke about.

It started to get near nine o'clock and one by one the operators started leaving to go home for the long weekend. There were only five of them left when a drunken and boisterous group from the Carpenters Union made their vulgarly obtrusive grand entrance into the bar. Big Sam knew one of the carpenters; they exchanged a nod of acknowledgement and wished each other a Happy Thanksgiving.

When John Chan attempted to leave, another carpenter spun his chair around and said, "Well, well, well look at what we got here, a real live Yamamoto Jap."

Chan returned a cold stare and briskly responded, "It's Thanksgiving. I'm not looking for trouble and if it makes you feel any better, I'm Chinese not Japanese."

The big mouth was Carl Pratt the local 21 Shop Steward who had earned a reputation for being a troublesome drunk. Pratt's drunken head was rocking like a wave as he slurred, "Chinese, Japanese it's all the same to me, a nip is a nip."

Chan was deeply insulted. The six-foot-two hundred-fifty-pound heavyweight towered over the slender one-hundred-forty-pound Chan. Slender in build, his wiry body appeared as if it were composed of stranded steel. Inspired by his size advantage and falsely encouraged by excessive alcohol consumption, Pratt challenged Chan to "take it outside." Chan was not frazzled as he returned an unfriendly stare saying, "After you, big guy."

They slowly exited the bar onto Eastchester Road as the drunken Local 21 sheep followed. Chan was standing in a boxer's stance, but his fists were open. Pratt screamed, "Here we go," and charged his smaller opponent. Chan propelled his limber finely tuned body in the air and kicked Pratt in the center of his flabby mid-section. As the breath exhausted from his body, Pratt folded in pain. The gentlemanly Chan waited for him to recuperate. Infuriated Pratt threw a wild, amateurish right hand. Chan blocked and grabbed Pratt by the throat like a vice. Gasping for air, his eyes bulged out of their sockets. A leg sweep would take the big man off his feet onto the cold hard concrete. Chan applied a painful wrist lock and placed his foot on the fat man's neck. Pratt was a beaten man.

Chan's narrow eyes were affixed on Pratt's beaten face as he spoke firmly, "This was not my idea. You misjudged me in every way. Is it over?"

"Yeah, it's over," Pratt moaned.

Chan continued, "I fought in the war on the same side you did. I'm a U.S. Army Veteran just like you. I may look different but I'm an American—just like you."

The crowd went back into the bar for a nightcap. Pratt drank coffee. Sam's curiosity took over; he turned to Chan and said, "John exactly what the fuck was that you were doing?"

Chan could sense the seriousness of this passionate question because no one had ever heard Sam Corvo use vulgarity, a very unusual trait for a construction worker. John responded," Well Sam, my Grandfather was a Kung Fu fighting master in China; he taught my father who in return taught me, my brothers and even my sisters. I'll teach my little one as soon as he is older."

Sam was an amateur boxer, and viewed Chan's skills as a sensational, almost magical, discovery.

When Sam arrived home that evening, the kids were sleeping. Annabel had finished her housework and was relaxing, reading a magazine. She greeted Sam with a kiss. "So," she remarked, "Did you and the guys have a nice time?"

"Well," said Sam, "It was the most interesting night with the boys I've had in a long time."

Annabel inquired "How so?"

Sam told her, "Sit down and I'll tell you the whole story." Annabel listened to every word; she couldn't believe her husband became so impressed by John Chan beating someone up. Sam told her that one day when Daniello is older, he was going to ask John to teach him his self-defense techniques.

Annabel replied," Do you think he will do it?

Sam said, "He did say it was reserved for family members, but I think it's worth a shot." Finally, exhausted, Sam went to bed.

Grandpa Joe Corvo was eighteen years older than his son, Sam. At six foot two, he was deemed tall for a Sicilian.

His unblemished skin and steel blue eyes misled many people into believing he was Sam's older brother. Grandpa Joe was a master mechanic, adroit in rebuilding gas, diesel motors and any transmission manufactured in America. Daniello relished hanging out in the shop with his Grandpa. The child was always given menial tasks such as fetching the grease gun, moving the oil draining pan, getting parts and handing Grandpa his tools. At age five, he could identify all the sizes of the sockets and wrenches by sight. His favorite assignment was pushing the button to make the lift go up and down.

Daniello's brother, Joe, joined a neighborhood boxing club for kids. Joe was seven years older than Daniello and enjoyed sharing his newly acquired skills with his idolizing little brother. He set up a makeshift ring in the living room using four wooden chairs as the ring post. Sam had bought his sons sixteen ounce boxing gloves for Christmas. A cautious father Sam constantly cautioned Joe to control the power of his punches. Joe knelt down and his little brother wailed away. When he became overzealous and sloppy, Joe would tap him on the head. "Jab, jab," he barked, "stick and move, never stay still." He taught his little brother to jab, throw a left hook and to hook off the jab.

Daniello was quiet to a fault. He loved to read, which awarded him an extensive vocabulary for a five year old. That September, Annabel enrolled him in a Catholic school two blocks from home. He was the youngest child in the class but the only student who could read. Daniello's shyness and quiet demeanor faded when he was the only student who knew the answer. He relished being smart.

The following May brought the much-anticipated boxing bouts dubbed by the elders as the Smokers. They were dubbed Smokers because many men smoked cigarettes, and in a short period of time the gyms air would be draped with breath-choking smoke. The men of the parish erected a boxing ring and the eighth grade boys were summoned to arrange the folding chairs resembling the boxing venue of Madison Square Garden. Danny Corvo celebrated his sixth birthday that May and had been practicing with his brother Joe for over a year. He was overly eager to fight someone his own age and size.

All the Corvo's arrived early so they could secure a ringside seat. The Smoker started at eight o'clock and the youngest kids were wisely scheduled to fight first. Each bout was two one minute rounds. The timekeeper was schooled to cut the round short if one child was really getting badly beaten. The overpowering Corvo boy's fights were all halted in thirty seconds.

The final match was with a much larger, older boy. At the commencement of the second round, his exhausted opponent sat on the corner stool laboring to catch his breath. Danny was trained to stand between rounds, gaining a physiological advantage. The crowd cheered as the bell rang for round two. Danny ran across the ring, riveting his opponent with a merciless barrage of blows. The bout was stopped twenty seconds into the second round as Danny Corvo respectfully embraced his badly beaten foe.

CHAPTER 2

The young Corvo kid continued as the class scholar in the second grade. His refined but unorthodox boxing skills made him the much talked-about attraction of the annual Smoker. The chairperson, Mrs. Lutz, suggested he be placed in the older group where he would face a more challenging group of boys. Annabel shed her lady-like persona and vehemently scolded Mrs. Lutz saying, "You are not going to punish my son because of his talent. If they're all afraid of him, tell them to stay home with their mommies." Mrs. Lutz gracefully apologized and the unfair suggestion was dismissed.

Joe Corvo decided to stop training at the neighborhood boxing club. Sam told his son, "Joe, boxing is good to learn so you can protect yourself but you don't want to hang around it too long… eventually your brains get scrambled." He promised to continue working with his kid brother until the day came that he too would lose interest. He switched from boxing to running track with his half Puerto Rican and half Italian classmate, Jimmy Perez. Perez had a remarkably attractive younger sister, Judy. Joe became smitten with her unique beauty. His intention of impressing the young Judy drove his enthusiasm for running.

The two Corvo brothers became running partners. When Danny informed Lieutenant Derosa that he spent a lot of his time running with his brother, the Lieutenant remarked, "I'm really glad to hear that Danny, because without lung capacity you will never survive underwater swimming. At my peak I could hold my breath for almost three minutes. I'd go under while the new guys watched. After a minute they panicked. I would stay under until they thought I was in deep trouble or dead. Then I'd surface, laughing my ass off." The young innocent Daniello grinned at the Lieutenant's venial vulgarity. He continued, "Of course I would have to explain to them that the only reason I could stay under so long was that I had great lung capacity because I was a daily runner. So as you could imagine I didn't have any trouble convincing them to run."

At age ten, John Chan agreed to teach the Corvo kid his military style method of self- defense. He included his son Chris, his niece and nephew. Danny was loose, flexible and ambitious. Chan's rules were simple. He insisted they not talk about training to anyone. Never brag, never show off and only use your skills to defend yourself. He told the boys with implied consequence, "Everyone is busy and so am I, so we will train only once a week for two non-stop hours. If you complain, you will not train. You will be given homework. If you don't do it, I'll know and you'll be dismissed from the class."

At the end of the first session, Mr. Chan took an old worn skip rope from his gear bag and started to skip. He started out slowly. After a few seconds the rope speed increased, faster and faster to a vanishing illusion. He crossed the rope from left to right, determined to increase the rate of speed. When finished, he threw the rope on the floor, pivoted to his worshiping students and said, "I'll be giving each of you your own rope. It will be the appropriate size for each of you. Learning will be your first homework assignment. See you next week."

At age twelve, Danny could cross the rope from a squatting position, a feat mastered by few, including the seasoned Mr. Chan. His Grandfather encouraged him to become a proficient mechanic. In similarity to his speed demon Grandfather, he developed a lust for danger. The pre-teen welcomed the few dollars his doting Grandfather gave him but he understood it was bribery to keep his interest.

Annabel became concerned that her son never got the praise he deserved in school because perfection was expected of him. A simple man, Sam humbly preached, "He aims high and always hits the mark. We're blessed."

Danny had reached puberty and his hormones were raging. When he and his few friends reached that age, all their conversations included the unexplainable attraction to the opposite sex. They held secret beauty contests rating their female classmates on a scale from one to ten. Jane McNamara was crowned the beauty queen of the seventh grade with a rating of nine.

Sam and Annabel's pleas to coerce Joe to attend college fell on deaf ears. He graduated high school and worked on the assembly line for the Fisher Body division of General Motors in upstate New York. He was making more money than most of his friend's fathers, a motivation that scorned higher education. The plant was a working man's paradise for poorly educated people and paid a salary commensurate with the savage harshness of the work. The sheet metal structures were not air conditioned and were poorly heated, adding to the brutality.

Rosemarie adored her younger brother. A sophomore in high school, she was driven to Pelham Manor in Westchester County for dance lessons. She was blessed with a unique beauty. Her slender five foot four body was unmistakable, with long flowing brown hair, greenish-blue eyes and all the right curves in all the right places. The boys pronounced that on a scale from one to ten, the teenage goddess was an eleven!

June tenth, 1959 was the day of the annual seventh and eighth grade dance. The event was held in the school auditorium on the second Saturday in June. Attendance was mandatory. The intent of the dance was to have the seventh and eighth graders improve their social skills. The boys had to wear a suit jacket, shirt and tie, and the girls had to wear a dress of the appropriate length. The music was provided by a disc jockey that played forty-five rpm records from the stage. The kids were privileged to request songs of their choice. Chairs were set up around the perimeter of the auditorium for the girls. The rear of the auditorium had a soda bar that sold soft drinks and snacks; the admission fee was fifty cents.

Danny and his friends knew they had to attend but they all had one minor problem—none of them could dance. Danny's quiet shyness eventually gave way to his passionate desire to dance and hold number one, Jane McNamara.

He asked Rosemarie if she could teach him to dance. She said mockingly, "Why do I need to teach you, Mr. Einstein? All you have to do is watch and you'll get it." "

"Come on Roe," he pathetically begged, "I only have sixteen days and I don't know any of the steps or moves."

Rosemarie cuddled her little brother and said, "Sure I'll teach you, anything for my little brother." In three days he was ready for the annual dance.

Danny Corvo was slender in build but tall for a twelve year old. His facial features were chiseled like those of an older boy. With piercing blue eyes and a perennial tan, he gained constant attention from his doting female classmates.

When dance night arrived he was motivated; shined shoes a Windsor tie knot and a dark blue sport jacket.

He met up with his friends at the local candy store and they walked the one block to the school auditorium. They paid their admission and had their hands stamped so they could leave and regain entry. His friend Bobby remarked, "Look, what did I tell you? The girls are dancing with each other and all the guys are hanging around like a bunch of monkeys."

They all laughed but Danny was infused with a new level of confidence. He knew how to dance! He approached the adorable Jane McNamara who was sitting with her friends and said, "Hi Jane, would you like to dance?"

She smiled. Her voice became an artificially induced lullaby as she softly sang, "Sure I would love to dance…. but not with you." The eight grade boys chuckled, and the girls giggled but none were foolish enough to make eye contact with the hurt Corvo kid.

Danny's pride had been maimed but he was able to keep his keen wit. He stood before her at an intimidating closeness, bowed like a gentleman and sarcastically replied, "Thank you very much; I'm glad I was able to entertain you and your friends. Oh, I'm sorry, let me take that back, your faggot friends." He quickly turned, making eye contact with the suddenly silent cluster of eight grade boys. His eyes glittered with rage as he belligerently said, "Just as I thought—a bunch of pussy faggots." His eyes readjusted to capture Jane's attention. Suddenly frightened, she lowered her head attempting to avoid his expression of anger. Danny gently placed his index finger under the chin of the young beauty, forcing her head to rise and encounter unwanted eye contact. Jane's casual sarcasm mutated into fear as her tear-filled eyes requested forgiveness. Danny said coldly, "Who's laughing now?"

Danny hurriedly walked past the line of seated girls. He felt someone grab his arm; it was Amy Winter. She spoke in a soothing caress. "Danny, don't let her ruin your night. I would love to dance." Deeply hurt and suspicious of her motive, he abruptly pulled away and said, "Yeah, I know you want to dance, but not with me, ha ha." She timidly placed her arm around his waist and held his hand as they began to dance. Danny gazed into Amy's hazel eyes and now realized that he and his friends rating system had failed. Her eyes sparkled with brilliant animation and a new number one was born.

The DJ announced that there would be a fifteen-minute intermission and the next dance was to be ladies' choice. Amy told Danny that she was going to go see her friends during the intermission and coaxed him to do the same.

The DJ made his announcement. "May I have your undivided attention? All the girls are to stand in the middle of the dance floor and all the boys should find a seat against either wall. Its ladies' choice. When everyone's where they should be, I'll give the girls the green light to make their choice."

With everyone in place, the DJ played a slow ballad. He addressed the girls and said, "Ladies go pick your partner."

Amy swayed her way over to Danny, put out her hand, and they began to dance. Danny saw Ben Nolan, an aggressive eight grader staggering his way toward them. Spinning Amy in graceful motion he gave Nolan his back.

Nolan's fingers repeatedly tapped Danny's shoulder with annoying persistence, his breath reeking of tobacco and alcohol. "I'd like to cut in," he drunkenly muttered.

Amy repeatedly shook her head no, and whispered in Danny's ear, "I don't want to dance with him."

Danny ignored Nolan until he tapped his shoulder a second time and demandingly grumbled, "I said I want to cut in!"

Danny grasped Nolan's tie, thrusting his face closer until they were nose to nose. He grunted, "Do yourself a real favor and go back to your faggot friends and leave us alone." Corvo's face was twisted in anger as his harsh command evaporated Nolan's suicidal bravery. "Go," Danny repeated, and the intoxicated Nolan retreated to his herd of cowardly friends.

Amy gladly agreed to exchange phone numbers, writing his number on the palm of her hand. When she took his hand to write her number, Danny smiled and quipped, "You don't have to write it down, just tell me your number and I'll never forget." He never did. A friendship of inseparable structure was about to begin.

In mid-August, Amy's parents formally met the Corvo boy. Mr. Winter closely analyzed his muscular body and asked his wife, "Are you sure he's only twelve?"

She answered, "Not only is he only twelve, he's also the smartest boy in the class. When they were in the second grade, Sister Mary Dennis had each student read a page from their reader. She then asked the student to tell her in their own words what they read. When it was Danny's turn he recited the entire page word for word. He has what they call a photographic memory. They wanted to have him skip the seventh grade but his Mother wouldn't hear of it."

"Why?" he responded.

Mrs. Winter said, "Because he's the youngest kid in the class and she believed that would be robbing him of part of his childhood."

Mr. Winter paused to reflect on her answer. He replied, "Now that makes sense. Most parents wouldn't see it that way but it really does make sense."

In January of 1960, Danny Corvo was accepted into the Bronx High School of Science. Amy had blossomed into an attractive young woman. Her autumn brown hair was long, wavy, and lay casually over her slender shoulders, highlighting her hazel eyes and petite facial features.

Around this time, Amy developed a cough that persisted for over a month. It was the end of May, and most of the eight grade kids were still fighting colds and viruses. It was unusual for that time of year. Danny walked her home one afternoon and she complained about being cold. She had feverish chills. Her condition rapidly worsened, and two days later she was admitted into Westchester Square Hospital. Sister Delores started each day with a prayer for the speedy recovery of Amy Winter. In Catholic schools it was a well-established practice to pray for the sick.

Annabel knew that Amy had pleurisy, a serious lung infection that flooded the lungs with fluid. Sam informed Annabel that Mrs. Hoffman, the wife of a casual friend, Nelson, had died of breast cancer. He said, "The poor guy has five daughters. News like that makes me realize how fortunate we are." Annabel's eyes became flush with tears at such awful news.

The next morning, Danny ran to Amy's house in hopes of obtaining encouraging news from one of her parents. He waited outside nervously until he heard the distant church bell, leaving him ten minutes to get to school. Desperate for some news, he rang the doorbell. Disappointed that no one answered, he ran to school.

Sister Delores started the class in her usual low-key way. First a loving salutation of, "Good morning, class" to which the class responded, "Good morning, Sister," followed by the Pledge of Allegiance to the Flag. A prayer for the speedy recovery of Amy Winter followed.

At lunchtime, he returned to Amy's house and anxiously rang the doorbell, hoping this time someone would answer.

Mrs. Winter opened the door. She could read the distress in the young boy's eyes and said, "Danny you don't have to run here all the time; your parents will worry about you unnecessarily. Amy is fighting hard. She's really sick, and has a lot of fluid in her lungs. The doctors are going to try something new this afternoon; I'll call your Mother later in the evening and fill her in." She hugged Danny, gave him a kiss on the forehead and told him to go home and eat his lunch.

He did his homework, skipped rope, ate a snack and went to the garage. Grandpa Joe was always happy to see his blue-eyed Grandson. He would say with sarcastic reverence, "Hey good-looking kid, how are you doing?" He gave Grandpa an update on his friend Amy and shared his worrisome feelings. Grandpa administered a dose of encouragement by telling him that she was in a good hospital and the doctors there knew their stuff. "Today," said Grandpa Joe, "We're going to start work on that old Indian motorcycle and when we get it running and safe for the road, I'll teach you how to ride." Danny's face bore no sign of enthusiasm. Grandpa continued, "But you know it's going to take a few weeks to get her right. Also your mother and father can't catch me teaching you how to ride—they want you to be older." Danny forced a gratuitous smile, but remained unmoved by the very special good news.

Mrs. Winter called Annabel at eight o'clock, informing her that the doctors inserted a drain tube through Amy's ribs into her lung. The doctors were hoping to drain the infectious mucus, reduce the fever, and ultimately improve her breathing. Annabel told Sally Winter that she would continue to pray and believed that the doctors had a good plan.

Annabel's face smiled confidently as she said, "Well, Danny, it looks like the doctors have a really good plan; hopefully the fever will break by tomorrow." She explained the drain procedure and its purpose, adding that the doctors were optimistic. Finally, the boy felt relaxed and was able to sleep.

The next morning Danny left for school with a renewed enthusiasm. Today was the day he hoped to get some good news. He kept mulling it over in his frazzled head, "They have good doctors, they know what they're doing, and everything's going to be fine, fine just fine."

He waited in line with the rest of the class until it was their turn to enter the school. The bright early morning sun polished the façade of the old Church's walls of brick. The sky held an array of oddly-shaped clouds over the City. It was a Friday near the end of the school year; graduation was a few weeks away. The beautiful day beckoned for good news.

When they entered the classroom, Sister Delores wasn't in the room. Everyone knew that if Sister was sick it wouldn't be long before the Principle, Sister Andrews arrived to substitute. No one wanted to get caught fooling around by the ultimate disciplinarian. The class sat motionless in their hard wooden seats. The monitors opened the windows and the classroom door leading to the hallway. The class recognized the sound of the Nuns' long clanging rosary beads as they made their way up the stairs. The Nuns huddled in the hall like a bunch of plump penguins. Sister Dolores breathed rapidly, nearing hyperventilation as she involuntarily wailed. Something was wrong, very wrong.

Comforted by the other Nuns, Sister Dolores composed herself and entered the classroom with Sister Andrews. Sister Dolores told the class to rise and face the American flag as they proceeded to say the pledge of Allegiance. Sister Andrews intervened, her eyes swelled with tears, her voice cracking on every syllable. She spoke with a nervous stutter saying, "Today we must pray for the repose of the soul of Amy

Winter. She went to the Lord early this morning." The Nuns wept and the girls in the classroom screamed.

The boys pasted their teary eyes on Danny Corvo. His eyes darted from left to right as he hastily made his way to the front of the class. He muttered, "No, no, no." Sister Andrews secured Danny by the arm. The powerful boy detached himself from her affectionate grasp, shouting, "I have to go, I have to go." Hastily he left and no one knew his destination.

The troubled boy anxiously ran to German Stadium in Throggs Neck, a six mile journey from school. He sat by the water facing the Whitestone Bridge. He wept in desperate despair, unable to understand how everyone could be wrong, everyone, even those "really good" doctors at the hospital. He needed to speak to someone who could help him comprehend what happened and why. He boarded a bus to Westchester Square and ran the rest of the way to his mentor, Lieutenant Derosa.

When Lieutenant Derosa answered the door, he could see his prize student was morose and deeply troubled. The boy was shaking and wailing. The Lieutenant surmised someone in his family must have died. He embraced the whimpering boy and ushered him in to the comfort of his living room. He said, "Calm down, I can't help you unless you talk to me, tell me what happened."

The constant bawling impeded Danny's speech. He was on the threshold of hysteria. Derosa held him tightly to his chest. Finally, the distraught youngster grumbled, "Amy's dead. She died this morning in that fucking good fucking hospital. Why, why, why?" he cried.

The Lieutenant gave him a glass of ice water as he labored to suppress his own grief. Danny was sad and mad at the same time. He was by nature a fighter, a kid who would never give up, but who could he be mad at? There was no revenge to be had, no wrong to right and no fight to fight.

Danny rubbed his tear-filled eyes and asked his mentor the very difficult question, "Why did God allow this to happen?" Derosa, a World War II veteran, was prepared for the question but disheartened by his student's grief. His face winced as he softly whispered, "I've asked myself that same question over and over; every time I'd hear that one of the guys I taught got killed, I asked the same question."

Danny repeated the question like a puzzled child, "So do you know why?"

After a long deep breath, the Lieutenant continued, "No. No mortal man can answer that question, but I have my own theory. God created the world and everything in it, including people. He could have had total control over all of us like puppets, but he decided to give us free will. In exchange for free will, we are all on our own. We can choose to be good or we can choose to do evil. God does not control us in any way. Sometimes we're in the wrong place at the wrong time, or get a terrible disease, but God does not interfere. It's the price we pay for free will." Danny's eyes were pasted on Derosa. His sobbing paused as he waited for the conclusion. Derosa continued, "It's the only explanation I can come up with Danny, but you should never give up on God." Danny became despondent as he held his face in his hands and continued sobbing. The Lieutenant called his parents and drove him home. He would never be the same kid again.

Eventually Danny resumed training with Mr. Chan, and swimming with Lieutenant Derosa. It was early July and the Indian motorcycle restoration project was completed. His innovative Grandpa built a rack to hold the rear wheel off the ground, and that's how he planned on secretly teaching his grandson how to ride. The rear wheel would rotate as the rider changed gears, it could accelerate and slow down, but it wouldn't go anywhere! He taught him the basics of how to start the bike, give it gas, use the clutch, apply the brakes, and shift through the gears. Grandpa sternly warned his Grandson to always respect any motorized bike because one fall could cripple or kill you. Grandpa Joe's rear rack invention kept the family from knowing Daniello was learning how to ride.

In August, a seventeen-year-old mechanic named Paulie Nartico came to Grandpa Joe's shop to borrow a torque wrench. Grandpa became acquainted with the kid from the neighborhood gas station where he worked as a mechanic's apprentice. Grandpa Joe asked, "So what are you working on now?"

Paulie answered, "I'm rebuilding a two eighty-three engine for my fifty-six Chevy. I went to Drivers' Ed, so I got my senior license two months ago."

Grandpa introduced Paulie to Danny and they shook hands. Paulie examined the boy's physical appearance with great admiration, and asked, "Hey, aren't you the kid that always running?"

A speechless Danny nodded affirmatively. When Paulie departed, Grandpa said, "You know Danny, that kid is one hell of a mechanic for seventeen. He puts a lot of the older guys to shame. His trick is that he loves working on cars and thinks nothing of putting in a fourteen hour day."

Labor Day was approaching and Danny became tormented by the plan that he and Amy had made to always see each other when school started. He no longer looked forward to going to the Bronx High School of Science and meeting new people. He didn't care if he was smart, and the future was too far away. His parents understood his mood swings and tried to speak in a positive way. They wanted their son to see that he still had his whole life ahead of him.

During the first week of school, he made friends with a boy who traveled on the same bus and train. Alan Singer lived a few blocks from the Corvo's home. Singer, an American mix of Jewish and Italian, had already made up his mind that he was going to be a doctor. When asked what his plans were, Danny replied, "To graduate high school and get a job." Singer's Jewish up-bringing prevented him from understanding anyone foregoing college. Alan told Danny that anyone who got into Science was beyond smart and that in time he would change his mind. Danny replied, "Yeah, that's what my parents are hoping."

Daniello Corvo had to compete with some of the brightest kids in the city. His parents were pleased that he had good grades and credited some of his accomplishments with his association with the Singer boy. Summer had arrived and the anxious teenager lusted to ride that Indian.

He drafted a close friendship with the Singer boy and with Paulie Nartico. His only remaining friend from elementary school was Bobby K. Having three friends in the densely populated Bronx was not a note-worthy accomplishment. He clearly remembered Derosa preaching, "Most so-called friends are like rainbows; you only see them when the sun is out. A few times in your life you may get lucky enough to find a friend that's like a star. That person can illuminate the darkest moments in your life."

Alan Singer persuaded Danny to play handball as an added exercise. Alan, a quick-witted lefty and Danny, an overpowering righty, created a chaotic duo for the other teams. The sleek build of Corvo's superior strength allowed him to blast the ball with a wave of destructive velocity. The opposing team would shelter the back of their heads with open hands in fear of getting hit.

It was the summer of 1963; Daniello Corvo turned sixteen. He was five foot eleven and weighed one hundred sixty-five pounds. He possessed abnormally large hands and the coltish build of a prizefighter, more so than a swimmer or runner.

It was that old Indian motorcycle that forged a close friendship between the quiet Corvo kid and the flamboyant Paulie Nartico. At twenty, Paulie was four years Danny's senior. He worked on cars and bikes at his mother's house where they lived. The ambitious young mechanic was the go-to guy for teenagers and guys in their early twenties who wanted to get more speed out of their car. Grandpa Corvo was the go-to guy for the big boys who had deep-pocket money to purchase top performance. Separated by the reality of economic boundaries, there was never a conflict of interest.

Paulie knew the reputation Danny had earned as a fighter. His finely tuned physique and lack of commentary disheartened the confrontational bullies of the Bronx. Unlike other people, Paulie admired his quietness, a quality he did not possess. Paulie, a pleasure seeker, had an idea; they just had to convince Grandpa Joe.

The Nartico epiphany was twofold: first they would have to convince Grandpa Joe that the Indian should be stored at Paulie's, affording him more work space. The second part of his plan was tricky and illegal. The two boys had become close friends and both lusted to ride, but Danny was too young to have a license. When Danny rode, he carried Paulie's driver's license, but Danny was taller and had blue eyes. Both of the boys knew they couldn't continue to ride without Danny having a license; it would only be a matter of time before one of them got caught. In 1963, photo ID's had not yet come to fruition. Paulie had a friend, Roy, who was in the employ of a newly formed company named Xerox, the pioneer in document reproduction. Roy made a photocopy of a license, covered over the individual's information with white strip paper and inserted whatever name, date of birth, and physical description required. In less than fifteen minutes, he produced a valid-looking driving license of the day.

Danny was helping Grandpa Joe when Paulie arrived unexpectedly. The Indian bike was stuck in the corner of the shop, claiming valuable work space. Paulie asked, "Hey Joe I've been thinking, you always help me out. So why don't we store the Indian at my garage? I have one garage that's almost empty; the only thing in it is my bike and some snow shovels." Grandpa Joe glanced at Paulie, mulling over his sudden proposition. After a few moments of silence, a wide smile gained control of his somber face as he said, "That would be a big help. I can use the room but you'll have to drain the oil and gas when the winter comes."

Paulie forced an obligatory smile and replied, "No problem, you got it." The boys walked the bike two blocks to Paulie's garage. Part one of the master plan had been completed.

Roy, the Xerox kid, was a Bronx visionary. He'd already made up a dozen blank drivers' licenses. Danny Corvo's name, address, height, weight, eye color and date of birth were inscribed on the document with professional expertise. He could now ride his beloved Indian motorcycle.

With their plan executed, they had to be very careful on what days and times they chose to ride. Grandpa Joe rarely worked on Sunday unless he had a high paying "rush" job. Danny reserved Sunday's in the summer for swimming at Orchard Beach by City Island or playing handball. Paulie rode with anyone who had a bike and sometimes made poor choices with the biker company he kept. There were a few rogue motorcycle clubs in the Bronx and neighboring Yonkers in 1963. Occasionally Paulie rode with a small club that called themselves Road Dust. The President of the club was a thirty year old, six foot, two hundred eighty pound monster of a man named Eddie Parelli, appropriately nicknamed Eddie Gaga. Eddie Parelli lived up to his newly anointed name, Gaga, a New York City slang word for crazy.

Eddie Gaga was trying to grow his club and vigorously searched for prospects. The larger his club, the more power he could wield. A new prospect had to undergo the consequences of the initiation period to gain the right of passage to earn their colors. They hung around with the club members in servitude and were at their beck and call. Prospects were given assignments they had to carry out if they truly wanted to earn membership into the club. Some assignments were menial, like getting beer, whiskey, food, and filling gas cans. The high-risk assignments meant assaulting someone or stealing a valuable commodity the club membership deemed necessary.

On a July Sunday in 1963, Eddie Gaga took one of his prospects to the Wall Bar in the Bronx.

The patrons of the bar were older, working-class people in their forties and fifties. They all dressed in dignified fashion; the men wore jackets and the ladies wore dresses. It was a friendly, quiet place. The Bar was famous for its very generous portions of homemade roast beef and over-sized hamburgers. During the week, the bar attracted a variety of customers, most of them hard-working blue collar men. Big Sam occasionally met his father for lunch during the week, when he was excavating in the neighborhood.

The well-dressed classy Sunday crowd was uniquely different from the weekly working crowd. Eddie Gaga and his prospect appeared out of place and formidable to the uneasy Sunday patrons, and that was exactly what Gaga sought. He thrived off his tough, scary guy persona. The two shabbily dressed bikers sat at the bar and Gaga ordered two pints of draft beer, a roast beef sandwich and an order of fries. The small balding bartender asked the prospect, "Anything for you?" He shook his head in a slow negative fashion. When the food was served Gaga asked the bartender for another plate that he handed to the prospect. Gaga picked up the roast beef sandwich and dug his teeth in until his huge massive jaws were crammed full of food. He chewed his food with a cannibalistic enthusiasm. After a long gulp of beer, he pivoted to the prospect and spit the food onto his empty plate. Using only his fingers the adoring prospect picked up the chewed food, put it in his mouth and ate it. They repeated the stomach-churning act over and over again as the visiting patrons became horrified.

The pistol bearing owner came out of the kitchen and insisted they leave. Gaga was finished with his game. The prospect paid the bill and they headed toward the front door. The silent patrons were relieved at their sudden departure. Suddenly, Gaga dropped his pants, exposing himself and "mooned" the customers by displaying his over-sized fat ass. He laughed with outrageous enjoyment as he made his way to his gleaming Harley-Davidson. It was just another fun day in the life of big bad Eddie Gaga.

It was the last Saturday in July. Mr. Chan was on vacation, Grandpa Joe was slow in the garage, and there were no swimming lessons until the following Saturday. Alan, Danny and Bobby met at the handball court in the park. The south court was occupied, so they patiently waited to play the north side. After a brief wait it was their turn to challenge for possession of the court. The overpowering duo won on the first attempt.

During the course of the second game, loud whistling and catcalls erupted from the south court. The players on the south side were having their male hormones teased. The instant jubilation was sparked by the arrival of the beautiful Hoffman sisters. Three of the five sisters were taking their one-year-old niece to the park. The child's mother was the youngest of the girls, who was not yet fifteen.

The three sisters were profoundly beautiful but the youngest one made boys cross-eyed with lust. Intrigued by their beauty, Danny asked Alan, "Do you know them?"

He replied, "No, not personally. But they're the Hoffman sisters. There's a total of five girls. Sadly, they lost their mother a few years ago." Somehow Danny recalled his father telling his Mom about a man named Nelson who had lost his wife and was left with five girls. It happened at the same time Amy had died and the name Hoffman remained embedded in his keen memory.

When lunch time came around, Danny asked Alan, "How did such a young girl end up with a one-year-old baby?"

Alan jokingly answered, "Well, you see, there are these birds and these bees and sometimes they get together and call for a stalk."

A sweaty and hungry Danny grumbled, "Cut the shit Doc, do you know what happened or not?"

Alan was sincerely surprised that his friend had never heard all the rumors and stories that circulated the prior year. But Danny was a loner and such news would rarely reach his ears. Alan became serious as he asked, "Really, you really don't know what happened? You never heard about this?"

Danny said, "I heard my Dad telling my Mom about this young girl having a baby but that's all I ever heard."

Alan remarked, "Danny, it's time to play ball. I'll tell you the whole story tonight."

By four o'clock, everyone headed home. Danny, dressed in shorts and sneakers, went for his self-imposed mandatory six-mile run. After dinner the threesome met at the park. Bobby K was busy talking to a girl who had him smitten. Alan and Danny sat in the back of the park near the checker tables. Alan said, "Hey, I almost forgot. You wanted to know about Dee Hoffman, the girl with the kid."

Danny's eyes widened with anticipation as he said, "Yeah, that's right. What's up with that?"

Alan said, "Dee, the youngest one had just started her first year at Columbus High School. She had an English teacher named Mr. Kadesh. The thirty-one-year old prick told her that she had a remarkable talent for writing and that with a little extra help she could someday become a famous author. Dee loved to write and use her imagination and was thrilled to hear that she had talent. Dee's mother had died and the father worked two jobs to make ends meet, so there wasn't really any set time she had to be home.

"One day Kadesh convinced her to come to his apartment for extra help. The phony bastard seemed to be such a nice man and interested in her talent, so she agreed. He started to drink and kept telling her that she was beautiful and smart. He gave her a drink of soda that contained muscle relaxers and sleeping pills. When Dee woke up, she felt fine but it was nearing five o'clock and she told Kadesh she had to leave. Kadesh had raped the kid while she was unconscious, cleaned her up and pretended nothing happened.

"When she got home, she noticed blood on her underwear. Absentmindedly, she thought it was that time of the month. That night she felt pain and discomfort and told her

57

older sister, Helen. After the drugs wore off, she recalled having her period two weeks before. So where did this blood come from and why? The older sister took her to Jacobi Hospital where it was determined that she'd been raped. Mr. Hoffman called the police. Kadesh was arrested and is now doing time in Sing-Sing Prison. I know this is the only true story because my mother was the attending nurse. Anything else you hear is pure bullshit."

That Sunday, Danny completed his prize fighter workout and decided to ride. He and Paulie gassed up the bikes and rode east on Pelham Parkway toward Orchard Beach. Beach traffic was heavy, but that was the advantage of having a bike you could navigate through and around anything. They rode to the end of City Island Avenue by Long Island Sound, parked the bikes, and stood by the pier watching the abundance of summer fishing boats. Paulie lit up a cigarette and Danny pronounced him an asshole for smoking. He could not understand why anyone would put that poison in their bodies. Paulie, the mentally immortal twenty one year old, smirked and said, "Well, Danny there are a lot of people that think we are assholes just for riding a motorcycle!"

Danny grinned impulsively saying, "Maybe we are, but you do both so you're a double asshole."

Paulie bobbed his head saying, "Okay you got me."

Danny told Paulie what that scumbag teacher did to the Hoffman girl. Paulie became unusually speechless and finally said, "You know, sometimes guys like that get killed in prison. The boys in the big house don't like pedophiles. You know what's really sad? I don't care how pretty she is, no guy's going to want her, that's for sure."

Danny responded," Really?"

Paulie said menacingly, "Really, really? You got to be kidding. Who would want a girlfriend that had someone else's kid at fourteen? Come on, Danny, wake up."

When they were about to leave, Eddie Gaga and a few of his boys from Road Dust pulled up and began making a U-turn to get back off the island. Gaga nodded, acknowledging Paulie's presence and invited him to ride along, saying, "We're going to the Wedge Inn on the Post Road. Follow us." Eddie Gaga loved giving the false impression that he had control over a large gathering of disciples. Paulie accepted the surprise invitation to hang out with the bad boys. Danny was clueless about Gaga and his crew, and mindlessly followed his friend.

When they arrived at the Wedge Inn, Gaga and his boys had their bikes parked in a single row. The revered President of the club always parked first, as his minions followed like chickens in a pecking order. The big man parked opposite the side entrance of the Wedge Inn so he didn't have to walk too far. Paulie and Danny arrived last, and parked at the end of the line closest to Boston Post Road.

Paulie introduced Danny to Gaga and his band of criminals. Danny was alert but remained quiet. Gaga labored to tuck his tank top into the pants of his oversized waistline, and said, "So where are you from?"

He answered, "The Bronx."

Gaga asked, "Where in the Bronx?"

He replied, "Up the street from Paulie."

Unappreciative of his blunt answers, Gaga snarled, "And I'm supposed to know where that is?" Danny shrugged his shoulders adding to Gaga's anger. Gaga continued his interrogation, "How old are you?"

He replied, "Eighteen."

Paulie's street-savvy intuition sensed that Gaga had reached the end of his short temper. He moved closer to the angry big man and whispered, "Eddie he's a standup guy. He just doesn't say much. Let's get something to eat."

Gaga's fat belly bounced in time with his laughter as he sarcastically said, "Maybe we ought to nickname him the Mute?" Gaga laughed as his boys parroted his lead. Danny smiled.

Gaga and his boys ate fast. They ordered a six pack of beer to go and handed the check to Paulie. Danny raised his eyebrows in disbelief and said, "He expects you to buy their lunch?" Paulie mumbled, "I have no idea what this is all about. I told him I don't want to be a prospect or join his club. I just want to ride."

Gaga plodded to the rear of the line, stopping to urinate on the seats of his guest's bikes. His fat face emitted a sinister laugh as he yahooed, mimicking the wild screeches of a rodeo cowboy. The quiet Corvo screamed, "Do you see what that fat fuck is doing?" He bolted out the side door and hurriedly walked across the parking lot to the first bike in the pecking order.

Paulie pleaded with him to go back inside the diner. Deaf to Paulie's emotional request, Danny stood before Gaga's meticulously shined Harley Davidson and kicked it over. The bike crashed onto the pavement.

Gaga's boys erupted, "What the fuck!" Eddie Gaga was smoking mad. His fat face reddened with anger as he ran toward Danny. The young, experienced fighter knew that boxing with this monster-sized biker was not a plan of victorious merit. If Gaga grabbed him, he would be giving him the edge and allow his minions to join forces. But Gaga wasn't the only one smoking mad. Danny visualized his Grandfather shining the seat that Gaga had just pissed on. He said to himself, "It's time for the Chan Plan."

The infuriated Gaga assumed a boxer's position as he lunged closer to his smaller opponent. Gaga's wild attack was met with a well-placed kick in the front of his face from Danny's oversized motorcycle boot. Instantly, the fat bully was out on his feet. Overwhelmed with an adrenaline-infused rage, Danny quickly kicked him in the head a second time on the way down.

The unconscious Eddie Gaga hit the pavement, lying flat on his fat-filled belly. A long switch-blade knife was visible in the fat man's back pant pocket. Corvo's rage was systemic as he retrieved the knife and cut Gaga's shirt from top to bottom. He walked past Gaga's boys, displaying their Club President's cut-up shirt in his hand. They remained silent as he walked toward his and Paulie's bikes. Paulie revealed a pistol from the front of his waistline for Gaga's boys to see. Armed with brass knuckles, they panicked at the sight of Paulie's 38 caliber revolver. Danny then understood the reason for their cowardly inaction. He picked up the six pack of beer, opened a few cans, and used the beer to wipe the two seats clean with Gaga's shirt. He rolled the big unconscious biker on his back and draped the urine and beer saturated shirt over the bloodied, broken-up face of Eddie Gaga. Gaga had sustained a broken nose, a broken jaw and was missing front teeth.

When they reached home, Danny decided that his bike riding days should be held in abeyance until he could ride legally. While they waited for the bikes to cool down, he inquired about the gun. Paulie told him that he was not a fighter, but was never going to let anyone beat on him. He said, "Danny, I know you're a smart and tough kid but if I didn't carry that gun today those guys would have put the both of us in the hospital or the cemetery."

Danny replied, "It's been fun but the way I see it, it's time to give riding a rest. At least for me it is—you do what you want."

Surprisingly, Paulie agreed, "Yeah I'm gonna put mine away for a while too, but don't think that the fat man isn't gonna come looking for us."

Danny said, "Hey, I told him I lived up the street from you."

Paulie managed a smile as he said, "Now, that's a good thing. He thinks I live in Throggs Neck, which is eight miles from here." The following day, the boys drained the fluids from their bikes and stored them in Paulie's garage.

At the dinner table, Sam told his youngest son that he had good news.

Danny inquired, "What's that Dad?"

Sam replied, "Next weekend, I'll be excavating about three blocks from here up on Bronxdale Avenue. It's a side job for old man Civetta. I'll be using his machines and you're going to be my helper and man on the ground. He pays cash, and I'll probably be able to have you run the dozer." Danny had spent time as his dad's co-pilot, moving the joy sticks and pulling the levers, but he never dreamed of being the operator. He was at ease to know that this dreadful day had ended with good news.

CHAPTER 3

Labor Day weekend passed as Danny Corvo continued to delay making a decision about attending college. What he did know was that he had to stay in motion; sitting still was not a comfortable choice for his over-active mind. On Thanksgiving Day, confused and frustrated, he decided to go to the cemetery. He had to run at a marathon pace not to be late for Thanksgiving Day dinner. Confused and anxious, he went anyway.

Danny concealed his secret cemetery visits from his friends. It had been four years; most kids would be over it by now, but Danny Corvo wasn't most kids. His blessed memory cursed him into reliving events that others would have long forgotten. He took solace in knowing that if he needed advice, Lieutenant Derosa or his sister Roe were available to talk.

At the Thanksgiving Day dinner table, Sam boasted about all the professional training his youngest son had completed. He was a proud father. Paying accolades to Mr. Chan, he told everyone how he witnessed him defend himself against a much larger man all those Thanksgivings ago. Danny chuckled to himself, "Boy, Dad, do I have a story for you."

Alan Singer was dubbed Doc by his friend, Danny Corvo. He'd already been accepted into Columbia University's pre-med program and tried feverishly to convince his closest friend to register for college. Finally, he said something Danny would not forget. He told him that he could go to college part-time and still have a job. Doc was pleased when his close friend agreed to consider the option he proposed.

As the school year ended, the Corvo family orchestrated a block party to celebrate Danny's graduation. His parents agreed that taking the summer off would give him a well-deserved rest. Lieutenant Derosa had gotten married and he attended the party with his wife, Teresa. He offered Danny a job teaching swimming as his substitute two Saturday's a month. Danny was proud that the perfection-seeking Lieutenant was impressed by his ability. He had been under his tutelage for thirteen years!

When the guests left, Sam summoned his youngest son into the privacy of an unoccupied bedroom. His face was without expression as he said, "You know, Danny, a man couldn't ask for a better son than you and Joe, but I'm compelled to tell you something. I've been thinking all through this party. Yes, you should take off for the summer and work with Grandpa, but remember you're only seventeen and a lot of jobs require you to be eighteen. So don't think that when September rolls around, employers are going to be knocking your door down. I spoke to the shop steward but he says things are slowing down and maybe he could get you in the apprentice program in about a year."

A year seemed like an eternity for the anxious seventeen year old. He briskly responded, "Well, Dad I have seventeen hundred dollars saved up from working with you and

Gramps. I was thinking maybe I should go to college at night and take a few business-related courses."

"I like that idea," his pleasantly surprised father replied, "You know you're really smart and you should give it a chance. But I'll pay for the courses you take—that's part of my job."

"No way, Dad, I have seventeen hundred dollars saved," repeated the proud son.

Sam Corvo stared at his son in a deliberate silence. His face was as Danny had rarely seen it. He crimped his lips as his eyes squinted into a sudden look of frustration. Almost a minute of speechless silence passed. Finally his plump cheeks regained a glimmer of a grin as he said, "Danny, Joe didn't want to go to college so I gave him money toward a car. Your Mother and I are paying for Rosemarie's college and we are going to pay for yours, we planned on it."

Danny looked at his dad admiringly and said, "OK, thanks, Dad, but just remember I'm going to be rich one day with or without college, and you and Mom are getting every penny back with interest—a lot of interest."

Big Sam forced a smile and said, "One step at a time son, one step at a time."

On the first Saturday of July, Danny had to meet the Lieutenant to learn Coronary Pulmonary Resuscitation. All swimming instructors were required to learn CPR by both the State of New York and the High school. Danny paid close attention as his snap-shot memory absorbed the mandatory material. He received his certification after the eight hour course. Now he could teach people how to swim and he'd added another life-saving skill to his resume.

It was the third Sunday in August. Bored, Danny decided to go to Orchard Beach and spend the day swimming and getting some sun. Up early, he put his transistor radio, two towels, swimsuit and four pieces of fresh fruit in his backpack. Orchard Beach was a mind-cleansing seven mile run from his house.

While running on the busily traveled Pelham Parkway, he saw a car slow down and the driver offered him a ride. The car was driven by a tall blond guy named Kenny. Danny vaguely recognized him from playing handball. His passengers were three teenage girls of splendid appearance, and there was plenty of room for a good-looking guy. Thoughtlessly, the impatient Danny grumbled, "Thanks but I need the road work."

One of the girls hung out of the rear window, using her dangling breast as bait. She pleaded, "Come on just get in." Danny returned an expression of amusement but kept running.

He arrived at Orchard Beach at eight thirty. The beach was already starting to fill up and the parking lot was two thirds full. This was not uncommon for the end of August, as people from the Bronx and Manhattan crowded the beach to enjoy the last days of the precious summer weather. Danny camped out at section thirteen, a Morris Park hang out. In their juvenile Bronx mentality, section thirteen was the crown jewel of Orchard Beach, with its rock jetty and views of Long Island Sound. Diving off the jetty was never a good idea for an inexperienced swimmer or for young children. There wasn't a lifeguard assigned to the jagged jetty and "No Diving" signs were posted to discourage swimmers.

Danny changed into his swimsuit, spread a towel on the sand, and clicked on his transistor radio. Girls were always striking up a conversation with the good-looking blue-eyed Corvo kid. By the end of summer he wore a suntan that accentuated his wiry, ripped physique. Uncommon for a Bronx teenager, Danny possessed a tremendous respect for the opposite sex, a value he had learned from his gentlemanly father. He was always polite and well-mannered; even to the McNamara girl who suddenly had a crush on him. He had dated during his senior year of high school but was unable to find a girl that shared or cared about his interests.

When noon arrived, section thirteen was over-run with sun worshipers. Danny had camped out close to the jetty where he enjoyed the view of Long Island Sound and City Island. When he saw the outline of the quaint fishing village of City Island, the Gaga showdown came to the forefront in his keen memory. He could not afford to be careless. He knew that one day he and Eddie Gaga would stand face to face.

Four carloads of boys and girls in their teens and mid-twenties arrived from One Hundred Eighty Seventh Street; the fabled little Italy section of the Bronx. Their coolers were full of beer, soda, and bags of Italian specialty food from Arthur Avenue. The drinking age in America was 18, but you had to be 21 to vote. These kids were not interested in voting but drinking was a common priority that consumed their free time. By two in the afternoon, their accents became thicker as they became dangerously drunk.

Danny was getting ready to call it a day. His stomach rumbled, with the sound of emptiness, but his undeniable lust for the water compelled him to take one last swim. He walked onto the jetty and lowered himself into the water, avoiding the risk of diving into the jagged rocks. Once in, he swam underwater for a long time, stunning himself at the great distance he surveyed.

Some of the kids swimming around him from Little Italy didn't speak any English; others did but had a heavy Italian accent. Danny became amused as he listened to their comical conversations. Two of the boys, Tommy and Nicky, were clearly twins and spoke unaccented, perfect English. They were both drinking beer and unmerciful at poking fun at each other. Nicky had passed the threshold of intoxication as his slurred speech made a mockery of the English language. He repeatedly ignored his brother's advice and carelessly dove off the jetty. Tommy screamed, "Listen, you dumb bastard, I know you're a good swimmer but there's rocks and boats all over the place. Plus you're shit-faced."

Nicky slurred, "I'm shit-faced because I've been drinking. You're shit-faced because you look like shit all the time."

His twin brother responded curtly, "Fuck you—drown."

All the boys from little Italy were drunk and started to get annoyingly loud. The girls catered to them with a motherly tenderness, trying to avoid unnecessary conflict. Tommy continued to curse at his brother as he tried to halt his brother's reckless dive off the jetty. Every time Nicky surfaced, his fearful brother frantically started screaming, "Don't you see all these boats zooming past your head? You're going to get you head knocked off. You got to stop the shit." It didn't take long to prove Tommy right. After Nicky finished another bottle of Ballantine beer, he dove off the jetty and started taunting his brother and friends.

Nicky dove under the water to swim back toward the jetty. Tommy watched in great despair as his biggest fear came to fruition; when his brother surfaced, a small motorized rowboat clipped Nicky's unsuspecting head. The driver knew he had hit something but wasn't sure what it was. Fearfully he exclaimed, "What the fuck was that?" The driver shut down the boat's motor and manually tried circling to see what he had hit.

The people on the jetty who had witnessed the violent impact erupted into loud wailing screams, "They hit Nicky, the boat hit Nicky, he's under water, he's gonna drown."

Frightened for his brother's life, Tommy pleaded, "Someone help; help my brother's drowning. Help, Dio, please help." Tommy could not swim and knew if he attempted to rescue his twin he would drown.

Danny had just finished putting his belongings in his backpack when he heard the alarming cries for help. He ran to the top of the jetty ,waving his hand over the water like a wand demanding, "Where did he go down?" Tommy pointed to where he last saw his brother. Danny dove in.

The water wasn't too deep near the shoreline of the jetty. It became ghostly silent as everyone watched in fearful antic-ipation. The sobering agent of fear set in as they prayed for God's help. A few seconds passed timelessly like a broken clock, an eternity for the praying on-lookers.

Finally, Danny Corvo surfaced with Nicky in tow. The drunken young man was unconscious and Danny had no idea how long he'd been under water. Tommy and a few friends assisted the courageous stranger in carrying Nicky's body out of the water. The body of the boy was motionless and it became logically apparent that he was dead.

But the bellicose character of Danny Corvo wouldn't sur-render to death. He commanded, "Put him down right here, on his back." Ignorant about what had to be done, the others sheepishly followed his instructions. Danny began CPR to pump water from the drunken victim's lungs. He pushed and pushed with an unrelenting persistence until Nicky's mouth released water and his head moved. The seemingly dead boy was now breathing and would be given another chance at life thanks to the valiant, untiring efforts of a brave young stranger named Daniello Corvo.

Danny was hugged and patted in the most affectionate way. He hated it. Nicky's brother, Tommy, was stupefied, but relieved at the sudden twist of fate. Tears streamed down his cheeks as he muttered, "You are the bravest guy I ever met, a hero. No one would take a chance diving in that water but you did. Thank you, thank you." The large gathering of spectators applauded his heroic deed.

Nicky was wobbly on his feet but the shock of a close encounter to death sobered him. He waddled his way to Danny and extended his right hand for a handshake of gratitude. He held a towel on his bleeding forehead covering the gash. He softly mumbled, "I need to know your name, I owe you big time."

Danny replied, "My name is Frank." Nicky nodded and said, "My name is Nicky Galliano, do you have a last name Frank?" Danny didn't want anything from anyone and was reluctant to give his real name, so without thought he instinctively responded, "My last name is Derosa."

Nicky asked, "Where do you live, Frank Derosa?"

With a believable certainty Danny answered, "Throggs Neck, I live in Throggs Neck."

The neck-stretching crowd got larger as news of the heroic deed swept across the small beach. A police car arrived as a Medic attended to the wound on Nicky's forehead. Danny picked up his backpack and hastily walked toward the Men's changing room. Tommy's inquisitiveness was aroused as he yelled, "Hey Frank, where are you going?"

Danny answered reassuringly, "I'll be right back. I'm just going to get out of this wet bathing suit." That was the last time anyone saw Danny Corvo on that day.

He slipped his shorts over his wet bathing suit and began his long run home. Reaching Pelham Parkway, he darted in and out of the side blocks that he knew so well. He had no plans of being seen. He asked himself, "Why did these guys want to know my name?" Running at the fast nervous pace of a hunted prisoner, he was two blocks from Lieutenant

Derosa's house. Dreadfully anxious, he decided to stop and see if anyone was home.

Teresa answered the door and welcomed the dripping wet boy into her home. The always-alert Derosa could read his student's face like a magazine. Something was wrong. As they entered the den he asked, "OK, what's the problem?"

Danny told the Lieutenant how he had saved Nicky Galliano's life but given them the wrong name. The Lieutenant made a facial gesture indicating approval of his heroism. Curiously he asked, "What name did you give them?"

Danny's stoic expression became a childish grin as he bowed his head and answered, "Yours."

Derosa broke into sudden laughter. He convinced his prized student that it was no big deal and these kids would probably not be able to find him. He embraced him and said, "I'm proud of you. You saved a kid's life. Even if they find you, there's nothing to be concerned about... relax."

Danny knew he did a good deed but he wanted to avoid publicity. The Lieutenant continued, "If you really don't want all the pats on the back, I'd be cautious about going back to Orchard Beach for the next few weeks. If you do go back to that beach, you better go to section one and leave section thirteen alone. You know section one is where all the colored kids go, but you can fit in with that Sicilian skin." Calmer, Danny headed for home.

Daniello Corvo had a genuine reason for avoiding the spotlight—Gaga and company. He had no fear of Gaga individually, but was wisely concerned about being brought down by eight or ten bikers. He knew how to fight but the odds were stacked against him. In spite of the jokes that his family and friends made, he knew that he really was not Superman. He was worried that a story about his rescue of Nicky Galliano would end up in the *Daily News*, revealing his true identity.

Nicky Galliano had to answer to his father for the big gash on his forehead and why they were home so late. Tommy had to answer why he did not have a gash on his forehead and why he came home late as well. Mr. Galliano was the highly educated son of Mob royalty; he had the controlling interest in ten construction companies throughout the five boroughs. His self-appointed surrogate controlled all the business activities in New York. Mr. G, as his close friends and associates called him, was an elusive, invisible gangster. He was tough on his boys and wanted them to stay out of the incriminating aspects of the family business. He set up legitimate enterprises for them to run and earn a respectable living. But he had a rule about the twins fighting. "No one gets to fight one of you. You fight as one, four arms and four legs."

Tommy replied, "Dad we didn't have a fight. You know I would never leave my brother. He had an accident."

Gus's voice grew horrifically loud as he cried out, "Accident, accident, what kind of accident?"

Tommy began to visibly shake as he said, "He was swimming off the jetty at Orchard Beach. When he came up for air, a small motorboat whacked him on the head. He went under. I thought he was killed." Tommy spoke rapidly trying to rid himself of the explanation his powerful father demanded.

Catching his breath he continued, "Dad out of nowhere this really well-built young guy came running onto the jetty and dove in to save Nicky. He dove under and in no time flat he came up holding Nicky around his neck and shoulders. Tony R. helped me pull them onto the jetty, but Nicky wasn't breathing. This guy who dove in, his name is Frank, he told us to lay him on his back. It was unbelievable. He kept working on him, Dad; pumping and pushing on his chest until water came out of his mouth and his head moved. Everyone started cheering;

Nicky was breathing. It was amazing. He told us he was going to change into something dry and then he just disappeared."

Mr. G gazed at his two sons, happy that they were both alive and home safely. Without hesitation, his investigation continued as he asked, "How old was this guy? Did you get his name?"

Nicky answered, "He said his name was Frank Derosa and that he lived in Throggs Neck. I think he's about nineteen or twenty."

Mr. G. appeared calmer. "Derosa, huh? That's a common Italian name. You know we have to find this kid. Maybe there's something I can do for him. A good kid like that is hard to find. Who knows, maybe his family is up against it, and they can use a little money. Don't worry, I'll find him."

Paul Ryan, Mr. G's childhood friend, was a retired New York City detective who did investigation work for the Galliano family's companies and business affairs. He would summon Ryan to find this kid, Frank Derosa.

It didn't take the seasoned detective long to find Frank Derosa, the Lieutenant. Lieutenant Derosa assured the detective that he was not the young man who had saved Nicky Galliano's life. Annoyed at the detective's extensive query, Derosa said to Ryan, "I've answered all your questions which I didn't have to do. So, can I ask you a question?"

"Shoot," replied the impatient Ryan.

"What does Mr. Galliano want with this kid anyway? He didn't cause any harm, and he saved his son's life?"

Ryan answered, "Exactly, Mr. G is a very influential and powerful man. He's also very generous to those who do right by him and his family. He wants to reward the kid in some way—money, a job, that kind of thing."

Derosa replied, "Oh, I hope you find him. I'm sure the kid can use something. Good luck." The Lieutenant was momentarily tempted to insinuate that he himself might be able to find this mystery kid, but in true East Harlem style, refrained from surrendering any information.

Lieutenant Derosa called his close friend, the Captain of the 43rd Precinct in Park Chester. He inquired about Gus Galliano. Without pretense, the Captain told Derosa that Gus Galliano was a businessman who had alleged ties to the mob but never got his hands dirty. He had no criminal record, so for all intents and purposes he was on the up and up. Derosa believed that in America, any successful Italian in the construction business was perceived by society to be connected to organized crime.

The Lieutenant was partially relieved by the Police Captain's evaluation of Gus Galliano, but even the police couldn't know everything about an alleged gangster. It was difficult to separate the facts from the stigma of being a wealthy Italian. The government officials saw an unblemished criminal record and nothing more. The Lieutenant knew the one person he could depend on for valid information was his older brother Nick.

Detective Ryan questioned the twins and a few of their friends. Nicky's friend, Tony, remembered that this kid Frank was talking to a tall blond guy named Kenny on the Sunday of the accident. On the last Sunday of August, Detective Ryan drove Tony and the twins to Orchard Beach. They planted themselves in section thirteen and waited patiently to see if this Kenny character would show up. A little after noon, tall lanky Kenny arrived with his harem of girls.

Ryan carried a gold retirement shield that looked like any other detective's shield. He and the boys approached Kenny, who was busily spreading out his beach blanket with the girls. Ryan flashed his shield in front of Kenny's eyes and began speaking, "I'm Detective Ryan with the 43rd Precinct, and I need to ask you a few questions."

Kenny was startled and nervously replied, "Am I in trouble?"

Ryan assured him that he was not in any kind of trouble but that they needed his help. Kenny answered, "Sure, what can I do for you, Detective?"

Ryan spoke slowly and with conviction, "You were at this beach last Sunday when this guy," pointing to Nicky, "was saved from drowning by a guy named Frank. I need to know where I can find him."

Nervously Kenny replied, "Can I ask why?"

Detective Ryan answered, "The boy's father wants to reward him for saving his son's life. So help me out here, ok?" Kenny thought about it for a moment and went over every scenario in his mind. He couldn't find any reason not to cooperate with the Detective. Kenny told Detective Ryan that the boy who had rescued Nicky was Danny and that he hung around Morris Park and that he sometimes played handball on the weekends. Kenny was adamant about letting Ryan know that he really didn't know him personally. Like most Bronx kids, Kenny did not trust the police.

Lieutenant Derosa called Danny to inform him that a private detective hired by Mr. Galliano was looking for him. He told him to refrain from unnecessary worry, citing the rich father's gratitude. The Lieutenant told Danny, "I had this Mr. Galliano checked out; he's a very powerful businessman who has a lot of influence. If you ever have to talk to him, make sure you're polite and don't go into your dungeon of silence. Talk to the man; if you don't he will interpret your silence as disrespect." Lieutenant Derosa shunned his brother Nick's way of life but he needed his help. It was time he and his wife Teresa planned a trip to East Harlem to visit his family.

Concerned about the true identity and character of Gus Galliano, the following Sunday Frank and Teresa took the IRT subway from the Bronx to 125th Street in East Harlem. Frank's parents had moved to a first-floor apartment of a renovated Brown Stone owned by his brother, Nick. The apartment afforded their retired parents the luxury of a back yard where Poppa Derosa planted his treasured plum tomatoes.

Mama Derosa cooked a traditional Italian Sunday dinner. Frank's wife was humored by the amount of food Mama cooked for five people. Nick was charming, and spoke without his normal engagement of street-gut vulgarity. Frank had told his wife that his brother Nick was a successful real estate investor; a truism to a degree. When dinner ended Teresa, the dutiful daughter-in-law, helped Mama wash and dry the dishes. Poppa resorted to his easy chair for a brief wine-induced afternoon snooze. Frank and Nick made their way into the privacy of Poppa's garden.

Nick Derosa was not a man to easily surrender information about anyone, but Frank was his brother. Without preamble Frank said, "Nick I need your help with something."

The traditional Italian older brother was eagerly willing to help his kid brother. His head slowly bobbed affirmatively as he asked, "Sure how much do you need?"

Frank repeatedly shook his head, saying, "No it's nothing like that. I need information about someone. One of my students saved a kid from drowning up at Orchard Beach in the Bronx. The kid was knocking on death's door but this student of mine knew CPR and was able to save him. The kid's father wants to give him some kind of a reward but I don't know if I should allow this kid Danny to get too close to him."

Nick was puzzled as he inquisitively asked, "Frank I'll help you if I can. but why are you coming to me?"

Frank's face bore an emotional blankness as he dryly said, "The kid's father is Gus Galliano."

Nick looked bewildered. His dense eyebrows rose while his eyes appeared to bulge out of their deep sockets as he repeated, "Gus Galliano? Did I hear you right? You said Gus Galliano?"

Frank answered, "Yeah, that's what I said."

Nick's fingers firmly grasped his brother's shirt sleeve as he escorted him deeper into the garden farther away from family ears. Nick held his head back and looked up at the sky. He made a hand gesture for Frank to do like-wise, saying, "Look, see that big white cloud? That's Gus Galliano; clean and pure white from a distance. You can't see through it and you'll never know what's behind it. That's the best description I can give you. The man is clean in appearance, just like that cloud. You can't see through him because he's too smart, and you can't ever know what's behind his motives because he doesn't trust anyone. Gus Galliano is the smartest, shrewdest, and most powerful gangster since Joe Kennedy. If Gus takes a liking to this kid, he's going to have a pretty good life. As usual, little brother, everything I just told you stays between us. In other words keep your fucking mouth shut."

Frank smirked as he said, "That's really interesting, but in my opinion Joe Kennedy being a gangster is a little far-fetched."

Nick was easily angered. He scornfully said, "Take off your soldier-boy fucking tainted eyeglasses. Joe Kennedy made his fortune during Prohibition. He had fleets of trucks and plenty of Irish foot soldiers selling and transporting sugar, corn mash, and charcoal. He and some of his Wall Street cronies even figured out a way to manipulate the stock market. Don't let the newspapers fool you. And finally little brother, if it wasn't for the Chicago Mob, his son would never have become President. They fixed Chicago. Every corpse in the cemetery voted for Kennedy, giving him a win in Illinois."

Frank was curious to know more, so he wisely apologized and begrudgingly agreed that he was ignorant about the life of Joe Kennedy. His agreement erased Nick's spontaneous anger. Frank asked, "Did you ever meet Galliano?"

Nick pressed his lips tightly and shook his head no. He said, "Never. No pun intended but he's too far up in the clouds. I met his surrogate, Frank Persico, the Capo of everyone. You can't tell that to anyone either if you do I'm a dead man. But I can tell you this much with certainty. Gus Galliano graduated from Hofstra-University with an engineering degree. That's why he's deeply invested in construction. He started his first company at twenty five. He had one hundred employees and set it up that they all owned one share of stock in the company. He legally borrowed huge sums of money, buying vacant lots for his trucks and equipment. He eventually bought his own lumber yard.

"On pay day, his men received a paycheck and an envelope of cash. He had the accountant take one-half of each guy's paycheck and he used that money to pay back the bank loans. Remember his employees were listed as share-holder owners of the company, so the transactions were legitimate. The envelope contained the cash amount that was taken from their paychecks to re-pay the loans and a ten dollar bonus. The cash was money he received from his father's gambling and loan sharking business. He was laundering his father's mob money almost as fast as the old man made it. He was audited once and represented himself. Galliano made the IRS look like fools. Again, this is between you and me and is not to be repeated."

Detective Ryan circled the park three times, but there was no trace of Danny Corvo. When they passed the rear of the park, Nicky recognized the young man who saved his life sitting at one of the checker tables with his friend Alan. "That's him with the white tank top," said Nicky.

Ryan insisted the boys stay in the car. Detective Ryan approached the two boys playing checkers and flashed his gold shield. Ryan was blunt as he said, "You're the boy who saved a kid from drowning last Sunday at Orchard Beach, Right?"

Daniello knew he was in an undeniable position and replied, "Right."

Ryan shed his detective-like coldness and extended his right hand saying, "It's my absolute pleasure to meet you." Danny hesitantly shook his hand. Ryan continued as his voice gained an amicable tone, "My boss, Mr. Galliano is Nicky's father. He wants to meet the guy who saved his son's life."

Danny glanced over the detective's shoulder and could see the disobedient twins walking into the park. They both shook Danny's hand and Nicky gave him an unexpected embrace. Nicky made eye contact with Ryan who made a hand gesture that he should speak. Nicky said, "My dad wants to meet you and thank you personally for saving my life."

An uneasy Danny answered, "When? It's getting near supper time and I have to get home. You know how Italian fathers are about being late for Sunday dinner."

The unamused detective asked curtly, "So now tell us your real name. I know it's not Frank Derosa." Danny responded, "Daniello, my name is Daniello Corvo but most people call me Danny."

The detective scribbled down his name, address and phone number. He left saying, "Don't worry, kid, you'll be glad when you meet Mr. Galliano. He's a really cool guy." Tommy and Nicky nodded their heads and offered a smiled of reassurance. Ryan continued, "So tell me when you can meet him. I'll come and pick you up and take you back home."

Danny quipped, "Tomorrow, but you don't have to pick me up. Just tell me what time and where to meet Mr. Galliano."

The detective spoke privately with Tommy and Nicky until they agreed on a time. "Meet us at the corner of 187th Street and Arthur Avenue. Bring your appetite and don't worry. It's going to be a good day," said Ryan.

Danny ran Monday morning and ate a cautiously light breakfast. He remembered "bring your appetite" and knew if lunch was served it would be disrespectful to pick at the food like a plump squab pigeon. He ran to Pelham Parkway and took the Number 12 Fordham Road bus to Arthur Avenue. When the bus reached Arthur Avenue, he walked the rest of the way, embarrassed to be sweating when he met Mr. Galliano. The well-disciplined teenager arrived ten minutes early as did Detective Ryan. They shook hands in a business-like fashion and started walking down Arthur Avenue toward Victoria's Restaurant.

Danny read the bold red "closed" sign and remarked, "This is the place; it's closed." Ryan laughed heartily and said, "Kid, it's closed to the public on Mondays but it's never closed to Mr. Galliano—he's the owner." Ryan tapped on the vestibule glass as Tommy disarmed the security system on the inner door and let them in. Tommy and Nicky were wearing dress shirts and finely tailored pants. Mr. Galliano was seated at a corner table, accompanied by his stunningly attractive younger wife, Victoria. His hair was gaining gray but remained predominantly black. He had the rough weathered facial features of a sea merchant, with deep, dark-seated eyes that commanded one's attention.

Danny was wearing a pull-over shirt, shorts and sneakers. Embarrassed by his meager appearance, he felt the blood rushing to his face as he approached the table. Mr. Galliano sat with his back against the wall so he could plainly see any approaching person. It was an unbreakable habit he had learned as a young man from his father—never trust anyone. When Danny got close to the table Mr. Galliano and his wife stood up and greeted him with a handshake. Mrs. Galliano became uncharacteristically emotional as she offered the young, handsome stranger an embrace. Mr. Galliano directed Danny to sit between his two grateful sons. Danny's eyes were hypnotized by the opulently framed photos of Gus Galliano and the most famed entertainers of America. Directly over Gus's head was a larger-than-life signed photo of him and Frank Sinatra. Next were Dean Martin, Joe DiMaggio, Tony Bennett and a new arrival on the rock and roll stage, the fabulous Stevie Wonder.

Gus started to speak, "We are here today, young man, because you saved our son's life. My son is a stranger to you and yet you did what no one else would do. You risked your own life to save his. I can see that you're in good shape; you have an athletic body and you're obviously a good swimmer. My wife and I thank God that you were there with all your swimming skills. I have a lot of people who work for me but I've learned to be a good listener. I want you to tell me all about yourself."

Nervous in the presence of this powerful man, he shyly asked, "You want to know everything about me? Where do you want me to start?"

Mr. G's voice became shallow in register as he calmly said, "At the beginning son, with your real name."

Danny was very cautious as he started telling the Galliano family about his upbringing. He began with his real name and moved on to his early swimming lessons, boxing at the Smokers and working on cars and motorcycles with his Grandfather. When he told them that he just graduated from the Bronx High School of Science, Mrs. Galliano impatiently interrupted him saying, "Wow, Daniello that's quite an achievement. What college are you going to?"

He answered, "I did well in Science but I'm not a big fan of school so I'm going to work on cars until I decide."

She said reassuringly, "If you decide to go to college, Gus and I would be happy to pay your tuition in appreciation for your valor. It's the least we can do."

Danny's blue eye's widened in disbelief. "Wow, that's really generous, but I think I want to work for right now. But thank you, thank you so much."

Mrs. Galliano was impressed by the youngster's steadfast rebellion of such an offer. """

Mr. G interceded, "What other kind of work do you like, Daniello? Or do you prefer to be called Danny?"

The boy answered, "Most people call me Danny, except for my mom when she's mad—then I'm always Daniello." The Galliano's mused at his honesty as he continued, "My dad is an operating engineer. You know he runs big excavators and bull-dozers. That's **what** I really like but he was told that things are slow and I have to wait until they start an apprentice program."

Mr. Galliano grinned and emitted a low grade chuckle as he said, "Well, Danny I think I just might be able to help you." Danny watched quietly as everyone at the table joined in the impromptu laughter. The young hero didn't get it. Mr. G hired whoever he wanted whenever he wanted. It was a simple equation. The union bosses were his well-paid loyal allies!

Only the best prepared Italian food was served to the Galliano family. The slender Victoria was greatly surprised at the finely built young man's appetite. She remarked in startled astonishment, "Danny I thought my two animals ate like a lion, but I think you have them beat. How do you stay so slim?"

He replied, "There's never a day that goes by that I don't run or skip rope. Usually I do both."

Mrs. Galliano continued, "Well, you sure look great, so there must be something to it. Do you have a girlfriend Danny?"

Puzzled and surprised by the personal question he bluntly replied, "Not anymore."

In a mother's loving but prying fashion she asked, "So a good looking, well-built kid like you doesn't have a girlfriend right now?"

Tommy, a jester of annoying persistence, said, "Don't feel bad, my brother Nicky gets dumped by a bimbo every other week."

The Gallianos chuckled but Danny remained unamused, his eyes bouncing from one Galliano to the next, a visual scolding of the obtuse comment. Nicky sensed that his young savior was hurting over a romance gone wrong. Sympathetically, he said with a humorous flair, "Don't worry it will pass. I get over it every other week."

Mr. G's huge fist suddenly slammed the table, jostling the properly placed china. A quiet attention came over the room as he demanded silence and said, "I didn't bring this boy here to talk about romance. I want to talk about the future."

Mindlessly and without hesitation Danny grunted, "She didn't dump me, she died."

When lunch was over, Mr. G handed Danny a business card with his company name and a private phone number. He instructed him, "Go home and talk to your parents about college and work. Make sure you call me next week." He placed a sealed thank you card containing five hundred dollars in the boy's hand. Detective Ryan was ordered to drive the kid home. One by one the Galliano family embraced their newly found hero and bid him farewell. Tears sprang into Victoria's eyes as she apologized for the boldness of her very personal question. Her apology was sincere.

He asked Ryan to drop him off a few blocks away from his house to avoid a possible interrogation by his worried Mother. Danny feared the proud Lieutenant could absent-mindedly slip in the presence of his father. He called him that evening and updated him on the meeting and the fabulous dinner with Mr. Galliano and his family. A man of great common sense, Derosa reiterated what Danny already knew…it was time to tell his parents.

Joe was working the night shift and Rosemarie would be home late from a dance recital. Danny used this evening as a rare opportunity to clear his conscience and tell his parents what was going on. When dinner ended Danny told his parents that he had something really important to tell them. Annabel lovingly asked, "Is everything ok?"

"Everything's fine Mom, just fine," he softly answered. Removing the thank you card from his back pocket, he handed it to his anxious parents to read. Annabel put on her reading glasses and read it aloud, "Dear Danny, there are no words that can express our gratitude to you for saving our son's life. To our family you are one of God's miracles. We're indebted to you for all time, with love, Gus, Victoria, Tommy and Nicky Galliano."

Big Sam and Annabel created a duet of robust inquiry, as they said, "What happened? What did you do? Who are these people?" Danny explained every detail of the Nicky Galliano rescue, eventually satisfying his parent's curiosity. Sam Corvo gazed at his son and proudly said, "Son, you are a hero. We are so proud of you." When Danny flashed the five hundred dollars in cash, they became suspicious. In 1964, a really good paying job paid about five hundred dollars a month! Sam probed, "Did this man ever tell you what he did to earn a living?" Danny answered boldly, "He owns construction companies and the restaurant we were in today." Sam and Annabel became happy for their son, but a reward that size, even for saving a life, was not comprehensible to their blue collar mentality. They went to bed believing that their son saved the life of a wealthy businessman's son.

A few days passed and Sam ran into Lieutenant Derosa. His son's heroic feat consumed their conversation. Sam was grateful to the Lieutenant for teaching his son the newly acquired skill of CPR that enabled him to save Nicky Galliano. When Sam mentioned the five hundred dollars, a grinning Derosa remarked, "I'm not surprised. Gus Galliano is a rich, influential man. Five hundred bucks is chump change for him." The Lieutenant walked Sam through everything he found out about Mr. G and convinced him that his son would benefit from the relationship. With great emphasis, the Lieutenant repeated what the police captain had told him—"Mr. G. was on the up and up." As promised he could not mention the reassuring conversation he had had with his brother, Nick.

Danny worked with his grandfather who was unusually busy getting his clients' cars ready for the frigid northeast winter. Radiators had to be flushed and the summer coolant had to be changed to accommodate the predictably cold winter. The rear tires of his trusting clients had to be changed to snow tires. There was plenty of work for his aging grandfather, who was appreciative of the help of someone trustworthy.

Danny went to Bronx Community College and signed up for a block of night courses. Big Sam was a proud father who would be insulted if someone else paid for his son's education, so Danny harbored the Galliano family offer. He was obligated to call the elusive Mr. G the following week as he had requested. He was never easy to find, but Danny was able to leave his secretary a message. When Danny didn't hear anything for a few days, he decided to go to the restaurant and leave Mr. G a note. His note informed him that he was taking a few night courses at Bronx Community College and only had to pay a registration fee.

A week later, Detective Ryan arrived unannounced at Grandpa Joe's garage. After a brief salutation the Detective was formally introduced to his Grandfather. The Detective and Danny ventured outside where they could converse privately. Ryan was brief and abrupt as he said, "Listen, Mr. G had to go away on business. I spoke to him last night and he wants to see you when he returns in a few weeks. In the meantime he wants to know if you need anything."

Danny answered, "Did he get my note?"

"No," replied Ryan, "But I read it to him over the phone. He was pleased to hear you started college."

Danny said, "I'm just trying it for one semester. I owe that to my parents. When January comes, I'll see what I want to do."

Ryan responded, "Just remember, Mr. G can help you with college or a job. It's up to you. I told you he was a cool guy and not a bull shitter."

The Galliano's were so greatly impressed by the heroic Corvo kid's academic potential they invited him to dinner at their Riverdale estate. The luxurious fortress was protected by armed security guards, motion cameras, and trained guard dogs. He was made to feel comfortable in their lavish home. The Galliano twins were always present and never insinuated class superiority. At the tender age of twenty two, the twins owned and operated the largest salvage yard in the South Bronx. They offered their admired hero a job that he would thankfully decline.

Danny turned eighteen on May 17, 1965, and taught swimming class two Saturdays a month for Lieutenant Derosa. His mother and aunts spent the day cooking and preparing food for a family birthday party. Danny wrestled with the idea of buying a new car. He knew it would wipe out his bank account and he wasn't keen on the idea of taking out a loan. He knew Grandpa Joe would lend him any amount within reason, but he felt too guilty to ask. The eternally grateful Mr. G would probably lend him the money and not expect him to pay it back, but that wasn't the blue collar Corvo way.

As the party ended, his twenty-one-year old cousin, Tommy, gestured for Danny to join them. His face was expressionless as he said, "Danny, Phil and I didn't want to ruin your party but you're going to find out anyway…we got our notice to report to Whitehall Street. We're gonna be drafted into the fucking Army." The police action in Vietnam was turning into a full scale war and the American people knew it. It was just a matter of time before Danny Corvo and Chris Chan would get their "come on down" notice.

When the guests left, Danny asked his Dad if he had a few minutes to talk.

"Sure, what's up?" Sam replied.

Danny said, "I guess you and Uncle Pete and Uncle Tommy know the boys have to report to Whitehall Street for a physical. If they pass they're going to get drafted, right?"

Sam was slow to respond. He didn't want to say anything that wasn't factual. After carefully assembling the words of his response, he said dryly, "I'm not sure where this war is going, son. It was supposed to be a police action and now it looks like all hell is breaking loose. I sure wish President Kennedy was still around. There's something about this Johnson I don't like. I can't put my finger on it but I don't trust his judgment."

Taking another long drink of beer, he continued, "We know your brother is safe because of his bad ear. I can't believe the GM doctor didn't figure that out when they hired him."

Danny interrupted, "I remember what happened, Dad. Joe told us they put a hearing device on both ears so all he had to do was raise his hand when he heard the signal with his good ear."

Sam gasped as his memory became reignited and responded, "That's exactly what happened. Now I remember. Anyway as far as you go, I think you have plenty of time. From everything I'm reading, kids in college are exempt until they graduate, and at that time they can go for a masters and that will keep them out as well. I know you say you're going to college part-time but you're taking enough credits to be deferred at this time. So, if you want to avoid going to war, stay in college whether you want to or not."

Joe told his kid brother that the plant was hiring people to work the assembly line on the night shift and boasted that he could get him hired immediately. The summer was a few weeks away and the college semester soon ended. All Danny needed to know about assembly line work was that it paid well. He planned on attending college during the day and working in the evenings, from 4:30 to 1:00 in the morning. He could take the minimum credits in September and still keep his deferment. On June 20th Joe drove Danny to the automotive assembly plant; by 11:00 am he was hired. When Danny completed his ninety days as a probationary employee, he was presented with his union card. He was now officially a member of The United Auto Workers of America.

CHAPTER 4

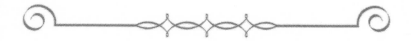

College and working the night shift evaporated Danny Corvo's free time, but his obsession with fitness remained unwavering. He brought his books to work, as the monotony of the assembly line was conducive to reading between jobs. Unable to rationalize forfeiting a healthy cash payment, he continued to teach for Lieutenant Derosa on his two assigned Saturdays. His newly acquired mentor, Gus Galliano, told him a man is more appreciative of his work if the government doesn't have their hands in your pocket.

The union had just finished negotiating a new contract with GM. The United Auto Workers gained paid holidays for Christmas Eve, Christmas Day, New Year's Eve and New Year's Day. The assembly line work was tiresome and monotonous. Learning that he would get paid for staying home was a welcome gift.

Danny and Doc Singer enjoyed their unique friendship but Doc was in Columbia University and had a heavy workload. Bobby K. began working as an apprentice in the plumber's union. He and his fiancée, Virginia, planned on getting married in spite of parental opposition to their age. Danny was happy for the young couple but surmised that, once married, the possibility of seeing each other would dwindle into a rarity.

The holiday season resurrected his grief at the loss of his childhood sweetheart like a never-ending nightmare. The young loner was hopelessly finding his way back into his dungeon of silence. His cousins, Phil and Tommy, knew that being drafted was imminent and chose to join the Marine Corps. They were proud to follow in the family tradition; both of their dads and Uncle Sam were Marines.

In late September, after basic training on Parris Island, the Corvo cousins were sent to Viet Nam. This holiday would bring a quiet sadness that had remained dormant since World War 2. The police action in Southeast Asia was transformed into the bloody Viet Nam War. Reality reared its ugly head and it didn't seem like the war was going to end any time soon. The weekly body count sent shock waves through a divided nation.

Sam and Annabel could feel that their heart-broken son was tumbling into a state of rabid depression. They engaged in positive conversations but were unable to encourage his participation. His appetite was kept in balance by his lust for exercise. They prayed that he would meet another girl capable of mending his shattered heart.

Joe had fallen in love with the twenty-one-year-old Judy Perez. Annabel enjoyed her company as they shared a love for the culinary arts. Danny no longer saw much of his older brother as he spent most of his time at the Perez house.

Christmas Day was frigid and the wind was unfriendly to pedestrians. It started to snow and quickly turned into an ice and snow medley of discomfort. At one o'clock, a tormented Danny decided that he had to go to the cemetery for Christmas Day. He plodded through the hostile elements, mentally avoiding acknowledgment of the physical discomfort. He knelt on the cold hard earth and embraced the headstone of Amy Winter. He relieved himself of his tears and began the long journey home.

Danny felt better after showering and changing into dry, comfortable clothing. He was finally able to think about what his parents had told him. Everyone had a good job and his enlisted cousins Tommy and Phil were ok. They were in a bad place, but thank God they were ok. For the first time since Amy's death, he embraced the future. We can learn from the past but we can't go back. We're powerless to change the past, but we can mold the future. When Annabel said grace at Christmas dinner, Daniello Corvo bowed his head and asked God to help him find a girl he could love for the rest of his life.

In March, Danny and Alan attended Bobby K's wedding. The two boys gave Bobby and Virginia one wedding card from the both of them with a generous monetary gift of forty dollars. The wedding was small and celebrated in a local catering hall. The boys danced with some of Virginia's girlfriends but thought none of them were worthy of pursuit. Danny was surprised to see the McNamara girl in attendance. She lived across the street from Virginia, and they had been friends since the first grade. Danny was unable to make the connection because they attended different elementary schools.

The once snobbish Jane McNamara had developed a physical attraction to the young well-built Corvo boy. She would dote in admiration, watching his muscular shirtless body glide effortlessly when he ran. His blue eyes were highlighted by the deep tan of his face. She was smitten. Jane regretted the way she spoke to him in elementary school, but that was five years ago. Surely he no longer cared, or even remembered.

Jane walked over to the table where the boys were sitting. Her smile was soft and inviting as she said in a velvety seductive tone, "Hi Danny, how are you doing? Do you remember little ole me?" Jane had blossomed into a desirable temptress. At nineteen years old, men would say she was easy on the eyes.

Danny was slow to respond as his eyes perused her body from head to toe as if he were searching his memory; finally he said, "How could I ever forget such a sweet well-mannered girl. Let me guess. You want to dance but not with me."

Jane became blush pink in the face; she couldn't believe that he never forgot her crass comments at the seventh grade dance. A girl of admirable charm, she attempted to make light of the incident, saying, "Come on Danny we were in the seventh grade, we were kids."

He concealed his anger as his voice softened to a low register saying, "Oh so that's it, we were only kids. You were so self-absorbed you thought it was humorous to humiliate me in front of our classmates." Danny stood close to her and continued to speak in a soft undertone. "So here's the way I see it; you're going to tell me you're a different person now, but I'm not interested in finding out. Go back to your company and enjoy the rest of the wedding. I'm half Sicilian and I don't forget and I don't forgive. Have a good night."

Alan thought Jane McNamara was a sex goddess and cried out, "For God's sake Danny, you probably blew a chance of a lifetime, what's up with you? She's gorgeous!"

Danny pivoted to make eye contact with his trustworthy friend and said curtly, "Not on the inside, not on the inside."

When the alcohol slowly evaporated, he went to bed and thought about what happened with Jane McNamara. He scolded himself. *I asked God to help me find a girl and then I act like I don't care.* He believed in destiny. If they were meant to be together, they would somehow once again meet by happenstance.

After his nineteenth birthday, in May of 1966, Danny put the possibility of being drafted out of his mind and bought a 1965 Pontiac GTO convertible. He knew he could store the car or sell it in the event he was drafted into the military. The car was a left-over model and the dealer took off another one hundred fifty dollars when he realized the young man was a GM employee.

Mr. G called and asked him to stop by the restaurant, so he proudly drove his new car to Arthur Avenue. It was a Bronx tradition for people to throw change in someone's new car as a way of wishing them luck. Mr. G opened the driver's side door and threw in a fistful of bills. He told Danny he didn't have a lot of time to talk but wanted him to know that he had work for him on Sunday's operating heavy equipment. Excited, Danny asked, "When and where?" Mr. G impatiently replied, "I just have to know if you want to give up your Sunday's this summer. I have a guy that will train you, yes or no?" Danny sensed his impatience and immediately answered, "Yes, of course, no problem, thank you." Mr. G said, "OK, it's done; I'll call you. Be careful driving that monster."

It wasn't a grueling task for Danny and his parents to figure out that Mr. G. was more than a successful businessman—he was connected. From the local barber shop to the local bars, everyone knew the name Mr. G but few people ever had a personal connection with him. Mr. G had a constellation of legitimate businesses and representatives, making it impossible for the Feds or the local Police to tie him to any illegal enterprises.

Gus Galliano had an intriguing pedigree. His maternal grandfather was Ignazio "Iggy" Savoca. He came to America from Catania, Sicily in the late 1800s. Iggy was one of the original "Mustache Pete's" of the newly born Sicilian Mafia in America. He was cunning and insidiously notorious. He was the "Don of Don's" in the Northeast but had one painful problem—he had five children and they were all girls! As the girls grew older and married, Iggy hopelessly searched for a son-in-law who could earn his confidence. When his youngest daughter Alicia married Stefano Galliano, Iggy felt blessed. Stefano was an educated street thug who was oddly ambitious. Iggy Savoca trained the young Stefano and the reign of power eventually passed from the Savoca name to the Galliano family. Mr. G. was Stefano's only child insuring him a symbolic throne in the hierarchy of the family. The young Gus was a perfect blend of his grandfather "Iggy" and his father Stefano. A college graduate, he was a gifted administrator who was both feared and loved by his underlings. He was appropriately dubbed "The Invisible Don." There was never a trace of evidence involving Gus Galliano in anything illegal.

The Police Captain had told Lieutenant Derosa that Mr. G was on the up and up because no one had any substantive evidence to the contrary. Mr. G paid his taxes on time and insured that his companies followed all the rules and laws set forth by the Department of Labor. He was smart, shrewd, and careful to a fault. The more he saw of Danny Corvo, the more he liked him. He admired the way the boy took pride in his physical appearance and well-being; he always hoped his boys would follow his example.

The Galliano brothers were older and altogether different kids than Danny Corvo, but they too admired his unnatural abilities. They wore the best of clothes and each of them drove a new Corvette sports car. The salvage yard was a successful business when Mr. G acquired it and with his closeness to multiple associations the business prospered. Danny introduced the speed-craving brothers to Paulie Nartico to have their cars race-tuned.

It was Saturday of the Memorial Day weekend in 1966. Tommy Galliano drove his twin brother to Paulie's garage to pick up his finely tuned Corvette. When they arrived, two bikers were pulling out of the Nartico driveway. Curiously, Nicky asked, "Hey, Paulie you work on bikes too?"

Paulie smiled and answered, "Speed is my creed. If you want it to go faster, I'm the one you're after." After they laughed at the pithy rhyme, the conversation remained on bikes and bikers. It wasn't long before the notorious Eddie Gaga's name came to the forefront. Tommy had heard of Gaga from one of his workers at the salvage yard. All the Gaga stories were exaggerated but filled with sick Bronx humor.

When Tommy asked Paulie if he knew Eddie Gaga, he replied, "Yeah, if you ride a bike, you'll eventually run into Eddie Gaga. I rode with him and a few of his boys a few times but I'm in no way part of his gang."

Then next question gagged the young mechanic like a strangulating choke hold on his throat. Tommy asked bluntly, "I heard Gaga got fucked up real bad by some young biker. I was told that he pissed on this kid's bike and the kid gave Gaga the beating of his life; fucked up his whole face. Did you hear that Paulie?"

Paulie quickly calculated that he was now standing between shit and syphilis. How should he answer that question? Did Danny tell them? Paulie's brain searched for a non-incriminating answer as his heart raced. Fearful, he hesitated but knew an answer had to be given. If Danny didn't tell them; should he lie to the Galliano brothers? Paulie quickly borrowed some time by responding, "Hold that thought. I gotta take a wicked piss, I need a minute." Paulie conceded to his street logic that they had to know. Otherwise the questions were too coincidental. When he got back, Paulie lit up a

Lucky Strike. He exhaled a cloud of the nerve-calming smoke and answered, "Come on, you guys know Danny Corvo is the kid that fucked up Gaga."

Tommy turned slowly to catch a glimpse of his brother's reaction and laughingly said, "I know now."

Frightened by his own violation of trust, he pleaded with the Galliano brothers. His face became pale and colorless as he begged, "Listen, you guys have to do me a favor. Whatever you do please don't tell him I told you. If he gets pissed, I'll end up losing a best friend or my life. What do you say?"

Tommy smirked as he answered, "No problem. We'll act like we don't know and see if he ever tells us." He refused to accept payment for his work as an act of penance for their promised silence.

Paulie had witnessed Danny Corvo give Gaga the beating of his life but even he didn't have the slightest clue about the extent of his younger friend's combative skill. Mr. Chan taught Chris and Danny every lethal military hand-to-hand fighting technique he had learned over a lifetime of training. The boys were adept at diffusing a person with a gun, knife, bat and any hand-held weapon. They were young and possessed a frightening but admirable degree of suicidal bravado. They were never careless, but always cautiously fearless. Mr. Chan had them execute these techniques from every angle until the boredom gave way to perfection. They practiced from the left hand and the right hand, high, low and in the middle. Mr. Chan's theory was drawn from an ancient Chinese belief. He said, "We don't always get to choose our opponent and we must be prepared to defend against all sizes. When you have gone over these techniques one thousand times, you will know them. When you have gone over these techniques ten thousand times, you'll have mastered them."

CHAPTER 5

I t was Thursday, June 9, 1966. Danny was looking forward to the eight-week plant shut down for the model changeover in early July. Collecting unemployment and sub-benefits from the Union, his benefit package provided ninety percent of his pay, for staying home. College didn't start until mid-September. He had a new car and free time. All he had to do was work for the next three weeks.

Thursday was pay night on the second shift, usually prompting good attendance. Danny was guaranteed a pretty easy job on pay nights so he decided to take an extra-long run of eight to ten miles. He ran from his dead end block to White Plains Road and onto the Pelham Parkway. He ran the parkway at a brisk pace until he reached the City Island Bridge. Reaching the approach of the bridge, he met Chris Chan who was on his way to City Island. Danny declined his friend's offer to join him in his run to the end of City Island, fearing he would be late for his job. The boys resumed running, Chris toward City Island and Danny toward White Plains Road.

Crossing Williams Bridge Road and Pelham Parkway, he glanced at his watch and saw that their conversation was longer than realized. He had to cut his run short and decided to exit at Mulliner Avenue, calculating that it would save him at least twenty minutes. Mulliner Avenue was frequently traveled by the High School kids from Christopher Columbus who resided in the Morris Park and Van Nest sections of the Bronx. He stepped up the pace, gaining enough time to get to his job. He crossed Lydig Avenue and saw that the long-awaited repairs had begun on the overhead IRT subway line. Running south on the left side of Mulliner Avenue, he saw the dismal silhouette of cheap construction shanties erected under that side of the overpass.

His pace was still brisk as he crossed lanes to the right side, avoiding the perilous-looking construction site. Approaching the overhead trestle Danny read signs prohibiting parking on the construction side of the street. There was one menacing-looking car defiantly parked on the left side of the street in the no-parking zone. The car was a poorly painted, dull black 1962 Pontiac Catalina convertible that had its name, "The Black Bitch," inscribed on the front fender in large white letters. It was illegally parked under the middle of the trestle in front of the makeshift shanties. He recognized the car from the neighborhood but didn't know the owner. He would soon find out, as his eyes focused on the black Pontiac. There was someone sitting in the driver's seat with his feet turned outward, resting on the pavement. He was obviously a man of massive size, as the driver's side of the car visibly listed toward the curb. The radio was playing very loud.

From across Mulliner Avenue he could hear the faint half-muffled sound of a girl's voice frantically begging, "Stop, stop, please stop, leave me alone, why are you doing this?"

The distraught girl bellowed loud alarming screams for help. Danny's eyes were blazing with alertness as he slowed his pace to a casual walk. He anxiously headed toward the rear of the Pontiac. The shanty door was partially opened. He could now see the screaming girl struggling to free herself from the grasp of two men. One man stood behind her. His left arm was firmly placed around the young girl's neck, interrupting her breathing. His right hand struggled to gag her feeble pleas for help.

The second male faced the girl, tearing her blouse with passionate desire. His left hand struggled, attempting to remove her undergarment. Restrained, she frantically attempted to kick her assailants as she rotated and twisted her body attempting to stop their vicious sexual assault. As Danny Corvo witnessed the assault on this young helpless girl, he became choleric with rage. Raw anger eclipsed his normal docile demeanor. Well-trained and adept at dealing with multiple adversaries, he knew the driver of the car had to be taken out first. Calmly he offered the driver a friendly salutation saying, "Hey how you doing?" Before the driver's lips could move a well-placed kick to the front of his face rendered him immediately unconscious. His nose spouted blood as his huge torso slumped to the pavement.

The attacker ripping at the girl's clothing was taller and leaner. His arms were blanketed with self-identifying tattoos. He saw Corvo behind him but his reaction time was retarded by the boy's sudden appearance. Danny kicked him behind the knee, causing his stance to falter and lose balance. He grabbed him by his long, girlish ponytail and pulled him to the ground. Holding onto the convenience of the ponytail, he savagely punched the man's face repeatedly in machine-gun tempo, breaking his eye socket. He too was instantaneously comatose.

The male holding the girl released her and pulled a knife. Danny pivoted to the girl and screamed, "Get going, get out of here." She started to run. But suddenly she stopped and turned to see what was going to happen next.

The man with the knife always thinks he has the advantage especially when his victim is unarmed. Danny backed away from the first lunge, and mockingly said to his tattooed attacker, "Come on you colorful little fat peacock. Let's see what you got." Angry and intimidated he switched the knife from his left hand to his right and lunged again. This seemingly vicious attack was just a mundane exercise for the highly trained Corvo. He crossed his hands over his attacker's knife hand, twisted his wrist and retrieved the knife, throwing it to the ground as he maintained a firm grip on the attacker's wrist with his right hand. He slammed down on his attacker's elbow with the palm heel of his left hand breaking his arm. The elbow protruded through the torn skin. The attacker collapsed to his knees, holding his arm as he screamed in agony. Now he was the one crying for help.

Danny looked over at the girl who remained motionless. He approached her slowly saying, "Are you okay?" She nodded yes. "Just give me a minute and I'll walk with you," he said. The knife wielding fat man was attempting to stand on his feet. This was not good. Danny punched the knife wielder with precision-placed blows to his head, rendering him unconscious. Devoid of remorse he picked up the girl's schoolbooks and brought them to her. She was troubled, trying to find the right words to say to the brave young stranger. She remained speechless and frightened by what they had tried to do to her, but more so, she was dumbfounded by the bravado of Danny Corvo. He told her, "Start walking and I'll catch up to you." Running back to the car, he removed the car keys from the ignition, discarding them into an empty lot.

Danny Corvo's training paid huge dividends. He had saved a girl from being raped, broke a knife attacker's arm and put three criminals into a semi-coma in under two minutes. Mr. Chan would be proud.

The girls blouse was badly ripped. Her bra had been compromised, exposing a portion of her young firm breast. Fleeced of her dignity, she crossed her arms, attempting to cover her skin. Danny glanced away, unbuttoned his shirt and gave it to her saying, "I'm sorry. It's a little wet but you better put this on and cover yourself up."

Unable to stop crying she managed a grateful smile and muttered, "Thanks." With the excitement behind him Danny realized that he recognized this girl. It was Dee Hoffman, the youngest sister with the little baby girl.

It was six blocks to the Hoffman house. The journey was silent. When they reached her home, Dee finally broke the silence saying, "How did you learn how to do all that stuff?"

Danny stared directly into her eyes, unable to understand the purpose of such a question. Pressed for time he answered, "From my father's friend. Listen, I have to go to work. I work nights. Give me your number and I'll call you tonight."

Her face became blank and expressionless; she was confused by his sudden request. She didn't understand what he wanted.

He continued, "Look these guys are not done. They're definitely going to come looking for me, which is okay, but you have to be on the alert at all times and protect yourself. These guys are bad dudes. Give me your number, please. I really have to get going."

Dee fumbled through her bag and took out an eye liner pencil. She wrote her number on the inside of a match book and handed it to him. She said softly, "My name is Dee Hoffman, What's your name?"

He answered, "Danny, Danny Corvo, I'll call you at eight thirty when I go to lunch." He started to walk away, then suddenly turned and said, "You may want to report what happened to the cops. I don't know. It's up to you."

Dee was the first one home that afternoon. Shaken and scared, she removed Danny's shirt, put on a clean blouse and waited for her sister, Lee. Lee was a freshman at Bronx Community College and was usually home about a half hour after her younger sister. One of their deceased mother's friends, Mary, babysat Dee's daughter, Abagail, until she came home from school. Life was not easy for a seventeen-year-old girl with a four-year-old child. Dee called Mary and told her she would be a few minutes late.

Lee arrived and recognized something had happened. She lowered her head to survey her younger sister's face. "What happened? You've been crying."

Dee told her sister the gruesome details of how three tattooed men had tried to rape her under the Mulliner Avenue train trestle.

Lee stared at her appraisingly and asked, "How did you get away. Are you okay?"

Somehow she was able to grin and said, "You know that guy that you describe as the crazy, good-looking guy who is always running?"

Puzzled Lee responded with a long, slow, "Yeaaah."

"Well, he was running down Mulliner and when he heard me screaming he came running over and beat the hell out of all three of them. Lee, it was like nothing you could ever imagine, he damn near killed them. There was blood all over the place. One of them pulled a knife on him and he broke his arm. I could hear the bone snap, and then he punched him over and over again until he was unconscious. I never saw anything like it in my life. It was making me nauseous. It was like watching a gangster movie," she said.

After relieving herself of the gory details, she became relieved and calmer, sedated by her confession. Her voice grew a softer tone almost a caress as she said, "Here's the thing; he suggested that maybe I should report it to the Cops. But if I do, isn't he going to get in trouble for what he did? I mean one of them could be dead. He beat them that badly."

Lee was quick to respond, "Slow down. What's this guy's name?"

"Danny Corvo," she replied.

Lee continued her interrogation, "Did you recognize any of those so-called men that attacked you?"

Dee lowered her head and said softly, "Yes one of them was Billy Caldo. He graduated last year. Remember he kept asking me out? I kept telling him no but he wouldn't give up. I even tried telling him I had a kid and he still didn't stop." Her throat lacked moisture from her frantic screams for help. Taking a much-needed sip of water, she continued, "Danny is going to call me tonight at eight thirty. He works the night shift somewhere. What should I do? After what he did, I really don't want him to get in trouble because of me."

Lee was a very pragmatic older sister. She thought about it for a moment, exploring the options and finally said, "Listen, Dee you went through enough shit with that school-teacher. The last thing you or this family needs is more negative publicity. You know how people like to gossip, and most of them suck. The three of them got what they deserved and it seems like none of them is going to mess with this Danny guy any time soon. Let it go."

Dee's face appeared refreshed as she said, "Thanks Lee, but I have to tell him that Billy Caldo's father is a number runner and is supposed to be in the mob. That's what I was told last year when he kept bugging me. I mean, if it's true that his father is in the mob, that's really scary."

Lee answered, "Tell him what you think he should know, but it doesn't sound like he's going to care anyway. Hey Dee, maybe you just found your knight in shining armor?"

Dee inhaled a deep worrisome breath and exhaled with a purposeful slowness saying, "What would he ever want with a seventeen year old who has a four year old kid?"

Lee's face was twisted in anger as she said, "Look in the mirror little sister. You're the most beautiful girl anywhere and you'll be eighteen in a few weeks, not a little girl anymore. Any guy that can't accept Abagail is not your knight in shining armor—it's that simple."

Shy and still rattled by the savage attack Dee sighed and whispered, "I'll just thank him and tell him about Caldo's father and that will be the end of that."

But Danny Corvo couldn't get the image of the young teary-eyed beauty out of his head. His anger had still not subsided. He had no feeling of guilt but worried about the girl. Would these three criminals blame her for the beating he gave them? Reaching work on time, he had fifteen minutes before the grueling monotony of the assembly line started. Bewitched by their identity, Danny decided to call Paulie and find out if he knew the tattooed bastards with the "black bitch" car. His alert friend knew the car but not the owner. He told Danny that his friend Peter owned a gas station in the neighborhood where they lived. He would make an inquiry.

Peter disclosed the owner of the "black bitch" was Billy Caldo, the son of a mob-connected enforcer and loan shark. Paulie relayed the daunting information to his friend. "The son lives off his father's reputation and acts like a tough guy but is not a big deal. The old man, on the other hand, is an altogether different story. He's supposed to be a mob enforcer who has cracked a lot of heads."

Danny's anger masked any underlying fear as he laughed saying, "Guess I better get a helmet."

At eight thirty, Danny made sure he had enough change to stay on the pay phone for twenty minutes. Dee answered the phone on the second ring. "Hello," she said in a soft-cushioned tone. "Hello this is Danny Corvo, and how are you feeling?"

"I'm still a little shook up but I spoke to my sister and I decided not to go to the cops. My family doesn't really need any more negative publicity. My dad works two jobs and this would really shake him up and not be too good for his health. It's not worth it. Thanks to you they were punished, and I hope they learned their lesson. Just so you know, one of them is a guy named Billy Caldo and his father is supposed to be some kind of a mob guy, so please be careful. Thank you so much for your help. I have to go," she said.

Danny was instantly annoyed at her dismissive tone and answered with a deliberate quickness, "Hold on, I have something you need to hear."

Dee paused and realized that she was being curt and rude to the stranger who risked his well-being for her. She inhaled deeply, calming her nerves, and replied, "Oh I'm sorry, sure go ahead."

Danny said boldly, "Since you're in such a hurry, I'll be brief. I already knew that Billy Caldo was the owner of the car. I also knew about his father. What you don't know is that they will never let that beating go without getting some kind of revenge. I told you, I'm not worried about me. I'm worried what they might do to you. When you go to school tomorrow, go a different way, although I don't think they'll feel like getting up early any time soon. I'll pick you up and give you a ride home. I'll be across from the front entrance. There is one last thing you should know."

Embarrassed by her own rudeness she asked, "What's that?"

"If you were three hundred pounds, butt ugly and had six kids, I'd have done the same thing and would still pick you up tomorrow. That's the way I was taught, that's the way I roll."

Dee Hoffman secretly applauded his gentleman-like manner. She had never known such a boy. Her voice became suddenly soft and friendly as she replied, "Thanks Danny, I'll see you tomorrow. I get out at two thirty. Thanks again, good night."

He answered, "See you then, good night."

In spite of his air of calmness, Danny knew he had to be careful. If there was one thing he knew for certain, it was that Caldo's father would seek revenge. He had one option. Go see Mr. G and tell him what happened. The remaining ten minutes of his lunch hour was just enough time to make one more very important call..

It was a Thursday night and Mr. G was still at the restaurant. Whoever answered the phone told him that Mr. G was unavailable to talk and directed him to call back. Danny pleaded, "Please tell him it's Danny Corvo I really need to talk to him."

Danny heard the gravelly-voiced minion say, "Hey boss it's the kid, Danny. Says he really has to talk to you. He sounds upset about something."

Gus Galliano was on the phone immediately. He asked, "Danny what's wrong?"

Danny's voice trembled with rapid nervousness as he asked, "Mr. G can I come and see you tonight after work? I can be there at 1:30 in the morning when I get out."

Mr. G answered, "It's my late poker night. I'll be here but what's wrong?"

Danny said, "I don't want to talk about it over the phone. I'll tell you everything when I get there after work."

Mr. G replied in a reassuring fatherly fashion, "Stay calm. Whatever it is everything will be ok. I'll see you in a few hours and don't drive like an asshole."

Later that night, Danny found the restaurant was closed but there were still rows of cars parked on the street from the Thursday night poker club. He knocked on the restaurant door and was let in by a well-dressed gun-bearing man. Mr. G excused himself from the game and ushered the kid into his private office on the second floor. Mr. G appeared uneasy as he began speaking, "So what's wrong, kid, that you would drive all the way over here at one thirty in the morning?"

Danny sighed in a nervous manner and began to speak, "Today when I was running, I saw these three guys trying to rape this young girl under the train trestle on Mulliner Avenue. I lost it. My brain short circuited. I thought about my dead girlfriend. Every fucked up thought I ever had rolled around in my head at the same time. I beat the shit out of all of them. I know I broke one of their eye sockets because I could see his eye hanging out of his head. The first one was easy. I kicked him in his face. He went right out. The last one pulled a knife. I took it away from him and broke his arm and then I punched the shit out of him until he was out cold."

Gus Galliano sat back in his chair, amused by the boy's heroic bravado. Staring in admiration, he nodded his head, indicating that he understood. His thumb and index finger were placed on his chin, his lips curled into an approving glimpse of a smile as he said, "Bravo, any witnesses?"

Danny answered, "Just the three of them and of course the girl they were trying to rape."

Gus continued in an authoritative tone, "No cops and no witnesses except for the girl, right?"

Danny nodded his head and replied, "Right."

Gus asked, "Did the girl call the cops?"

"No, she was raped when she was thirteen by her school-teacher and has a four year old girl. She told me I punished them enough, and that her family didn't need any more negative publicity. She also said that she didn't want me to get in trouble for what I did." His glimpse of a smile suddenly grew into a child-like laugh.

Gus said, "So what's the problem? What are you worried about?"

Danny answered, "The guy whose arm I broke is Billy Caldo. His father is supposed to be a bad-ass tough guy and I know he'll come looking for me." Mr. G now understood why the kid wanted to see him immediately. This could not wait.

Mr. G leaned over the table as he thrust his face closer to Danny, his long beefy fingers tapping the table in cardiac rhythm. He commanded, "Tomorrow you be here at noon sharp. Caldo and his piece of shit son will be here as well. After they apologize to you, you can go about your business worry free. After you leave, I'll decide how much money the Caldos are going to give this girl. It sounds like she can use some help." Resuming a smile he asked, "Is she pretty?"

Danny rolled his eyes in gleeful admiration. "Like nothing I've ever seen. She's absolutely gorgeous but that had nothing to do with it. I'd have done it if she was fat and ugly. I'm sorry I had to ask you to help me with this but I really didn't know where to turn."

Mr. G raised his voice and said sternly, "You never have to be sorry to ask for my help. You saved my son's life. Victoria and I told you, anything we can ever do for you is still not enough, understand? One more thing, not now but one day I want you to tell me how you became this fighting machine. I told you my ears have a lot of voices whispering into them. I thought the story about you and the biker was really funny but I didn't want to say anything just yet. But now I'm a proxy. So go home and sleep."

Danny nodded. Gus gave him an unexpected embrace of reassurance and he headed for home.

Dee Hoffman was having a restless night. She couldn't relieve herself of the bloody image of Danny Corvo beating those three men. She believed that they deserved to be stopped and punished but was intimidated by how easy it was for him. She started to frighten herself speculating that he actually enjoyed it. Just who was this guy who fought like a Gladiator? She pondered—maybe it was just another Bronx maniac, a nut. Twisting and turning she exhausted herself into a deep sleep. When she awoke, mysteriously her fear was gone. She convinced herself that only a genuinely good man would risk their own life to rescue a stranger. She had a barrage of questions she needed to ask him.

Danny arrived at twelve o'clock as requested. Entering the restaurant, he could see the well-dressed enforcer Caldo and his sloppily dressed overweight son sitting with Mr. G. The boy's arm was in a cast and his eye was covered with a huge bandage. The father was a formidable-looking man. His face wore a blanket of scars, trophies of all his street conquest. But in the presence of Gus Galliano, the great destroyer of men looked like a school kid who just got reprimanded by the principle.

Mr. G waved Danny to come over to the table. Everyone stood up. Mr. G embraced Danny and gave him a kiss on the cheek. The kiss signified family. The Caldos looked helpless. Mr. G instructed everyone to sit. He started to speak, "Danny, I told Mr. Caldo what his son and his two punk friends tried to do to that girl of yours. They want to apologize."

The young Caldo, frightened and desirous to be forgiven, muttered, "I'm sorry. It will never happen again. I deserved the beating you gave me. I'm sorry, please accept my apology."

Danny shunned the boy's extended hand. Unafraid and still seeping with anger, he rotated his attention to the father. His eyes were searing with hostility as he said, "I want your word that nothing will ever happen to that girl, nothing."

The feared enforcer offered his extended hand to shake. Gus signaled Danny a commanding gesture to accept his peace offering. They shook hands.

It was over. But Mr. G was not finished relaying his wishes in the matter. He gave the elder Caldo an icy stare saying, "So both of you understand. If anything happens to this kid or his girl, you'll become my enemy and I'll hunt you like a fucking rat. Understood?"

The Caldos replied in unison like well-rehearsed choir boys, "Understood Mr. G."

Dee Hoffman adhered to her savior's advice and walked a different route to Columbus High School. When school was dismissed at two thirty, she could see her handsome guardian standing across the street from the main entrance, but didn't see any car. He walked with a confident swagger as he crossed the street to greet her saying, "Hi, I had to park around the block. They posted all these no parking signs and I really don't need a ticket. So, is everything quiet?"

She answered, "Yes and No. Yes, no one tried to attack or kill me but some of the kids said they saw an ambulance pick up a bloody guy on Mulliner Avenue yesterday afternoon."

Danny said coldly, "Ok, sounds quiet enough for me." Those few words supported his belief that there were no witnesses.

The convertible top of the car was up, inhibiting anyone from seeing them. He walked to the passenger side of the car and opened the door for her. Dee commented, "Really nice car. So where did you say you work?"

Danny said in a teasing manner, "I didn't. But if you must know, I work the night shift on the assembly line for Chevrolet from Monday to Friday. During the day, if I'm free, I help my Grandfather at his speed shop for a few hours. Two Saturdays a month I teach swimming at Evander High school."

Dee exclaimed, "Wow, I guess you don't have much free time?"

Danny made a head gesture indicating that she was correct. "Where do you live?" she continued.

"On the dead end of Holland, practically my whole family lives there. They own almost every house, it's a quiet spot. Not that they're rich or anything. Everyone works and pays a mortgage but it just worked out that way, it's a pretty cool place," he answered.

Intrigued, she continued with a litany of mandatory questions, "So where did you go to school?"

"Science," he replied.

Her soft girlish voice emitted a loud, "huh?" Then she said, "Science, like The Bronx High school of Science?"

"You got it," he proudly replied.

She sighed again in dramatic fashion saying, "You have to be a wizard to get into that school. How come you didn't go to college?"

"Not my cup of tea. I did really well in Science and the faculty was all upset when I didn't go. For now I'm taking courses at BCC during the day but not in the summer. I need a break," he said.

Dee pulled a small round mirror from her purse and removed a particle from her eye. Danny stared in a hypnotic way, overtaken by her natural beauty. Relieved of the pesky nuisance she turned saying, "Now that's better, I can see. My sister Lee goes to BCC. You've probably seen her around. She's blond, blue eyes about five foot four. She looks a little like me I'm told. Well, we are sisters."

Danny grinned welcoming the opportunity to say, "Oh, so she's pretty too?"

Shrugging her shoulders in modest reply she said softly, "I guess. When I told her what happened yesterday, she knew exactly who you were."

Danny inquired, "Really, how so?"

Dee pointed her finger inches from his perplexed face saying, "I hope you have a good sense of humor. She refers to you as the good-looking, crazy guy who's always running."

Danny acknowledged the humorous remark with a robust grin and said, "I don't know about the first one but tell her the last two sound right."

Dee smiled at his humble comment. She finally seemed relaxed. Danny intentionally drove slowly so they would have more time to talk.

As they got closer to the Hoffman residence Danny resumed speaking, "You sure have a lot of questions. Did I pass the test?" Dee smiled and shrugged her shoulders indicating that she wasn't sure. Danny said coolly, "Ok I got it. By the way, a friend of the family knows the Caldos and he's going to speak to the father. He said to tell you not to worry. No one is going to bother you or go after me, so we're good."

Dee pivoted in her seat staring directly into Danny's eyes; she was puzzled by his comment. "What is your friend some kind of a gangster too?" she reluctantly asked.

Danny tried to hide his annoyance with her on-going parade of questions. He forced a wide smile and said, "The man's name is Gus Galliano, a prominent New York business-man. He owns construction companies, car washes and an Italian restaurant. Everyone respects him; please trust me, I have no reason to lie to you. Before you ask, I called him last night from work, right after I spoke to you. I had to drive over there after work and tell him the whole story. He's angry at the father for his fat son's behavior. Trust me." Danny glanced at the car's clock and knew he was running out of time. "I have to go. I'm gonna be late for work. I'll call you tonight at eight thirty to see if everything remains quiet."

Dee lowered her eyes and muttered, "Sure but just so you know, I may not be home. I only have a few days to buy a prom dress."

As the young beauty exited the car, Danny responded with a wink and thumbs up saying, "Hey, I hope you have a great time."

Danny throttled the car into high speed, seeking to avoid a response. He thought to himself; what was I thinking? A girl of her rare beauty is always going to have guys seeking her affection. Accustomed to loneliness, he tried to pass it off as no big deal. But it *was* a big deal because he was unable to get her face and voice out of his head. He kept telling himself that he wasn't going to call her.

Dee stood there and watched him drive away until his car was out of sight. Baffled and confused, she walked to Mary's house to pick up her little girl. On her way home, she held Abagail's hand and listened to the excitement of her

113

daughter's day. Dee, Abagail, and Lee arrived home at the same time. Once inside, Dee made Abagail a snack and put on the TV so she could watch cartoons.

Her older sister was bursting with anticipation as she asked, "So did he pick you up?"

Dee answered, "Yep."

Lee said eagerly, "Tell me all there is to know. I'm all ears."

Dee said, "He's really a perfect gentleman, I mean really. He even opened the car door for me. He has a new car, and works like three jobs. He graduated from Science and goes to BCC during the day but not in the summer. I know, my knight in shining armor! But there was one thing that was a little weird."

Her pragmatic older sister asked, "Like what?"

"He told me that he would call tonight at eight thirty when he goes to lunch. But when I told him I might not be home because I have to buy a prom dress, he seemed upset. Well, not upset but he had a weird look on his face."

Lee pushed her, questioning, "Did he say anything?"

Dee sighed, "He winked, gave me a thumbs up and said, 'hope you have a great time,' and then he zoomed off. I don't get it."

Lee took her younger sister by the hand and sat beside her on the deeply worn couch. After a prolonged deep breath she remarked, "Did it ever occur to you that on his end he's trying to get to know you and you just brushed him off by mentioning the prom? Listen, this guy that wants to take you to the prom is a jerk and is interested in only one thing. Do I have to spell it out for you? Dee, the devil is in the details. When you tell crazy, good looking always-running Danny boy about Abagail, you'll know for sure if he really wants to get to know you or not. He sounds like a genuine really cool guy. I think you should give it a shot. You know those knights in shining armor types don't come around every day. Sorry for being so long-winded, but that's what I think."

Without further preface Dee asked, "So what should I do?"

Lee's face radiated the look of a mischievous child. "Give prom boy a phone call and tell him to fuck off. If and when this Danny guy calls, tell him you changed your mind and that you're not going to the prom because the guy's a jerk. Next time you're, with him in person show him a picture of Abby and tell him who she is. Then and only then will you ever know."

Motivated, Dee memorized her wise older sister's instructions. She would give up going to the prom in an attempt to get to know the handsome heroic stranger who had rescued her.

It seemed like eight thirty would never come. Dee took her daughter for a long walk around the neighborhood, hoping the clock would magically rotate faster. At eight o'clock, she put Abagail to bed and waited patiently by the phone. Finally the clock struck eight thirty, but the phone remained silent. Ten minutes passed and Dee Hoffman began to feel that she had raised her hopes too high and was headed for immanent disappointment. Finally at eight forty five, the phone rang. Her impatient sister, Lee, answered with a humorous British accent saying, "Hello, Hoffman residence."

Danny chuckled at her flawed impersonation and said, "Hi, this is Danny Corvo, is Dee home?"

Continuing her poor British impersonation Lee replied, "Now you just hold on a bit, Mr. Corvo. I'll check for you." Lee tightly cupped her hand over the receiver to avoid being heard, and said, "Oh Dee, it's Danny Corvo, are you home or are you stupid?"

Dee snapped, "Give me the phone, coo coo girl." Dee's voice was soft and youthfully soothing as she answered, "Hello."

"Hi, it's Danny Corvo. Sorry I'm late with the call but I got stuck on a job. So did you get your dress?"

Dee hesitated arousing his curiosity and said, "Nope, I'm not going to need it."

Danny gleefully responded, "You're not going to need it. Why not?"

Dee paused again and replied, "Because the guy is a jerk and I'm not going to the prom just to say I went. And to quote you that's the way I roll."

Danny clenched his fist, snapping it in approval of the surprisingly good news. He exclaimed, "That's the way you roll?"

Dee was amused by his response and said, "So I guess you're calling to see if everything is quiet. Well it is, and I'm feeling better knowing it's over. Thanks again."

Danny surmised an attempted early dismissal of the conversation so he rapidly responded, "I'm glad you're ok. I have to relieve a group after lunch and I think I'll ask the boss to let me out early. I have swimming instruction tomorrow at nine so I'll probably stop at the Wall Bar, have a beer and a sandwich and go home and hit the hay. It's been a tough week."

Dee sighed, "Oh yeah, it's been tough alright. What time do you get home?"

Danny replied, "I should be sitting in the bar by twelve thirty and hopefully it won't be too crowded and I'll get out of there in a half hour."

She sighed as she said, "I have an idea. Why don't you stop by my house? I'll have a sandwich and a cold beer waiting. You just have to tell me what kind of sandwich and how many beers. We can sit on the front porch so we don't wake up the whole house."

Without a moment of hesitation he answered, "Any kind of sandwich and one beer is my limit. Are you sure you want to stay up that late?"

Dee answered, "I'm always up that late and I think it's the least I can do." She heard the sound of a sudden eardrum piercing whistle blowing in the background as Danny abruptly proclaimed, "Gotta go, see you at twelve thirty, bye."

Danny left work at eleven forty-eight, and drove as fast as the law allowed. He arrived at the Hoffman house at twelve twenty. The young beauty was sitting on the bottom steps of the wooden front porch. She was wearing blue shorts and a white top. Her hair was down, draped over her shoulders. His eyes were aglow with admiration. She looked like an angel. When he reached the steps Dee got up and they shook hands and sat down. She handed Danny a neatly wrapped roast beef on rye and a cold bottle of Miller High Life beer. Neither one would dare say it as both of them tried to conceal their feelings but they were both exactly where they wanted to be.

Danny munched the sandwich in rapid appreciation and said, "Really good sandwich, thanks."

Dee tossed her long blond hair in sultry motion and whispered, "You're welcome."

Danny stared, swallowing her beauty and offered her a slug of beer.

She answered, "No thanks, besides I won't be eighteen for another week. You don't want me to be arrested do you?"

He laughed in respectful response and asked, "So when's your birthday?"

The voluptuous beauty replied, "Next Saturday June eighteenth."

Danny looked up and started counting on his fingers asking, "Are you doing anything special for you birthday?"

She answered in absolute confidence, "Not really. I know my Dad will make a birthday dinner on Sunday, that's always the way we celebrate. I'll be with my family and that's enough for me."

Danny got up and tossed the sandwich wrapper and empty beer bottle in the trash can. He returned to his seat next to her and said, "I have an idea. Since we both had such a crappy week why don't we go to Rye Beach and celebrate your birthday on your birthday? We can stay on the beach for a little while and I know your little girl will love the rides. We don't have to stay all day. It will be fun I promise. What do you say?"

Dee cupped her head in her hands and started rubbing her face in short brisk circles. Shocked by his awareness of her daughter she remained unresponsive. Finally she turned to Danny, her eyes welling with tears and said, "You want to take me on a date and you want my daughter to come?"

Danny moved his face closer to hers and responded, "Absolutely, it will be fun. Have you ever taken her to Rye Beach?"

Dee wiped her eyes and softly answered, "No." Obviously upset she continued rubbing her forehead stopping only to stare at her handsome guardian.

He very calmly asked, "Talk to me, what's wrong?"

She inhaled a few deep breaths of the fresh summer air. Composed she finally started to speak saying, "I'll tell you what's wrong but you have to promise me you're not going to say a word until I'm done, Promise?"

Danny became intrigued by her willingness to share her innermost thoughts and whispered, "I Promise."

Dee answered with a cold boldness, "I'm wrong. When I was thirteen this creepy English teacher took me to his apartment because he told me I had writing talent. He drugged me and raped me. My sister took me to the hospital. The bastard was arrested but I became pregnant. I wanted to kill myself. The Minister and my father who is pretty religious convinced me to have the baby and I'm glad I did but now every boy thinks I'm some kind of an experienced sex machine." She started sobbing as Danny instinctively tried to hold her in a consoling way.

Startled by his sudden touch she pulled away saying, "Let me finish please. I was so drugged that I don't remember one second of the whole ordeal and I'm glad I don't but that's not what people think. I never had a boyfriend. Any boy that ever liked me ran for the hills when they found out I had a kid. The older boys wanted to go out with me because they thought I would be an easy lay, like I'm so experienced. I haven't even kissed a boy since the seventh grade. I'm branded the pretty little neighborhood slut and that's not what I am.... it's not."

Danny moved closer. He let her cry, avoiding any physical act of compassion. When she finished wiping her tears Danny began to speak saying, "Anyone who thinks that of you doesn't know the truth and they're pieces of shit; excuse my French. I don't have a lot of friends. I know a lot of people but that doesn't make them a friend. One of my true friends is a guy named Alan. We went to Science together. He's going to be a doctor so I call him Doc. He knew exactly what happened to you and for your information, he doesn't think you're anything but a beautiful girl who was taken advantage of by a creep."

Dee tried to comment but Danny waved her off. "Now, please let me finish," he scolded. "His mother was the attending nurse when you were admitted. When the rumors started, she told him the truth. A few summers ago you and two of your sisters were walking past the park. You had the baby in the stroller and a group of horny handball players started to whistle and hoot. It wasn't hard to know why. I asked Alan if he knew any of you. He told me you were the Hoffman sisters. That night he told me the truth about what happened to you. People are cruel and often talk when they should keep their mouth shut.

"All I know is this, every day I run it's the same route, up Morris Park to Eastchester to Pelham Parkway to the City Island Bridge. On the way back, I take the Parkway to White Plains Road to Van Nest Round trip is about eight miles. I run that route almost every day. I never, ever, ever run up Mulliner Avenue. This past Thursday, something made me turn up that block. I was at the right spot at the exact time you needed my help. I believe in destiny. You and I were destined to meet on that day at that time under those God awful circumstances." Waving off another attempted interruption he continued, "I'm almost done. I promise. So here we are. How about next Saturday the three of us go to Rye Beach and celebrate your birthday? And now it's your turn to talk," he said.

The light from the street lamp highlighted the blueness in her eyes and the silky softness of her skin. She spoke in a soft girlish tone almost a caress saying, "Danny, you seem like a really nice guy but we've only known each other for two days."

He smirked with a bold confidence as he answered, "Hah, I knew you were going to say that but think about this. My father and mother have been married for over twenty five years and are still happy. There has never been a day that my Dad doesn't kiss my Mom the minute he comes home from work. Sometimes she'll be by the sink, he'll walk up behind her put his arms around her waist and bingo—kiss on the lips time."

Dee smiled and said, "Ahh, that's so sweet but what does that have to do with us knowing each other for only two days?"

Danny rose abruptly and walked to his car. He opened the glove box and removed a small yellow pad of lined paper. He stood before her like a nervous grade school child preparing to read to the teacher. His face had a mischievous grin as he held a wordless pad in his left hand. "It's all written down right here. Everything there is to know about Danny Corvo by Danny Corvo."

Dee Hoffman smiled widely as she became amused by his humorous innovation. He read with the slow annunciation of a grade school student saying, "This explanation of me was written exclusively for Ms. Dee Hoffman. I like running, swimming and fighting. I really, really like beer, fast cars and you."

Dee placed her laughing face in her hands and said, "You are so funny so please continue."

His eyes were fixed on hers as he said boldly. "I will. Check this one out. Somewhere a long time ago, my mother and father only knew each other for two days. That's the way friendships start, one day at a time. Sometimes those friendships turn into something more, it happens all the time... one day at a time. Besides, if it makes you feel more comfortable, I'll pick you up every day until next Saturday and then we'll know each other for a whopping ten days."

Dee's face had a seductive smile as she said, "You Science guys are pretty smart. I have two more questions; one, how old are you? And two, I told you why I don't have a boyfriend. How come you don't have a girlfriend?"

Danny started rubbing his forehead with his fingers pressing deeply into the skin. The question halted his humor as he said, "I'm nineteen. I had a girlfriend in the eighth grade. Her name was Amy Winter. We were together every day. We made each other laugh. We did everything together; our parents gave up on separating us. One day she started to cough and in a few days she was gone, dead at fourteen. I became a loner. I figured if I'm not close to anyone there would be no grieving. I'm not ashamed to tell you that I cried until I ran out of tears. That's why I run. It clears my head. I still go to the cemetery sometimes and kneel by her grave. There were a few girls that I dated but I just never felt comfortable with any of them. I couldn't talk to them and worse than that I didn't want to. I know it sounds weird but I'm just telling you the truth."

Dee placed her open consoling hand on his broad shoulder saying, "I think you and I have had our share of bad times, your story just made me cry you know. I don't want to cry anymore and I don't want you to be sad anymore. Let's meet tomorrow and talk some more. You know for someone who doesn't talk much you sure were full of syllables tonight."

Danny laughed briefly and said, "I've said more to you tonight than I've said to everyone else all week. I don't know why but I'm comfortable talking to you. I hope you feel the same. Where and what time tomorrow? I get home from swimming class as eleven thirty."

Dee tossed her long hair in girlish fashion and said, "I'm comfortable too and I don't know why yet either. How about we meet here at eleven thirty and I'll introduce you to Abby. Her real name is Abagail but we all call her Abby."

Danny remarked, "Abagail—that's a pretty name. Just so you know my real first name is Daniello but my friends call me Danny." He raised Dee's hand to his lips and kissed it. He smiled and wittingly imposed a credible English accent saying, "Good night, Ms. Hoffman. I'll see you tomorrow."

Danny hadn't felt that good in a long time. He went to bed marveling about his new discovery and those hypnotizing deep blue eyes. Could it be that God did answer his prayers? Delia Hoffman could feel the caldron of love bubbling inside her. Something was brewing between them.

Danny pulled up in front of the Hoffman house at eleven thirty. Dee and her older sister Lee were teaching Abby how to skip rope. She proudly introduced him to her sister and then to Abby. When he was asked if he would like to try and skip rope he declined telling them that he was probably too clumsy and it's a girl thing anyway. The girls giggled. Danny squatted down and shook Abby's hand saying, "I feel like ice cream, how about you?" The child was very interested in ice cream on a hot June afternoon. He drove the two sisters and baby Abby to City Island for the best soft serve ice cream in the Bronx.

By the time they returned to the Hoffman house Danny had learned a lot about the family. He learned that Lee was nineteen, Helen was twenty and they both lived at home with Abby and their father, Nelson. Lauren, twenty two the second oldest was away at college and Rose twenty four was married and lived in Connecticut. All five Hoffman girls had blond hair, blue eyes and were naturally desirable.

The sometimes speechless Corvo kid wasn't left with much of a choice but to tell his newly acquired friends about his own family. He told the girls with absolute certainty that his dad Sam knew their father Nelson from the neighborhood barber shop. His father, Sam Corvo was an operating engineer. The neighborhood men dubbed him "Big Sam," a nickname he earned playing high school football. The Hoffman girls were German-American and humorously resisted believing Danny's mother was German. Danny insisted he'd inherited his Sicilian father's black genes and his mother's blue eyes. The girls laughed at his self-proclaimed defamation of his heritage.

At mid-afternoon Danny told the girls that he had to go home to help his Grandfather pull a transmission. Lee played with Abby to allow them a few minutes alone. They made plans to meet that night and the following day. He promised to pick her up from school every day until the end of the school year. They laughed, they hugged, they kissed; something was definitely brewing in the love caldron for Danny Corvo and Dee Hoffman.

Danny picked up Dee and her daughter on Saturday June 18th, her eighteenth birthday. It was a blistering sunny and uncommonly hot day for the middle of June. The three of them changed into their bathing suits and met on the beach. The beach was scarce of people for such a hot June Saturday. Dee wore a modest a one piece white bathing suit; she was angelic. Impressed by her perfectly-formed body Danny asked her if she worked out. She told him that going to school and raising Abby was enough work-out to stay an Olympian in Gold Medal territory. They laughed.

After lunch they ventured on every ride and attraction that permitted a four year old. The threesome laughed in frequent repetition. It was the most fun the two loners had in a very long time. When they arrived home the innovative Danny presented his new friend with a bouquet of long-stemmed roses he had hidden in his trunk on dry ice. She blushed and cried joyfully as it all seemed so surreal.

As they were saying goodbye, Mr. Hoffman arrived. Dee said excitedly, "Hi Dad, I want you to meet a friend of mine, this is Danny Corvo." The two men shook hands and exchanged respectful salutations.

Mr. Hoffman remarked curtly, "Corvo, are you Big Sam the engineer's son?"

Danny answered, "Yes sir."

Mr. Hoffman continued, "I remember you from the Smokers. You sure gave us spectators a treat. You were one hell of a boxer. So, how did you and Delia meet each other?"

Danny glanced at the blushing beauty and very calmly responded, "Well, Mr. Hoffman I guess you could call it happenstance. She dropped her books on her way home from school on the street where I was running. Everyone just kept walking past her as she scrambled to pick them up. I stopped and gave her a hand. We were going in the same direction so I walked her home."

Nelson said, "Sounds like you're a gentleman but then again you are Sam Corvo's son. Your dad is one heck of a good man, tell him I said Hello."

Danny smiled and nodded his head affirmatively saying, "I will thank you Sir."

As Danny attempted to leave, the child put her arms around him and said, "Thank you for the best day I ever had."

Danny squatted down and gave Abby a fatherly embrace saying, "We're going to have more fun days, Abby, I promise."

Danny had won the parental seal of approval from Mr. Hoffman. He turned to his youngest daughter and said, "He seems like a nice guy but only you can know how far your friendship can go. But I'll tell you this, you won't have to worry about anyone bothering you. That's for sure."

Dee smirked as she said to herself, "Oh my God if you only knew!"

CHAPTER 6

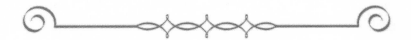

As the July Fourth weekend approached the Corvo family prepared for its annual Fourth of July block party. The quiet dead end block was the perfect party venue lacking the usual cacophony of a busy city street. It was in a sense countrified. The Corvo cousins Phil and Tommy were in Viet Nam but remained diligent in sending letters of hope to the family. Everyone was safe, healthy and solvent. There could be no reason to cancel the annual celebration. Dee had graduated high school and the Plant shutdown would begin right after the holiday giving the young couple the precious commodity of time.

Danny created an extensive list of guest which included Dee, Abby, her sister Lee, his friend Doc and Mr. and Mrs. Robert Kenny. The newly formed couple had been together for less than a month and Danny's parents had never met her. He fore warned his parents about her little girl expecting a tidal wave of unanswerable questions. The classy Hoffman family never made a foul or negative comment about the out-of-wedlock child. Nelson Hoffman was a hardworking man who had lost his wife and struggled to provide for his family. Sam Corvo knew Delia Hoffman was only a child when Kadesh drugged and raped her.

Annabel was a practical mother who hadn't seen her son happy in six years. She hungered to meet the Hoffman girl saying, "I'm going to hold and hug that girl and she will know that I love her from the very first time we meet. What a strong young women she must be; losing her mother and raising a baby. God Bless that girl."

Danny waited on the corner until he could see the three girls approaching Holland Avenue. He kissed Dee on the cheek and held Abby's hand as they walked to the party. When his parents sighted her for the first time Annabel whispered, "Sam she's an angel, look at her. My God her beauty is indescribable."

Danny could read the approval on his parents smiling faces as he said, "Mom, Dad this is the girl I've told you about; Dee Hoffman and her daughter Abby." Annabel hugged Dee and kissed her on the cheek in true European salutation saying, "Welcome to our home, I'm so happy I'm finally meeting you and Abby."

Annabel leaned over as Abby gave her a sudden hug. She melted. Annabel spoke softly, her prepared words as smooth as heated honey, "Hi I'm Danny's Mom, how are you?" The out-going child answered boldly, "I'm Abby, Danny's friend, we like to go for ice cream and take rides in the car, pleased to meet you."

"How smart," said the happy Mrs. Corvo.

The Corvo family's deep religious beliefs enabled them to accept Abagail as a gift from God. The Hoffman girls were showered with love and affection. Dee felt relaxed in their meeting, relieved the anticipation was over. Doc and Lee engaged in a long political conversation. Their political agreement and disdain for the same politicians led the way to a first date.

The following day Danny had gotten a call from Detective Ryan telling him that Mr. G wanted to see him and the girl Wednesday at noon. Dee reluctantly agreed to accompany him to the restaurant. She asked, "Danny, it appears to me that this man treats you like a son, are you related?"

He momentarily remained speechless and finally answered, "You're right, he and his wife treat me like a son and his boys treat me like a brother. I'll tell you why. Nicky was drunk at Orchard Beach and clowning around in the water when a small boat hit him in the head. He became unconscious and went under. He was drowning. I jumped in and pulled him out, gave him CPR and saved his life. I ran away because I didn't want any publicity. Mr. G sent his own private detective to find me. He did. When I met Mr. G and his family, they told me I saved their life too. He and his wife Victoria told me they would help me in any way possible. They even offered to pay for my college. For me meeting the Galliano family was like hitting the Irish Sweepstakes. End of story."

Dee cuddled closer and said softly, "Do you know what I think, Daniello Corvo? The girl that ends up with you is the one that hit the Irish Sweepstakes."

Danny pulled her close saying, "Well, Ms. Hoffman you can't lose when you're in a one horse race! So go and celebrate, you won." They embraced and kissed with heated passion.

The young couple drove to Little Italy to see Mr. G. When they arrived at the restaurant Danny instructed Dee to wait in the car. Mr. G was alone sitting in his usual chair, his back to the wall, always careful always aware of whom was approaching him. He hugged Danny and asked, "So where's the girl?" He answered, "She's in the car. But before I bring her in here I wanted to ask you, why did you tell Caldo that she was my girlfriend?"

Mr. G shook his head indicating the foolishness of the question. Without preface he replied, "It explains your actions and your crazy uncontrollable anger. It also allows me to put him on the hook for more money. Why should he give money to a stranger? But if she's your girlfriend he has to make amends for what his kid did. Understand?"

Danny didn't fully understand Gus Galliano's gangster mentality but nodding his head saying, "Makes sense, I understand, by the way; we've become pretty friendly, she's a sweet girl." Mr. G bowed his head in approval.

Dee wore a blue top and a white dress, not too long, not too short, a lady like garment. When Mr. G observed the young beauty swaying toward his table he could only say, "You kids are a match in heaven, one better looking than the other." He shook Dee's hand, and ordered them to sit. He motioned to his attentive waiter to serve lunch.

When lunch was finished Mr. G slid an envelope across the smooth linen tablecloth. He gestured for Danny to take possession. His dark eyes darted back and forth from Danny to Dee finally settling on her. "Young lady we just met but I guess by now Danny told you about our friendship. He saved my son's life, and more so he saved my family from ruin. Losing a child is the worst hardship life can throw at you. My wife and I love this young man like a son. You're his friend so our love spills over to you as well. Those three bastards tried to do something terrible to you and they have to pay. I could have had all of them thrown in jail but Danny told me that's not what you wanted so I listened to him. The beating Danny gave them was partial payment; in that envelope is payment for your pain and suffering. It's yours, use it wisely."

Mr. G hugged and kissed Danny on the cheek. He took Dee's hand and kissed it in a royal manner. She was touched never having a grown man treat her in such a dignified manner.

When they got back into the car Danny handed her the envelope. She opened it slowly and counted the money. She stared at Danny and screeched, "Holy smoke Danny, there's fifteen hundred dollars here." She brushed her hair aside so her face was in full view saying, "Are you sure your friend's not a gangster?"

He made a circular hand gesture of uncertainty saying, "I'm not sure of anything except this, I'm glad I decided to run Mulliner Avenue on that day."

Dee squeezed his hand, "So am I, so am I," she said softly.

Dee asked Danny to be the custodian of the fifteen hundred dollars fearing that someone in her family would find it and force her to disclose how she got it. Understanding her dilemma he planned on depositing the money in the safety of his Grandpa's gun safe. The excitement of Mr. G's generous gift had the young couple driving aimlessly around the Bronx.

Danny asked, "You know when Mr. G asked me your name I wanted to say Delia, it's really a beautiful name. How come you don't use it?"

She responded, "I do sometimes, but my sisters started calling me Dee for short and it kind of stuck. You know Lee's real name is Leanne but we call her Lee for short. See what I mean?" Danny raised his eyebrows and said, "I do, but I think Delia is a really pretty name." Her angelic face was rosy with delight as she childishly sighed, "So call me Delia, Dee whatever you want… long as you call me." They kissed at the traffic light and received an avalanche of horn blowing from the impatient Bronx motorist.

The young couple became inseparable. He would start working for Mr. G on the coming Sunday, July 10th and was looking forward to operating the excavator. He would start working at six in the morning and be finished at two thirty granting him leisure time in the evening.

The following Saturday was training with Mr. Chan and his son Chris. Training was always intense; rest was not part of the curriculum. Danny's abundance of running and skipping rope kept him in the aerobic condition required to complete a Chan training session.

When Danny arrived, Mr. Chan and Chris both had an unusual look on their face; something was up. Mr. Chan announced I have good news and bad news for you two. He exposed his biggest grin a rarity and began to speak, "Well tough guys, starting next month we will be training with ten police officers from the NYPD. These guys are not any of the donut eaters. They're part of the Mayor's tactical patrol force and are all in great shape."

Danny grinned and asked, "So what's the bad news?"

"It's going to be tougher and longer but you boys will be fine. They will respect what you know, therefore they will respect you. Also, they agreed that you two can come to the shooting range when we get to firearm training," said Mr. Chan.

Danny exclaimed, "Whoa, that's sounds great, but who's going to teach that?" Mr. Chan's grin widened as he proudly proclaimed, "I will. Oh, I forgot to tell you boys, during the war I was a trained sniper." Danny was looking forward to training with the NYPD guys in August but for now he had to concentrate on working the excavator on Sunday.

He rose extra early on Sunday morning not wanting to be late for a Mr. G assignment. Driving directly to the job site on Bruckner Boulevard he anxiously waited for Mr. G's operator to arrive. The operator was Benny Longo an older man in his late fifties who claimed to be a life-long friend of Mr. G.

There were two John Deere excavators and one bull-dozer on site. Benny was a grizzly bear sized man with broad shoulders, an unusually wide forehead and tree trunk fore-arms. His unusually high-pitched voice did not match his physical appearance. When he started to speak Danny had to gag his laughter. He threw Danny the keys to the excavator and said, "Hey kid, get up in the cab with me and I'll watch you for a bit to see if you know what you have to know. Start digging a trench along the painted line it goes for about two hundred feet, got it?"

Danny nodded yes and began to dig. Two minutes later Benny shouted over the chattering sound of the loud diesel engine, "Stop the machine and let me off. You're as good as I was told. We'll be out of here in no time and get paid for the whole day."

At eleven o'clock the project was complete. Benny praised the young operator and told him to go home. Guilty about leaving early he approached Benny and said, "Benny there's one thing I can't do and that's lie to Mr. G. I can't accept pay for a whole day when we only worked five hours. Sorry, no can do."

Benny's laughter was also comically high-pitched as he said bluntly, "Listen, Mr. G is going to be elated that we fin-ished the job early, less wear and tear on the machines. Also, he pays us for the job not how long it takes, get this; if we didn't finish until ten tonight we still get the same pay. So stop thinking we are doing something wrong."

Alan had asked Danny to play handball on the follow-ing Friday afternoon. They hadn't seen much of each other so Danny agreed. Proud of his physical dexterity he invited Delia and Abby to come and watch. Dee was pleased to be invited to watch this 'guy thing' but told Danny that she couldn't get there until around one o'clock.

Alan and Danny held the court in brilliant dominance for over an hour, it was getting near one o'clock. Once again they heard salacious innuendoes from the other court. Alan said with great assurance, "Guess your girl's here." The hormone-ravaged boys were tantalized by her unique beauty prompting their whistles, gestures and immature comments. The foolish admirers watched Dee and her daughter walk into the handball court to greet Danny. He crouched down and held the youngster in his arms. Rising to his feet, he embraced and kissed the beautiful attraction that was his. The Gaga story had circulated and it grew a fearful respect for Danny Corvo. The uncontrollable admiration the boys had for Delia Hoffman was wisely harbored in their subconscious minds. The whistles and taunting became a thing of the past, never to be repeated.

They spent all their free time together during July of 1966. Abby came to love Danny the same way any happy kid loves their father. Quiet to a fault Danny always had a story for little Abby Hoffman. He played games with her, took her for walks and ice cream was always on his menu.

The young mother could see the relationship between her little girl and Danny was becoming an unbreakable bond. She became happy and scared in the same instant. She asked herself, "What happens if he gets tired of me? What happens if he finds someone else who doesn't have any kids? He never told me he loves me. What if it's just infatuation and nothing more, then what?" She had to tell him she was becoming afraid and why.

It was nine o'clock on Sunday night. Danny had worked all day excavating and was looking forward to spending time with his girl. Benny Longo had handed him an envelope and said, "This is from the boss, he pays us once a month." Mr. G had paid him three hundred and twenty dollars in cash for four Sunday's, eighty dollars a day. Danny was overjoyed knowing he had to work forty hours on the assembly line to clear one hundred and ten dollars.

The young couple was sitting on the front porch engaged in meaningless young lover's chit-chat. She knew, now was the time to talk to him about her feelings. Danny had taught Dee how to drive a standard shift car. She passed her driver's test on the first try and was enthusiastic about buying a used car. Danny told her about all the decent used cars Grandpa Joe and Paulie were able to locate.

When the topic of purchasing a car came to center stage, he could sense that her mind was somewhere else; puzzled by her lack of interest he asked, "So what's wrong?"

Dee cupped her hands around his face and said, "I don't know how to explain it, but I'll try." He removed her hand from his face as she continued to speak, "When I was walking home from school that terrible Thursday I could never imagine in a million years how my life would change. I met you; we became friends, best friends. You saved me from another suicide-prompting disaster and it's been great, almost too good to be true; the best days of my life. But I'm worried."

Danny raised his finger to his lips gesturing that she should stop speaking and said curtly, "Worried, why?"

She answered with bold conviction, "Abby is becoming too attached to you. What happens if you find someone else; someone without a kid, someone with no baggage. I don't think it's smart for me to make her think you're always going to be around every minute of every day. Also, I have to find a job. I can't keep leaching off my father. When I'm working days, you'll be in school. When I'm home at night, you'll be working. Your weekends are so busy we won't have any time together. Don't you see what I'm saying?"

Danny lowered his head as his fingers aggressively massaged his forehead. His voice lowered to a soft register as he muttered, "I understand your concern but I don't understand what you want to do. Help me out here; what do you want us to do?"

Her eyes teared up as makeup ran down the young beauty's face. She said bluntly, "I think we should give it a rest for a week. I want to see how Abby reacts. I want to see how she feels, the questions she asks. You asked me to trust you and I did and now I'm asking you to trust me, it's only a week. We can meet next Saturday night, right here at nine o'clock."

He got up and stared into her eyes. It was not a look of love but one of contempt. Delia stood up and put her arms around him. Danny stood with his arms limp at his side unwilling, to return her embrace.

She softly whispered in his ear, "It's not even a week, trust me. I'll be waiting for you, next Saturday at nine o'clock. I have to find out. Please don't be mad."

Her words "give it a rest," cast Danny Corvo into self-condemnation the inescapable route to his dungeon of silence. As Danny walked to his car, Doc and Lee were returning home from the movies. They had been dating since the Corvo Fourth of July bash. As they both waved hello, Doc yelled out, "How's it going Danny, what's the hurry?"

Danny winked and gave them the thumbs up, climbed into the convertible without opening the door and drove off. Doc knew something was wrong.

Lee approached her troubled younger sister cautiously attempting to avoid a screaming match that would wake up their father. With a sincere softness in her voice Lee asked, "Dee, Danny looked upset, out of character, what's wrong?"

The young mother explained her innermost feelings and fears to her closest sister. She expected a long philosophical lecture but didn't get one as Lee said quietly, "You two will work this out and I'll tell you why. That boy loves you with every ounce of strength that God gave him and then some more. Everyone can see it, even Dad. I understand your concerns but love will prevail, it always does. Stay calm, give him a chance. Love you, goodnight."

Danny was confused, depressed, sad and angry at the same time. He drove to Paulie's to see if he was still hanging around the shop. It wasn't unusual for him to work until midnight even on the weekends. He was young, married with a daughter, and had an uncontrollable desire to please his very demanding Italian spouse. A fifteen hour workday became commonplace. Danny put up the convertible top and locked his car.

Paulie was still working and was glad to see his good friend. He called out sarcastically, "Hey stranger where have you been?"

Unresponsive to the question he answered, "I came for the Indian."

Paulie asked, "Hey, is everything all right, you look a little fucked up?"

"Come on, you know the deal everything is never all right. I need the bike." he answered. Paulie got the bike, primed it, started it and gave it to his anxious friend. He rode around until two in the morning trying to figure out what triggered Delia's madness. Danny arrived at the only reasonable explanation, "she's a woman and the answer is there is no answer."

When Danny got up on Monday morning, he pushed himself to run twenty miles stopping briefly to take in water. His mother sensed something was wrong and his defiant silence was the evidence. She knew not to push him. He worked in the shop with Grandpa Joe until he had to run again and again. Grandpa Joe also knew something was wrong; girl trouble.

By Wednesday, Annabel's motherly love and curiosity defeated her will to remain silent. She asked, "How come you're not with Delia and Abby. You haven't seen them since Sunday. What's wrong?"

He said coolly, "Don't know; she's scared."

Annabel convinced him to listen to her motherly counseling about the workings of the female mind. She demonstrated humor in her explanation of female wisdom, arousing a brief smile. Annabel listened intensely to every detail, every word that her son would tell her. She assured Danny that in her valued opinion, he was making too much of too little, a mountain out of a mole hill. Delia had some very genuine concerns according to the infinite wisdom of his mother.

Annabel made them a cup of tea and ordered her youngest son to sit across from her in the kitchen. Her expression was not one of a loving mother but one of a scolding principal. She said sternly, "I want you to listen to me very, very carefully, Daniello. In order for me to help you, you have to be willing to help yourself. I can't help you unless you level with me and your inner self. There is only one question that you have to know the answer to and it's a simple one."

Danny nodded as she continued, "Do you love Delia Hoffman? That's the big question. You don't have to answer me but you do have to answer yourself. I know you two have only known each other for two months, but I fell in love with your father after three weeks. When you answer that question it becomes even less complicated; if the answer is no, there's nothing to talk about and nothing to worry about. However, if the answer is yes another question will arise."

Impatient, he snarled sarcastically, "What's that?"

Annabel picked up her tea cup and clutched it in both hands; she moved closer and said, "Did you ever tell her? You know we girls are quite intuitive but we can't read minds."

Danny's voice trembled with emotion as he responded, "Mom I love that girl more than myself, Abby, too. I just don't know why she can't see it."

Annabel answered, "Danny you've heard the old saying, actions speak louder than words?" He nodded affirmatively as she continued, "Well in the case of love that's not always true. Actions, good deeds and good intentions can be misinterpreted or unintentionally discarded. Saying I love you ends all speculation and conjecture; it's simple to understand. Just say, I love you."

Danny loved Delia Hoffman but in his once-broken heart, he felt that she was the beneficiary of all his generosity and heroic deeds. He wasn't worried about giving more than he would get but she too never whispered those three little words. Now he is confronted with another dilemma. He was just given advice from an unimpeachable source—his mother.

He decided to talk to his sister Rosemarie. Rosemarie also recognized the great change in her little brother since his budding romance with the Hoffman girl. He was beyond the boundaries of happiness and she wanted to keep him there.

She listened to Danny's explanation of what happened and tried her very best to counsel him. She said, "Tell me if I have this right." You want to tell Dee that you love her but, and it's a big but, you want to make sure that she loves you too. Am I getting the idea, Danny?"

He grinned boyishly and answered, "Yeah you got it." Rosemarie took a deep breath and said, "I have an idea that just might work."

Danny asked excitedly, "What?"

Roe answered, "Nat King Cole." Danny very slowly pronounced each syllable of the famous singer's name, "Nat… King…Cole. We're going to get Nat King Cole to tell Dee that

I love her and then she'll tell me that she loves me. Roe you're not smoking weed are you?"

She laughed in a loud tone and said, "Between you and your brother, I probably should be smoking something but for now I'm clean. Listen, Nat King Cole sang the song, 'When I Fall in Love.' You have to listen to it. In the song he sings that when he falls in love it will be forever and when he gives his heart it will be completely. At the end, he sings, 'And the moment that I feel that you feel that way too, is when I'll fall in love with you.' So give her the forty five, we'll black out the name and title. Make her promise to listen to the whole song.

"At the end of the song she will hear, 'And the moment that I feel that you feel that way too, is when I'll fall in love with you.' When she hears those words, and by the way he sings those lyrics twice at the end of the song, she's going to have to tell you that she feels that way too or she doesn't. I know it's a little corny but it's romantic, beautiful, and just what she needs to hear."

The love-struck young man developed an instant eagerness for the idea and inquired, "Where can I find that forty five?"

Roe said reassuringly, "In my room. Wait here, I'll go and get it."

It was Friday, August 5, 1966. The sun was a bright orange blaze and it radiated a skin blistering heat. The temperature surpassed ninety degrees by ten am. The love-struck youngster didn't waste any time. He blacked out the name of the artist and the song, put it in a large manila envelope with cardboard so it wouldn't bend and placed in the Hoffman mailbox by six thirty in the morning. He attached a note which read, "Delia, Please listen to the end, no stopping please. I'll be home all day working with my grandfather, let me know what you think. You can call the shop number. Thanks, Danny."

He learned the Hoffman's received their mail between ten and eleven in the morning. What the great believer in destiny didn't know was that Delia went for a job interview in Manhattan and wouldn't return home until midafternoon.

Many years before, when the boys were young, Grandpa Joe had built an outdoor training area behind the far end of his garage. It had a concrete slab for lifting weights and skipping rope, and welded angle iron to secure a heavy bag.

By two o'clock Danny Corvo convinced himself that Roe's idea was flawed, a failure of great expense. Downhearted he removed his work shirt, replaced his work boots with sneakers and started skipping rope on the concrete slab behind the garage.

Delia arrived home from her interview at two fifteen and walked directly to Mary's house to pick up Abby. When she arrived home Lee handed her the envelope from Danny. Dee was ambivalent to open it but knew she didn't have a choice. Good news or bad news, she had to read it. Seeking privacy she went down into the basement where her father had stored the old portable record player. After reading his note she plugged it in on his work bench. Her curiosity made her heart race. She thought to herself, "What in the world is this boy doing?"

She set the volume to low so only her ears would be privileged to hear whatever Danny had sent her. She knew from the beginning lyrics exactly what he was trying to tell her. Once again her eyes swelled with tears, but these were happy tears of gratitude. Rosemarie, the perennial romantic, had guided her little brother straight into Delia Hoffman's heart. After listening to the words, "'And the moment that I feel that you feel that way too, is when I fall in love with you,'" all her doubt was erased.

Delia was still wearing the dress and blouse that she wore to the interview. Running upstairs she yelled in a begging manor. "Lee, please watch Abby, I'll be back as soon as I can." Kicking off her high heels she slipped into her tennis shoes and started running the seven blocks to the Corvo house.

The temperature was flirting with one hundred degrees. The eye-catching beauty was a comical sight running in a formal dress and tennis shoes. She received whistles of admiration before finally reaching the dead end. She began walking up the long hot black topped driveway.

Danny was behind the garage skipping rope and out of her sight. Grandpa Joe smiled at her presence. He said, "I guess you're looking for Danny?" He put his index finger in front of his lips, "Shhhh come here I want you to see something." Quietly he walked Delia into the last bay of the garage where a small window faced the workout area. At five foot four she was not tall enough to peer through the glass window.

Grandpa Joe gave her a stool; she carefully stepped onto the stool and watched Danny skipping rope. She was aghast at his level of professionalism. She had never seen anything like it the speed challenging the eyes to find the rope. Faster and faster he crossed the rope at will. When she saw him cross the rope from a squatting position, she couldn't control herself and blurted, "Holy shit." Blushing, she apologized to Grandpa Joe.

Dismissive of her language, he said proudly, "That's why I wanted you to see it. He never shows anyone; you know, that's his way."

Dee watched for a few more seconds. He stopped skipping and in angry conquest slammed the rope to the concrete floor. Grandpa Joe held her hand and helped her off the stool. He whispered, "Shhh, now go and talk. I'm going into the house."

Danny was shirtless and drying himself off with a beach towel. Dee walked closer, startling him. She put her arms around him. Looking up at his sweating face she said, "Kiss me."

Danny was momentarily alarmed but gladly followed her command. It was a long kiss. Dee placed her hands around his face saying, "Do you feel it, that I feel that way, too?"

After another long kiss, Danny knew it was the perfect time to say what he had rehearsed so many times. He said in proud response, "I could tell you that I love you and I do but more than that I'm in love with you." Tearfully she whispered, "I'm so in love with you, I hate myself for getting you upset."

Danny drove Delia home as they made plans to meet after dinner that evening. She said mockingly, "By the way Danny, I thought skipping rope was a girl thing?"

Danny surmised that she must have seen him thanks to his big proud Grandpa, so he answered, "It is, I'm just better at it." He motioned for Dee to come back to the car. He whispered, "I love you and I always will." Blowing a symbolic kiss, she slowly sounded out the words, "I love you too and I always will."

That night, the encounter on the front porch was about the future, their future. Delia told him that she thought her job interview for a position as a receptionist in Manhattan went very well. When she told Danny it paid sixty five dollars a week, he said, "I almost forgot to tell you. Wait until you hear this. Mr. G paid me eighty dollars a day for the excavating work. I counted the money twice; I couldn't believe it. Eighty dollars a day, in cash. I know Sunday's pay double time but that's still a lot of money."

Dee shook her head and smiled, "Maybe you can ask him if he has any job openings. I know this really hard working German-American girl who's looking for a job." Dee's comment was meant in jest.

Danny defused her laughter by saying, "You know, Dee sometimes things we say in jest become a reality. He has eight, nine, maybe ten companies. Who knows, maybe he can use someone like you. Besides, I don't like the idea of you going all the way to Manhattan for sixty five dollars a week. I'm going to ask him."

Dee insisted that she was only kidding but he reiterated that it was a noteworthy idea and there was nothing to be lost in the asking. Danny left early that Friday night, knowing the following day was the first undercover training session with Mr. Chan and the NYPD. Delia knew he was physically spent and didn't think anything of his early departure.

Danny arrived early at Mr. Chan's. He and Chris exchanged salutations with the ten NYPD tactical patrol officers. Men in their late twenties and early thirties, they appeared physically empowered. Despite their physical appearance they possessed only the bare basic knowledge of self-defense. The two boys had the policeman enthusiastically impressed with their knowledge and skill.

Sergeant Malone, the group team leader, asked Danny his age and how long he had been training. He told him, "I'm nineteen and have been training since I was ten."

The Sergeant answered, "Well, I'm glad you boys are on our side of the law. I wouldn't want to deal with the physical battle of arresting either of you." The NYPD tactical patrol force's first impression developed into a genuine respect for the knowledge and skills of these two clean cut boys.

On Monday, Danny went to visit Mr. G and his wife in Riverdale. He asked Mr. G if he could have a word with him privately.

Gus Galliano was in a rare fine spirit as he laughingly asked, "So who did you beat up now?"

"No, no it's nothing like that; first I wanted to make sure that there wasn't a mistake in the pay you gave me for operating the machinery. Eighty dollars a day in cash is a lot of money," he said.

Gus smiled, "Its right, that's what I wanted. Is there anything else?"

Danny answered, "I hate to ask you but I was wondering if there was a job you knew about for Delia. She's really smart and is really good at bookkeeping and accounting. She went for a job interview but the job is all the way down in Manhattan."

Gus lashed out, "How many times do I have to tell you not to be sorry for asking." His large open hand patted Danny gently on the cheek a welcomed gesture of assured calmness. He said, "Let me talk to Victoria, I'm sure we can use her, don't worry. Most of these girls today are prima donnas and they don't last long with Victoria's Sicilian temper. You know she's really easy to work for but some of these kids think the world owes them a blow job. They come in late, don't finish what they started, and call in sick. It doesn't work that way. I'll call you in a few days."

The days passed and he was ordered to stop by the restaurant. Mr. G. wanted to speak about Delia and a few other things he had on his mind. Always respectful, he arrived early and was escorted to the private office on the second floor.

After a customary greeting Mr. G began to speak, "Life is full of opportunity, timing is everything. Let me start with this girl friend of yours. I have an office building in one of my supply yards on Eastchester Road. That's where we order, store and track all our construction material. Victoria needs someone immediately to learn that job so she can spend more time processing the payroll. She needs someone who is ambitious but more importantly someone she can trust. It pays seventy-five dollars a week and is close to her home."

Danny rose from his chair in jubilant surprise and said, "Thank you. You won't regret hiring Delia."

"Sit back down and allow me to finish," he quipped. "I want you to stop calling me Mr. G. It's too formal. That's for people who need a constant reminder of who's is charge, not you. Call me Gus." Danny nodded in a repetitious slowness indicating that he understood. Gus continued, "Remember what I told you, timing is everything. One of my heavy equipment operators got himself in a tussle with a guy that was screwing his wife. He killed him. Sounds like the right thing to do, but now he's going away for a long time. I need to find a replacement."

Gus rose from the table and walked around to sit next to Danny. Once seated, he put his hand on the young man's shoulder and asked, "So do you want to operate heavy equipment or work on the boring assembly line for the rest of your life?"

Danny sighed and said, "You always think of me, you're like another father. It's really an easy choice. I'll drive up to the plant tomorrow and tell them I'm changing jobs. When do you want me to start?"

Gus shook his head in displeasure and said boldly, "Hey kid, listen to me. Tomorrow you don't go anywhere. Keep collecting your unemployment check, it's your due. When it runs out then you can tell them. Don't be in a hurry to throw away your own money. You can start work on Monday. I'll let you know what job site to report to and you have to bring your girlfriend to the yard on Eastchester to meet with Victoria. Do that tomorrow morning between ten and eleven understand?"

Danny answered politely, "I sure do, and I thank you again."

Gus was grinning as he said, "Don't be so quick to thank me the job only pays forty dollars a day. Now we have some unfinished business to talk about."

Danny innocently replied, "We do?"

"You never told me how you learned to fight like a pro. You know being in good shape and well-built doesn't mean you can handle yourself. I heard that biker story more than once. Some say you took out the fat fuck in less than a minute. So what's the story?" he queried.

Danny squirmed in his chair in nervous response and said, "This is awkward for me. Can I tell you the short version?"

Gus became amused. He answered quickly, "Danny boy, you know I'm not about bull shit so tell me the short version."

Danny promptly answered anxious to finish what he swore not to tell anyone, "Well, Gus, my father has a Chinese friend and he was a martial arts master, a sharpshooter, and a military technique genius. I've been training with him since I was ten years old. He kept no secrets from us and that, in a nutshell, is the story."

Gus smiled and replied, "Hmmm, now that makes some kind of sense. That degree of skill had to come from somewhere. You mentioned that he didn't keep any secrets from us. Who were the other people?"

Danny lowered his head knowing that he would now have to divulge another piece of his sworn secret and said, "His son, Chris. No one else that started with us lasted. They couldn't make the grade and were dismissed from the class. The training is brutal on a good day." Gus's inquiry had finally been satisfied and they bid each other farewell.

CHAPTER 7

D anny drove Delia to meet Mrs. Galliano at the Eastchester office. If Delia didn't know the reality of their relationship, she would have thought Victoria was his mother. She had a parental admiration for him. It was apparent that she was proud and wanted him to succeed. She told Delia that she heard so much about her and was delighted they were finally meeting.

A new chapter started in the lives of Danny Corvo and Delia Hoffman as they both began working for the very powerful and influential Galliano family. The following Monday was the assigned start date and both were anxious to demonstrate the skills they had acquired. Their work was close to home, paid very well and gave them time to spend together.

Delia was pleased when she received her first official paycheck. She grossed seventy-five dollars and netted sixty-two dollars and seventy cents. When she asked Danny to see his check, he laughed and produced a wad of bills. Gus paid him two hundred dollars cash in order to avoid a disturbance of his unemployment payment.

The happier they were, the faster the time eroded into memories. Danny took Delia to meet with Gus's sons, Tommy and Nicky, at their junk yard in the South Bronx. Tommy had told Danny that he had the deal of a lifetime on a car. A 1965 Chevrolet Impala had been totaled in a crash and the Galliano brothers happened to have a stolen identical 1965 Impala in the yard. It was just a simple matter of swapping the vehicle identification tags and the stolen car became legal. The wrecked car gets put in the crusher and sold for scrap. The brothers charged a grand for a twenty five hundred dollar car and everyone wins.

Delia didn't know much about cars or their prices but she did know that this deal was suspiciously too good to be true. Danny told her that the brothers Galliano had some good luck and they wanted them to be a partial recipient of that luck. She accepted his far-fetched story with a grateful smile and was wise enough never to ask again.

Danny escorted Delia to pick up the car. Nicky's salutation was brief as he asked Danny to join him in the office trailer. Nicky remained forever grateful that Danny saved his life but beyond that he admired him. Nicky had been working out with light weights and following a daily regimen of calisthenics Danny Corvo provided.

Nicky looked uneasy as he asked, "How did you two get here. I didn't see your car?"

"We took a cab so she could drive the car home. She's happy," said Danny.

Nicky continued, "Danny, I'm worried about Tommy. He's becoming a party animal. He smokes weed and drinks like a mother fucker and I understand that, I mean I was a fuck-up too. He's hardly ever here and all I do is cover up for him with the old man. All the chicks and fucking around that's one thing but I think he's doing some heavy drugs."

Nicky locked the trailer door from the inside saying, "Don't worry I'll just be a minute. I want to show you something." He opened the huge bank safe that concealed a cash box and an assortment of guns. Nicky hastily moved some boxes around and said, "Check this out, see these bags that's fucking heroin. Look in this one, fucking needles; I don't know what to do."

Danny was unprepared for such news and replied, "Let me think on it but we have to do something. This is bad." Nicky embraced Danny saying, "Thanks bro, let me know. I wanted you to see it first-hand. We may have to go to the old man to get him some help before it's too late."

Delia drove Danny to her house where everyone was excitedly waiting to see the new car. When she pulled up the family was cheering as her grinning father threw good luck change into the car. Danny stayed for dinner to help celebrate the happy occasion.

Danny's mind was drifting through a maze of options thinking about Tommy Galliano. He shared some his thoughts with Delia, but this was different; he didn't want her mind to speculate. It was bad enough that she knew the Galliano's power exceeded that of white shirted businessmen. Delia was a very young mother but she was not street wise. She could never understand guns in a safe; wads of money or narcotics. Danny needed advice but who could he talk to and trust?

Lieutenant Derosa grew up on the mean streets of East Harlem and knew first-hand the perilous death trap of heroin addiction. He was a life coach for Danny Corvo filled with worldly wisdom and experience one cannot learn in college. His blunt reply lacked hesitation as he said, "The first thing you have to find out is how deep your friend is into this heroin. How long has he been on it, how much does he take? If he's hooked, you know, addicted, it's bad. Heroin is one of the hardest drugs to get off of once you're hooked. If he stays on it and doesn't get help it's only a matter of time. He'll get some bad shit or OD, you know overdose. Then someone will find him dead."

Danny said curtly, "With all due respect, I knew most of what you told me, you know about the dangers and all that but how do I get him help."

Derosa's voice rose into a loud register. "You and the brother have to confront him. Look at his arms for needle marks. Open that fucking safe and show him his shit. Tell him he's going to die. It's that simple. His father has tons of money. He has to go to a professional rehabilitation center. There is one other possibility; maybe he's selling it, which isn't good either. In either event, you and the brother have to confront him. If there are no marks on his arms, he's probably dealing."

Tommy spent time at the yard in the mornings, then disappeared after lunch. Unannounced, Danny showed up early the following morning and relayed Derosa's advice to Nicky. Tommy sat in the trailer sipping coffee in his usual unconcerned manner. His once-chubby face was sunken from the sudden weight loss. The air was thick with silence as Nicky opened the safe. Tommy was nervous as droplets of perspiration formed on his thick forehead. He was uneasy about the presence of Corvo. He attempted to cut through the silence and apply humor saying, "I know Danny don't need a gun, so what's up?"

Nicky was frothing with rage as he threw the heroin packets and needles on the desk shouting, "This is what's up. What the fuck is wrong with you? You want to fucking die?"

The startled heroin user became defensive and said, "I don't really use that much. I'm ok. Don't make a big deal over nothing. I know what I'm doing."

Danny's face twisted with anger as he grumbled, "That's the oldest story in the addicts' handbook. It's eighty degrees at eight in the morning. What's with the long-sleeve shirt? Do you think we're going to get snow?"

Tommy had a profound physical fear of Corvo and found no consolation in his sarcastic humor. He became teary-eyed. He joined his hands as in prayer and said nervously, "Please don't tell the old man. I can stop, I know I can, just let me prove it."

Nicky scooped up the packets of heroin and flushed them down the toilet. The hypodermic needles were slammed to the floor and broken into pieces by his boot heels. Nicky was unable to regain his composure as he shouted, "Take the fucking shirt off." There were visible marks, but not the tracks of the typical junkie. Nicky and Danny agreed to give him a week to get clean.

Nicky retrieved a snub-nosed 38 from the gun safe and placed it on the desk with an uncomfortable force. He spun the gun in short circles until the barrel posted on his brother. His voice became deviously soft as he said, "You tell them hippie assholes that if they come around here peddling that shit, they're going into the crusher; and I don't give a fuck if they're still alive when I put them there!"

Danny left, concerned about Tommy's true condition. All junkies lie and both of them knew it. Mr. Galliano had been like a second father to him, and that made Danny feel especially guilty about remaining silent. He convinced himself that it was only for a week and if things didn't improve the old man was going to be told anyway.

He stopped by the yard on Friday morning before going to the job. Nicky reported that his brother was diligent and it looked like he's getting his act together. Relieved from the guilt he headed to work.

151

Tommy straightening himself out on his own meant Gus would be spared the distressful details. His mood tilted toward happiness, allowing him to daydream about spending time alone with his girlfriend. He was off that weekend, so they made plans to take Abby to Jones Beach on Long Island.

Some say, if you want to make God laugh, all you have to do is tell him that you made plans. The Corvo family phone rang at two thirty in the morning. Sam Corvo rose from his slumber and answered the hallway phone. Good news is never announced at two-thirty in the morning.

Danny could hear his father whispering, "Oh my God, I'm so sorry Nick, let me go and wake Danny."

But Danny had been awakened by his father's voice; he overheard the preface of his father's conversation and knew something unfortunate had happened. He anxiously whisked the phone from his father's hand and answered, "Hello Nicky, what happened?"

Nicky was trying to speak but the wailing gave way to incoherent gibberish. Danny pleaded, "Nicky please slow down I can't understand you." Taking rapid deep breaths, his voice became clearer as he muttered, "Tommy's dead, he crashed into a cement column down by the Tri-borough Bridge. He must have been doing a hundred; there are car parts all over the place. I don't think there's nothing left of his body. He's gone, Danny. My brother is gone."

Danny told his parents that he had to drive to the Galliano Estate in Riverdale. His wise mother persuaded him to wait until the morning and allow the desolate family to grieve.

Early Saturday morning, Danny told Delia that Tommy Galliano had been killed in a car crash. He arrived at the Galliano estate at eight fifteen. The iron gates at the front of the Galliano estate were opened and protected by men with guns. Two police cars were parked at the top of the circular drive by the main entrance.

Victoria greeted Danny with the frightened face of a lost child. Her beautiful face was bleached of color. No parent could be prepared for this kind of tragedy. Gus greeted him with the forceful embrace of a grieving father. His face was without expression, like the motionless lines of a marble statue. He spoke with a cold preparedness saying, "Danny, I always told the boys and you too; don't drive like an asshole. The cops told us he was doing over a hundred miles an hour, God help him. I cried all night. You saved us from a day like this when you saved Nicky. After that miracle, who would have ever thought that something like this would befall this family? I think I'll do what they do in the Jewish faith—a one-day wake, tomorrow Sunday. We can have his mass and funeral on Monday. I can't have Victoria sit there staring at that closed box for three days and three nights; it will kill her."

Danny tried to mimic the strength that was Gus Galliano but his youthful eyes soon welled with tears as he muttered, "I want to know if there is anything I can do to help. I know words don't really do much at times like this, but if there is anything I can do I want to do it. I loved that kid like a brother."

Gus rested his heavy hands on Danny's shoulders and said, "I know you boys became close like brothers and I always approved of that friendship. Too bad Tommy couldn't follow your obsession to work out like Nicky did; even thought they were twins they were different. He was wild."

Victoria summoned her husband into the kitchen and told him the wake was to be held on Sunday only; from three to six pm and from eight to ten pm. The Pastor arranged the mass for Monday at ten am. The burial would take place at Saint Raymond's Cemetery on Tremont Avenue and a luncheon was arranged at Alex and Henry's restaurant in the South Bronx. Gus refused to have one of his restaurants be a reminder of his son's death.

When Danny started to leave the grasp of Gus's oversized hand propelled him back saying, "Danny, I know that I'm not your father and I would never infringe on that relationship but I want you to know that I have grown to love you like a son."

Danny embraced the grief-weary Gus Galliano saying, "I love you too. Thank you. That means the world to me."

The wake of Thomas Galliano became the venue that introduced the Corvo family to the Galliano's. The educated and sophisticated Gus Galliano portrayed the quiet, somber demeanor of a confident businessman. From his introductory salutation through his praise for their son the Corvo's were star-struck with his presence.

Nicky Galliano's reputation for being a cold and hard-shelled portrait of his grandfather was not visible. The whites of his eyes were red and moistened with clear flowing tears. He offered a hand of friendship while apologizing. He said dryly, "Thank you for coming. Please excuse my lack of self-control, but I'm having a hard time. You know this son of yours is like another brother to me."

Annabel gently held Nicky by the arm and said, "I don't know if Danny ever told you but he had a twin brother who also died. I'm happy you two boys have each other."

After the funeral luncheon, Danny told Delia something that would become etched in her memory. His face was sullen. His words were clearly annunciated as he said, "On the day of a funeral it doesn't matter if it's beautiful and sunny or cloudy, rainy, dark and gloomy. It doesn't matter if the person was young or old. It doesn't matter if they took a long time to die or if they died suddenly. Funerals always suck."

CHAPTER 8

As the sunny days of August 1966 gave way to early autumn Mr. Chan gave the boys his September itinerary. Unexpectedly the Tactical Patrol Force Sargent reserved the gun range for every Saturday in September. Danny was now burdened with the uncomfortable task of asking Lieutenant Derosa to be excused from his Saturday obligations. Derosa not an easily excitable man acquiesced to his unprecedented request.

Sargent Malone reserved a gun range in Stormville, Duchess County, New York. Malone knew the owner, a retired N.Y.P.D. Detective who always gave preference to his brothers in blue. The range was almost fifty miles from the Bronx the center of the boy's universe. Any place north of Yonkers was viewed by Bronx kids as a baron wilderness. The wilderness characteristic of the range had many invisible advantages. The boys could be trained to shoot under the guidance of Sargent Malone and never be seen by anyone. The indoor range provided a training venue that protected them from inclement weather. The weapons they would eventually shoot were not available to the everyday citizen.

The force members were professionally trained with a handgun. It was now the boys turn to begin an apprenticeship in arms training. They would first be trained to shoot a long barrel 22 revolver. The experienced force members shot their assigned 38 caliber revolvers.

Mr. Chan was a teacher who paid close attention to detail especially when it came to firearm training. His years of marksmanship level training immediately allowed him to notice that some of the force members were closing one eye while shooting their revolvers. Annoyed at this amateurish trait he spent over an hour lecturing and demonstrating why that was the incorrect way to shoot. He said, "Timing is crucial in any combative situation but when firing a gun, time is of the essence. In a street fight you may hit your opponent first and knock him out, that's an easy one. But every now and then, you will hit someone first only to find that they are unaffected by your power. They either have a steel jaw or your blow didn't properly hit the target.

"However, when you are compelled to draw and fire your gun, you better go first and hit the target. You do not have time to close one eye to take aim. You have to go first and that's why leaving both eyes open is paramount in you being successful and staying alive. For those of you who have developed this terrible amateurish habit you have much work to do. When you start shooting the proper way; with both eyes open you may at first glance see a shadow. It will appear like a double barrel; that will soon go way with practice. Does everyone understand?"

Mr. Chan gave the three "One eyed shooters" to Sargent Malone for his corrective guidance and observation. The boys had next to no experience shooting a firearm, but they also had not developed any poor shooting habits. After basic gun aiming fundamentals, the six officers and the two boys would shoot and reload at their individual targets until each of them spent one hundred rounds. The targets were placed seventy five feet from the shooters. Mr. Chan explained that having all the rounds end up in a space no bigger than a fist should be their goal. The fist simulated the human heart, the desired target in combat.

Danny had placed eighty percent of his expended rounds in the imaginary fist. Chris placed a few in the fist area, which was normal for the average beginner. Danny Corvo was never average in anything he pursued. Mr. Chan had seen it over and over in the years of training him. There was never a technique or a takedown that Danny didn't master first. By the end of the day the talented Corvo kid had also fired the police issued 38 caliber revolver. He spent over an hour painstakingly making adjustments for the kickback from the higher caliber revolver. He taught himself never to become frustrated when learning something new. He concentrated and listened to Mr. Chan's instructions down to the finest detail.

By mid-September 1966, everyone knew the basics and safety procedures of shooting a high powered rifle. The rifle of choice was similar to the M15 used by the United States military in Viet Nam. Mr. Chan believed that actions spoke louder than words. The members of the patrol force were the touted elite of the NYPD. Their ego was larger than life and some of them had to be convinced that Chan was as knowledgeable with a rifle as he was with his hands. The no nonsense instructor sensed their dubiousness and wasted no time.

He started the session with a brief talk, saying, "Well, gentleman I'm going to tell you that shooting a rifle is not as glamourous as one might think. Actually it can be quite boring. The key to success in firing this rifle is in your breathing. When I take aim I inhale ever so slowly, when I have the target in the crosshairs, I breathe out and fire. Let me show you what I mean."

Chan loaded a thirty round clip into his rifle and took aim at the target one hundred feet away. Putting his rifle down, he asked Sargent Malone to examine the target to guarantee that it had not been previously fired upon. When Malone returned to the firing line Mr. Chan took aim and fired thirty rounds at the distant target. When the clip was spent Chan smiled with delight and said, "Come on let's take a walk and see how I've done." The first bullet breached the target and the other twenty nine followed. Thirty rounds fired into one hole a seemingly impossible task.

Danny returned from the gun range and escorted Delia and Abby to a fish restaurant on City Island. After putting Abby to bed they walked to Holland Avenue seeking quiet time together. The Hoffman house always possessed heavy weekend traffic of young male admirers. The young couple enjoyed the quiet refuge of the Corvo back yard. They planned a much anticipated trip to Jones beach for the following day. The weather was uncommonly warm for mid-September.

Delia rested her head on Danny's shoulder and asked, "Are you ever going to tell me where you have been going these past three Saturday's?"

He forced a smile and said, "You know I give you a lot of credit. You actually waited three weeks."

Delia remarked boldly, "Yes, I know, but now my patience is worn thin. I really would like to know. The curiosity is killing me."

Danny replied, "This stays between you and me." Her cute girly smile vanished as she made a head gesture of serious affirmation. "I've been training with ten cops who are assigned to the Mayor's tactical patrol force. I'm taking a course with them on the use of firearms. Mr. Chan was able to get me and Chris included for free. It seemed like a good opportunity. Choose your words carefully because I'm a pretty good shot," he jokingly said.

Delia sighed loudly saying, "Okay, one more question. Why?"

Danny answered, "Well, you see, I have this beautiful, smart, talented German girlfriend. One day we're going to start a business and make bushel baskets full of cash. We're going to need a lot of money because there are a lot of kids on the horizon. I'm going to need a State pistol permit in order to protect all our loot so we can afford to have all these kids. You need to have extensive training in order to get a pistol license so I thought I'd start now before all the money and kids."

Delia hugged him and whispered, "That's really sweet Danny; I love you and all your craziness."

Saturday, September 24, 1966 was the last firearm training session. Danny's breathing technique when firing his rifle had reached a level of professionalism enjoyed by few. He observed Mr. Chan as his keen mind photo-copied his every move. He mimicked him to a flaw; his accuracy was unparalleled by anyone except the master Chan.

By the end of Saturday number four, he too, could shoot one or two holes in the target and have the remaining rounds follow. He attained the expertise of a Marksman. The Tactical Patrol Force acquired a deep admiration for the nineteen-year-old Corvo kid.

CHAPTER 9

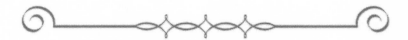

October of 1966 was an election year for the notorious Road Dust motorcycle gang. Eddie Gaga had sworn vengeance to the young kid that smashed his face in three years prior. The club had grown but Gaga's failure to retaliate against the kid who disfigured his face made him lose credibility with the membership. Other members now sought the Club Presidency and boasted they would never let anyone assault a club member let alone the president. Gaga had to know Paulie Nartico was the pathway to finding the young kid who tarnished his reputation as a bad ass.

It was the Friday night before the three day Columbus Day weekend. Gaga and three of his loyalist found Nartico and his wife Gloria at Charlie's Inn in Throggs Neck. Gaga befriended Paulie in front of his wife. He coaxed the easily rattled mechanic into speaking to him privately.

Gaga was more of a showman than a bully. Outweighing the slender mechanic by over a hundred pounds he demanded Danny Corvo be brought to his club on Zerega Avenue. He threatened to cut up his wife promising to rape her while he watched. Paulie's 38 special was neatly wrapped around his ankle holster; no one was going to touch his wife. The threat pushed Paulie to the threshold of suicidal courage as he said in a cold tone, "I don't see the kid too much anymore but leave my wife out of it."

Gaga snarled as he loudly insisted, "Do me and you a favor and bring him to the club." Paulie dismissed himself in silence and rejoined his wife. As soon as Gaga and his boys left he too would leave; time was of the essence.

Gaga had never heard the old expression, "Once bitten twice shy," but it applied to him in every way. Eddie Gaga knew young Billy Caldo, the mob enforcer's son and two of his crew were broken up by one guy. He knew that guy was the same person that broke his face. Gaga had many opportunities to find Danny Corvo but was discouraged by a deep inner fear.

The uneducated Gaga was a surprisingly street-wise politician. To secure his presidency he had to convince the club members that he would punish the kid that smashed his face. The ultimate bully, he was always tough when the odds were stacked in his favor. He knew without doubt that his fat, out of shape, alcoholic, drug infested, cigarette smoking ass could not physically deal with Corvo. His threat to Nartico was empty rhetoric in a desperate attempt to reestablish his tough guy persona with his accompanying minions. If Nartico didn't produce Corvo, he would then emerge as the revenge Gaga sought; a much easier target than the formidable Corvo kid.

If the thrill-seeking Gaga had done just a little more research he would have discovered that Corvo was held in high esteem by the Galliano family. There wasn't a rogue motorcycle club suicidal enough to go against the Galliano family. Although the Road Dust club had grown in numbers they were not yet high on the biker's food chain. It would have been prudent for Gaga to step down as president and let someone else run the show. His unharnessed imagination could have produced believable reasons why he had to give up the presidency; but his drug-fueled synthetic tough guy persona shaded his ability to reason.

Paulie had a very restless night. He knew too well the ramifications of reneging on a promise to the bully, Gaga. He carried a gun but never used it. The pressing question at hand was, could he? The following morning a sleepless fear drove him to the Corvo garage. After exchanging good morning salutations Paulie motioned to Danny to join him in private conversation.

Danny could see the perspiration forming on his forehead and said, "What's up? You're here way too early." Paulie's voice quivered with despair as he said rapidly, "We got big trouble. Gaga and three of his boys cornered me at Charlie's Inn. I thought after three years, the fat fuck would let it go. But no, he's losing cred with his boys, and is trying to hold on to his presidency. He wants me to bring you and Delia to his club so they can fuck you up and rape her. He threatened me too; saying that he was going to do rape my wife if I didn't show up with you. The mother fucker is bat shit crazy."

The well-trained physically fit Danny Corvo didn't share a moment of Paulie's fear. But the threat against Delia moved his spirit from angry to vengeance. His self-control became paralyzed. Just who did that fat bully bastard think he was fucking with? Danny knew he had to act quickly but first he had to examine his options very carefully.

He was reluctant to go to Gus who could have Road Dust dismantled with a phone call but didn't want to risk being viewed as a user; a once-brave hero who chooses to hide behind a powerful friend. Sergeant Malone could provide police support but Paulie would then have to file a formal complaint against Gaga. Paulie could never submit to that logic. The third option was to ask Nicky Galliano for help and advice.

On the surface, Nicky's business was squeaky clean, but the tentacles of his father's influence and power were far-reaching. Danny never forgot the words Nicky said to his brother, "And you know I'm not fucking kidding," about putting his brother's drug suppliers in the car crusher. It was so believable. Mr. Chan could never understand why his student gambled with his future by riding a motorcycle illegally at the age of sixteen. If he didn't ride with Nartico the Gaga incident would have never happened. He was sure Lieutenant Derosa would share the same sentiments as Chan. He had a decision to make and time was running out.

He immediately dismissed any further thoughts of involving the Police. Why would he admit to an illegal activity when he never got caught? It was too complicated. He became ambivalent about involving Nicky. Nicky was Gus's only living son and his help could indirectly involve the family name. It was apparent that Corvo and Nartico had to deal with Gaga on their own. Danny went for a long, mind-cleansing run. He had to devise a viable solution. Gaga had to be stopped, that was the easy part if he could only find him alone.

Danny wasn't solitary in thinking about a viable solution to the Gaga malady. Paulie didn't possess the skills, heart or stomach for fighting like his friend Corvo but something had to be done to stop the fat man Gaga. Fear is a strange motivator. Paulie feared for his safety and the well-being of his wife. He knew the Galliano brothers and had attended Tommy's funeral. Nicky viewed him as a friend of a friend because of his relationship with Danny Corvo.

Perplexed by his predicament, he drove to the junk yard and summoned the advice of Nicky Galliano, hoping that his advice would morph into help. It was the only plan that made sense. He and Danny could not deal with Road Dust alone.

Nicky's greeting was amicable but not devoid of questions. He was a street kid and had a keen ability for reading people. "What brings you to the junk yard on this beautiful day? What's wrong?" Nicky asked. Paulie asked if they could talk in the privacy of his office. When Gaga's name surfaced Nicky reminded him that he knew the whole story and asked bluntly, "Again, what's wrong?"

The nervous mechanic had difficulty in expressing himself; he stammered and stuttered, an easily aroused symptom from his childhood. Nicky gave him a shot of vodka and ordered him to calm down and answer his question.

Paulie explained his surprise meeting with Gaga and his two minions. He repeated what he recollected as Nicky listened intently impatiently motioning with his hands for Paulie to continue. The threat against Paulie's wife gained his closest attention. The threat against Delia Hoffman changed his expression. His face twisted into a choleric rage. In Nicky Galliano's heart, Danny Corvo was his brother. He had a myopic view on how to deal with threats to his family; no forgiveness, no letting it go, only revenge. His business was legitimate but he was Gus Galliano's son. Gus always instructed his twin boys to support each other in a confrontation. Nicky chose not to seek his father's advice but knew he would get his blessing to help Danny Corvo.

Paulie was intrigued at how easily the young Galliano could sway from angry and enraged to cool and calm. Nicky's face was cold and expressionless as he said, "I know exactly how to handle this problem, but I'm going to have to talk to Danny."

They shook hands as Nicky assured the excitable high-strung mechanic that Danny Corvo would never find out about their conversation.

From the first moment they met, Danny Corvo felt obligated to protect his beautiful Delia. She had experienced a childhood devoid of the love and guidance of a Mother. Danny loved her and protecting her became ingrained in his nature. Anyone who threatened his beloved Delia would be putting their own life in imminent danger. At nineteen, he was six foot one and weighed one hundred and eighty-five pounds of sleek muscle. His fighting skills made him lethal.

Miles away in a junkyard in the South Bronx, Nicky Galliano planned a way to protect Danny. Danny had heard Nicky tell him over and over that he loved him like a brother. Just words, he thought. Nicky acquired a deep admiration for Danny's physical prowess and was appreciative of his guidance. It was evident that Nicky Galliano had eradicated his bad habits and had become physically fit. He owed much of his life-altering success to the kid who saved his life. His brotherly love was sincere, causing him to feel morally obligated to protect Corvo.

Danny had not yet arrived at a solution to deal with Gaga and his minions. The thought of killing him was foremost on his mind. He felt like a captive bird trapped in a pair of large, over-powering hands. But he had the skill and the means to carry out his mission. No one was going to hurt the people he loved. He needed a plan.

He was surprised to see Nicky Galliano show up at his job site. It was lunch time, plenty of time to talk. Nicky didn't waste any time. "Danny," he said, "I hear this fat fuck Gaga is threatening you and Delia. Don't ask me how I know; just listen. I have a plan."

Danny looked angry but inquisitive. "What?" he grunted.

Nicky replied, "Gaga and his crew are like the girl scouts compared to the bikers I deal with. I give my collection work to this guy, Pete. He's the President of a club from Yonkers. These guys don't fuck around and Gaga and his boys are scared shitless of them. Between me and old man, they make a lot of money. I'm going to ask Pete to meet with us. I'll tell him the whole story. I'm sure he'll come up with a way to diffuse this phony tough guy Gaga."

That evening Nicky and Danny met Pete at the junk yard. Danny could sense a mutual respect between them. Danny didn't utter a word; Nicky became the steward of the conversation, telling Pete every detail starting with the ass beating Danny gave Gaga three years ago.

Pete's beer belly bounced in laughter as he turned to Danny and said, "So finally I get to meet the kid who broke the big mouth's face. You gave me and my guys a good laugh, my pleasure." Danny forced a respectful smile as he nodded and shook Pete's hand.

Pete's plan was directed at the heart of the threat. He and his highest ranking members would confront Gaga at the Zeraga Avenue club. Gaga and some of his members would be invited to follow them to the junk yard. Danny and Paulie would wear with the colors of Pete's club and wait in the junk yard with the rest of Pete's crew.

The Road Dust boys couldn't disrespectfully decline to follow Pete and his boys to the junk yard. They knew there would be immediate consequences for a disrespectful decline. They felt an eerie curiosity about why they were being invited to the yard; a party, celebration a business deal? No one knew.

Upon arrival everything appeared as normal as a junk yard could feel under the cover of darkness. It was a chilly

October night and Gaga sweated in mid-July fashion when he saw Corvo and Nartico. The panic on his face was evident as he looked at his men with despair. Pete's raspy voice began to speak loudly, "I guess you know why you're here. You threatened two of my boys and their ladies. The boys are one thing but the girls are something altogether different. So I got bad news and good news. The bad news is that you can openly apologize to the boys and take back your bullshit threat. The good news is you can fight with Danny and be allowed to park in the handicapped zone for the rest of your fucking life. Speak."

Gaga had on his whiskey balls and knew he couldn't back down in front of his boys. He snarled, "I'll fight him."

Face to face they stood the fat Gaga and sleek lean Danny Corvo. The rules were that there were no rules. Gaga lunged forward, a rerun of the fight at the Wedge Inn parking lot. But this was a bigger, more developed Corvo. Gaga absorbed another guided front kick to the stomach as he painfully fell to his buckled knees. Danny patiently waited for the fat man to regain an erect posture. Gaga's minions watched in disbelief. Every strike was guided with accurate precision as Gaga's face became saturated in his own blood. A final barrage of hammer fist blows left the bloody fat man unconscious on the blacktop.

Danny's energy was in reserve as he called out Gaga's right hand man, Louie Discola, "Hey, I hear you're the other tough guy looking for me, so here I am. What do you say Mr. wanna be President?" Discola, another large obese biker, carried a back-breaking beer belly. Pete intervened saying, "Louie get smart; apologize and go the fuck home." But Louie also possessed whiskey balls and lusted for the club presidency. He too chose to fight.

Louie glared at Pete and said, "No rules, right Pete?"

Pete answered, "No rules."

Louie reached into his back pocket and pulled a knife, Danny waited. Most aggressive attackers blinded by anger and alcohol make the same mistake. Louie lunged with an untrained amateurish body movement. Angry about the sudden appearance of a knife, Corvo became unbridled fury. Punches and knee kicks made head and face contact in rapid, precise succession. In a few horrific moments, Discola's face was also bloodied and broken. He held his hands to his mouth as his loosened teeth trickled to the junkyard pavement. Pete commanded his boys to intervene. Discola was about to lose his life.

Three months later, Eddie Gaga moved to California. Shortly after Gaga's departure Louie Discola was found shot to death. No one was ever arrested for the murder and no one cared.

CHAPTER 10

It was July 4th 1969. The annual Corvo Independence day bash was planned to be memorialized by all. Danny and Delia had been working for the Galliano family for the past two years and were saving for their wedding. He had earned an engineering degree from Pace University in Westchester while Delia studied accounting courses in the evening. Victoria Galliano developed a parental affection for the young motherless beauty.

Many things had changed in the past two years. The Corvo cousins, Tommy and Phil, finished their tour in Viet Nam and were home to stay. Doc Singer was attending Flower and Fifth Medical School, Joe Corvo and Judy Perez were wed and expecting a child. Danny's sister, Rosemarie was attending Fordham Law School and planned on taking the New York State bar exam in September. Grandpa Joe was a spry seventy-two years old and enjoyed the untiring energy of a teenager.

This year was an over-crowded celebration. Lieutenant and Teresa Derosa, Mr. and Mrs. Chan, Chris Chan and his girlfriend, Doc and Lee Hoffman, Paulie and Gloria Nartico, the Hoffman girls and all their men attended. Nicky Galliano was the surprise quest accompanied by his fiancée a striking red headed professional dancer.

The inventive Corvo men created a dance floor by sectioning off forty feet of the street with a string of Christmas lights. A local Disc Jockey played songs of the fifties and sixties as the over-abundance of guest crammed the dance floor with the restricted movement of penned cattle.

Danny Corvo and Delia Hoffman often spoke about marriage but were not formally engaged. The ear-deafening music paused as the DJ announced, "Delia Hoffman, please make your way to the dance floor." Delia became noticeably addled as she looked at her sister's and muttered, "Wonder what he's up to now?" "Don't know," Rose said in a wide grinned smile, "But I think you should go and find out." The giggling Hoffman girls gaped in amusement as Delia swayed her way to the edge of the black topped dance floor.

Without comment Danny escorted her to the center of the street. He placed his arms around her and motioned to the DJ to play Nat King Cole's, 'When I fall in love'. Her eyes welled with tears as she laid her head on his chest. As they danced, the boys clapped and the girls shed copious tears of joy. Danny waved his arm and the DJ halted the tear-jerking love song. He released Delia, knelt on one knee and asked her to marry him. She gently cupped her hands around his face. Lowering her voice to a soft caress she proclaimed, "Yes, Yes, Yes"! He placed the ring on her finger as family and friends chanted, "Kiss, kiss, kiss."

Phil and Tommy were wildly celebrating their military freedom as their ingestion of beer and whiskey mockingly glamorized the horrific deeds of war. Some tales of the young weary soldiers were humorous while most were tragic. Like so many other Americans Danny couldn't understand the United States involvement in the war. The dead mutilated bodies of our young soldiers were being flown home at an exhausting rate. Men of draft age were protesting all over the American landscape. He never participated in any protest believing that in doing so he would be disrespecting our soldiers who fought so valiantly to protect our right to protest. How does anyone validate blaming our soldiers when most were inducted into the Army against their will?

Danny Corvo a pragmatic young man calculated his future very carefully. He earned his engineering degree, was engaged to the women he loved and was making an inconceivable amount of money rarely earned by someone of his social status. He planned on returning to college in September to pursue his Master's Degree.

But love can make the smartest of men do the dumbest of things. In mid-October Danny received a letter from the Selective Service Board notifying him that he was re-classified 1A, available for the draft. He carelessly failed to take enough credits to classify him as a full-time student, making him eligible for the draft. An appeal to the Draft Board on the grounds that he was still a college student was denied.

Lost for a remedy he spoke to every confidant in his life beginning with his father. Big Sam an ex-Marine was not a proponent of the war. He did, however, have a deep-seated belief that no one was so privileged that they could dodge the draft.

All his options had unintended consequences. He could Marry Delia the mother of a child and become legally and automatically exempt. But moving up the wedding date to avoid induction into the Military could cast doubt on the sincerity of his love; if not now in the future. His other option was to go to Canada with Delia and be labeled a draft dodger by everyone that knew his name. Mr. G had contacts in Toronto a predominantly Italian town. Finding work for him was not a problem, but he would be ashamed and tormented. The third option was to do nothing and wait until December 1st, the date of the initial draft lottery. He dreaded sharing this unexpected awful news with his fiancé.

Danny consulted with his most trusted counselor on female affairs, his sister Rosemarie. She believed that Delia's emotional state was in some ways fragile. With that information in the forefront she advised her younger brother to wait until the December first lottery. It was a case of simple logic; if you get a high number and don't have to go it will all be pleasantly over. If that doesn't happen then you have to deal with it.

If more than one thing was going wrong Grandpa Joe preached, "Misery loves company." Lieutenant Derosa read in the New York Mirror that Mr. Kadesh, Delia's rapist English teacher was being released from prison in March of 1970. The op-ed explained that Kadesh the son of a wealthy businessman had hired one of America's elite law firms and they were awarded a reduction in his penalty based on a technicality. Derosa had to relay the sickening, vile information to his star student.

The cool and inconspicuous Derosa stopped by the garage the next day with the fabled claim that he just wanted to say hello. Danny was always glad to see one of his mentors as he remained eternally grateful for the skills acquired under his tutelage. The Lieutenant had purchased a new phonograph for his wife that was neatly stored in the truck of his car. He coaxed Danny to stop working for a moment to examine his new purchase. Danny acquiesced to his request but demonstrated his impatience. Derosa assured him it would only take a minute. When they distanced themselves from eavesdroppers Derosa started to speak, "Bad news, the scum-bag who raped Delia is getting out in March on a technicality. The article claims that he will be moving South with his parents but who really knows what he will do. Here's the article, read it for yourself."

As he read the article, Danny shook his head in disgust. His face became reddened with anger as he snarled, "Un-fucking believable. What a country, letting out that piece of shit. Delia's going to panic. I'll have to conceal it for as long as I can. Mother Fucker!"

Derosa offered words of regret but could sense the angry young man was unraveled. Danny Corvo felt his Camelot world falling apart. First the draft, and now the impending release of Kadesh. Danny was dumb-founded that the infinitely wise Lieutenant did not offer any advice. He didn't have any.

Big Sam and Annabel were worried about the draft lottery but tried their best to mask their feelings. Danny could see straight through their smiley-faced disguise and now had to disclose more unwanted news. His parents were livid at the news. Big Sam's kind pattern of behavior became un-done as he cursed the American judicial system.

Annabel had a much different view of what the Kadesh release meant to her. She became childishly sulky; her mind wildly speculated as she grumbled, "What happens if he decides that it's his right to have visitation rights with Abby? What happens if his father's lawyers can get a judge to agree? Some of these Judges are bought and paid for and Delia's family could be faced with the trauma of seeing him on a regular basis. Abby would have to be told her pedophile father wasn't killed in a car crash. This is an elephant-sized mess." The possibility of being drafted was dwarfed by the Kadesh debacle. Danny knew one thing was for certain; he would protect Delia Hoffman from harm and grief regardless of the consequences.

Danny could remember Mr. Chan telling him and the tactical police force guys that, "We don't get to choose our opponent but we have to be prepared at all times." Those words orbited around in his head as he strained to find a solution. Kadesh was just a different type of opponent. To be victorious, he had to employ a new strategy even if that meant redirecting his moral compass. The wonderful American legal system had failed him. Left with little choice, he sought the counsel and advice of Gus Galliano.

Gus and Victoria Galliano watched the same news programs as the rest of America and were also worried about Danny being drafted. They too saw the piles of body bags containing the dead bodies of young American boys returning home to be buried. The Galliano's never trusted any aspect of the United States government and believed the war was a tragic mistake.

It appeared to them that only the poor and uneducated kids got drafted. Gus vowed not be vocal until the December 1st draft lottery results. If they were favorable, he would remain gladly silent, if unfavorable he would offer an alternative plan Danny couldn't abruptly dismiss. Gus admired Sam Corvo; a hard working stand-up guy and a good father. He would never attempt to intrude on that sacred relationship. Gus knew his place in Danny's life; he was an advisor, a teacher and a friend. Gus Galliano was the best friend a kid could ever find.

Danny called the restaurant and told him he had a pressing issue that had to be resolved and needed his guidance. Gus never missed an opportunity to ask, "Who did you beat up this time?" Danny's silence gave creditability to the seriousness of the matter. Gus invited Danny and his fiancée to dinner at the Riverdale Estate.

Victoria was pleased with Delia's work ethic and had become a mentor of motherly statute. The wealthy mother of two boys lusted for the companionship of a daughter. Delia Hoffman learned easily and earned Victoria Galliano's trust a rare achievement. Many handsome salesmen frequented the office of G & G construction. Delia was disciplined enough to never make eye contact with any of them. Victoria was a keen observer and developed a deep admiration for the young beauties one of a kind faithfulness. Delia Hoffman was becoming the daughter she always wanted.

It was a chillingly damp and drizzly Tuesday night. Halloween was only a week away and the ritzy section of Riverdale was decorated for the occasion. Paper ghosts, goblins, mummies and mock graveyards were erected everywhere. The young couple drove her 65 Impala to the Galliano residence a visible demonstration of their sincere gratitude. When dinner ended Gus excused himself and summoned Danny to his study. He told the ladies, "We have some boring construction stuff to go over. Don't worry, we'll be back in time for desert."

Gus knew there was a problem. Holding problems in abeyance annoyed Gus Galliano as did inaction and coward-ice. He impatiently asked, "What's going on?"

Danny told him the details surrounding the upcoming release of the scumbag Kadesh. He shared a condensed ver-sion of his mother's perspective implying that Kadesh might demand visitation rights. His eyes glittered with wrath as he said, "It's bad enough I got the draft hanging over my head, but this is unheard of. How do I ever tell Delia about Kadesh? Hiding the draft from her is hard enough, but this one is worse. I could be in Viet Nam and this piece of shit could be walking the streets of my neighborhood. Delia and her family would be tormented; I can't deal with this shit."

175

Danny abruptly got up from his seat and placed his closed fists on Gus's desk. His face was cold. As he observed Gus's reaction, his voice shed its angry tone. "I could kill this guy but I can't get close enough to him. If I could I would."

Gus was unmoved by his angry bravado and said sternly, "My boy, you can deal with anything that comes your way. I know you have the ability to kill, but you're not a killer. Killing is serious business. You may need a little help but trust me you can deal with this problem. The great American legal system, it's rigged to help the rich. Look at these kids getting killed in this bull shit war; you think their parents are rich? No way do the rich kids go to Viet Nam." Gus stood up to tuck his shirt into his pants. He asked, "What prison is this bastard in, do you know?"

Danny answered, "I'm not really sure."

Gus replied with a dry certainty, "I'll have Ryan find out. Now go back to your girlfriend and send Victoria in here. Don't act like anything is wrong."

Gus wanted to insure himself that killing Kadesh was the only solution to the problem. When Gus explained the imminent release of Kadesh to his wife, she became unhinged. Her face twisted in angry disbelief as she said, "Please tell me there's a way to stop this from happening this can't be. These kids are going to get married; they can't have this albatross around their necks."

Gus responded calmly, "First I have to have Ryan find out where he is. Then we have to peruse the inmate population to see who is capable of doing the job."

Victoria answered coldly, "The job. By job you mean who is going to kill the son of a bitch?"

Gus said, "Exactly, it's the only solution. Funny, that's what the kid said. These child predators get shanked all the time and now with an early release it will all make sense. One more thing, what do you think I should tell the kid?"

Victoria replied, "Tell him to trust you and that everything will be alright. Tell him Ryan will arrange for Kadesh to have a fight with another inmate and that will interrupt his early release. When the bastard is dead, you can tell him that the fight got out of hand and Kadesh got killed."

Gus waved his finger at her as his head nodded approvingly saying, "And you wonder why I love you, my Sicilian beauty. I'll call Ryan when the kids leave. Let's go have desert."

Ryan's contacts easily uncovered that Kadesh was imprisoned in the Ossining Correctional Facility, known as Sing-Sing. Sing-Sing prison was located thirty miles north of the Bronx. Ironically, it was not too far from the assembly plant where Danny had worked. Sing-Sing presented Ryan with many options in dealing with Kadesh. Six of the prison guards were from the Bronx; three of them were "dirty" and welcomed the extended income of bribery.

Eddie Spencer surfaced as the logical choice to help initiate the fall of Kadesh. He was single, a ladies' man and a degenerate gambler. His most appealing attributes—he borrowed money from the family's loan sharking business and was not a good gambler. He continually sought ways to reduce his rapidly increasing debt. Opportunity would soon be knocking on Eddie Spencer's door.

Ryan met Spencer at the Rivera Club in Yonkers. Gus never physically approached anyone he hired to perform work for him. There were always a constellation of delegates, surrogates, and low level in-between guys shielding Gus's appearance as if he didn't exist; just the way he liked it. When Ryan informed Spencer that Kadesh was the mark, he became interested. Pedophiles were the most hated creatures in the prison system. All the guards knew about the eminent early release of Kadesh and were privately ordered to remain silent. Information of that nature had to be kept off the cell block floor. If leaked, it could cause a riot. Wardens never wanted to be obligated to answer for a riot or a murder under their watch.

Ryan informed Spencer of the murderous task at hand. Spencer gave Ryan a list of every inmate that had the opportunity to mingle with Kadesh. The plan was simple. Spencer would give a fiberglass knife to the inmate of Ryan's choice. A fight would pursue in the shower and Kadesh would be stabbed to death. In Sing-Sing, inmate eyewitnesses did not exist. They agreed to meet the following week.

The name Johnny Holmes aroused the interest of the retired detective. Holmes was a black contract hit man that had a satisfactory past with the family. He was serving six life sentences and could never become eligible for parole. The father of six, Holmes would be guaranteed that his family was financially solvent, the bait he could not ignore. He loved his children and had an open disdain for pedophiles. Spencer would be the one to offer the contract to Holmes, guaranteeing him there would be no prison personnel to witness the murder and that his wife would be given twenty thousand dollars in small non-traceable bills.

The plan initially satisfied Gus Galliano's fail-safe standard but he chose not to give the order. He knew the plan had merit but it was too obvious. He decided to master-mind a plan that could not pierce his veil of innocence. He had a preference for the insidious, prompting him to summon the service of Tony "Pimples" Capobianco. A brilliant scholar of medicine, Capobianco became a hired master of torture. The diabolical "Tony Pimples" combined rare toxins and lethal chemicals that, once injected into the bloodstream, stopped the heart. The pre-paid Coroner would arrive at the conclusion that the person died of a massive heart attack.

Capobianco's work was simple and untraceable. He would supply Ryan with his deadly potion in a hypodermic needle. The needle would pass from Ryan to Spencer, the Correction Guard. Once Spencer had possession of the deadly needle, it would be passed to Holmes.

Holmes had sold and used heroine before his imprisonment for multiple murders. Injecting Kadesh was not a concern; neither was murder. Johnny Holmes, the master assassin, lost his conscience when he reached puberty.

In the steaming mist of the prison shower, Holmes forced a wet towel over the front of his short pudgy victim's face, avoiding visible marks. The back of Kadesh's head was smashed into the shower wall and rendered him unconscious. Holmes injected the deadly needle under his armpit. The pre-paid Coroner deemed the bruise on the back of his head to be a result of the sudden-death fall.

On Thursday, November 13, 1969, two weeks before Thanksgiving, the pedophile was pronounced dead from a massive heart attack in the shower of Sing-Sing prison. The Coroner validated a heart attack as the cause of death. Gus Galliano told Danny Corvo that although he was not a very religious man he believed in "divine intervention." He said calmly, "See, we sometimes worry about nothing. Now that bastard has to answer for what he did. He's going to rot in hell."

The story of Kadesh's death was carried by all the New York City newspapers but never made it to the front page. The Hoffman family was secretly relieved by the sobering news. Abby would continue to be protected from the truth about the rapist who was her biological father. The Hoffman family wanted Danny Corvo to be the only father Abby ever knew.

179

On Saturday, November 22nd 1969, the Corvo family rented the Church hall to celebrate the christening of Joe and Judy's first child, Joseph Corvo the third. Grandpa Joe was honored to have their first child named after him. Big Sam was promised that their next child would be named in his honor.

Danny was secretly relieved that Kadesh was dead, but the December first draft lottery haunted him. Every day he awoke, the draft lottery was foremost in his mind and challenged his ability to concentrate. Even the powerful Gus Galliano could not engineer a deferment for him. Infiltrating the Selective Service Board required extensive planning with willing politicians. In this case, there simply wasn't enough time. Danny was a believer in destiny, and he knew the lottery could change his life. He vowed to conceal the pending draft from Delia Hoffman.

CHAPTER 11

A deeply in love woman can always sense when her man is troubled. Once again, like the hands on a clock that inevitably repeat the hours of the day he slowly retreated into his dungeon of silence. Thanksgiving Day dinner was a giveaway. The Corvo family invited Nelson Hoffman and two of his daughters, in addition to Delia and Abby. The families enjoyed the uniqueness of each other's humor. The well-prepared holiday dinner was bountiful, reminiscent of a Roman fiesta. But a troubled Danny hardly ate and became disengaged from the family gossip and high-spirited political arguments. His photographic memory made him a debater of unquestionable statute. His lack of interest in the ensuing debate aroused Delia's suspicion.

When Danny excused himself to use the bathroom, Delia followed him. Taking him by the arm she steered him into the private confines of the kitchen pantry. She put her arms around his waist and said, "Danny you're scarring me; you're not eating or talking what's wrong?"

His face mustered a slight smile as he answered, "I'll be ok, I promise. I just had a couple of tough days on the job." He kissed Delia on her forehead, realizing his worrying was self-induced and premature. He garnered a laugh by saying, "You know I don't like the idea that you can read my mind. You're scaring me, Ms. Hoffman!"

Danny worked the Friday after Thanksgiving. Work was a natural stress-reducer that kept his mind off the impending lottery. It was three days away. At lunchtime, a gleeful Victoria informed Delia that they were going Christmas shopping; it was the busiest shopping day of the year.

Shopping with Victoria Galliano was like exploring a new world. They rode in the back of a limousine to stores the under-privileged Bronx girl thought only existed in fashion magazines and fairy tales. Shopping in Manhattan's plush, high-end stores was routine for Victoria but for a poor girl from the Bronx, it was an introduction into a whole new world. Victoria's affection toward Delia made her treasure how fortunate she was to be Danny Corvo's fiancée.

The weekend was gone, and the moment that would mold Danny Corvo's future was about to unfold. He was grateful to be working that Monday. Work, like running, diverted his thoughts. He made arrangements to meet Delia at nine o'clock after Abby was put to bed. By eight o'clock the drawing of the lottery numbers had begun. Danny watched the drawing with his worried parents. May 17th, his birthday drew number 112. Danny Corvo was going to be drafted.

The Corvo family had lived through the anxiety of Phil and Tommy serving in Viet Nam. They were now both home and unharmed. Sam and Annabel embraced their son and offered words of encouragement. His father said, "At least you know that basic training is going to be a joke. No one is going to be in the shape you're in, not even the drill sergeant." Danny was unmoved by his father's attempted humor but managed to muster a smile. All that remained was prayer.

Danny dreaded the task of telling his fiancée the result of the lottery. He arrived at the Hoffman house at nine o'clock, and drove to a small quiet coffee shop on the far end of City Island. The café was patronized by few on the Monday after Thanksgiving. He requested a corner table where the deeply-in-love couple could speak privately.

Danny held Delia's hand and began to speak, "You know I love you more than anyone, including myself."

Delia tried to respond but he muffled her attempt with a low soft, "Shhh." She moved her face closer to his, anxious to hear every word. Danny continued, "I screwed up big time. I didn't take enough credits this semester and I've been classified 1A."

Delia put her hands up to cover her mouth. She cried out, "Oh my God. What does that mean?"

He replied, "The lottery numbers were drawn tonight. My birthday drew number 112. I don't know how soon, but I'm going to be drafted."

Unexpectedly Delia Hoffman's face became statuesque. She refused to cry but became angry. Her voice gathered a scornful tone as she said, "Danny, I'm not losing you to this dumb war. Let's get married... like tomorrow."

Softly he replied, "You and I are going to have a proper wedding, the kind you deserve. No one is going to think I married you to avoid the war. All marriages are tested somewhere along the way. I hope our marriage is never tested but if it is, I never want to give you reason to think I married you to avoid the war. I love you too much for that. I'll get through it fine. No war is going to get the best of me." Delia knew by his cold facial expression and brash tone that arguing with him at that moment was pointless.

There would be an abundance of advice doled out during the days ahead. Gus laid out a plan for him that was tempting, almost too hard to ignore. One of Gus's associates in Toronto would provide Danny and Delia with an apartment. Danny would have a job operating heavy equipment and Delia would be given a clerical job. Delia could travel home once a month to visit both her family and the Corvos. The families could visit them in Canada without consequence. Gus Galliano called the plan "a no brainer" but remained deeply concerned about Danny's unique stubbornness.

Danny may have miscalculated his college credits, but he was as mentally fit as he was physically. His love for Delia Hoffman was deep and at times appeared unreasonable. He would never consider having Delia and her daughter live with him out of wedlock. He could never use this very special love for self-gain. He viewed Gus's plan as visceral rather that factual.

Monday, December eighth was the feast of the Immaculate Conception. Danny attended church intermittently but eight years of Catholic education often influenced his moral compass. He attended early mass that morning in his search for guidance. At noon, he drove to the United States Marine Corps recruiting station on Fordham Road and joined the Marines. His decision was now final and everyone's words became meaningless, empty dialogue.

That evening, Danny confronted his parents and shared the news about joining the Marine Corps. Neither of them was surprised; it was a family tradition. He informed them that the tour in Viet Nam was only for nine months. Annabel silently contemplated, "Only nine months, only." It was going to seem endless. Annabel knew what every combat soldier's mother knew; she was in for nine months of heart-thumping sleeplessness.

The draft was a forced induction into the United States military and Danny Corvo was a man who resisted being forced to do anything. Why would he accept being inducted into the Army when he could choose to be a Marine? When told, Delia forced a smile and said, "I know, I can read your mind, remember?"

Danny offered reassurance saying, "The faster I go in, the faster I'll be home." He was ordered to report to Parris Island, North Carolina on Monday, January 26, 1970.

Gus invited the young couple to his home in Riverdale. He knew Danny would be leaving soon and wanted to give him some going away assurances. Danny was pleased that Nicky and his girlfriend were present. They had developed an unbreakable bond of trust. Nicky was a keen businessman. He remained physically fit but was always in awe of the kid who saved his life. Danny seemed to be two steps ahead of everyone. Nicky often teased Danny, telling him, "You know bro, if you weren't so good-looking you could become the light-heavyweight champion of the world."

Danny agreed in comical fashion saying, "Yeah, if they let me use my feet."

Before dessert was served, Gus summoned both boys to his office for "some guy talk," a ploy to free them from the bondage of their women. The Galliano's witnessed an unbreakable bond developing between their son and the Corvo boy. Both boys worked long hours and were starved of free time but somehow they were always together.

Gus had a stern, scolding look on his face when he began to speak, "Don't interrupt me. Danny, I know you are a physical masterpiece but war is a dangerous venue. No one

185

wants to hurt you. They all want to kill you. You're always saving someone. Delia from being raped, Nicky from drowning and the list goes on. It's wonderful, almost spiritual; but war is dangerous. I know why you refused my offer to go to Canada and I understand, but we all need you to come home in one fucking piece. I want you to promise me you're not going to be John Wayne. Look after yourself; no one is going to give a fuck about you. I want you to promise me."

Danny's head jolted back as he roared with laughter. Composing himself, he said curtly, "Gus with all due respect, if I get killed trying to save someone, what are you going to do? Send Ryan up to get me?"

Gus's wit was pithy as he snapped, "No, I'm not sending anyone. I'm gonna put a million dollars in the collection basket for security. Then I'm gonna kill myself and when I get up there I'm gonna slap the shit out of you."

Danny smirked and said, "Gus, I'm taking care of me, don't worry. I got to get home and marry Delia. That's most important to me and I think the both of you know that."

Gus continued, "Bertrand Russell said, 'War does not determine who is right, only who is left.' So Danny boy you have to make sure you are one who is left. The best-prepared soldiers die in war so we have to talk about some of the unpleasant possibilities. You know whether you're careful or not you could get killed." Danny made a head gesture indicating he agreed. Gus added, "God forbid but if anything happens to you Delia will be taken care of as long as she stays single."

Danny thought Gus was making a joke but his stern expression said otherwise. He inquisitively asked, "Single?"

Gus answered, "Yes single. It's disrespectful to take care of another man's women. Why are we even talking about this? Everything will work out. Don't be too long you two." Gus left the boys and went upstairs.

Nicky thrust his face closer and said, "You know that you're like family to us, so I want to give you some more insurance. The newspapers print that my father has his fingers in a lot of pies. Some people say he's a gangster, a Don. I prefer to say he's a shrewd businessman who does business with a much diversified, versatile group of successful people. My father cannot be held responsible for the business ethics or morality of his associates. He's no different than Joe Kennedy. When you get home, we're going to start a construction company on Long Island. Pop bought a lot of waterfront property in a place called the Hamptons. He wants to build luxury homes the size of mansions for the elite of Manhattan. You're the guy with the engineering degree and will be the President of the company. What do you think Mr. Engineer?"

The tough street fighter became teary-eyed as he absorbed the deep trust the Galliano family placed in him. He inhaled deeply saying, "Sounds great, but right now I have to take one step at a time."

Nicky felt his emotional state and said jokingly, "I know. I just wanted to give you another reason to get your ass back here in one piece. Remember, no fucking John Wayne." The boys embraced and returned to the dinner table for desert.

Christmas of 1969 fell on a Thursday. Sam and Annabel invited enough people to fill a ballroom. Danny may have been stubborn about a farewell celebration but he couldn't dictate to his parents on the number of guests they invited to their home for Christmas. The harsh reality of war was somehow overshadowed by the pleasant family gathering. Danny and Delia were off the Friday after Christmas and decided to take Abby to Rockefeller Center in Manhattan.

Victoria Galliano had told Danny about Angelo's Restaurant on Mulberry Street in Little Italy. She told him about the famous actors and actresses that frequented Angelo's and suggested he take the girls. "Make sure you tell them Gus Galliano sent you," she said.

Danny was in an unusually good mood considering his impending induction into the Marines. When the check came Delia grinned childishly as her face became blush red. Danny asked, "So what's so funny?"

Delia didn't respond as her grin became girlish laughter. When Danny opened the fine leather check folder he read the words, "To our favorite couple, hope you enjoyed your dinner."

Danny asked, "Did you know?"

She said, "Yes, but I was sworn to secrecy. They are the sweetest people."

Danny roared with laughter and said, "I've heard Gus referred to as a lot of things but never sweet; that's a new one!"

The year 1970 had arrived and Danny was given two weeks' vacation beginning the week of January 12th. He would use that time to bid farewell and get his affairs in order. The 65 Pontiac and his Indian motorcycle were stored in Paulie Nartico's spare garage. Paulie promised to start the vehicles periodically and change the oil. He wouldn't accept any money from Danny; he too petitioned, "Just get your ass back here."

Lieutenant Derosa's humor made a mockery out of any sad aspect of saying goodbye. His jokes were lude and rude designed to distract from the moment. He had a contagious optimistic attitude. All was calm all was bright. Derosa assured his star student that basic training in the Marines would be a mundane task for a man of his many talents and unparalleled condition.

Mr. Chan was coldly pragmatic about anyone going off to war. He had experienced the horrors of battle in World War II and knew that quite often the best-trained men don't make it home. His advice was to never be complacent and never become so relaxed that you didn't always know what was going on around you. He told his student, "War is the most stressful situation a man can face. Your great physical condition will be a huge asset. There will be many a sleepless night. War is hell on earth. Whoever said that wasn't writing poetry. Don't forget, always know your surroundings, it could save your life."

By Friday, January 23, 1970, Danny had spent some time with all the family and friends he loved. He spent his last weekend with Delia and Abby. He remained diligent in reminding her that he was going to basic training, not Viet Nam. That information somehow shrouded the inevitable and enabled them to remain calm. He said jokingly, "Hey, what happens if I get lucky and end up in Germany? Please stop worrying, we have to take one day at a time."

Delia's eyes were unblinking as her soft eyebrows melded together. "Germany... hmmmm, can I trust you around all those blond-haired blued-eyed beauties?" she said.

Danny gazed at her affectionately and said softly, "There will never ever be another woman for me—never, no matter what. Now scoot on over here and give me a kiss."

Early Monday morning, January 26, 1970, Danny Corvo took a cab to the Kingsbridge Armory and boarded the bus for his long journey to Parris Island, North Carolina.

CHAPTER 12

Danny understood the rules and hard work at Parris Island as a stepping stone to getting home. The training wasn't banal and mundane as some veterans predicted. Challenged, he pushed every drill. Running ten miles at five in the morning was a well-rehearsed routine but the over-stuffed Marine backpack was an added challenge.

The Drill Instructor, Sergeant Edmund Thatcher, a fifteen-year veteran of the Corps, could recognize physical exceptionalism by simply watching his men breathe. Running, jumping, climbing, hauling and fighting, the grinning blue-eyed Private Corvo always seemed to be just having fun. He worked hard and rarely broke a sweat, a testimony to a fine conditioned athlete.

Week four brought the introduction of hand-to-hand combat. As emphasized by Mr. Chan, Danny observed each technique with purposeful concentration. Chan had stressed the importance of this type of training as a matter of life or death.

Sergeant Thatcher paired up his "wanna be" Marines. Danny's partner was Jimmy Reilly a twenty-five-year old heavyweight Golden Glove boxer from Chicago. When the verbally abusive Sergeant asked if anyone had experience in hand-to-hand combat Jimmy Reilly proudly raised his hand. A dubious Private Corvo remained silent.

Thatcher asked, "So, what kind of training have you done, Cupcake?"

With a loud clear energetic hooray Reilly shouted, "I trained boxing, Sir. I was the heavyweight Golden Glove champion in Chicago, Sir."

Thatcher grunted, "Nice Reilly. Unfortunately the Cong don't wear boxing gloves, there's no referee ,and no one min- ute rest. No one's going to sit you down on a stool to fix your boo boos. If you throw in the towel, you'll die. The only rounds you'll be experiencing are lead ones looking to take your fucking head off or put a hole in your heart."

Dethroned by the harshness of Thatcher's commen- tary Reilly maintained a respectful level of enthusiasm and responded, "Sir, yes Sir, thank you Sir."

Sergeant Thatcher instructed his men to sit down and pay close attention to what he was about to tell them. His voice low- ered as he began to speak saying, "By now all of you know that you're training to go to Viet Nam. Depending on whom you ask, you will get an array of answers about who you'll be fight- ing. Some will tell you we are fighting communism. Others will call the enemy Gooks, The Cong, Nips, the North Vietnamese and sneaky mother fuckers. They will all be partially right but I'm going to tell you first hand who you will really be fighting."

Thatcher's facial expression transformed from cool and calm to red-faced anger. His voice grew loud and clear as he screamed, "You'll be fighting the fucking devil." Suddenly his register lowered to an unfamiliar softness as he continued, "Did you hear me boys? You'll be fighting the devil. Now

191

somewhere in grade school, all of you heard the expression, 'You can't fight fire with fire.' Well I'm here to tell you that's exactly what you are going to have to do if you plan on living. You're going to fight the devil with the devil. In each of us, our personalities are governed by three phases of our being, the Parent, the Adult and the Child. I can remember sitting in a bar knowing I had to get up at 0600 hours. At 0200 hours both the Parent and the Adult start preaching. Drink up and go— you had enough. Then that little fucking Child chirps up and whispers, 'Ahh, fuck it,' so you stay and get foolishly wasted."

The seated marines were comforted to recognize that Thatcher had a human element and was sharing a personal story. The gravelly-voiced Sergeant continued, "What no one ever dared to tell you is that inside the child portion of our personality is a little fucking devil. My job is to awaken that little devil inside of all of you. War and the devil have no con-science. You'll do what you have to do to survive and to win this war. When I'm done training you the little devil inside of you will be wide awake and ready to go. When you go home, you can put your devil to bed, but it will be refreshing to know that he's there at your beck and call if you should ever need him. The young indoctrinated Marines cheered their Sergeant's words with great enthusiasm. Hoorah.

Danny paid close attention to every technique the Sergeant displayed. Reilly was a formidable partner at six-foot-two and weighing in at two-hundred-twenty pounds. He was a man of large stature, a wide skulled, thick boned, blue-eyed Irish giant. Once again Mr. Chan's words echoed in Private Corvo's ears, "It's not how you look, it's what you got!"

At first encounter Reilly was impressed and surprised at Corvo's performance. There was nothing being taught that Corvo did not execute mindlessly with blinding speed and precision. The day's drills in hand-to-hand combat were Mr. Chan's beginner fundamentals garnished, with a lot of hoo-rah's and screaming.

After lunch, Sergeant Thatcher moved on to knife defense techniques. By this time, Jimmy Reilly was both mentally and physically spent trying to keep pace with Corvo. Annoyed at his own flaws, Reilly asked, "Hey Corvo, how do you do this stuff so easily? I mean, like everyone is learning slow and having trouble understanding, except you. What's the deal?"

"Well," said the grinning Corvo, "I'm dumb."

"You're dumb?" asked Reilly, "What is that supposed to mean? And if you're dumb, what the fuck are the rest of us?"

"Smart," he gleefully responded.

Reilly studied the grinning arches of Corvo's face and muttered, "You're fucking with me, right?"

Corvo snapped, "Big-time! I'm just trying to cheer your dreary, negative and depressing ass up, Champ."

Reilly enjoyed Danny's dry wit and unique sense of humor. He savored being called Champ. He knew Danny had experience that he just wasn't ready to share. The golden glove champ from Chicago and the fighting machine from the Bronx, New York would become inseparable friends. They shared photos of their girlfriends back in the States, often boasting about their faithfulness. It wasn't uncommon for their fellow Marines to endure a drunken off-key rendition of "When a Man loves a Woman." In time Danny would divulge all his past training with Jimmy Reilly, but first there had to be a trust of irrefutable merit.

Sergeant Thatcher called Private Corvo into his quarters after the first day of hand-to-hand training. "Sit down Corvo," said Thatcher.

Danny made direct eye contact and replied, "Thank you, sir."

Thatcher continued, "I watched my boys fumbling and stumbling to learn the knife techniques which is customary on the first day and then I watched you. It was second nature to you, ingrained in your subconscious like you have been doing this kind of stuff all your life. So what's your deal Corvo?"

The quiet Private replied, "My father and two Uncles were Marines, Sir. They insisted I learn how to protect myself from when I was really young. My two first cousins were Marines. They just finished a tour in Nam. I didn't have much of a choice but to learn, Sir."

Thatcher said, "Tomorrow you and I will train privately. I like what I see."

Sergeant Thatcher didn't have any physical advantage over his young Private. Their bodies were similar as was their measurement of height and weight. Danny was chiseled and cut from all the years of swimming and training during the early formative years of his life. Sergeant Thatcher carried the lower abdomen bulge of a beer drinker. He ushered Private Corvo to a small matted area in the Officers Club anxious to evaluate his skills. The seasoned drill instructor was out-maneuvered at every turn. Corvo was too fast and his spontaneous movements always gave him the upper hand. He could deflect and reverse any technique Thatcher employed.

Thatcher was a Drill Instructor. It was in his makeup to dramatize his authority; yelling, screaming, making fun of his boys and calling them names with a female connotation. He loved, "Cupcake," "Sweetheart" and his favorite, "Sugar Buns." But after all the dramatics of being the Drill Instructor, Thatcher loved the Corps and had a great love and admiration for these men who choose to become a Marine.

Many Drill Instructors would have been tormented by the great fighting skills of a Danny Corvo but Thatcher was wise. The Sergeant viewed Private Corvo as an asset to both his squad and the Marine Corps. Danny would soon become squad leader. Thatcher very humbly told the squad, "Off the record men, if this guy can whip my ass you all better stay on his good side." That comment aroused the young marine's great desire to watch the first Danny Corvo/Jimmy Reilly boxing exhibition in the weeks to come.

The M14 was replaced by the M16, also referred to as the assault rifle. A 45 caliber pistol was provided as the standard issued side arm. Danny had fired both of these firearms when he trained with the NYPD tactical patrol force. Learning how to disassemble the M16 and put it back together was child's play for Private Corvo. The humble private could perform the tedious task blindfolded but chose not to demonstrate that ability to anyone.

Sergeant Thatcher was not surprised by Private Corvo's shooting ability. Thatcher tried to coax the talented Private to become a Marine sniper, he declined. The Corvo plan was simple; serve my country, go home to Delia Hoffman, get married and have many children.

With only a few days left before graduation, Thatcher set up the "Fight of the City Boys." Corvo from New York versus Reilly from Chicago. The two stripped down to their Military issued underwear and were given a pair of soft shoes and ten ounce boxing gloves. Reilly's pride overshadowed his fondness of Danny. He believed with the greatest of confidence that Corvo did his thing but boxing was his thing. After all he was a Golden glove champion. Reilly was in for the disappointment of his life.

Sergeant Thatcher was the designated referee. He would allow them to fight three, three minute rounds. When the bell rang for round one Danny charged across the ring. Reilly was only a few steps out of his corner and the mauling Corvo was all over him.

Halfway through Round One, Thatcher momentarily stopped the bout and said, "What's wrong with you two? Take off your medals and those dog tags, you're gonna cut the shit out of each other." The fighters complied and the round progressed.

When Round One was over, Reilly, breathing heavily, reclined on the corner stool, his weary arms draped over the ropes. As he peered across the ring, he could see an unattended Corvo standing in his corner. Round Two produced a stronger and faster savage attack by Corvo. The Chicago Golden Glove Champ was knocked down and took a standing eight count from Thatcher.

When Round Two ended, the well-conditioned Corvo continued to stand. Reilly knew he had a supreme opponent. Beaten and discouraged a battered but brave Jimmy Reilly came out for round three. Danny then demonstrated to his squad the true brotherhood of the Marine Corps. He danced and slipped Reilly's punches very rarely countering. Reilly knew his friend was saving him from the humiliation of hugging the canvas. Danny's hand was raised in victory. The squad kept screaming, Corvo, Corvo. Danny put his thumb and middle finger to his lips and whistled loudly, the crowd became silent. He diverted their attention from his glorious performance by chanting USA, USA, USA. Everyone followed as he and Reilly embraced.

Two days before graduation Sergeant Thatcher once again called Private Corvo to his quarters. Thatcher said, "Sit down Danny." He then handed his squad leader a bottle of beer, "Don't worry I cleared it with your Sergeant. You know, Corvo, you were a true Marine from the first day you set foot on this Island. God knows you're chock full of talent but what amazes me most is that you're humble. I know you and Reilly are good friends but believe me if it was the other way around he would have tried to knock your ass out. You and the rest of the boys will be leaving soon after graduation, probably to Nam. We may never meet or see each other again. I just wanted you to know that meeting you was one of the best learning experiences of my career. Before we part company I have a question and I hope you'll answer it, but of course you don't have to. Who taught you all that stuff?"

Prepared to satisfy the Sergeant's curiosity the Private grinned saying, "My father has a Chinese friend, Mr. Chan, a veteran of World War II. He combined the mastery of martial arts with his military experience which took it to a whole new level. I started with him when I was ten and that's why I guess it really is ingrained in my subconscious."

The Sergeant embraced him and said, "Danny, I get constant reports from the Nam. It's not good. Don't be a hero and keep that little fucking devil awake at all times."

Danny returned home after the graduation ceremony. He arrived in New York on Sunday, March 22, 1970, wearing his Marine Corps issued camouflage. It was noon on Palm Sunday. He rode the IRT subway line to Bronx Park East and walked to the Hoffman house. As he turned the corner, the Hoffman family started to cheer. The marine private had to control himself from tearing up. He appeared pugnacious in his Marine Corps crew cut. He held Delia in his left arm and Abby in his right. He swung them in small circles with the dizzying motion of a merry-go-round. He put Abby down and concentrated on kissing the anxious full-bodied lips of his sensual fiancée.

Victoria gave Delia a surprise vacation the week following Easter. She wanted the young, very-much-in- love couple to spend time together. She knew too well the uncertainties of war. Her younger brother was engaged to be married prior to being drafted into the Korean War. He never made it home.

With his future bride by his side, the handsome Marine made his rounds visiting friends and family. Their love was as visible as the amazing impression of a darkened sky full of stars. That wonderful week of freedom and love rapidly dwindled down to a few precious hours.

With his duffle bag in tow, the Marine Private boarded the first of two buses to the Kingsbridge Armory to join the assemblage of his squadron. His distraught fiancée tearfully accompanied him to the local bus stop. They shared a long final kiss. He cupped his large hands reassuringly around her thin teary eyed face and said, "I love you Dee and don't worry; nothing can stop me from coming back to you. We got a lot of babies to make." She forced a grin but her heart was already aching.

On Monday, April 6, 1970 at ten am, Private Daniello Corvo and his squad boarded a plane to California. The next morning they boarded another plane for the gruesome fifteen hour journey to Saigon Airport the gateway to death in South Viet Nam. Hoorah!

CHAPTER 13

Private Corvo and his company of Marines landed in Viet Nam at 8:45 a.m. Wednesday morning. Even well-conditioned Marines from the Southern states couldn't imagine the airlessness of the Viet Nam jungle. The blistering heat was melded with a relentless unfamiliar clamminess. A short journey in Humvees brought the boys to their destination. It looked like a tent city.

On Thursday morning, April 9, 1970 Privates Corvo and Reilly boarded their assigned helicopter to perform reconnaissance duty. The mission entailed searching for wounded and dead American soldiers and returning them to base. The Chopper was assigned to cover a ten-mile radius from the camp. All passengers were warned to be prepared to encounter enemy fire. The six Marines were issued metal 'butt shields' to sit on as it was not uncommon for helicopters to receive ground fire aimed at penetrating the under body of the craft. In the absence of the protective shield soldiers were being hit with the guided shells and being maimed. Others lost their lives. It had become a mandatory directive for all passengers to use the shield. Father Smith a twenty-eight- year old Army Chaplin requested a ride to a venue located twelve miles away from camp. The Marine pilot, a Captain, granted the Chaplin his request but warned it may not be a pretty ride.

A half-hour after take-off Private Reilly spotted a dead American GI floating face down in a shallow murky pond. The body was waterlogged and featured the helium filled character-istics of an inflatable cartoon. The highly-decorated pilot was on his third tour of duty. He told the group, "Well gentleman, this fellow has been floating there for about a week. Hold your nose and don't soil your clothes." A weighted harness was low-ered and maneuvered around the corpse. The Captain gave the command, "OK boys bring him up." The body barely got off the water when it split in half. The stench was unfamiliarly peculiar and nauseating. Danny pivoted to the Chaplin and said, "Are you ok Padre?" The Chaplin didn't answer; his boyish face had already turned cadaver grey as he began to puke. Private Reilly became amused and said, "Hey Danny, having fun yet?"

The Padre reached his destination a few pounds lighter and much wiser. He had vowed to never swear but on this day he swore to never request a ride with a recon team for the duration of his tour in Viet Nam. The Captain called for a watercraft to retrieve the body of the split floater. It was not reassuring to hear the seasoned Captain exclaim that it hap-pened all the time. It didn't take Reilly and Corvo too long to witness first-hand the unspoken horrors of war. The craft returned to the base with four dead GI's. One of the causali-ties looked like he was fourteen. He was a seventeen-year-old volunteer whose proud parents had signed a release to allow their son to become a United States Marine.

U.S. Marines were on patrol every day seeking out the enemy. The days were generally sedated in comparison to the natural camouflage of the darkened night. The Cong liked to strike and create havoc under the cover of darkness. During the calm light of day the Marines played football, softball, played cards or wrote letters. It sometimes felt like a peaceful place but their ears were trained to tune in for the call to duty siren. Reilly the Chicago golden gloves champ made sure he brought his boxing gloves. He dismissed any dreams of revenging his loss to Corvo but enjoyed the punishing workout.

The next few weeks brought tension filled nights of action as the causality count became insurmountable. Private Corvo and Reilly both had registered kills but never spoke about it. Danny was beginning to understand the silence of his father and two uncles. He recalled telling Gus Galliano that he wanted to kill the rapist Kadesh but couldn't get close enough. Gus's blunt remark that he wasn't a killer became embedded in his brain realizing that now he was one.

Corvo and Reilly befriended a twelve year old Vietnamese boy, Bao Dao, whose parents were killed at the hands of the American infantry. His grandparents cared for the emotionally lost child and his younger sister but nourishment was not plentiful. Corvo and Reilly intervened and carefully smuggled leftover food for the struggling Dao family.

Bao was fluent in English. With the name, Bao, ending in a vowel, Corvo had to endure the wrath of Reilly's street wise sense of humor, as he proclaimed the child a slanty-eyed Italian. Corvo's keen wit could not be underestimated. He informed his Irish pal that "Fucko" was an Irish name and it too ended in a vowel.

The shattered orphan enjoyed playing catch and wrestling with his new-found friends. Reilly allowed the child to wear his boxing gloves and taught him the basics of punching. The well-built Corvo flipped the boy like a rag doll, earning his undivided attention. Young Bao visualized Corvo as a true-to-life American superhero. The two Marines became the big brother Bao never had.

Delia and Annabel were faithful in sending Danny letters of interest and gossip from home. He was grateful, but kept his responses brief and unrevealing. On May 15, 1970 Private Corvo received a tin of home-made cookies from his two favorite girls. Sunday, May 17th, was his twenty third birthday.

Danny's twenty-third birthday began with the loud shrills of the call-for-duty siren, a day he would never forget. The Cong had launched a massive ground offensive to the north side of the camp. Private Corvo and Reilly along with three other Marines were assigned to a Chopper attempting to foil their advance from the rear of the attack. Six Choppers carrying forty Marines opened fire to the rear flank of the insidious attack. Many of the Cong were instantly killed, while survivors fled to the safety of the thick jungle foliage.

The Captain spotted two Cong who dropped their weapons and raise their hands to surrender. The chopper was immediately grounded. Corvo and Jennings were sent on foot to bind their hands and make the capture. They were approximately one hundred feet away. The Chopper took fire from rebels camouflaged in the heavy brush, startling Corvo and Jennings. Their initial reaction was to assist their men in the aircraft. Simultaneously, the two fleeing Cong picked up their weapons and fired at Corvo and Jennings. The Marines in the Chopper opened fire, instantly killing the supporting rebels who emerged from the brush.

The two Cong started to run for cover in the bushy richness of the jungle foliage. Corvo and Jennings pursued the two escapees with determination. Out of ammunition and exhausted, the two Cong were captured. Their hands were tightly bound behind their backs and they were forced onto the deck of the grounded Chopper. After their feet were also tied, they were forced into a kneeling position.

Private Corvo's Chopper was one of the six that had an interpreter aboard. This massive daytime attack was a bizarre move and Sergeant Reynolds was going to get to the bottom of it before the aircraft landed. The seasoned Sergeant's face was frosted with anger as he instructed the interpreter, "Ask the one with the gold tooth where their camp is located."

The interpreter asked the question as both of the prisoners looked at each other and laughed. They laughed in defiant length. Reynolds mumbled, "Mother fucking gooks," as he grabbed the prisoner by the throat and instructed the interpreter to ask the other one. In spite of Reynolds deadly hold, both prisoners resumed their suicidal laughter.

The veteran Sergeant was humiliated. He turned to Private Reilly and said, "Private, slide that door open about a foot and a half." The dutiful Private responded, "Sir, yes sir," and slid the door to the requested position.

Once again Reynolds instructed the interpreter to ask the same question but once again they resumed their defiant laughter. Reynolds' face became angry as he snarled, "Corvo, turn that little ugly laughing hyena around and face him toward the door."

Private Corvo placed a vice grip hold on the prisoner's shoulders as he turned his face to the open door. Reynolds gestured to the interpreter to resume questioning saying boldly, "Tell his friend to watch what I'm going to do. Tell him to watch very carefully."

A look of frightened disbelief could be seen on the interpreter's face as he relayed the message. Reynolds screamed above the sound of the rotors, "Hey Captain bring her up a little higher."

He responded, "Roger that."

When the craft reached the desired height Reynolds picked up his right foot and booted the prisoner out of the Chopper. The captured prisoner screamed until his lifeless body became imbedded in the soft silty Vietnamese mud. Reynolds wasn't quite done. Satisfied, his voice became a low shrill as he continued, "Now, ask laughing boy again."

The face of the once amused prisoner was blanched of color. The trembling prisoner lost control of his bowl movements. After providing his captors with the much needed life-saving information he too was booted from the Chopper. Sergeant Reynolds interrogation methods were heart palpitating and barbaric, but they saved American lives. War is hell! Hoorah!

Danny and Jimmy Reilly put on a boxing show for the mind-distracting amusement of their brother Marines. After both of them sustained unnecessary bloody gashes in their chest, removing their medals and dog tags became a hard-learned habit. Marines are men of big hearts and great courage, so it wasn't surprising when Danny and Jimmy were challenged. The two accommodated their fellow Marines but let them learn the hard way about removing the metal objects that hung around their neck. Once the metal tag broke skin the fighter would hastily call time and remove his tag. Eventually they all got the idea.

Danny was held in high esteem by his squad members. His physical athleticism and a witty sense of humor made him the centerpiece of Marine jargon. Marines were fit and their physiques were well balanced. Corvo maintained the muscular sleekness of a professional fighter. The most seasoned and toughest of Marines were all leery of Private Corvo. He maintained a quiet demeanor and never raised his voice. The squadron had a standard testimonial, "If Corvo ever blows and loses his temper, we're getting out of Dodge."

August 1, 1970 was an unusual non-eventful Saturday in the camp. The men washed their uniforms and hang them up on rope lines to dry. The vapor-filled air of the jungle prevented the drying process from becoming complete. It was awful. The squad used inactive Saturday's as the reminder day to write home.

By mid-day letters were written, the siren was silent, and the young hyper marines were bored. Reilly brought out the gloves and started to gather participants. Reilly refereed the first three bouts until Sergeant Reynolds arrived at the makeshift ring. The Sergeant took control of the ring and refereed the next two bouts. The Main Event was about to begin, Corvo verse Reilly. Reynolds called the boys to the ring and instructed them to hang their tags and neck jewelry on the corner post.

Danny was in a jovial mood that day and danced circles around his best buddy. Mimicking Cassius Clay he jabbed Reilly's round Irish face and touted, "What's my name, what's my name?"

The reddened face Reilly answered, "Crazy Corvo, King of the streets." The Marines howled with laughter knowing the two bosom buddies were putting on a show. Halfway through Round Two the blasting siren ended the show. Reynolds shouted, "Saddle up on the double, boys, we got work to do."

The fighters scrambled to grab their gear and clothing. In less than two minutes, the young Marines boarded their assigned Choppers. Company B was under attack ten miles north of the camp and requested air and ground support. Reilly the fearless Irishman shunned eminent danger and cried out, "Hey Corvo, having fun yet?"

Danny applied his standard answer, "One day closer to home, bro, one day closer."

The pilot had a visual on the ensuing battle. Opening fire, he sought a drop zone for his twelve Marines. The chopper doors were ajar on both sides in preparation for a rapid descent to the ground. The drop zone was on the north side of a small but deep waterway. Reducing altitude, the pilot proceeded past the open water. Sergeant Reynolds spotted enemy shell launchers. He shouted, "Captain we have incoming at eleven o'clock."

The Captain strategically maneuvered the craft but a propelled shell grazed the tail end of the chopper. The unbalanced chopper became unsteady and returned a barrage of unguided fire power. The ground attack became overwhelming as the chopper took another hit and started to spin out of control. Two of the Marines jumped to the refuge of the open water below. The chopper was hit for the third time and suddenly exploded into a combustion ball of tiny metal fragments that rained down on the calm, murky waterway. The two Marines were still free-falling above the water when the chopper exploded. Any chance of survival for those remaining on board was a physical impossibility.

The following morning, a recon team escorted by heavily armed aircraft, searched for the remains of the Captain and the twelve Marines. The Cong had done their damage and moved on to the safety of the thick jungle.

The recon team placed the bodies and fragments of the dead Marines in plastic bags. The bodies were charred and fragmented by the fiery explosion that dissected the dead Marines. There was no accurate method available to identify the remains of these fallen soldiers. It became a grueling guessing game about what body part went with each soldier.

All eleven Marines who remained on the destroyed chopper were fragmentized. The re-con team recovered body parts, partial uniforms, jewelry and tags. The list of the fatalities was released to central control in alphabetical order: Captain R. Bashford/PFC P. Cashing/PFC D. Corvo/Cpl. J. Dellaforte/PFC R. Fitzsimmons/PFC J. Hickey/PFC R.Higgins/PFC J. Murray/ Sgt. E.Reynolds/Cpl J.Jones/PFC L. Tossini. Missing in action were PFC F. Jennings and PFC J. Reilly. In mid-August an Army patrol stumbled on the partially decomposed and muti-lated body of PFC F. Jennings. In the absence of any tangible evidence, PFC James Reilly, the Chicago Golden Glove champ was deemed MIA.

CHAPTER 14

T he remains of the eleven Marine casualties aboard
the destroyed chopper were tagged and flown to the
Dover Air Force Base in Delaware. They were placed
in the Charles C. Carson Center for Mortuary Affairs, the
final processing venue. Once identified and labeled, their
personal belongings would be returned to their family members. When the body's identification was certified, the Marine
Corps notified family members within twenty four hours.
It was Marine protocol to send two Casualties Notification
Officers of equal rank or higher to perform the dismal task.

Recon teams have a tedious and time-consuming task
properly identifying the remains of soldiers killed in an
explosion. In this tragic event, it was the personalized shirts,
tags and ID's that made their job remotely possible. The families of these fallen Marines would not receive any news until
Tuesday, August 4, 1970.

That morning arrived along with the sweltering heat that
had persisted for the past week. Grandpa Joe was in the front
of his garden tending to his beloved Sicilian plum tomatoes. At

nine in the morning, the partially shady garden was bearable from the wrath of the August sun. Close to the street, Grandpa Joe watched curiously as the dark green military sedan approached, searching for a suitable parking spot. Grandpa Joe had parked his customers cars near his shop, eliminating parking spaces in front of the Corvo house.

The vehicle slowed down, searching for the proper address. Eventually it parked three houses down from the Corvo Victorian. Grandpa Joe sensed something was wrong. Why would a Military vehicle park on this dead end? When the two Marines in full dress uniform exited the vehicle, he prayed that tragedy had not reached the home front. The two Casualties Notification Officers walked directly to the front entrance of the Corvo Victorian. The spry mechanic hurriedly left his garden and followed the two Marines to his son's front door.

Annabel was preparing potato salad when the doorbell rang. She yelled, "Just a minute I'll be right there." Walking into the front hallway she could faintly see the silhouette of the two fully dressed Marines behind the lace curtains of the vestibule as her heartbeat with a frenetic rapidness. She felt a sickly warmness engulf her body. Blood rushed to her face as she opened the heavy inner door. She quickly studied the faces of the two young Marines standing before her. They didn't have to speak. She knew.

Thoughtlessly she asked, "How can I help you?"

Their faces remained cold and expressionless devoid of emotion. Before they could speak she held her hands to her face and began to wail.

Grandpa Joe opened the door behind the insensitive Marines and asked, "What's wrong?"

They spoke directly to Annabel, "Ma'am, are you related to PFC Daniello J. Corvo?"

Breathing heavily, she whispered, "Yes, I am. I'm his mother."

Grandpa Joe tried to avoid what he already knew but hoping his instincts betrayed him asked again, "What's wrong?"

The Officer continued to focus all his attention on the dead Marine's mother. He spoke with emphatic clarity and said, "Mrs. Corvo, we're sorry to inform you that your son, Private Daniello J. Corvo, was killed in action on Saturday August 1st in the Viet Nam Theater. The United States Marine Corps sends their condolences. The Corps will supply everything necessary to give Private Corvo an honorary funeral."

Brushing the two Marines, aside Grandpa Joe held his traumatized daughter-in-law in his consoling arms. Somehow the distraught mother found the strength to compose herself. She accepted the manila envelope containing Danny's personal belongings and a letter of instructions from a Colonel Dillard.

When the two officers departed, the heartbroken Mother and Grandfather continued to sob, knowing the worst was yet to come. She asked her sister-in-law to call her children, Joe and Rosemarie, and insisted they come home as soon as possible. She took a cab to her husband's job site.

Big Sam was working on Bay Chester Road in the North Bronx. It wasn't a large site, so Annabel didn't have any difficulty finding him. Clutching their son's dog tags and gold cross in her hand, she approached her bewildered husband.

Surprised by her sudden appearance Sam didn't pay much attention to the dog tags or cross. He asked, "What are you doing here, is everything alright?"

She swung their son's tags and cross in front of his face like the pendulum of a clock and muttered, "They killed Daniello, they killed our son; he's gone." Her legs became rubberized as she slowly collapsed to her knees. Big Sam loudly moaned in horror as he fell to his knees consoling his grieving wife.

John Chan was oiling one of the machines when the operator shouted above the loud clanging roar of the diesel engine, "Hey John, Corvo and his wife are holding each other crying. Someone must have died." The logical inclination was that the eldest Grandpa Joe had died. He rushed to their side and asked softly, "Sam what happened?"

Sam Corvo's face was a river of clear-flowing tears as he cried out, "John, they killed my boy. Danny is dead." The unemotional Mr. Chan clutched his friend in his arms and succumbed to grief. He loved his student Danny Corvo as a father loves a son.

The grieving parents held hands the entire ride home. Their world of everyday contentment was rattled into deep despair. Telling Joe and Rosemarie was going to be another phase of dreadful unendurable pain.

When they arrived home, Joe and Judy and baby Joseph were waiting on the front porch. Rosemarie was called and summoned to come home. Joe embraced his parents; his face laden with mournfulness he said, "Grandpa told us; what are we going to do now?"

Sam held his oldest son and said reassuringly, "We're going to be strong the way Danny would want us to be. We still have a family to take care of—we have to take care of each other."

Rosemarie pulled up and began to cry before exiting the car. She knew the sudden request for her presence meant something horrible had happened. Logic persuaded her into believing something had happened to her grandfather. When she saw Grandpa Joe walk down the driveway, she knew her instinct had been deceived. She screamed in loud anguish, "Not Danny, please dear God, not Danny."

Sam called Doctor Sherman, who was close enough to make a house call and administer a sedative. Joe directed his teary eyes at his mother and said, "Mom, someone has to tell Delia. I'll go and tell her." Annabel thanked her son and gave him two sedatives to take with him.

Joe's sobbing was insuppressible as he drove to the Eastchester Road complex where his future sister-in-law worked. His eyes were red with bereavement. He had difficulty getting into the secured building until Victoria heard his last name. She casually said to Delia, "Dee, your future brother-in-law Joe is here. I hope everything is alright."

When Joe walked into the office, Delia sprung up from her chair and rushed to greet him. Victoria watched with cautious anticipation, knowing this unexpected visit might not be good news. Delia asked the dreaded question no one wanted to answer, "What's wrong? What happened?"

Joe regained some of his composure. After taking a deep breath, he said without preamble, "Danny was killed Saturday morning. His body is in Delaware. God damn this fucking war."

Victoria Galliano, the rock of the great Gus Galliano, shed her tough veneer and succumbed to crying and sobbing. The threesome embraced until the tragic news infiltrated Delia's fragile nervous system, causing her to collapse. When Delia regained consciousness, Joe gave her a glass of water and one sedative. The other was given to Victoria Galliano.

It all seemed so surreal. How this brilliant, multi-talented fighting machine could be gone at the age of twenty three was incomprehensible. Logic told the grieving Corvo family that war has no conscience and is indeed hell on earth.

Gus Galliano had lost one son to a drug-induced car crash. The young Corvo kid had saved the life of Gus Galliano's remaining son. Deep in his heart, he thought of Danny as another son. Receiving the news of Danny's death, Gus retreated to his private chambers and wept in quiet solitude. The business plans he had cleverly masterminded for Danny and his son were disfigured into a shattered dream.

With the exception of Delia Hoffman, Lieutenant Derosa took the news hardest of all. He had witnessed his gangster older brother kill two men when he was only a child. As a grown man, he acquired an acute disdain for the taking of a life. He too would be prescribed heavy doses of sedatives to ease the pain of Danny's death. The Lieutenant told his friend Sam Corvo, "You know, I loved your son as if he were my own." Sam nodded signaling that he understood. Derosa continued, "No disrespect intended, but we should have sent them to Canada. This war is a lost cause and now this. God help us."

Gus Galliano called the Corvo residence, offered his deepest condolences to Annabel and asked to speak to Mr. Corvo. Sam was handed the phone and Gus said, "Sam, this is Gus Galliano. I'm lost for words. I know from losing Tommy there are no words to ease the pain not even a little bit. I want you to know that I'll never forget what that boy did for my family. If it wasn't for him, I wouldn't have any kids. If there is ever anything you or family need please don't hesitate to call me. I mean that sincerely from the bottom of my heart."

Sam was grateful and said, "Thank you, I know Danny admired and loved you and was always grateful to have you has a friend."

Gus responded, "Thanks, I have a suggestion for you as the man of the house."

Sam nervously asked, "Sure, what is it?"

Gus replied bluntly, "Don't put your family through a three day wake; cut it short, two at the most. I did that for my Tommy and I know it was better for his mother."

213

Sam respectfully gave great thought to Gus Galliano's suggestion. The letter from Colonel Dillard explained in unwanted detail the complexity of the recon mission. Bodies recovered from an explosion mandated a closed casket. That was the cold hard truth. Sam very carefully assembled the words that would commit his wife to a one-day wake.

Private Corvo's remains arrived at Riggio's funeral home at noon on Wednesday August 5th. The wake would be held on Thursday August 6th from 2 to 4 p.m. and 6 to 8 p.m.; the funeral mass on Friday August 7th was at 10 a.m. The remains of Private Daniello Corvo were to be buried in Saint Raymond's Cemetery, not far from his childhood sweetheart, Amy Winter.

Delia Hoffman was dressed in black from head to toe, reminiscent of an old Sicilian widow. She wore a black hat with a closely knit lace trim covering her eyes. The funeral director was given some symbols of love and affection to be placed in the closed casket with Danny's remains; torn in half movie tickets, Christmas cards, birthday cards and the 45rpm Nat King Cole record, "When I fall in love."

The heavy dose of sedation given to Delia could not halt the hurricane of newly formed tears. She was haunted by Danny's words at Tommy Galliano's funeral, "It doesn't matter if it's a nice day or a rainy day on the day of a funeral. It doesn't matter if the person died fast or slow, was young or old. Funerals always suck."

Nine-year-old Abby Hoffman insisted that she be brought to the funeral parlor. Delia told her she could come with her Grandpa but her stay would be limited to a few brief minutes. The child, dressed in bereavement black, gained the undivided attention of the somber mourners. Delia held her hand as they courageously approached the casket to kneel and pray. Delia abruptly rose from the kneeler and pulled her stubborn daughter like a dog on a lease. When she released Abby's hand the confused child ran back to the casket. The congregation's eyes became pasted on the child's unpredictable behavior.

With the sweet innocence of a child, she placed her ear on the casket and softly whispered, "Come on Danny stop teasing me. No one could kill you." After a momentary hesitation she closed her small fragile fist and knocked on the hard oak casket, saying softly, "Will you please come out and stop fooling me." The mourners were further bereaved by the child's innocent gesture. There wasn't a dry eye in the room.

Saying goodbye is never easy when it's forever. Outside the funeral parlor, the Marine Band bagpiper played, "Oh Danny Boy." The ceaseless flow of tears made their way to the warm August ground as Delia Hoffman tried to absorb the finality of the moment.

The despondent nature of the funeral mass retarded the passing of time turning brief moments into hours. Doc Singer, Nicky Galliano, Lieutenant Derosa, his brother Joe, and cousin's Phil and Tommy Corvo carried the casket of the slain Marine. At Saint Raymond's Cemetery the casket was slowly lowered into the ground. A procession line was formed and the mourners were each given a red rose to cast onto the coffin. Grandpa Joe's weakened body was supported by his son, Sam, as he painstakingly shuffled to reach the casket. He paused in final adoration of his grandson and muttered, "My little Danny is gone, gone with the wind."

The Corvo family held a buffet luncheon in their home. Friends and family gathered to honor the memory of the young Marine. Respectfully many expressed their sorrow but words could not begin to relieve the loss of a son. Delia Hoffman drew strength from Annabel but it was the prescription sedatives that got her through the day. Sam and Annabel were newly blessed Grandparents and somehow would have to find the strength to carry on.

CHAPTER 15

Five days after the Marine helicopter explosion, the lone survivor was captured and imprisoned in South Viet Nam. The North Vietnamese identified the soldier as Marine Private James Riley. His escape and recapture earned him a transfer to the infamous Hoa Lo Prison in North Viet Nam. Hoa Lo Prison was dubbed the "Hanoi Hilton" by its many brave captives. The inmate's unbreakable spirit flourished thanks to the great American sense of humor. Contemptuously the prisoners dubbed the cesspool of a prison, "Heartbreak Hotel," "Hells Hole," and "Fiery Furnace." Those names painted a clear picture of the camp's torturous treatment.

The young Marine found himself bound in a four by four foot steel cage. Starved and beaten he was awakened by a tooth-less face slapping North Viet Cong prison guard. His English was poor and limited. Unable to properly pronounce R's, the toothless prison guard thrust his face closer and commanded, "Wiley wake up. We have many questions to ask you."

The young re-captured Marine diligently answered all of Lieutenant Cho's questions. "Wiley, what is Captain's name?"

He answered promptly, "Joe. Joe DiMaggio." His fellow prisoners held their mouths in restrained silence. In spite of their poor physical condition some found it difficult to smother their laughter. All his answers had the same false, sarcastic narrative but he was believable.

When day one of the interrogation was over his caged comrades exclaimed, "Wiley, you are one good American bull-shitter. Welcome to the Hanoi Hilton."

Wiley became the young captive's new calling card. It would be their united ability to spit in the face of torture that kept some of them alive. But many died due to the daily regimen of beatings, torture, starvation and illness. The Paris Peace Talks were initiated in an attempt to end the war and soften the harsh treatment of POW's. The long-term inmates of the Hanoi Hilton believed Hanoi never really got the message.

Before the end of 1970, the prisoners were permitted to walk about and engage in simple exercise. Any attempt of one on one interaction was met with the consequence of solitary confinement. The North Vietnamese version of solitary confinement was stuffing the prisoner in an air deprived fifty-five gallon metal drum. The twenty foot high wall was a deterrent to the most courageous and incorrigible prisoner. Prisoners of the Hanoi Hilton remained tortured, underfed, and beaten. Only the strongest of the strong would survive this man-made hell.

The slow passing of time was torturous in itself, but it was now Monday, Christmas Day, 1972. Life would go on for the Corvo family after the loss of young Danny. Over two years had passed, but the emptiness remained. Many changes had ensued and much remained the same. For most of the people who knew and loved the deceased Marine, life strangely remained the same. The everyday routine of Bronx living would continue like the ticks of a fine-tuned clock. Grandpa Joe, in his mid-seventies, continued to pursue his labor of love—making cars go faster. Some days, the simplest of events brought tears to his eyes. His memories were haunting, as he sometimes imagined hearing young Danny's voice saying, "I got it Grandpa, take a break." He would miss hearing that voice and watching him apply the skills that he so patiently taught him as a child.

Joe and Judy had a second son that they graciously named Daniello. Rosemarie was a Defense Attorney working for a Manhattan based law firm. She was engaged to be married in August of 1973. Doc Singer was a surgeon practicing at Mt. Saini in Manhattan. At the tender age of twenty seven, his reputation for brilliance was widespread. The demand for his services was becoming untenable.

It took Delia Hoffman six months to get off of the prescription sedatives after the loss of her beloved guardian angel. She became insecure about facing the future alone. The thought of single-handedly raising her daughter Abby as she approached the teenage years worried the young beauty. Her sisters encouraged her to go out on dates. Her closest sister Lee preached with unyielding justification saying, "You can't spend the rest of your life missing Danny. He would never want you to be miserable. You're young and have your whole life ahead of you." Those words didn't resonate until she heard them from Annabel Corvo.

In May, Delia Hoffman went to the dentist for a routine cleaning and yearly exam. Her regular dentist was on vacation. His replacement was a young, attractive dentist who became immediately smitten with the young beauty. He called her at work the following day and asked how she felt. Surprised,

Delia said, "There's nothing wrong. It was only a cleaning and the exam was fine. Is there something I should know?"

Doctor Blatner chuckled and replied, "No, everything is good as you say. I was just wondering if you would like to go to a Yankee game?"

Delia responded curtly, "We don't even know each other. Thanks, but no thanks. Sorry, but I have work to do."

The smitten young Dentist wouldn't give up so easily. The son of a wealthy Connecticut businessman had a privileged upbringing. Raised in the lap of luxury and accustomed to getting his own way, his persistence was unescapable. The following day would bring a special delivery of twelve long-stemmed red roses. The note read, "I'm sorry if I upset you. You're right we really don't know each other so how about a cup of coffee?" The note was signed, Matt Blatner.

Lee convinced her younger sister to accept the Dentist's invitation to lunch. Delia agreed to meet him for lunch on the following Friday. She made it clear that her demanding job would restrict their luncheon date to one hour. Dr. Blatner accompanied her to a local diner about five minutes from her job. Dr. Blatner had graduated from Johns Hopkins magna cum laude. He was confident and touted many of his personal achievements during their brief encounter. He professed to be an athlete of professional statute. He asked, "So from what college did you graduate?"

Delia smiled and replied, "I didn't. I'm just taking courses at Bronx Community to enhance my accounting skills."

The young Dentist became condescending with an air of parental criticism, "You know, in order to excel in life, you really need a good college education."

Delia looked at him defiantly. Her unblemished face became rosy with anger as she said, "Then perhaps you should screen your dates before you ask them out. Oh, and by the way, I have a daughter who will turn ten soon. I had her when I was thirteen; but don't worry she's going to college. I can find my own way back and don't call me again. Oh, one more thing, I hate roses."

When Delia returned to work, her abrupt manner and curt answers told the tale of her first encounter with a man. Victoria said mockingly, "So, it went that good, huh?"

Dee answered, "He's a well-educated, self-centered jerk who thinks the world owes him something."

Victoria laughed and said, "Every mother thinks it's great when their daughter dates a doctor or a lawyer. The truth is most of them are exactly what you said, self-centered jerks. And they really look down on any of us girls who don't have a college education."

Delia, appreciative of her insight replied, "Boy, you hit the nail right smack on the head."

Delia Hoffman turned twenty three that June. She tried to display an air of calmness and demonstrated a manner of happiness for her unsettled child. Abby was ten years old and still had trouble believing that her "Daddy Dan" was gone. She became a constant reminder of Danny's absence.

In July, Delia was leaving work when the summer sky suddenly opened into a torrential gush of cool rain. Her 65 Impala was strategically parked under the shade of an old oak tree a distance from the side entrance to the building. She patiently waited under the canvas canopy for the surge to subside. A young lumber salesman approached and offered to walk her to the car under the protection of his oversized umbrella. Innocently Delia accepted his offer, got into her car, thanked the young man and drove home.

Two days later, the young Italian lumber salesman walked into Victoria Galliano's office. Upon his departure he stopped at Delia's desk and said, "Hi I'm Anthony Rango."

Delia glanced up and said, "Hi, I'm Delia Hoffman, Mrs. Galliano's secretary and bookkeeper. What can I do for you?"

He replied, "Oh, I'm sorry. No, nothing really. I just wanted to say hi. You do remember me from yesterday?"

Delia said, "Sure, you were the gentleman with the umbrella. Thanks again." Her eyes quickly returned to the financial document she was amending. Anthony Rango waved an unacknowledged goodbye and left the building.

He returned the following week and spoke business with Victoria Galliano. When his business was completed, he once again approached the young beauty's desk. After a prim salutation, Anthony Rango said, "Please don't think I'm being too straight forward, but I was thinking about you."

Delia became annoyed and sternly responded, "Now why is that?"

He handed Delia a long narrow package, the contents concealed in colorful wrapping paper and said, "My Company has me giving out these umbrellas, embossed with their logo on it of course, to our best clients. I thought you might be able to use it, just in case. It's really a cool umbrella and it can easily accommodate two people."

Women found Anthony Rango to be attractive, as did the grieving young beauty. Her female intuition cautioned that the umbrella was a "break the ice" ploy by the young, well-spoken lumber salesman. She would test him.

As Rango touted the practicality of the umbrella, she interrupted him with a twang of sarcasm. "Two people under one umbrella, that's great. I have a ten year old girl and an umbrella that size might just come in handy."

The sassy salesman blushed and said, "That's cool. So you're married?"

Delia parried his question and remarked, "My man was killed in Viet Nam last August."

Rango lowered his head in a prayerful manner and offered his condolences. He gently placed the umbrella on a clear corner of her desk and quietly departed.

Anthony Rango visited the Galliano Company every week. Every visit produced another practical gift and friendly dialogue. Victoria didn't appreciate Rango's over-abundance of confidence. She perceived him as an apprentice gigolo. He flirted with every female that came into his view and remained a persistent predator.

Delia was lost, emotionally drained, and critically lonely. She cried herself to sleep more often than not. Her sister, Lee, was right—Danny was gone and she had to move on. The constant doses of Rango's praise caused her to become receptive to his friendship. As time went by, Delia dropped her guard and gave in to the advances of the handsome Rango. He was very kind to her daughter and she soon believed that this was as good as it gets. Delia Hoffman and Anthony Rango were engaged in July of 1972. They planned to be married in February of 1973.

When the news hit the Corvo family, they were happy for Delia and Abby. They never met her new fiancée and could not acquire a desire to do so. Sam and Annabel agreed that life goes on but to resurrect old feelings would be self-destructive. Delia respectfully visited Annabel and shared her plans for the future.

Annabel graciously gave Delia her blessing but declined to attend the wedding. She said, "I'm sure you must understand. We envisioned you and our Danny walking down the aisle. We were overjoyed when you two kid's fell in love. It would break our hearts to watch you walk down the aisle with another man. I hope you truly understand." Delia wept in the arms of the only resemblance of a mother she ever knew

Annabel Corvo. She left the refuge of the quiet dead end street of Holland Avenue and moved on with her life.

Nelson Hoffman was a hard-working man of quiet demeanor. He pretended to accept Anthony as his new future son-in-law and never uttered a word to anyone about his deep-felt concern regarding the man's alcohol consumption. He too noticed his propensity to gape and stare at other women. He could not grasp his daughter's attraction, as there were few similarities between Anthony Rango and the late Danny Corvo.

Lee Hoffman was the only one to recognize her younger sister's ambivalence toward her February 24th wedding. She decided to confront her younger sister. Late the following evening the two sisters were alone in the living room watching Johnny Carson. This would be Lee's chance to probe. She patiently waited for the commercial, lowered the volume on the TV and asked, "Dee, do you ever get nervous and wonder if you are making the right decision?"

Dee folded her arms across her chest and answered, "Look, I know it's a big move. I went over it in my head a thousand times. Abby seems to like him, he treats me really good, he has a good job, is kind of good-looking, so what should I wait for?"

Lee remarked, "I just want to make sure you gave it enough thought. You know you're my favorite sister." Dee smiled and offered a long embrace. Lee continued, "So, Do you love him?" Startled by the straight-forwardness of such a brazen question, she paused and responded, "If the question is, do I feel the same way about Anthony as I did about Danny the answer is not yet. Hopefully I'll get there some day. Remember, you're the one that told me I can't live in the past." Guilty and unsure of the credibility of her own advice Lee forced a smile saying, "Everything will be great, don't worry you know how I am about protecting you."

The wedding invitations were all returned and tallied. There would be a total of seventy people in attendance. The Galliano's gave Delia a very generous gift but declined to attend. Victoria's explanation was a re-cast of Annabel Corvo's—it would just feel too weird.

Annabel awakened the morning of the Hoffman/Rango wedding in a state of deep depression. The thought of Delia Hoffman belonging to another man revitalized her dormant sorrow. Delia was Danny's girl. Why did God allow this to happen?

The ceremony began at one o'clock. At 1:30 p.m., Delia Hoffman became Mrs. Anthony Rango.

Annabel's depression did not subside as she groaned, "Sam, I'm never going to Church again. This wedding makes me think that there is no God." Her depression and sentiments about the wedding were self-destructive. Her loving husband held her and once again they relived the torment of losing their son.

After a prolonged silence, Sam said, "I'm not giving up on God because Delia got married. Please don't say those kinds of things. War and this government killed Danny, not God. Remember the whole free will theory? We can't become atheists. We still have a son and a daughter, two beautiful grandchildren and our parents are still alive. What are we going to do when Rosemarie gets married in August... stay home? Take a pill and calm down. You'll feel better tomorrow."

CHAPTER 16

The Paris Peace Accord orchestrated the long-antici-pated end to the Viet Nam War. February 27th was a day applauded and celebrated by all of America. Prisoners of war from both South and North Viet Nam started being released under Operation Homecoming. POW's were fur-nished with brand new gray uniforms supplied by the North Vietnamese. The first group boarded C141's and were flown to Clark Air Force Base on Luzon Island in the Philippines. Once there, they were required to reveal their name, rank, and serial number for the record. They were given a physical and a well-anticipated Texas-style steak dinner followed by creamy old-fashioned American ice cream.

After a few days of rest, the men boarded a C141 and were flown to Andrews Air Force Base in Camp Springs, Maryland. This base served as the distribution center for the POW's returning home to their families. Soldiers in poor physical condition were admitted into the military hospital for treatment. There, they welcomed the long-awaited oppor-tunity to communicate with their families.

On Thursday, March 29, 1973, the last remaining twenty-seven prisoners from the infamous Hanoi Hilton prison boarded a C141 and were flown to Luzon Island. These men were in the poorest physical condition of all the soldiers flown to the Island. The torture and starvation was visible on their emaciated bodies. Their skeletal make-up protruded through the skin. Many had severe nervous conditions and would shake like a drug addict in need of a fix. Others had missing teeth and broken bones that were never set to heal properly, causing unsightly physical deformities. These beaten, battered, underfed, and undernourished men were the strongest of the strong. Unlike so many of their brother prisoners, they had survived.

"Wiley," the six foot one boxer, was reduced to an empty shell of a man. His once overly-defined muscles clung to his bones. His once handsome face was sunken below the cheek bones; his eyes had lost their luster, empty of life. The endless beatings left the ugly marks of uncontrolled sadism. Somehow he endured. Something stronger than torture kept him alive. That unexplainable something was his love for a woman.

Seventeen of these soldiers were deemed physically capable to be flown to the States. "Wiley" and nine of his captive brothers remained behind until they regained enough strength to make the long journey home. "Wiley" and his nine brother prisoners were placed in the hospital dorm. Ten hospital beds were placed side by side, affording these men the comfort of each other. They had suffered the inhumane cruelty of the "Hanoi Hilton" and somehow inspired each other to survive. These ten men were dubbed by the hospital staff as the "Hanoi Ten Pins." They would say like bowling pins you can knock them down, but as soon as you turned around, they would be up in automatic fashion.

By day four the "Hanoi Ten Pins" had already began to reap the benefits of good hospital care and nourishment. Dialogue between the men had resumed giving the attending medics hope. The new mission of the "Hanoi Ten Pins" was to heal, eat, laugh and joke their way back to the States. The nursing staff had used their personal ID's and dog tags to record the personal information of these men. All of them were now able to speak or communicate by nodding their heads.

Before they could be released, the staff was obligated to follow military procedure and ask each of them a three phase question. What is your full name, rank and serial number? They started on the left with "Coco" Rodrigues. Corporal Rodrigues was a dark skinned Portuguese that his buddies nicknamed "Coco." Sergeant Hayes asked, "Coco, what's your, name, rank and serial number?" He answered with enthusiasm, "Edwin Rodrigues, Corporal U.S. Army, 6421889. The procedure was continued from left to right, recording and verifying the verbal response of each soldier, letter for letter, number for number. Getting this information wrong was not an option.

Sergeant Hayes and his assistant admired these courageous men but many of them were not easy on the eyes. Finally they reached the last of "Hanoi Ten Pins," James "Wiley" Reilly. Sergeant Hayes said, "Well, Wiley you are last but not least. Tell us your name, rank and serial number?" Wiley answered, "Daniello J. Corvo, Private First Class U.S. Marines, 1862445."

A shocked Sergeant Hayes quickly pivoted to his assistant Private Cummings and cried out, "Holy shit, something's way out of whack here." He approached the side of the bed and placed the Private's dog tag in his hand. It read James J. Reilly, 1891872.

The Sergeant asked again, "Soldier, please don't fuck with me. What did you say your name was?"

The soldier replied, "Daniello J. Corvo, United States Marines."

"That's what I thought you said." Sergeant Hayes continued, "How did you end up with Reilly's dog tag?"

Private Corvo struggled to prop himself up to make eye level contact with the Sergeant and whispered, "Reilly and I were friends. We took our tags off to box. A few minutes into it the siren sounded. I've been thinking about this for over two years; either we just got mixed up in the heat of the moment or one of the guys decided to fuck around and switched the tags. That's all I can figure. But I can tell you this—I'm not James Reilly."

Sergeant Hayes reported this major discrepancy in information to his Captain. Angry and displeased, Captain Mueller personally visited Private Corvo. He was given the same information and explanation as that given to the Sergeant. He asked Private Corvo if he knew what happened to Reilly. Danny paused and offered a head gesture of affirmation saying, "When the chopper first got hit, I tried to get him to jump. There wasn't much time, maybe a few seconds. I jumped along with Jennings. The rest of my guys were blown up. When I surfaced from the water I could see copter and body parts all over the place. It was a fucking nightmare." The Captain thanked the Private and told him to rest. He assured him that he would soon be going home to the States.

Captain Mueller knew this error in identification was a major problem. The Reilly family had been praying and hoping for the return of their son. With the war officially over, they anxiously waited for news of his release. The Corvo family had spent over two and a half years mourning the death of a son that was still alive. They had a wake and buried him. Heads would roll.

Captain Mueller was ordered to notify Colonel Dillard, the head of the Causality Notification Team. Colonel Dillard listened intently as Captain Mueller relayed Private Corvo's summary of the chopper explosion. Dillard was aware of the complexity of a Recon Team's mission when it involved an explosion. Switched dog tags gave birth to a new nightmare.

Once again two Causality Notification Officers were dispatched to the Corvo residence. Colonel Dillard flew to New York and became the catalyst of the task at hand. Colonel Dillard landed at La Guardia Airport in New York on Wednesday, April 4, 1973. This was the same day Private Daniello Corvo and his nine prison mates landed at Andrews Air Force Base in Maryland. The Colonel spent the night at Fort Schuyler Naval Academy in the Bronx a twenty five minute car ride to the Corvo Victorian. Dillard had to be absolutely certain that Private Corvo was home in the States before consulting with the Corvo family.

Early Thursday morning Colonel Dillard received official notification from Andrews that Private Corvo had arrived at the military base hospital. His physical condition was reported as poor but stable. A Naval Officer drove the Colonel to the Corvo residence at ten am.

Grandpa Joe was test driving a customer's car and paid very little attention to the Official Naval vehicle pulling into his block. They parked the eerie four door sedan directly in front of the Corvo Victorian. Colonel Dillard accompanied by Navy Lieutenant Everett entered the vestibule and rang the Corvo doorbell.

Annabel could see the silhouette of two military men through the faded lace curtains. Confused and curious she entered the narrow hallway and made her way to the vestibule door. She opened the door and said, "Can I help you?"

Colonel Dillard asked with a degree of uncertainty, "Mrs. Corvo?"

She answered, "Yes, what's this all about?"

Taking a deep breath the Colonel replied, "Mrs. Corvo I have the most shocking news I've ever had to tell a soldier's Mother."

Annabel's eye's widened in great anticipation. She prodded, "What is it? Is it about my son?"

"Yes, Ma'am, it's about your son, Private Danny Corvo" he replied.

"What, what is it?" she asked.

The stern-faced Dillard continued, "There has been a terrible case of mistaken identity."

Annabel's arms flailed as she hugged the statuesque Colonel. He continued, "Your son and a buddy were boxing and they somehow put on each other's dog tags. Mrs. Corvo, your son is in the Andrews Air force Base hospital in Maryland. He's alive and doing well."

Overjoyed, Annabel collapsed in Dillard's arms. Lieutenant Everett hurried to the vehicle and retrieved the first aid kit. He administered smelling salts to revive the overly-excited mother.

The two officers accompanied her into the first floor apartment and administered a sedative to settle her flustered nerves. Dillard offered to assist her in notifying Mr. Corvo. Without preface Annabel said coldly, "My husband died of a heart attack six months after we buried our son."

After giving them that information, Annabel ran into the rear garage and embraced her startled father-in-law. Her fair-skinned face was pink with excitement as she said, "Pop, there was a mistake. Danny's alive. He was a prisoner of war all this time, but he's alive."

After the two officers left Annabel and Grandpa Joe began the joyous task of telling their family the shockingly good news. Annabel's joy was stifled as she muttered, "Oh my God, we have to tell Delia. And worse than that, we'll eventually have to tell Danny."

Joe Corvo drove his mother to Maryland the following day, Friday April 6th. He volunteered to tell Delia Rango that a tragic mistake had been made and that her former fiancée was alive. Anthony Rango was a recent recipient of a handsome inheritance. The Rangos had purchased a classy Tudor home on Tenbrook Avenue in the ritzy 'Indian Village' section of the Bronx. It was close to Delia's job and it was an upscale neighborhood.

At one o'clock in the afternoon, Joe drove to Delia's workplace to tell her and Victoria Galliano the bizarre news. Joe weaseled his way into Victoria Galliano's office without Delia's knowledge. He politely asked about Mr. Galliano and Nicky. She informed him that Nicky was married and Mr. Galliano had developed diabetes and had been in a deep state of depression since the loss of Tommy. She said bluntly, "Losing Danny didn't help either; I know that you know to Gus your brother was another son."

Joe smiled and said, "Well, Mrs. Galliano I'm not a doctor but what I'm going tell you is going to make Mr. Galliano and you feel awfully good."

Confused and puzzled she said, "So what are you waiting for? Tell me already."

Joe waved his clenched fist and said, "Danny's alive. His dog tags were switched with his friend, Reilly. He's alive. He's in the Military hospital in Maryland. We're going to see him tomorrow."

Victoria crossed her arms across her chest and said, "Dear Mother of God." Overcome with sudden joy she hugged and kissed Joe Corvo. Her well-preserved face became beautified as she said, "I must have told Gus a hundred times I just couldn't believe that anyone could kill one of God's miracles. You know, I always believed that your brother was truly one of God's miracles."

The happiness left her face as she whispered, "What are we going to tell Delia?"

Joe said softly, "The truth."

Delia had her head buried in the typewriter. Joe Corvo approached her desk and began a self-induced clearing of the throat. Slightly irritated, she looked up and said, "Joe Corvo, how are you? Is everything ok?"

Joe's face was expressionless as he said, "I need to talk to you."

Victoria knew Joe's message was going to be damaging to Delia's already fragile state of mind. She waved them both over and said, "Why don't you two use my office so you can have some privacy." The two went into the office and sat down by the window facing Eastchester Road.

Delia said, "Joe this is weird, what's wrong?"

Joe responded, "Nothing's wrong but what I'm going to tell you is shocking and it's probably going to hurt."

She said, "I'm a big girl, Joe, and after losing Danny there's nothing you can tell me that I can't handle."

Joe's face grimaced. "Well, Dee speaking about Danny, that's what I have to talk to you about."

"How so?" she blurted.

"Danny and his friend Reilly were boxing on the day their chopper got blown up. Their dog tags got switched when the siren went off. Danny jumped out of the chopper into the river and was captured three days later. He was a prisoner of war. He's alive."

Delia sprang out of her chair and instinctively embraced him. Hysteria was setting in as she screeched, "I have to go to him. I have to see him. Where is he?"

Joe firmly responded, "You're married, Dee and I have to tell that to Danny. This is so fucked up."

Delia listened to Joe's sobering logic about how they couldn't change history. She was so emotionally distraught that she fainted and had to be taken by ambulance to Jacobi Hospital.

Victoria Galliano followed the ambulance to the hospital. As a courtesy to Delia, she called Anthony Rango to inform him of his wife's admittance. Then she drove to her Riverdale Estate, anxious to tell her distressed husband the startling good news.

Gus was in his study listening to opera. When Victoria entered the room, Gus sensed the exuberance of her mood. He said softly, "Bella ragazza, I can see the happiness in your face. Share with your old broken down man the good news of the day. What is it that elates you?"

Victoria leaned in to give her husband a kiss on his head. She carefully maneuvered a chair closer to him and said, "Do you remember me telling you that I always thought Danny was one of God's miracles?"

"How could I forget? Why do you bring this up?" he said.

She continued, "Remember when he was sixteen, he hospitalized that big biker guy? And how could we ever forget what he did to Caldo and his two punk friends that tried to rape Dee. Then there is of course the unbelievable rescue of our Nicky."

Gus became momentarily petulant at the resurrection of the beloved boy's heroism. He continued to speak in a low whisper, "Vic, I think about Tommy and Danny every day. That's part of my depression; so tell me what this is all about?"

Victoria ignored her husband's obvious annoyance and said, "Guess who is going to come and visit you in person soon? In about two to three weeks."

Gus snarled, "The fucking Easter bunny. Would you please tell me what all the grinning and giggling is about?"

She sat her petite body on his lap and prodded his chin with her finger until their eyes met. Then she said, "Joe Corvo came to see me today. Danny was never killed. He jumped into the river one hundred feet below before the helicopter exploded. He got captured three days later but they never killed him. He's back in the States and recuperating in the Maryland Army Hospital."

She stood before him awaiting his reaction. Suddenly he bounced from his chair with juvenile energy and kissed her. Gus was reenergized, as the demons of his depression quickly withered away. Suddenly his smiling face lost the curves of joy as he said, "He's going to flip when he finds out Delia got married. What a fucking mess this is going to be."

Victoria reported that Delia had to be hospitalized after learning that her former fiancée was alive. Gus paid little attention to her concern and said blatantly, "I'll try to convince Danny not to kill her fucking husband, but it's not really a bad idea under the circumstances. This Rango is a scumbag." Victoria never underestimated her husband's ability to retrieve information about anyone. He had his fingers in many pies and there were many people trying to win his confidence.

The following morning, Joe Corvo drove his mother to the Andrews Air Force Base Hospital in Camp Springs, Maryland. Dillard had informed the Corvos that the young Marine was stable but needed much rest and nourishment before he could be transported to New York. The Corvos understood nourishment to mean that he needed to eat. No parent or sibling could be prepared for what they were about to see.

A Military guard accompanied them to the third floor dorm to meet with their loved one. The attending guard was young but spoke with the congeniality of a seasoned veteran. He said softly, "Try not to be alarmed. These guys have had some rough years. Believe me, your son will bounce back, but he's going to need some time." When the guard escorted them to Danny's bedside, the widowed mother became inconsolable. Three IV's were being pumped into his body while he remained in a deep, much-needed sleep. His face was sunken at the cheek bones. This once masterpiece of a body devoid of visible muscle had been beaten into a sketchy skeleton. Annabel could see very little a mother would recognize. He looked like a different human being. They sat in gloomy despair and decided it best to conceal Delia's marriage until his health improved. They patiently waited for Danny to awaken.

Two hours passed before Danny awakened. His voice was reduced to a raspy whisper as he said mockingly, "So how was my funeral?"

Annabel's blue eyes welled with tears as she answered, "Awful. The past two and half years have been awful."

They took turns very gently embracing and kissing their loved one. Then Danny asked the dreaded question, "Where's Delia?"

Joe very cleverly responded, "Danny, she has not been good since your funeral. We know how much you two love each other but we didn't tell her yet."

The young marine's eyes blazed with anger as he moaned, "You got to be kidding, why not?"

Joe said, "She's been mentally fragile ever since she thought you died. Her doctor thought it would be a good idea to let you put on a few pounds, lose those damn IV's so she doesn't start thinking you're not going to make it. I love you, brother, but please, let's give it another week. Now you have an incentive to eat like a pig."

Danny pressed his lips in firm affirmation gesturing his agreement. He muttered, "I waited almost three years. If that's going to be better for Delia, I can wait another week. She kept me alive in that hell-hole, you know."

Danny struggled to prop himself up to eye level with his brother and mother. Annabel surmised the cross-examination was about to begin and so it did. He appeared to accept the reasoning behind Delia's absence. Only bleak traces of familiarity remained on his sunken face but his mind was robust with precision. He seemed calmer as his face labored to arch a glimpse of a smile. His eyes repeatedly pivoted from mother to brother and asked, "So where's Dad? Is he working?"

Annabel inched closer and wrapped her hand around her son's. Her eyes welled with tears that soon spilled down her face. She squeezed her son's hand and said softly, "Danny, Daddy died six months after your funeral. It was quick. The Doctor said he suffered a massive heart attack. Your father was taken from me, but now I have you back. We have to stay strong for each other. That's what your father would have wanted."

The hardened Marine remained momentarily unresponsive. The killing fields of Viet Nam had inoculated him from displaying the tearful grief of an ordinary civilian. His eyes continued to pivot from his sobbing mother to his older brother. His eyes were cold. Without emotion he grunted, "My father died from a broken heart because of this senseless fucking war. Is everyone else okay?" After a brief reassurance they departed for New York.

Anthony Rango became infuriated when he found out what caused his wife to be hospitalized. He reacted with an unharnessed vengeance and without regard for his wife. Flush with someone else's money, he traded Delia's cherished 65 Chevrolet and bought her a new one. He called Victoria

Galliano, and informed her that his wife would no longer be working for her company. The wise Victoria knew Rango was a deceitful and jealous bastard motivated to try to erase the memory of Danny Corvo.

Soon after Rango's call, Delia secretly visited Victoria and begged for forgiveness. She explained in apologetic detail that it wasn't her idea but she didn't have much of a choice. She lived in a beautiful house, her daughter was privileged to attend Catholic school, and she was pregnant. Victoria obsessed; maybe Gus was right—killing the bastard might not be a bad idea.

It was Sunday April 8th. Gus Galliano insisted without query that he be driven to Maryland. Victoria called Annabel and told her of their plans. Annabel warned her to be prepared for the dismal representation of the young man they loved. She explained in acute detail the story Joe had devised about Delia.

The Gallianos accepted Danny's ghostly appearance with the nonchalance of a seasoned coroner. But Gus felt heartbroken listening to Danny's plans for him and his fiancée. On the ride home Gus said, "Danny is the toughest kid I ever met. Sorry, Nicky but you know that's true."

Nicky answered, "I know, Dad, you don't have to convince me." Then he added, "But as tough as he is, I'm not sure if he can handle this mind-boggling twist of fate."

The following Saturday, Joe Corvo set out alone to tell his brother the unthinkable news. Danny had made substantial progress, gaining six pounds, and he was relieved of the IV therapy. When Joe arrived, he was sitting up eating lunch. His voice had regained some of its normal pitch as he offered a pleased salutation. Joe kissed his kid brother on the cheek, and pulled the heavy metal chair closer to the bed. He spoke of the family, joked about Grandpa Joe's juvenile behavior and talked about the void of losing their father.

Danny politely listened to his older brother. Finally he asked, "When is Delia coming?"

Joe's face turned gray, and his lips quivered as he spoke. "Danny I don't know how to tell you this. I couldn't tell you last week because you had to regain some of your strength." Danny's eyes were fixed on his brother's like the cross-hairs of a sniper's rifle. Joe began to whimper as he painstakingly continued, "Delia was the most distraught girl after your funeral. She had to take tranquilizers for six months just to get through the day. Everyone told her to move on with her life, even Mom. She got married in February of this year. I'm so sorry Danny; so sorry."

Danny absorbed the punishing information in silence. Joe watched his tormented brother for over an hour until he finally broke the silence. In astute clearness he said, "Married, hmmm, nice. She saved my life, you know. If I didn't have the thought of her to keep me going, I'd have died for sure. But that's how I feel right now....dead. Who did she marry?"

Joe tried to parry the question but Danny's persistence was lethal. "A guy named Anthony Rango. He's a salesman for a construction material company. They live in a big Tudor on Tenbrook; he does pretty well for himself," he said. Danny laughed with an artificial sincerity and said, "If I had known all this shit I'd have stayed on the chopper. I'd be better off."

Joe rose from his chair and hastily put on his jacket. His stood and reaffirmed his older brother status as he said firmly, "Don't say that Danny. You, too, have your whole life ahead of you. I have a six-hour ride so I'm going to get going. But you should know that when I told her what happened, she wanted to see you. I told her that she was married and couldn't change what had happened. You're my kid brother and I have to tell you the same thing; it's over. You have to get on with your life

239

as well." Joe leaned in and kissed his unresponsive brother goodbye. Danny Corvo retreated into his dungeon of silence.

Danny was a natural fighter. All his life he had to have something to fight for; a purpose, a person, a goal. He lost Amy to illness and now Delia, Abby, and his father to the war. He believed the news of his own death had killed his father. What would his new mission be? Where would it take him? Who and what would he seek to fight?

CHAPTER 17

The tormented young Marine lay in his hospital bed trying to make sense of it all. In the distant background he faintly heard Ray Charles singing, "Born to lose." He thought to himself with a morbid rationale, *maybe that's it—I was born to lose.* He evoked self-prescribed torture by revisiting the events of his life. Sammy, his twin brother died, Amy Winter, his first love died, he lost his military deferment through carelessness, he refused Gus's offer to work in Canada and avoid the draft. These lifetime events, carelessness, and poor decisions led to his imprisonment in the harshest prison in the known world, and a complete debilitation and destruction of his magnificent body. The torment reached its summit with the death of his father and the loss of his life's inspiration… Delia Hoffman.

Private Corvo was scheduled to be released from Andrews Hospital at the end of April. He dreaded the thought of having his friends and family see him in this emaciated state. A true fighter never ponders suicide, but the idea of dying became attractive. Somehow, someway there had to be something or someone that could reignite his immense enthusiasm for life. His mother constantly reminded him of the blessings bestowed on their family. She said with a motherly softness, "Losing your father was awful, especially for me, but everyone else is still alive and healthy. We are blessed with the addition of your two nephews Joe and little Daniello." Danny remained encapsulated in a combat soldier's coldness as he said, "Yes, I know I've been blessed with an abundance of loss, pain and a generous dose of sadness. My plans have turned to ashes. I'm sorry but that's how I feel."

A man blessed with a brilliant mind, Danny realized that any chance for a good life had to start with regaining his health. He forced himself to eat and persuaded his family to stay home April 22nd, Easter Sunday, and forego the long journey to Andrews. Monday, April 30th was his scheduled release date. Annabel tried to conceal his homecoming for fear of a media blitz. A news reporter from the *Daily Mirror* had been to Andrews and was intrigued by the Private Corvo story. The young Marine's ability to survive the one hundred foot drop into the river and avoid the chopper explosion was a journalist's dream. His escape, recapture and survival in the Hanoi Hilton would produce another chapter of this exciting story. The switched dog tags and his physical maltreatment, accompanied by the mental torture of losing his father and fiancée, would be a read no romantic could resist.

Private Daniello Corvo arrived home at 2 p.m. The quiet dead end in the Bronx was spilling over with people and the unexpected, uninvited news media. Reporters from *The News, Post, New York Times* and *The Mirror* were all infatuated with this old-fashioned heartbreaking tear-jerker.

Danny had regained some of his body weight, but still weighed an undernourished one hundred forty seven pounds. He required the assistance of a cane to walk. His family members were unable to conceal their shock and sorrow. The only people with dry eyes were the news reporters. Grandpa Joe hugged his grandson and forced him behind the gated entrance to his driveway.

When the gate was closed behind him, Danny paused and addressed the reporters. His eye's rotated from one to another like a fine-tuned periscope. He said curtly, "Come back in a week and I'll talk to you. Right now, please have the decency to give me a chance to become reacquainted with my family. I have two little nephews that I never met before so please back off." Corvo family members were overwhelmed with happiness to hear their loved one speak with such grandiose clarity.

On May first, Danny's picture was plastered on the front cover of every newspaper. *The Daily Mirror's* headline read, "A bittersweet homecoming." *The Daily News* printed, 'Super Flying Marine is home'. *The New York Times* would show the emaciated Marine standing next to his grandfather. The headline read, "The long road home."

The Corvo phone rang incessantly. Each newspaper requested a private interview with the returning Marine. The romanticism of a young, good-looking marine losing his true love stimulated their literary appetite. Their persistence was unrelenting. On May 8, 1973 Danny met with one member from each newspaper. He told his story in factual sequence beginning with the Reilly boxing match to the present day. The New York Post reported asked, "What is your biggest regret?" he answered bluntly, "That I didn't die in the explosion. I'm finished talking now. This interview is over."

The newspapers wrote that the Private Corvo story made the Kleenex Company richer. The hardest of men teared up reading the saga of the young marine. He remained in a chamber of quiet solitude and refused to see anyone except his immediate family. Aware of his ghostly appearance he begged everyone to give him a chance to regain his health. His refusal to give an audience to Lieutenant Derosa and Mr. Chan upset Annabel Corvo. She knew her son had hit an all-time low.

Delia Rango threw up when she saw the front page of the *New York Times*. In a fearful act of self-defense she blamed her pregnancy for the vomiting. Her private time was spent in a state of tearful depression as her blood pressure surged and heart raced. The family doctor knew exactly what was ailing the young pregnant beauty. She wanted to erase being married to Anthony Rango and no longer wanted to have his child. She longed to return into the arms of the only man she ever loved. A sudden fall in the garden eradicated any concerns about having a child. The fall caused a miscarriage.

Gus Galliano was the closest resemblance of a father Danny knew. With the respect a crowned Prince shows to a King, Danny pleaded on the phone for more time before making a personal appearance.

Gus was not a stranger to the obscure effects of depression and said, "Danny, you gave me back hope."

Danny asked, "In what?"

Gus answered, "In everything. Your return has cured my depression. I'm eating well; I feel good and have some big plans for my two boys. So you keep getting better. Eat well so you put muscle back on that masterpiece of a body. When you're ready you come and see me."

Danny said abruptly, "Thanks Dad, I'll be there soon." He reflected on Gus's words, "my two boys" and instantly caught his misspoken salutation. He apologized with a sincere reverence saying, "I'm sorry—I didn't mean to say Dad, it just came out."

Gus spoke in a soft clear tone saying, "You don't have to apologize. You know by now Victoria and I both consider you another son." Those words traveled deep into the young marine's soul and reinstated a reason to live.

Annabel, the ever-loving mother, never gave up on her son. He was depressed and a one on one talk with her youngest child was overdue. Once again they sat across from one another sipping a cup of tea. Annabel said, "Danny I know you're not going to say much but the least you can do is listen. Ok?" Danny returned a positive nod of acceptance. She continued, "You're home now and anyone can recognize a heartbroken man. You see the happiness of everyone around you and remain expressionless. It's almost like you don't understand what all the jubilance is about."

She edged her chair closer and held his hands as he forced a glimpse of a grin. She continued, "That's because you have no idea what we went through. There I am cooking potato salad and the doorbell rings. I see two men in uniform standing in the vestibule. When I opened the door I knew. They didn't have to speak, I'm a mother and I knew. We buried you Danny. The whole family buried you. A closed casket, bits and pieces. That's what they made us believe was left of our son. We cried, took tranquilizers and your father and grandfather drank heavily. The thought of losing you cost your father his life. It was the most horrible event of a lifetime.

"And Delia, she was worse than anyone that poor girl. She got so skinny I thought she was going to die. You can partially blame me for her getting married. I told her in no uncertain terms to get on with her life because that's what you would want. I knew how much you loved that girl and I didn't think you would want her to punish herself for the rest of her life. Would you?" Annabel paused to take another gulp of warm tea to clear her throat.

Danny remained stoic and said, "Keep going Ma I'm all ears."

Annabel continued, "Can you put yourself in our position? Imagine someone making you think I was dead or your father, or brother or Rosemarie. Imagine how you would feel. Then imagine the incomprehensible shocking joy to find out it was a mistake. My heart is still racing."

Danny pushed his chair back, got up from the table, and whispered, "Thanks, Mom."

Annabel's voice grew unrecognizably loud almost hostile as she cried out, "Thanks Mom, that's all you can say?"

Danny repositioned himself in front of the table. He became ashamed of his disrespectful manner and said calmly, "Ok, so tell me exactly what I should say, and while you're at it, tell me how I should feel. What do you want me to say?" His face twisted into the look of a spoiled child as he shouted, "I'm so happy Dee got married while I was caged up and chained like a fucking animal." Danny's eyes began to swell with tears. His voice became soft and low, "I'm sorry Ma, I'm trying but I'm lost. Losing Amy was easy compared to this. She died. I lost Delia to my own stupidity. I don't blame her—I blame me. I should have listened to Gus and gone to Canada."

Annabel embraced her son and wept on his shoulder, saying, "I just want you to be okay, Danny. Please try."

He whispered, "I will, Mom; I will."

Annabel stepped away and asked, "Don't you have any desire to see Delia?"

Emotionally unsettled, his temper flared as he returned a cold hard stare and said, "Why? I'm not fucked up enough? I'm going to send her a letter. Joe will bring it to her so her husband doesn't get to read it. Then I'm getting out of here. I'll visit from time to time, but I'm leaving the Bronx. I weigh one hundred sixty five pounds and I'm going to start training in a few days. I'll be gone in a few weeks."

On Friday May 18th, Danny Corvo got behind the wheel of his 65 Pontiac and drove to visit the Galliano family. Paulie Nartico had serviced Danny's car and it appeared show-room new. Gus and Victoria Galliano couldn't take their eyes off their fabled hero. His presence in their home was of miraculous dimension. Gus had his personal chef on site to cook Danny's favorite meal, fettuccini with olive sauce and steak pizziola. Nicky and his wife were not in attendance as Gus explained that they were out in the Hamptons on Long Island planting the seeds with the town board for the development of their waterfront land parcels. There would be a break before dessert as the two men retreated to the sanctuary of Gus's private study.

There, Gus began to speak. "I don't know how you do it but when I saw you in the hospital, my heart dropped. And those pictures in the paper didn't help any either. Look at you now. You look marvelous. Tell me your plans."

Danny was quick to answer the question he hoped was asked. He said, "Gus I need to work and make money but I can't stay in the Bronx. Losing Delia has got me all fucked up. I have so much anger inside me I'm afraid I'm going to blow. I know it's not her fault but that doesn't ease the broken heart syndrome."

Gus glared at Danny with a look of puzzlement and said, "Broken heart syndrome?"

Danny replied, "That's what the Marine Head doctor called it."

Gus said with a boisterous arrogance, "He should have called it fucked-up war syndrome."

Danny answered, "Yeah that too but 'broken heart syndrome' was the phrase of the day." Danny leaned over the table closer to his mentor and said, "Remember when I told you I wanted to kill that scumbag Kadesh? You told me I was tough but I wasn't a killer."

Gus muttered, "Yeah, I remember."

Danny said boldly, "Well, I am now. To the best of my recollection I must have killed at least forty of them gook mother fuckers and I didn't lose a minute of sleep. Gus, I need to work, and more importantly I need to get out of the Bronx."

Gus remained silent and gathered his thoughts. Finally he said, "Before you left I told you I had plans for you and Nicky, and they don't include killing people so calm down. I know Nicky told you a little about my plan. The time to initiate the plan is now. You have a clean last name and the news media is making you out to be a war hero. That will all work in our favor. The FBI takes out their magnifying glass as soon as they hear or see the name Galliano; that's why we're going to use your lily white clean last name Corvo. We're going to start the 'Corvo Construction Company Inc.' You will be the president and own one hundred percent of the stock.

"Your first job will be on Long Island where you can live since you want out of the Bronx. I bought a beach house in the Hamptons last year. You can live there. You'll be building a shopping mall in Moriches. When the economy improves, you'll build luxury homes for the elite of Manhattan. I have two dozers, one excavator, and two dumps with trailers. They're getting lettered up this week to read, 'Corvo Construction Company.' So how does that sound for a plan?"

Danny gasped and said, "Wow, how am I ever going to repay you?"

Gus smiled and said, "I told you a thousand times—you already paid me, remember? Listen, you're going to be working your skinny little ass off and making money for the family."

Danny sprung from his chair and embraced the father figure he loved.

Memorial Day became Danny's target date to resume his training program. He had visited Lieutenant Derosa and Mr.

Chan on the Saturday of Memorial Day weekend. Both of his teachers saw a disturbed and angry young man. They knew not to preach while he remained in his dungeon of silence and agreed he needed a sabbatical from the Bronx. The haunting reminder of Delia Hoffman was everywhere. He needed a change of scenery; the Hamptons, with its over-abundance of beautiful women, appeared to be a good choice.

On Sunday May 27th, Danny begrudgingly agreed to meet his two old friends, Bobby K. and Doc Singer. They met in the Wall bar to shoot pool and have a few beers. Danny violated his long-standing self-imposed two beer rule; a visible sign of his depression. These were two of the few people he revered from his childhood. His unforgiving destiny would somehow always haunt him.

While waiting for his turn to shoot pool, he saw Delia and her daughter exiting the local bakery, walking toward her father's house. He closely watched her every sway with euphoric admiration. Delia Rango appeared more beautiful than his photographic memory remembered. With a rapid abruptness, he embraced his two old friends and said, "I have to get out of here. I can't do this."

Bobby K had noticed his broken-hearted friend's visible adoration of his lost sweetheart. Doc aborted his idea to convince Danny to stay when he saw Bobby K's finger across his lips, indicating that he should be quiet. Danny left, knowing it was time to write Delia.

Early Memorial Day morning, Danny stretched and began a slow jog. His body had been so deteriorated that full-out running would take some time. Slowly jogging, he made his way to Saint Raymond's cemetery. He sat by Amy Winter's headstone. Drawing his legs to his chest, he placed his head on his knees. Lost for a solution to his unforgiving destiny, he began to weep. Passersby offered their condolences to the young mourner.

Suddenly he felt a tap on his shoulder accompanied by a soft familiar voice, Mrs. Winter. She said, "Danny please stand up. I want to look at you." He stood and embraced Mrs. Winter asking, "How are you and Mr. Winter?"

She answered, "We're as good as can be expected. It really never goes away."

Danny nodded and replied, "I know. I came here today to get some inspiration from Amy. I know it sounds weird, but somehow she always guides me. I have to write a letter to my former fiancée who, as you and the whole world knows thanks to the newspapers, is now married to someone else. I needed some food for thought. I have to go now. Please give my best to Mr. Winter." Danny slowly jogged home. He was now prepared to write his farewell letter to his beloved Delia.

His letter read:

Dear Delia,

I don't know how or where to begin but I'll try my best. I don't blame you for anything that happened. I have only myself to blame. I was so infatuated with making money for our future that I failed to pay attention to my college schedule. Gus offered Canada and I refused because I loved your father and didn't want to disrespect him.

When the chopper was hit the first time, I knew it was going down. I could see the mortar shells being launched, one after another. I tried to convince Reilly to jump but he hesitated, causing him to lose his life;

lucky guy. After being caged like an animal for over two years, I no longer believe in destiny. I believe in luck. Unfortunately mine has not been too good.

I know you were always grateful that I rescued you from Caldo and his perverted friends. Now it's my turn to thank you. If it wasn't for the memory of your face, your smile, the sound of your voice, I'd have never survived that hell hole. My desire to see and hold you gave me more courage than I ever thought I had. I truly wish I never found the guts to jump; it would have been better for the both of us, but thank you.

This War has turned out to be a colossal nightmare for this once-great country. We never employed the military protocol and procedures to truly defeat the enemy, causing many of our young men to die without reason. America has lost face and credibility with the entire world. I promised myself that if I made it through the Hanoi Hilton I would do everything in my power as a civilian to prevent America's engagement in unwinnable wars. Somewhere in my future, I plan on running for Congress. It's the least I can do for my brothers that lost their life. For now, I have to take it one step at a time.

I've taken a job with Mr. Galliano. If I don't stay busy I'm going to crack. I have

251

developed new skills that Mr. Galliano may need me to use someday. By the time you read this letter, I'll be long gone. I'll be working construction at the very far end of Long Island and up in Massachusetts on a place called Cape Cod. I love the Bronx but I can no longer stay here—too many memories.

I wish you every happiness life has to offer. I had so many plans. I was certain Abby would be a doctor or a lawyer; she's really a bright kid. I hope you and Mr. Rango are able to send her to a good college. I know I'll be ok because I can feel everything inside of me getting colder by the minute. I'll take my life into my hands and I will use it. There will be another song to sing and I will sing it. I'll have all the things that I desire and let passion flow like rivers to the sky. Stay well.

Sincerely yours,
Danny

On Sunday June 24, 1973, Danny Corvo packed his clothes and personal belongings into the trunk and rear seat of his car. He returned his Indian motorcycle to Pauli Nartico for storage. Rising at five a.m. Monday morning, he began his long journey to the Hamptons. As planned, his brother would personally deliver his letter to Delia.

When noon arrived, Joe Corvo drove to the Rango residence on Tenbrook Avenue. Delia answered the door, her face was colorless and without expression. She was thin, pale and the musty grey color of sickness. When she saw it was Joe Corvo her expression changed, her face gained a slight rosy color of excitement. She surmised that whatever Joe was going to say had to have a connection with Danny. She said with bland enthusiasm, "Joe Corvo, how are you? Come on in."

Joe politely declined and said, "I have a letter for you. It's from Danny. He said it was personal and wanted me to hand it directly to you. I certainly didn't read it but I don't think anyone else should see it."

Delia gave Joe a farewell kiss on the cheek and closed the door. Anxiously, she ran to the privacy of her sewing room and opened the letter. The contents of the letter were distressing to her. She was hoping that somehow, some way, her guardian angel had a plan to rescue her from the life she had chosen. Danny's forgiveness reinforced her belief that he no longer loved her. Her sadness morphed into a deep depression. Once again, she secretly used alcohol and prescription sedatives to function.

The Galliano beach house was magnificent. It had a one hundred eighty degree view of the Atlantic and its own private beach. Danny unpacked his belongings and headed for the beach....his beach. The Atlantic water was still cold at the end of June but Danny Corvo was a marine. He had regained most of his body weight and muscle tone. His face regained its handsome shape and his steel-blue eyes could pierce a girl's heart. A long chilling swim momentarily abated his depression. If only the sand dunes, beautiful sunsets, and the magnificent Atlantic could clear his head of Delia Hoffman. Somehow her presence would always be with him. She was branded into his keen memory and etched into his soul.

Tuesday morning he drove to the Moriches job site to receive delivery of his construction equipment. He watched proudly as the equipment bearing his name rolled off the heavy-duty trailers. The first driver asked, "Excuse me, can you tell me where Mr. D. Corvo is? I have to have him sign for this delivery?"

Danny boastfully answered, "You came to the right guy. I'm Danny Corvo. Where do I sign?"

He finally understood the monumental degree of Gus's generosity. It was at that moment that he recognized the enemy. For the first time his opponent became tangible. He now knew who and what he had to fight. Establishing a successful business was the only way to pay back the Gallianos. Anyone who tried to interfere or infringe on the success of his business would become his enemy. He recalled his brother Joe telling him that Anthony Rango was a successful businessman. His dormant ambition soared as he swore to crush anything and anyone that threatened the success of his business.

Nicky had already procured the building permit and followed protocol by having had it posted on the property. The sign read, "Coming soon: The Moriches Mall." Danny contacted the surveyor and began excavating the following morning. By ten a.m., the surveyors had delineated the footprint of the future mall. He started to excavate without hesitation, digging from dawn to dusk, stopping briefly to put some much-needed nourishment in his stomach. There was no weekend fun on the beach, only work. Taking advantage of the dry, mild weather, he labored for sixteen-hour days, including Saturday and Sunday. In seven days, the job site was prepped for the cement contractors. Wednesday was July 4th and Danny had promised his family that he would come home for the traditional holiday party.

The holiday traffic going to Long Island was stop and go, bumper to bumper. Danny left the Island at five a.m. and headed for the Bronx. He arrived at his parents' home at 7:45 a.m. After the morning salutations and a brief breakfast, Danny drove to Riverdale. He updated Gus and Nicky on the Mall project.

Gus said, "Ready for cement? Didn't you sleep? That's remarkable."

Danny answered, "They want to open by Labor Day, September 3rd. I have two months and intend to be done early. The less time it takes, the more money we will make."

Nicky shook his head in laughter and said, "You truly are a fucking nut, but I love you Danny boy. I'll call the Union boss tonight and see if he can get a crew out there early tomorrow morning. He owes us, so I think we should be alright."

Danny mingled with his family and friends, giving a well-rehearsed appearance of being happy. He enjoyed the at-ease conversations with his two mentors, Lieutenant Derosa and Mr. Chan. Annabel was content to see her son frolicking with his family and friends. The last time Danny had attended a July 4th party, he proposed to Delia Hoffman. Now she was married to someone else and Danny Corvo was shackled by her memory. He pretended in theatrical fashion that life was good. Behind the smile of many beers he was an emotional cripple, unable to accept the loss of Delia. Slowly his sadness fermented into raw anger. He dismissed himself from the firework display, alleging he had an early commitment the next day. He took advantage of the daylight for his long ride to the Hamptons.

The concrete crew arrived at the job site at 7 a.m. The cement forms were put in place by noon. The crew needed one inspection and the foundation would be complete. Bobby Higgins, the town building inspector, was a former marine and had great admiration for the young Corvo. He'd read the heartbreaking story of Private Corvo and was happy to oblige his request for a same day inspection. Danny remained relentless in his pursuit to complete the project early.

Even the powerful Gus Galliano couldn't broker an agreement to get the framers to work on Saturday and Sunday with one days' notice. The carpenters arrived on Monday, and Danny placed them on a twelve-hour-a-day schedule with the promise of being off for the weekend. The job was masterfully coordinated as the completion date was re-estimated to be August 17th, two weeks earlier than originally predicted.

If Danny had remained a United Auto Worker, it would have taken him one year to earn $12,000. Building the Moriches Strip Mall ahead of schedule earned the young engineer $16,000 in salary and profit in less than two months. He had promised his parents that he would become wealthy with or without college. Under the guiding hand of Gus Galliano he was on his way.

On Saturday, August 25, 1973, Rosemarie Corvo, the young attorney, married Robert Benson an attorney from Austin, Texas. Rosemarie and Robert had met while he was lecturing at Fordham Law School. The last place on earth Danny wanted to be was at a wedding, any wedding. But Rosemarie was his sister, a teacher, and a best friend. He returned his invitation excluding any mention of an escort.

At the wedding, Danny was seated with his cousins and their wives. He conducted himself as a happy-go-lucky bachelor to bolster the spirit of his only sister. The single girls were infatuated with the handsome young bachelor. The smitten young girls avoided ballroom etiquette and boldly asked him to dance. He obliged, smiled, and made them laugh, but none of them aroused his curiosity. He gave Robert and Rosemarie one thousand dollars in cash, a gift that made his sister deeply suspicious of his true relationship with the Galliano family. The following morning he departed for Long Island.

CHAPTER 18

In 1974, the recession and oil embargo crippled the American economy and devastated the U.S. stock market. The plan of constructing high-end homes for the prominent rich of Manhattan was put on hold. Corvo Construction set their sights on government contracts. Road building and bridge repair were a priority that could not be overlooked by Uncle Sam. Gus Galliano's influence with the construction unions set up the Corvo Construction Companies ability to underbid all its competitors. The young businessman continued to save and invest his money. He interpreted the low stock prices as a once-in-a-lifetime buying opportunity and purchased large blocks of stock that yielded high paying dividends, such as Consolidated Edison. He was young and knew that the American economy was cyclical. Time was on his side.

In early 1975, he purchased a large East Hampton water-front lot from Gus Galliano. The price he paid made the purchase a gift in legal disguise. His self-induced solidarity provided him ample time to construct a small beach house. He engineered the waterfront house to be constructed on deep pile-driven piers to avoid the potential of damage during hurricane season. His engineering skills were well learned and applied to architectural perfection.

In June of 1975 Danny received a courtesy call from Doc Singer informing him that he was getting married in early September. Danny offered congratulatory well-wishes to his school friend and curiously asked, "Who's the lucky girl?"

Doc was remiss and said, "No, no. first things first. I want you to be my best man and I won't take no for an answer. What are you going to say?"

"We don't answer a question with a question Mr. Debater. Who's the lucky girl?" Danny repeated.

Doc began humming a quiz show song and blurted, "Leanna Hoffman."

Danny became angry at his old friend's insensitivity. He said curtly, "Doc you're putting me between the rock and the hard place. I know Delia is going to be there, and that's the last thing either one of us need."

Doc answered with sympathetic reverence saying, "You're like a brother. I had to ask."

Danny continued, "I think Bobby K. would be a better choice. I'll send you and Lee a magnificent gift. Please try and understand. By the way, how is Delia doing?"

Doc was startled by his sudden inquiry and said, "It's not so good Danny. This guy is a piece of shit. He's a degenerate gambler, drinks heavily and I'm pretty sure he sees other women. Let me take that back—I know he fucks around with other women."

Danny's unresponsiveness was long enough for Doc to ask, "Danny, are you still there?"

"I'm here, just thinking to myself. Why does she stay with him?" he said. Doc paused momentarily before saying,

"I think she feels trapped and probably doesn't know everything I told you, especially the fucking around part. I'm sure when she find out, it will be splits-ville. You know, Danny, she thinks you hate her guts."

Danny was hesitant to speak. He was not prepared to respond to such a comment. Finally he said, "Doc, I'm making so much money sometimes I feel like I'm stealing. I say this to you only because I know I can trust you'll keep it to yourself. There are a lot of people that I hate, and some I really hate, but I could never hate Delia. I don't want to sound childish, but her face slaps me in the face every morning. There's no shortage of girls out here, believe me, but I'm just not interested. I can't really explain it. One last question and I'm only asking because you said he was a piece of shit. Is he abusive?"

Doc knew that Rango hit Delia after the miscarriage, blaming it on her infatuation with Danny. The passive Doctor chose to lie and answered, "No."

Danny briefly thought about attending the wedding and observing Mr. Rango in the flesh. When the adrenalin rush subsided, he dismissed the idea. He rationalized that Delia had never tried to contact him and her claim to be miserable was merely self-pity. She didn't leave Rango, so it was indeed over.

In late August, Danny came into the Bronx to visit his family. He spent time with Bobby K. and his family. The four half-Irish half-Italian Kenny children were pointedly adorable. Upon leaving he gave Bobby K. a wedding card for Doc and Lee containing five hundred dollars in cash. Danny steered himself and Bobby to a quiet remote area of the yard. He spoke softly almost an inaudible whisper saying, "Bobby I need a small favor."

Bobby knew he certainly didn't need money so he inquired, "Sure, just tell me what you need."

Danny replied, "I hear this Rango guy is a piece of shit. You're the best man and Delia is the Maid of Honor so you will have the opportunity to talk to her. Very casually, try to find out if this Rango guy is ever abusive. Doc said he isn't, but when I asked, I could tell he was hiding something. Let me know."

Bobby K. was not pleased by his covert request but he acquiesced with a forced grin, saying, "I'll use my Irish charm and find out everything I can."

When Danny departed, Ginny's eyes teared up as she muttered, "What a shame. I feel so bad for that guy. Do you see the way he loves to play around with the kids? He and Dee were so happy together. Anyone can see that he's still pretty messed up in spite of all his success." Bobby slowly nodded his head in agreement and said, "You're right. Danny would give up every penny if he could erase what happened. You know, Ginny, he's still crazy in love with that girl. We should never have gotten into that fucking war."

The Singer/Hoffman wedding became history and his trust-worthy friend reported that Delia didn't give any indication of being physically abused, but she was in a miserable marriage.

By the end of October, Danny had procured his pilot's license and purchased a used twin-prop four-seat aircraft. His private plane proudly displayed the name of his company, Corvo Construction. The plane purchase was part of the master plan to construct luxury homes on Cape Cod, Massachusetts.

In October of that year, a letter was sent from the NBC television network to Danny's mother's address on Holland Avenue in the Bronx. The producer never forgot the heart-breaking story of the brave young marine who jumped to safety from a helicopter, only to be captured and imprisoned. The NBC researchers discovered that the young marine was physically fit, and had aspired to become a very successful businessman. The heartbreaking story of losing his fiancée, accompanied by his success, aroused a great desire for an updated interview. Many Americans never forgot the photo of the emaciated young marine holding on to his grandfather. This was a true story of the American spirit overcoming adversity.

Danny agreed to meet with the producer and two of his writers. Truly fascinated by his enormous success, they agreed to pay him for a TV appearance on the Johnny Carson show. The Johnny Carson talk show remained the most widely watched late night program on national television.

The first pre-show interview was inundated with personal questions regarding his rapid accent to success. One journalist asked, "Mr. Corvo, in a nutshell, would it be correct to say, you survived a one hundred foot jump into a river and survived the most horrific prison in the world for almost three years. Is that account of what happened correct?"

Danny answered, "Yes, Sir."

The bold journalist continued, "You then came home ill and sickly, regained your marvelous physique, started your own construction company and have been successful ever since."

Danny answered, "That's true, depending on how you measure success."

The puzzled writer asked, "How so?"

Danny gave the journalist a crippling stare and remarked, "Money can't replace losing someone you love. You know that old saying, it's better to have loved and lost than to have never loved at all."

"Yes" the journalist answered.

Danny replied, "Whoever said that is full of shit. No love, no loss. No loss no pain. That's the way I see it now."

The seasoned journalist knew to withdraw from the topic and asked, "Is it true that you have a pilot's license and have your own private plane at twenty eight years old?"

Danny burst into a loud laughter and answered, "Yes, me and thousands of other Americans. Please don't make a big deal about something as mundane as owning a used airplane. Incidentally, please call me Danny; you're old enough to be my father so you can dismiss with the Mister." Danny possessed a skill for forcing the most persistent of men into rapid retreat.

After the initial interview, the producer salivated at the idea of Danny Corvo being a guest on the Johnny Carson show. He was a good looking, well-built marine, exceptionally intelligent, witty, well-spoken and a war hero; a producer's dream. They chose the Friday after Thanksgiving, November 28th for his appearance.

Mr. Levine, the NBC producer, reiterated that millions and millions of Americans watched this show. He said, "You know, young man, this telecast will be an opportunity for you to popularize your Company. Make it a point in a very humble way that your goal is to construct luxury homes in both the Hamptons and on Cape Cod. You watch and see—people will respond. You're an admired war hero, young man."

There wasn't a living soul in the Bronx that didn't tune in to the Johnny Carson Show on that Friday night. The exception was Anthony Rango and his degenerate friends. Friday night was his night to go bowling with the boys, drinking and carousing with the girls. He and Delia had been living apart for over a month. He sustained the mindset of a single adolescent devoid of responsibility.

The jealous Rango knew his wife watched the Carson Show every night at 11:30. After a belly-full of food and drink, he ventured to the Tenbrook house. The arrogant playboy planned on catching his wife watching her ex-fiancée on TV. He peered through the curtains of the front window, waiting for Danny Corvo to enter the Johnny Carson stage. Angry, the jealous drunk charged into the living room screaming, "So I guess you're really happy to watch your fucking war hero on TV. Shut that fucking TV off now before I kick it in."

Thirteen year old Abby had become an independent teenager who loathed her erratic step-father. She rose from her chair and approached him in a confrontational swagger shouting, "Why? Why do we have to shut it off? You don't even live here anymore. We watch this show every night. What's wrong with you?"

The excessive alcohol consumption refueled his anger as he raised his fist saying, "You little ungrateful bastard. You go up to your room now."

Petrified of his violent display of anger Delia pleaded, "Abby go upstairs and do as you're told, please." It was at that moment that Delia knew this loveless, sham of a marriage had to end. She raised her voice and said, "You don't come home for weeks on end and now you want to tell us what to watch on TV. I'm getting a divorce. You are an animal."

Rango's face became twisted with hate as he levied his pudgy fist at her unsuspecting face. She fell to the floor, striking her head on the corner of the large, bold coffee table. A halo of blood formed around her head as she lay motionless on the floor. Frightened that she may have been seriously injured, the cowardly Rango fled in his car.

The constant screaming and fighting had young Abby accustomed to sleeping with ear plugs. At two a.m. she awakened to use the hallway bathroom. Noticing that the TV and lights were still on downstairs, she descended into the living room. She saw her mother lying unconscious on the floor, her head gushing blood. The panic-stricken teenager ran into the street screaming, "Someone help me. I think my mom is dead. Someone please help!" No one answered her tormented cries for help.

She called her grandfather, Nelson. Still half asleep, a very tired Nelson Hoffman answered the phone, "Hello." Abby's breathing became deep and rapid as she grumbled, "Grandpa, call an ambulance. Mommy is unconscious on the floor."

Her drowsy grandfather said, "Stay by the phone. I'll call the ambulance and then I'll call you right back."

Nelson dressed military style and drove to his daughter's house. The ambulance had arrived and Delia's gurney was being placed in the vehicle. Nelson inquired about her condition saying, "I'm the girl's father. Is she going to be ok?"

The reluctant ambulance attendant answered, "Sir, I'm not a doctor. We have to take her to the emergency room as fast as we can. You can meet us there."

Nelson Hoffman put his granddaughter in his car and drove the few blocks to Jacobi Hospital. He was bewildered by the absence of his son-in-law and asked, "Where is Anthony?"

The young teenager's eyes blinked in nervous rhythm. She began to cry as she said, "I don't know. He came into the house late last night and they were fighting. It's the first time he's been home in a month. He left like he always does when they fight."

Nelson Hoffman had just experienced the meaning of a rude awakening. Discovering that they were living apart reaffirmed his belief that their marriage was in trouble.

That same night, on television, Johnny Carson's praise of the young marine gained Danny recognition as a war hero with the news media. Danny was cool and calm and answered every question with the utmost respect. He followed Mr. Levine's advice and interjected the name of his company at every opportunity.

Johnny said, "Now Danny I want you to do me a small favor?"

Danny answered, "Yes Sir."

Johnny continued, "Let's make it two favors. One: stop saying Sir and call me Johnny."

Without further thought, Danny instinctively replied, "No problem, Sir."

A soft hum of laughter encased the studio. Johnny gestured for the crowd to remain silent. He held up the front page of the newspaper showing a frail, undernourished Marine being supported by his elderly grandfather. Johnny said, "This home-coming photo was one of the saddest I've ever seen printed anywhere." Returning his attention to Danny he said, "Could you please show the audience what hard work and determination can accomplish."

Puzzled Danny said, "Sure, what do you want me to do?"

Johnny said, "Give all of America a treat and take off your shirt."

Danny raised his eyebrows, but acquiesced, saying, "Mr. Carson, you do know it's November?" The easily humored audience was stupefied at the young marine's physical appearance. He was a poster specimen of a magnificent man. When Danny departed, Johnny Carson praised the young marine and promised his audience he would return to the show in the spring.

Danny was travel weary and spent the night with his mother in the Bronx. He had planned to spend the weekend and return to the Hamptons early Monday morning. Breakfast was wonderful. Annabel invited everyone to enjoy the company of their newly acclaimed "celebrity" relative. The caffeine-fueled conversations gave way to the jokes and laughter of Danny's newly found stardom.

At ten o'clock Doc Singer called asking to speak to Danny. Annabel said, "Danny, its Doctor Singer. He wants to speak to you. Guess everyone knows you're here."

Danny took the phone and said sarcastically, "I know I looked fat on TV. What's going on?"

Doc said, "You were great Danny, but I didn't call to break your balls. I have some bad news."

He answered, "What else is new, shoot?"

"Delia is in the hospital. She fell and hit her head last night. She's in a coma. That's not all; her dirt bag husband abandoned her over four weeks ago. He hasn't paid the mortgage, electric bill, phone bill, and worst of all, they have no health insurance."

Danny inquired, "How bad is she?"

Doc inhaled deeply as he said, "It's too early to tell but there are no signs of her coming out of it anytime soon. She's in Jacobi. If she doesn't come out of it by tomorrow, I'm going to have her transported to Mount Sinai in Manhattan."

Danny's never-ending love for Delia over-shadowed his ability to reason. He paused and said, "I'm on my way."

Danny put on a fake smile and returned to the breakfast table. Very casually he stood behind his mother. Grasping her thin shoulders in his over-sized hands, he softly whispered in her ear, "Ma I need to talk to you alone. I'm going to walk down the hall to your bedroom. Don't make a fuss. Just come."

Annabel procrastinated a few moments before leaving the table. Entering the bedroom she said, "What happened? What's wrong?"

Danny's face was troubled, an easy read for his alert mother. He said excitedly, "Delia fell and hit her head on a coffee table. She has been in a coma since last night. She's in Jacobi. Before you say it, I know it's none of my business and that's what I wanted to tell Doc. I thought differently when he told me that the husband abandoned her and Abby a month ago. She has no insurance and the asshole hasn't paid any of the house bills. I'm confused Mom. What do you think I should do?"

Annabel motioned with her long thin index finger for him to come closer. She held his boyishly sad face in her hands and said, "Daniello my son, there is nothing wrong with visiting an old friend who is in the hospital. I'll pray, and when she comes out of that coma and sees you she will be the happiest women in the world."

Danny gently joined his hands with his mother's and asked, "How do you know that?"

Annabel lowered her voice to a whimper and calmly replied, "Because she never stopped loving you, never. She made a mistake under very harsh circumstances. We pushed her to get on with her life but she never ever stopped loving you and she still does. You listen to me, Mr. successful engineer, that girl still loves you and you can that take to the fucking bank. There, I said it… fucking bank and it felt good!"

Danny kissed his mother on the forehead and said, "Thanks Mom but let's leave this between us for now."

Danny arrived at Jacobi by 11 a.m. where he met Doc, his wife Lee, and Mr. Hoffman. Mr. Hoffman was teetering on an emotional melt-down. Seeing Danny, he composed himself as they embraced. He said, "I'm so happy to see you and I'm so happy you're here."

Danny inquired about Abby and was told that she was distraught. The family agreed it would be better for her to remain home while the mother was listed in critical condition. Doc made arrangements with the administrator to allow the small group a few minutes in the intensive care ward. Doc claimed that Danny was Delia's husband. Mr. Hoffman whispered in Lee's ear, "His mouth to God's ears."

Sunday was a very difficult day to hire a transport service to move a patient. The Hoffman girls and their spouses visited their youngest sister. Abby remained sheltered from the truth in the confines of her grandfather's house. Danny visited late Sunday afternoon before heading back to his business on Long Island. He instructed Doc to keep him abreast of any change in Delia's activity. He temporarily moved back into the Galliano beach house, where he had access to a telephone.

On Monday, December 1, 1975, Delia Rango was transported by private ambulance to the Head and Trauma Unit of Mount Sinai hospital. She was placed in the intensive care ward to undergo a battery of tests. Doctor Singer consulted with Doctor Matt Schwartz, a world-renowned head and trauma specialist. Schwartz examined Delia and reviewed her records as a courtesy to his friend and colleague. Schwartz informed Singer that a procedure to reduce the interior swelling of the brain might become necessary, if she didn't awaken in a few days. Shockingly, he informed his colleague that the fall was caused by a forceful blow to the side of her head. "To every action there is a reaction," he said with great certainty.

It was a dangerous procedure that could only be performed by an experienced surgeon. The cost of the surgery, hospital stay, and after care was estimated to be between eight and ten thousand dollars. Nelson Hoffman was a working man who struggled to raise his five daughters without a wife. He now faced the tragic reality that he might have to sell his house.

Doc Singer visited with Danny and shared the test results and the prescribed procedure. He knew Delia was struck on the head by a forceful blow, probably a punch. All the evidence indicated that the blow was delivered by the hand of Anthony Rango. Doc knew that Danny's Sicilian appetite for revenge would be nourished by such news. He was perplexed about how and when to relay that information to his always protective friend.

Finally, Doc said, "This guy Schwartz is one of the best neurosurgeons in the world but he commands a hefty fee." Danny stared at his friend without a response. His face arched into a boyish grin as he said mockingly, "Describe hefty."

Doc answered, "Eight to ten thousand."

Danny replied, "Eight to ten thousand, huh, no wonder why they wear a fucking mask. How soon does it have to be done and what is your gut feeling of how she will end up?"

Doc hesitated in answering the puzzling question. Finally he said, "Schwartz wants to give it a few days but if surgery is deemed necessary I'm confident he's our best choice. There's never a guarantee in these types of surgeries but he's the best chance we've got. We're having a family meeting tonight to see if there's a way we can come up with the money to move forward. Even if she doesn't need the surgery, the hospital stay and the testing are mounting up to big bucks. We have some time but not a lot."

Danny's business alliance with the Galliano family had great earning potential. The twenty-eight-year-old Corvo had crossed the threshold into the top five percent earning bracket of the United States. Under the guidance of the fatherly Gus Galliano, he'd invested his money wisely and with great success. He no longer viewed ten thousand dollars as a large sum of money.

Doc was astonished at his friend's nonchalant lack of concern for what he deemed to be a large sum of money.

Danny was anxious and said abruptly, "Two questions—who do I make the check out to, and how much of a deposit does this best in the world doctor require?"

Doc was pleased. He dreamed of the day Danny Corvo would be reunited with his dejected sister-in-law. He said cautiously, "I know if I ask whether you are serious, I'll end up in a coma next to Dee so I'll just answer the questions. Half in advance is customary. You can make the check out to the Mount Sinai Medical Group and I will fill in the amount required as soon as we know."

Danny said, "That's fine but can anyone meet me by the Hotel on the Bronx side of the Whitestone? I'll bring the check tonight."

Doc answered, "No problem. I'll tell everyone about your kindness and cancel the meeting. Lee and I will meet you, but be prepared to be slobbered over. Thanks Danny. I'll meet you at seven thirty."

Danny had just taken a giant step in getting back the life he missed. All the money in the world couldn't replace his beloved Delia. Two problems remained. Would Delia survive without permanent damage? Secondly, what shall they do with Mr. Rango?

As Doc predicted, his wife was a grateful but tear-filled woman. She embraced Danny, sobbing, "We can't thank you enough for helping my sister. I tried to rehearse the words I would say to you but there aren't any. Don't ask me why but I never gave up on my dream of you and Delia being together."

Danny was coy and answered bluntly, "Slow down, Lee, your little sister is still married."

Lee boldly lunged closer as the pitch of her voice fluctuated nervously. "My sister is done with that dirt bag. She's going to get that mockery annulled; you watch and see."

Lee never stopped believing that Danny Corvo was her little sister's knight in shining armor. Doc Singer directed his wife to go start up the car while he bid goodnight to his old school friend. When she exited the hotel, Doc said, "Promise me you're going to stay calm."

Danny appeared confused as he said softly, "I am calm. What are you talking about?" Doc rubbed his brow as he searched for the right words. The moment of truth had arrived. He said, "Doctor Schwartz believes that the fall was a result of a blow to the head. It certainly wasn't Abagail so it had to be Rango. It had to be him. No one else was there. There were no witnesses. When Dee awakens, if she acknowledges these facts, I'm having him arrested."

Danny stared at Doc with a prolonged silence. Suddenly his face bore a sardonic grin as he said, "So that's why Lee is talking about an annulment, and that's why he doesn't come to see her; hmmm, interesting. But let's not jump to conclusions, Doctor Singer. We must remember that in America we are all innocent until proven guilty. First things first; we have to wait and see if she comes out of this coma, then you can worry about Mr. Rango." They embraced and headed home. It was at that moment Doc knew the well-trained combat Marine had already planned the demise of Anthony Rango.

Corvo Construction was performing fire debris removal and demolition on a burnt-out apartment building in Flushing. The necessary permits had been procured and his seasoned crew required little supervision. Danny had wisely hired Corporal Rodrigues, one of the "Hanoi Ten Pins." He was out of work but had extensive experience in the construction industry. Rodrigues also possessed a federal pilot's license, an added bonus to his resume. The circumstances of this project afforded him the daily opportunity to drive into Manhattan.

It was Thursday December 4th, and medically, time as running out. With her vital signs stable Delia was moved to a private room. A few days had passed without any activity from the comatose patient. The hospital staff recognized Mr. Corvo as a personal friend of Doctor Singer and granted him off-hour visitation privileges. Every visit started and ended with a kiss on the forehead. Danny's departing words became a solemn ritual. "I love you. Please come back."

Doctor Schwartz notified the family that surgery was scheduled for Monday, December 8th. The following day, Danny took the nerve punishing journey to Manhattan. He arrived at eleven a.m., two hours prior to the hospital visiting hours. The dutiful Nurses performed their test, changing IV bags and monitoring Delia's vital signs. He slid his chair closer to the bed, speaking in a low decibel whisper. "Hey kid, we're never going to be apart again. I'm here to stay but you have to come back to me. I can't make it without you."

As Danny gazed at her face he thought her eyes fluttered. Could it be? He placed his hand on her pale, colorless face and lovingly caressed her cheek. Unexpectedly the door opened and a young girl entered the room. She exclaimed, "Excuse me, are you a doctor?"

Without removing his eyes from Delia, he answered, "No I'm just an old friend paying an old friend a visit."

The girl's voice quivered as she said, "Danny, Danny is that you?" He pivoted in abrupt response to the sound of his name. Years had passed but there was an instant recognition of the girl. He rose from the chair ever so quickly and said, "Abby?"

The young beauty's eyes were swollen with tears as she answered, "Yes it's me. I can't believe you're here with my mom. I've been praying for a miracle and I think my prayers have been answered. God it's so good to see you. I can't believe it's you."

Danny and Abby engaged in a long awkward embrace. At fourteen, she was no longer the little girl he remembered. In a fatherly fashion he said, "I'm not going to ask you why you're not in school but if you need a ride home, I'll drive you."

She forced a smile and said, "My grandpa should be here any minute and I'll travel home with him. It's only two trains. Forgive me for staring but I still can't believe you're here."

Danny gazed at her appraisingly saying, "You look just like your mother did when she was your age; same expression and smile. By the way, that's the biggest compliment I can give a girl. I'm praying she comes out of it soon. Your mom and I have a lot to talk about."

Abby walked to her mother's bedside and kissed her on the forehead saying, "Mom you better snap out of it soon. You shouldn't keep Danny waiting. He's a celebrity now, you know."

They shared a laugh and embraced as he handed her a business card with his private phone number saying, "I don't give this number out too often but I want you to have it. Keep me aware of her condition and if you need anything call me. I really have to get back to the job site before the bridge traffic gets too heavy. I'll try to come in again tomorrow."

Abby sat in the chair Danny had left so close to her mother's bed. She held her mother's hand while in waiting for the arrival of her grandfather Nelson. It was 3 p.m. Visiting hours ended at 4. Slowly, she reached over and stroked her mother's hair. Unexpectedly she felt an ever so slight movement in her hand. The anxious teenager began to stroke her mother's face with her hand when she saw her eyebrows raise. Delia's eyelids began to flutter as her eyes opened with a lazy slowness. Her eyes blinked rapidly as she labored to focus. Abby said, "Mom, can you hear me? It's Abby."

She felt her mother's grip tighten on her left hand. She repeated, "Mom, can you hear me?"

Delia's eyes widened as she whispered in a raspy low register, "Abby, where am I?" The excited teenager bolted up from the cold metal hospital chair and kissed her mother on the forehead. She panted like a water-deprived puppy, saying, "Oh Mom, thank God, thank God you're awake. You're in the hospital." She pressed the alarm button on the side of the bed to notify the nurses.

Instantaneously three nurses arrived exclaiming, "What's wrong?" Abby screamed, "My mom's awake. Thank you God!"

The Head Nurse informed Doctor Schwartz of the change in the patient's status. Doctor Schwartz had finished a scheduled surgery and was preparing to go home. Surprised by the sudden change in his patient, he entered Delia's room. He asked Delia a sequence of questions and ordered her to perform various menial tasks. She was able to blink her eyes and follow his light from left to right. She squeezed his hand, moved her toes and crossed her legs. Schwartz was delighted. He asked her, "What's your name?"

She responded, "Delia."

"Delia what?" he asked.

She answered, "Delia Hoffman."

Surprised by her answer Schwartz said, "Isn't that your maiden name?"

Delia's eyes squinted as her lips puckered in childish defiance. She said, "Not anymore." The wise doctor reserved comment and told the nurses station to insure that Doctor Singer was notified of the good news.

Nelson Hoffman arrived in time to receive a verbal report from Doctor Schwartz. He was emotionally ecstatic over the good news and entered his daughter's room. He approached the bed and reached down to cuddle his youngest daughter. He said, "Thank God you came back, Dee. We were all so worried. Thank God....no surgery. How do you feel, sweetie pie?"

Delia's face became rosy with excitement as she said, "I feel weird but a good weird. I had this crazy, crazy dream that of all people Danny Corvo came to see me. He was caressing my face and telling me he was here for me. I know it was only a dream but it was so real."

Abby's face blossomed into a smile as the adoring teen-ager said, "So Mom, you really enjoyed your dream?" Delia repeatedly nodded yes, as Abby continued, "I'll tell you why it felt so real." Delia turned her head, anxious to get an expla-nation. Abby's face reflected the stoic look of an older woman as she said with a cool bluntness, "It felt real because it *was* real. He was here." She proudly dangled the revered Corvo construction business card in front of her Mother's puzzled face. "Look he gave me his private phone number and asked me to call him if there was any news. Boy, do I have news for him." Delia put her hands to her mouth as tears made their way down the all-too-familiar path on her face.

The Head Nurse told Nelson and Abby that Delia needed to rest. She informed them that Doctor Singer was on his way and they were welcome to come back when visit-ing hours resumed at eight o'clock. Doctor Singer and Nelson agreed that it would be wise to wait until the morning to call Danny. It was a long grueling ride that everyone knew the travel weary marine would be unable to postpone.

Doc Singer arrived at his sister-in-law's bedside at 9:30 p.m. Not fully awake Delia responded to the Doc's question, "Hey Dee, how are you feeling?"

She answered, "I'm tired but I feel good. I can't believe that Danny came to see me but I was still sleeping. Do you think he'll ever come back once he knows I'm ok?"

Doc's cheeks rose, forming a smile of reassurance and he said, "Definitely, he will be here tomorrow morning so get a good night's sleep."

On Saturday morning Abby had to be the one to call Danny Corvo. Excited, she swayed impatiently waiting for him to answer the phone. Finally she heard his voice, "Hello." With robust enthusiasm she said, "Danny, Mommy's awake. She came out of the coma last night shortly after you left. I didn't want to call you last night because it's a long drive and I knew that's what you would do. You needed to rest too you know. Please don't be mad at me."

Abby welcomed Danny's loud familiar laughter, "Ha, ha. I could never be mad at you for letting me sleep. But just so you know, I'm getting dressed as we speak. I'm going to fly into Westchester Airport and take a car to Manhattan. If you or anyone else meets me there, I can give you a ride home. Thanks kid, I'm on my way."

Danny made an impromptu detour to the local florist, boarded his plane, and flew into Westchester Airport. He arrived at Mount Sinai at noon. The Hoffman sisters and their spouses were in the visitor's lounge waiting for visiting hours to commence. Danny was graciously received by everyone. He asked the family if he could be the last visitor, implying that he needed some private time. It was impossible for the family not to acquiesce to the wishes of the very generous Mr. Corvo.

Delia was miraculously much improved in a short time. Love can have a powerful influence on illness. She received her family with tears of joy and yesteryear's long-lost hardy laughter. One by one they departed from her room. Lee was the last to leave, but not without pontificating some of her overprotective discourse. She said, "Danny is on his way, he'll be here shortly." Dee could feel her heart rate accelerate and said, "Are you sure?"

Lee answered reassuringly, "Without a doubt. But no one has seen or heard from Anthony. Is there anything you need to tell me?"

Delia sighed in dramatic fashion and said, "Please go to the house and take my clothes and personal belongings and bring them to Daddy's. Abby knows where everything is. I'm never going back to that house or near that bastard again; never!"

Angrily Lee asked, "He hit you didn't he?"

"Please just get my stuff for now. I'm supposed to be resting and staying calm. Once I'm home, we'll talk some more. Please."

Lee kissed her sister and said, "I think that crazy, good-look-ing guy who's always running should be here by now. Stay calm. Love you."

Delia coaxed the nurse to assist her with an application of make-up. Anxiously she waited for her beloved Danny to enter her room. Slowly the door opened. All she could see was an over-sized bouquet of assorted flowers obstructing the view of his face. Unsuccessfully she tried to hold back her tears. Danny handed her the flowers and wiped her eyes with his handkerchief. It had been over three years since they'd gazed into each other's eyes.

When Delia attempted to speak, Danny raised his finger to his lips, "Shhh, don't say anything. You need to rest. You look unbelievably beautiful, as always."

Laughing and crying, she muttered softly, "You're full of it. I look terrible." He smiled and answered, "Ok, you look like shit; now does that make you feel any better?" Delia smiled again as Danny leaned closer and gently placed a kiss on her parched lips. He continued to speak, "Seriously, you have to rest and get out of here. Today is not the day and time to talk about the past. However, I must ask you. Do you remember when Abby was little and told us that we couldn't be happy without each other; she was right wasn't she?" Delia slowly nodded yes. He continued, "Rest and get out of here. I'll come and see you when I can. I promise, but it's a grueling drive and I'm super busy."

Delia motioned with her index finger for him to come closer to the bed. With tears flowing down her face she whispered, "I never stopped loving you, and I never will. Can you really forgive me?"

Danny put his large calloused hands around her face and said, "There's nothing to forgive. We had some bad luck, but destiny gave us today."

Delia's memory was sharpened by the comment and she remarked, "Destiny? In your letter you wrote that you didn't believe in destiny anymore, only luck. Do you remember?"

Danny laughed boisterously saying, "Yeah, I remember, but I'm older and wiser now."

Delia grinned at his pithy wit and said, "One more thing; did Doc tell you I'm getting an annulment?"

He said bluntly, "Yes. Now go and get some sleep. I'll see you as soon as I can, maybe tomorrow."

Danny drove Abagail and Mr. Hoffman back to their home in the Bronx. He declined a family dinner invitation explaining a prior commitment with Nicky Galliano. The combat marine's interpretation of an annulment was the polar opposite of his beloved sweetheart Delia. Rango was the catalyst of Delia's life-threatening coma. His alcohol-enraged jealously had prompted the near-fatal blow to her head. It was embedded in Danny Corvo's creed to never condone a man abusing a woman... especially his woman.

The Gallianos were elated at the possibility of Danny and Delia reconciling. Gus referred to their separation as "the unspoken collateral damage of war." Danny was a good earner for both himself and the Galliano family. A reunion of the two young lovers could only bring more success to the already successful Corvo Construction Company. Once again, Danny and Nicky excused themselves to speak in the privacy of Gus Galliano's study.

Nicky looked suspiciously at Danny and said, "I'm really happy Delia's ok but she's still married. What's the plan bro?"

Danny pulled his chair closer. He spoke in a low whisper. "If it was just the marriage thing it would be easy but it's not that simple. That piece of shit smashed her in the head, that's why she went into the coma. I have it all calculated in my head. I'm going to find him and kill him. Please don't tell me the bullshit that I'm not a killer. I killed many a gook, and unlike the traumatized guilt-ridden veterans that take pity on themselves I sleep quite well. He tried to kill my women and I'm going to kill his faggot ass."

Nicky shook his head in a slow motion from side to side gesturing his dissatisfaction and finally said, "Ok, you're a big boy. Tell me this plan you have calculated in that Da Vinci head of yours."

Without preface Danny said, "I just need a little help from Ryan."

The faithful friend answered, "Not a problem. What exactly do you need?"

"Need to know where he hangs out and when. Once I know his MO, he's done" said the angry marine.

Nicky rose and walked aimlessly around the study, searching for a way to reason with his angry friend. When he returned to the table, he sat next to him and said, "Listen to me... Let's get him arrested and put in jail. Then he will drop dead just like Kadesh."

Unaware of the circumstances surrounding the Kadesh murder, Danny became stupefied at the outlandish comment and said, "Like Kadesh? So now you're God? Come on, Nicky, give me a break. I'll take care of it. That's what I was trained to do."

Nicky laughed with a deliberate defiance and said curtly, "Kadesh didn't have a heart attack on his own. It was a set up a wedding gift from us Galliano's to you. Don't forget your darling little Delia is the daughter my mother never had. Could you imagine if he wanted visitation rights with Abby? No way could we allow that to happen." Nicky spent the next half-hour painstakingly explaining every detail of the Kadesh murder. Danny's eyes had a frightening intensity as he listened to every word.

When the climax of the malady unraveled he said, "I'm impressed; nice work, Nicky, and thanks. But this one is mine. Trust me it's a piece of cake."

Nelson Hoffman summoned the help of his neighbor who owned a large commercial van. Early Sunday morning, Nelson and Abby were driven to the Tenbrook house. As suspected, there was no sign of Anthony Rango. Nelson, Abby, and his neighbor, Rocco, hurriedly removed all of their belongings and piled them in the van. At day's end, the boxes of personal belongings were boxed and stored in Nelson's basement.

All the Hoffman girls were married and living on their own. A lonely Nelson welcomed the return of his youngest daughter and granddaughter. Abby spent the rest of the day sorting through their belongings and placing them in the bedrooms. The young teenager was pleased to learn that this time she would have her own room.

At the same time, Nicky Galliano thought about how to help Danny. Nicky never believed that committing a murder was "a piece of cake," as Danny suggested. Concerned for his angry friend's freedom, he summoned the counsel of his wise father.

The following morning, Nicky returned to his parent's house to consult with his father. He shared Danny's proposal and plan. Gus sat back in his chair, rubbing his brow and shaking his head. Unpleased he remarked, "Believe it or not, I understand why he's thinking this way. When I was his age, I probably would have done the same thing. But this kid is different. If this kid plays his cards right, he can become big, a Congressman or a Senator. He has all the ingredients to become an elected official. He's a war hero. The fucking news guys eat him up, they love him; plus he's scary smart. Tomorrow, Monday, you'll drive me to the job site and I'll try and reason with him. He has to stay clean, that's all there is to it."

Danny spent Sunday afternoon at the hospital visiting with Delia. The conversations were centered on Abby's future and Danny's company. There wasn't a word spoken about Mr. Rango or their flawed marriage. He was informed by the nurse's staff that Delia might be released as early as Friday December 12th. This news did not leave him with much time to execute his plan.

Gus and Nicky arrived at the Long Island job site at eight thirty Monday morning. Danny ran to the car and respectfully embraced Gus, saying, "So I guess you're here to counsel me on the effects of murder on my lily white conscience. Or you're here because you want me to take you to breakfast?"

Gus gave Danny Corvo a look he had never seen before and it registered an unusual fear with him. He thought to himself, "Maybe I should just listen, this is serious."

Gus grumbled, "Get in the car."

Danny and Gus sat in the rear while Nicky drove. Gus instructed Nicky, "Take me to that diner I like. It's about a half hour drive; we should be done talking by then." Turning his attention to Danny, he continued, "I told Nicky that I know and understand why you want to kill this piece of shit. I had him checked out and I know he's a scumbag. I just don't want to see you throw away all we worked for. Let me give it to a pro. He'll disappear and that will be the end of that. Marry your girl. Make some kids and get rich. What do you say?"

Danny's face was cold. He shook his head, implying disagreement, and said, "Please hear me out. I love you and Nicky. I think you know that. I don't want to sound rude to you but I am a pro. I killed more people than anyone you know and that's a fact. I have to kill him; then and only then will Delia really believe that I forgave her. I'll never tell her and never talk about it but she will know. Also, I'll work my ass off for you and always respect your guidance but I need to do this. I'll remain the lily white war hero and I'll tell you why."

Danny Corvo had the unique talent of penetrating Gus Galliano's hidden sense of humor. Gus let out a deep loud belly laugh and said, "You're a piece of work. Ok, tell me why?"

With his piercing blue eyes concentrated on Gus Galliano's face, he boldly answered, "Because it ain't a crime if you don't get caught. I call it my PED plan."

Confused Gus repeated, "PED?"

Danny said, "Yes, PED… Plan, Execute and Disappear, it's Marine lingo."

Gus digested everything he was told without comment. A long interval of silence passed until Gus said, "Seems like you have your mind made up and there's no changing it. Just remember, if you get caught, you'll go away for a long time. Jail isn't fun."

Danny smirked and boldly responded, "Been there done that… remember? I'm feeling eggs. What say you?"

Gus answered, "Not now, but sometime I need to hear the whole plan. Let's go eat. Hey Nicky, I really wish I didn't let you go swimming that fucking day, life would have been so much easier without fucking Johnny Weissmuller." Danny laughed knowing there was a degree of acceptance of his plan by his powerful mentor.

Detective Ryan reported that Anthony Rango was shacking up with a cute nineteen-year-old drug-using hippie. She and Rango had rented a small cottage in Edgewater Park. This remote section of the Bronx was a small waterfront summer community. Most of the houses were vacant during the winter months, making it the ideal location to capture Mr. Rango. Ryan verified that Rango departed every morning at 4:30 a.m. before the sun came up. Part one of the plan was complete.

On Wednesday morning, December 10th, Corporal Rodrigues flew the Corvo Construction jet from Islip Airport to Hyannis. Islip was an uncontrolled airport that did not require permission to take off and land. Rodrigues reached Hyannis Airport at 10 a.m., requesting permission to land, and announced to the control tower that he was Daniello Corvo. He then provided tower control the ID number of the Corvo Construction plane. Private Coimbra, one of the "Hanoi Ten Pins," lived in Wellfleet, a small Portuguese fishing village. He provided car service and lodging for Rodrigues.

There was no car manufactured in the world that Nicky Galliano couldn't steal. On Wednesday at 4:10 in the morning, Nicky provided Danny Corvo with access to the rear seat of Rango's car. At almost 4:30 to the second, a hung-over and tired Anthony Rango unlocked his '74 Cadillac and plopped into the front seat. One insidious blow on the head from

283

Detective Ryan's leather-bound lead club rendered Rango instantly deprived of his senses. Danny took control of the car and drove to the Galliano salvage yard in the South Bronx.

Rango was put in a cargo container as the two waited for him to regain consciousness. The Cadillac "girl finder" of Mr. Rango would be put into the crusher and sold for scrap metal. Finally at 5:15 a.m., Anthony Rango regained consciousness. He awakened to the crystal blue eyes of a revengeful and hostile Danny Corvo. Frightened, the cowardly Rango pleaded for his life saying, "I got money. I don't know what this is all about, but I got plenty of money. You can have it all. Just don't hurt me."

Danny spoke in a low whisper and said mockingly, "You have plenty of money, eh? So how come you don't take care of your wife and kid?"

Rango's eyes widened with fear. He said, "Who are you? What do you want?"

Danny asked, "You don't know who I am?"

Rango answered, "Fuck no, I never saw you before. Who are you?"

Danny moved closer to Rango and very softly said, "I am Divine Intervention. I was put on this earth to shelter Delia Hoffman from scumbags like you and I'm very good at it. I'm going to give you one chance to live. Why did you hit my woman?"

The petrified playboy desperately began to cry as his drug-infested brain finally calculated that this man was Danny Corvo. With fear-driven remorse, he pleaded, "I didn't mean it I was drunk. I swear it will never happen again."

Nicky handed Danny a pair of welder's gloves. As Danny slowly put on the gloves, he smiled at Rango saying, "This is from Delia." Rango was knocked out from the first blow and was struck two more times before meeting the metal boiler plate floor. Nicky reminded Danny that it was getting late. He added, "Finish it; we don't have time to fiddle fuck around."

Danny responded, "Destiny doesn't fiddle." He propped Rango up to a sitting position. His clean, sharply tailored pants were drenched in his own urine. Corvo grasped his head in his oversized hands like a vice and swiftly snapped his neck. Rango was dead.

Rango's body was wrapped in a blue tarp and placed in the trunk of the full sized Cadillac. The body was dumped under the same Mulliner Avenue trestle where Danny had saved Delia from being raped all those years ago. Heroin and cocaine were placed in Rango's pockets and a dead rat was forced into his partially opened mouth. The world would never miss a drug dealing rat.

Nicky became very uncomfortable with the military style execution of Rango. This technique was employed by savvy marines and could ultimately draw attention to Danny. Nicky had to counter the technique to remove any possible suspicion of Delia's former fiancée.

They removed Rango's body from the trunk of the car in a few short seconds. Time was of the essence. Danny re-entered the passenger seat of the car. Nicky approached the body and unfolded the top portion of the blue tarp. He pulled a silenced 45-caliber automatic pistol from his waistband and shot Rango twice in the head; closing the tarp he entered the car.

Danny remained silent for a few blocks and finally asked, "What was that all about?" A grinning faced Nicky answered, "Insurance."

Danny asked, "Insurance? How so?"

Nicky replied, "The devil is in the details. When the cops find the scumbag with two holes in his head and a rat in his

285

mouth, they'll know he was executed and why. In the absence of a bullet, it could appear that he was killed by a trained member of the military. We don't want anyone looking at you, now do we?" Danny's face was cold, but he burst out laughing. He slowly shook his head and muttered, "I should have let your dumb ass drown."

With the Rango mission completed, Danny was driven to Wellfleet to stay with Coimbra and Rodrigues. At eleven o'clock Thursday morning, he attended a meeting with the Town Engineer of East Harwich. They discussed plans for the development of two waterfront lots on Pleasant Bay. Rodrigues, posing as Daniello Corvo at the Wednesday morning Hyannis Airport landing, was documented. There was now a written record and eyewitnesses that Daniello Corvo was in fact on Cape Cod when Mr. Rango met his fate.

CHAPTER 19

Danny was ordered to stay on Cape Cod for another week, eliminating any suspicion of his geographical location. Corporal Rodrigues was driven back to Long Island to run the construction crew in his absence. It seemed to be a rock solid plan that met with Gus's approval.

The ill-fated Rango's body was found early Thursday morning by an elderly woman walking her dog. The pure-bred German Shepard barked incessantly at the tarp concealing Rango's body. Over-powering its frail owner, the obsessed dog's paws clawed into the tarp's surface to reveal the flesh of a blood-drenched human head. Unable to control the powerful dog, the woman frantically screamed for help. A young construction worker en route to the subway station assisted the panic-stricken woman in controlling her dog. Once home, the frantic woman called the police and reported her bizarre discovery.

The discovery of the mob style murder of Anthony Rango didn't make the front page of any newspaper. Viewed by the press as the murder of a small-time drug pusher, the story was reported in the rear section of the newspapers. The lack of publicity was always a good thing for those who committed the murder.

The police investigation revealed that Anthony Rango was married and lived in the Bronx on Tenbrook Avenue. His neighbors informed the detectives that the deceased man's wife had suffered a fall and was in a coma and that their young daughter was temporarily staying with her grandfather. The Detectives followed Delia Rango's medical trail from Jacobi hospital in the Bronx to Mount Sinai in Manhattan.

At ten a.m. on Friday, December 12th, two Detectives traveled to Mount Sinai Hospital in Manhattan to inquire about the present condition of the late Anthony Rango's wife. The Detectives were surprised and encouraged that Mrs. Rango had regained consciousness; the next of kin had to be notified. Delia was still in a weakened condition. The Head Nurse suggested that the Detectives speak to Doctor Schwartz before informing Mrs. Rango that she was now a widow. Schwartz gave the Detectives the address and phone number of Delia's father, Nelson, ensuring them that he could direct them to Rango's parents. He asked the detectives if they could return later in the afternoon after he administered a mild sedative to his patient.

The two detectives returned promptly at 2 p.m. Delia became wide awake in anticipation of a visit or call from the man she so deeply loved. Doctor Schwartz accompanied the detectives into her room after persuading them to allow him to relay the news. After a brief introduction, Delia became distraught. She believed the harmful hand of her maniacal husband had reached Abagail. Doctor Schwartz assured her that although her daughter and all her family members were fine, there was indeed bad news.

Doctor Schwartz was a surgeon and short on words. He said, "Delia, early this morning your husband's body was found not too far from where you live. He was murdered; shot in the head and had heroin and cocaine packets in his possession. The detectives have a few questions they need to ask you. Are you up to it?"

Delia's face grimaced in sudden surprise as she heard the dreadful news and she nodded affirmatively. Detective Poli was puzzled by her lack of emotion and said, "I'm sorry for your loss, Mrs. Rango. Are you sure you don't want us to come back at another time?"

Delia said, "I'll be ok. Just say and ask what you need." The seasoned detective continued, "Were you aware of your husband being a drug user?" She brushed her hair to the side, allowing her face to be in full view. The detectives were momentarily distracted by her beauty as she answered, "My husband has not been home for over a month. Prior to that, he came and went as he pleased. We were not happy. He was planning on getting a divorce. I was planning on getting an annulment. I don't know anything about what he did as far as drugs go, but I do know he was not the same person I married. He hasn't paid any of the bills for the past two months. He's the reason I'm in here. The Friday night after Thanksgiving, he barged in unexpectedly and started yelling and screaming at me and my daughter. As usual, he was intoxicated. My daughter ran upstairs to her room as he demanded. I can still see his fist approaching my face, but I couldn't get out of the way. He punched me in the head, and when I woke up I was here. That's all I remember."

Satisfied at her brief summation Detective Poli responded, "Thank you, I understand; get some rest."

When the detectives departed, the phone rang. It was Danny. Delia told him that Anthony had been shot to death

and that his body was found under the Mulliner Avenue trestle. Danny responded in a cleverly imposed surprised fashion
saying, "Really?"

She answered, "God forgive me, but I don't care. The
detective said that he had drugs in his pockets and a rat
stuffed in his mouth..... Strange."

Danny replied, "Drugs are ruining a lot of people but the
rat in the mouth means he was a snitch. It seems to me that
he was probably dealing drugs and ratted some people out to
save his own hide. Are you're ok?"

Delia said boldly, "Yes I'm absolutely ok. I just don't want
to go to any service or funeral. I know it will look bad but I
just really don't care. Do you have any ideas?"

Danny paused for a moment and said, "Stay in the hospital until it's over; talk to Doc. Tell him what's on your mind
and he will arrange for you to stay."

Delia's voice softened as she asked with a cute, girlish
persistence, "Are you coming into the city?"

Danny sighed. "I wish I could, but I'm still on Cape Cod
and probably won't be back down in New York until Tuesday
or Wednesday. I'll call again tomorrow; get some rest and
don't forget to tell Doc what's on your mind."

Doc easily arranged for Delia to remain in the hospital,
citing the loss of her husband as a traumatizing event capable
of interrupting her recovery. Anthony Rango had a wake on
Sunday and Monday and was buried on Tuesday, December
16th. Anthony's parents informed the Detectives that they were
aware of the troublesome marriage but had difficulty believing that their son would hit his wife. The Detectives assured
them that, based on his death, there would be no necessity for
any further inquiries.

Danny remained on Cape Cod pursuing permits and
arranging for preliminary septic system tests. He faithfully

called Delia, keeping her abreast of his work activities, and inquiring about her health.

Freed from the grip of her poor judgement, she became relieved after the burial of her late husband. She was released from the hospital on Thursday, December 18th. In the absence of a divorce, she received a life insurance payment of fifty thousand dollars and complete ownership of the Tenbrook Avenue house. Haunted by unpleasant memories, she put the property up for sale. The asking price was the generous sum of sixty-five thousand dollars.

Danny finished the Cape Cod business and flew into Westchester Airport. His brother Joe was still working on the night shift and arranged to pick him up at 1 p.m. Danny was happy to see his sister-in-law and two nephews. Joe asked, "Have you spoken to Delia recently?"

Danny answered, "Sure, just about every day. I'll probably stop by and see her today if Mom lets me out of the house."

Joe chuckled and said, "That was something about her dirt bag husband. I know her marriage was in shambles but that had to be a big surprise."

Danny exhaled loudly and quipped, "Joe, the guy had a rat in his mouth and drugs in his pocket. Someone put two bullet holes in his head. He abandoned her and then came home to beat her into a coma. She may have been surprised but under the circumstances she may have been pleasantly surprised."

Judy spun from her front seat making close eye contact with her brother-in-law saying, "From a woman's point of view I can understand how an abused woman wouldn't care one bit. He didn't get killed that way because he was an altar boy."

Danny placed his hand on her shoulder and said, "Amen to that."

At 2 p.m. he arrived at the Hoffman house to visit the girl he so deeply loved. Mr. Hoffman was working and Abagail was in school, affording the reunited couple an opportunity to speak privately and with open frankness. Delia wore a New York Yankee baseball cap to conceal the portion of her scalp that had been shaved to suture the deep wound. She proudly wore the engagement ring Danny had given her. A long embrace, followed by a long overdue kiss, seemed surreal to the reunited couple.

Delia said in a tired voice, "I still can't believe that you're here. I love you so much."

Danny grinned and replied, "I love you too."

The young couple sat on the living room couch holding hands. She began to speak. "So what do we do now?"

Danny answered, "Get married, have a bunch of kids and love each other every day for the rest of our lives."

Her face became rosy pink and she said, "When?"

He answered with absolute certainty, "Next year in June, on the anniversary weekend of our first date."

Delia edged closer, resting her head on his shoulder. "Are we going to have the same big wedding you originally planned?"

Danny laughed boisterously, "A big wedding? We're going to have a huge wedding at the Marina Del Rae in Throggs Neck."

Delia made a fresh pot of coffee and seductively gestured for him to follow her into the kitchen. They sat face to face at the small round kitchen table. She opened up the half-torn envelope Joe Corvo had personally delivered. She began waving the letter Danny had written her saying, "Danny, I have a question about something you wrote in this letter."

He answered, "Now there's something that hasn't changed; you have a question. Fire away."

She gave him a long loving stare and slowly said, "What does the ending part mean? The part that reads, 'I will have all the things that I desire and let passion flow like rivers to the sky.'"

Danny reached in and joined hands saying, "You really don't know?"

Delia nodded, gesturing that she really didn't understand.

He responded, "Those words are not mine they were in a song called MacArthur's Park. I was certain that you would make the connection. The next line of the song is, 'And after all the loves of my life, I'll be thinking of you and wondering why.' I wanted you to know that no matter where I went, or what I did, or who I did it with; I'd always love you and never be able to forget you. That's what I wanted you to know." The two reached over the small table and once again engaged in a long seemingly endless kiss.

Continuing to hold both her hands, Danny said bluntly, "If it's ok with you, I don't want to talk about anything that happened in our lives from the day I left for Nam until today. We both made mistakes that we regret and I want to eliminate that period of war time from our lives. It's counterproductive the only thing that matters from this day forward is our life together... our future. What say you?"

Unexpectedly she answered, "I agree. I don't want to talk about any of it either, but I have a few things to say and I need you to let me finish without interruption. I need you to promise not to interrupt even for one word."

Anxious to hear what she had to say, he agreed and said, "Sure no problem. Go ahead. Speak your mind."

Delia released his hands from hers and rose from the table. Pouring herself a glass of ice water, she stood before him. Her eyes were fixed on his as she said, "I love you more than I love myself. I would sacrifice my life to save yours and I know you would do the same for me… you already have. There is nothing in this world I wouldn't do for you. But I'm not dumb. It seems to be a little too coincidental that the piece of shit Anthony was found dead in the same spot where we met. What are the odds of that?

"So here's what I want you to know. I love you, but if you were the one responsible for killing that bastard or if you had him killed I'm not going to love you—she hesitated and then said, "Any less." Her voice cracked with nervous emotion as she paused for a moment to take another gulp of water.

Danny smirked as he thought, "My little sweet Delia is sounding an awful lot like Victoria."

Delia resumed speaking. "In fact, I'd somehow have to figure out the impossible; a way to love you more, because if you played a role in killing him, you once again rescued me. This is something I don't ever want to bring up again and it sure fits into your timetable of silence. I want you to know that I really don't care. I just care about us being together for the rest of our lives. I lost you once and I'm never going to lose you again.

"Don't answer, don't say a word. I just wanted you to know. Nothing you can do will ever make me stop loving you. Lastly, if you really decide to run for political office, I have over one hundred thousand dollars you can use to run your campaign. From here on out, it's you and me against the world. I love you."

Danny rose from the table and placed his hands on her frail shoulders. He gazed into her deep blue eyes, his face without expression, as he said softly, "Don't worry I'm not going to grace your theory with an answer. But I must tell you this… I am a highly-trained combat soldier. I believe that we are who we are because of where we were when we were there. I was highly trained before I stepped one foot onto Parris Island or landed in Viet Nam. You saw that first hand on the first day we met. So there is one thing in life you can always be certain about, and that is me protecting you from the horrors of this world."

PART 2

A society gets the criminals it deserves.
—Val Dermid

CHAPTER 20

T he deed had been done.

Anthony Rango was dead.

Delia Hoffman was a free woman.

Gus and Victoria Galliano delighted in the re-united Corvo/Hoffman long-awaited wedding plans. They viewed the young couple as an extension of their family. Victoria planned a banquet for New Year's Day, 1976. Gus closed his Little Italy restaurant and his personal chef was summoned to cook on sight at their Riverdale Estate.

The Galliano Estate was opulent and protected in every way. High intensity flood lights and cameras surveyed the court-yard and walkways. Trained German bred guard dogs were on duty. The walls of the massive dining hall were garnished with expensive art. The gleaming teak floors were adorned with fine rugs imported from Persia. The Galliano estate was a palace, a home fit for a man of great power and fortune.

The Galliano's son, Nick, and his wife, along with Danny and his bride-to-be received a verbal invitation. Scripted invitations were extended to Congressman Morano and Bishop Pestoni.

New Year's Day brought an unwelcome mixture of icy rain and snow. The roads were slippery but passable. Dinner was scheduled to be served at 2 p.m. and the guests were instructed to arrive at 1 p.m. for cocktails and hors d'oeuvres. The always-respectful Danny would bring Victoria her favorites, a box of imported Italian chocolates and a bottle of semi-sweet Riesling wine.

Danny was innately punctual and Nicky was always annoyingly late, a trait that the Gallianos had become accustomed to. Nicky arrived with his wife Sonia at 1:15 p.m. Sonia was an unusually fair skinned, tall high-spirited girl of Hispanic persuasion. She gave up a promising dancing career to become the wife of Nicky Galliano, a handsome man of great earning potential. Gus would sarcastically congratulate them for being "only a little late."

The doorbell rang at 1:30 p.m. and the two young couples were anxious to see who Gus and Victoria had also invited. The lady of the house greeted her friend and spiritual advisor Bishop Pestoni. The Bishop apologized for his tardiness, citing the poor road conditions. Victoria was an overly-generous parishioner and had established a Christmas fund for New York City orphans. Through her husband's connections and influence with the labor unions, it was not uncommon for her to raise a million dollars for the annual New York City orphan fund.

The Bishop had married Nicky and Sonia, so a formal introduction was not necessary. Victoria then introduced Danny, saying, "Bishop Pestoni, this is Danny Corvo, the brave young man who rescued Nicky from drowning, and this is his fiancée, Delia Hoffman, whom I spoke to you about a few weeks ago."

The short stout Bishop extended his thick, pudgy hand, prompting a handshake. The Bishop's face bore a childish grin as his eyes appraised Delia. "Young lady, sometimes life is not so kind, but God is good. Everything is going to be fine for you, just fine."

Delia's radiant face managed a glimpse of a smile and she responded, "Thank you." She found herself in a state of befuddlement. What was he talking about?

Dinner at the Galliano's was always a culinary masterpiece, a feast. The Italian chef's expertise was studied to impress the most exquisite taste. It was a near-impossible task for the guests to restrain themselves from over-eating. The tantalizing thought of multiple desert offerings would tempt the guest's already content palates.

At 3:15p.m. the doorbell rang again. This time Gus Galliano excused himself from the dinner table and greeted the newly arrived guest. Gus's loud greeting echoed through the dining hall as he said, "Congressman Morano, I'm glad you were able to stop by for desert. Give me your coat."

When the Congressman entered the dining room, he instructed everyone to remain seated. The Congressman was over six feet tall, a physical trait donated by his Irish mother. He had a full head of peppered hair and wore finely tailored clothing. His tall, slim appearance and dutifully focused eyes portrayed the look of unquestionable authority. He introduced himself to all the guests and cleverly gave the insinuation of a down-to-earth, ordinary man.

Nicky, the family clown since he had learned how to speak, whispered in Danny's ear, "Now this is interesting, a holy man and a politician at the same dinner table."

Danny returned a smile. In a cautiously low voice, he muttered, "Never underestimate the brilliance of your parents—dumb didn't get them here." Nicky grinned as he very slowly nodded his head in agreement.

The desert and expresso represented an exquisite finale for the Galliano banquet. Victoria excused herself from the dinner table and requested that Bishop Pestoni accompany her to the family study. In a few moments, Victoria returned to the dining room and motioned for Delia to join her. As the two women walked away, Danny noticed the Congressman gaping at them with admiration, his eyes carefully aimed like a high powered scope at their every sway. Danny held his tongue but thought to himself, "They're all the same low-life pieces of shit, no respect."

When they entered the study, Bishop Pestoni was seated behind the large mahogany desk. The short, stout Bishop rose and motioned with his pudgy index finger for the two women to sit, one to his left and one to his right. He looked at his dear friend, Victoria Galliano, and smiled. Turning to Delia he said, "Now young lady, I know that by now you must be over-whelmed with curiosity, so I will not linger with my words. When you sustained that terrible head injury, Victoria came to me and asked to have masses said for your speedy recovery. I obliged as is my duty as her Pastor, but I also took it upon myself to have a number of Novenas scheduled in your name. Thank God our prayers were answered. You look wonderful."

Bishop Pestoni, his chubby, well-fed face glowing with pride, turned his attention to Victoria. "Shall I tell her or would you like to be the bearer of the good news?"

Victoria girlishly chuckled and responded, "Bishop you are on such a roll; please continue."

The Bishop bowed his head in acceptance and once again concentrated his attention on a very, very confused Delia Hoffman. The Bishop resumed speaking, "Delia, from the very first day you woke up from the coma, you expressed a desire to have your marriage from that evil man Rango annulled. As you must know, Victoria is an extremely bright woman who loves you dearly. Moreover, she is persistent almost to a fault." Victoria raised her eyebrows at his blunt comment but respectfully remained silent as the Bishop continued. "Distraught and upset, she came to me on the very day you awakened from the coma. She relayed to me your desire to have that unholy marriage dissolved, annulled. Her great enthusiasm inspired me to initiate the paperwork without pause or hesitation. Unfortunately, as of all matters with a legal connation there would be a fee. Victoria gladly paid the vast sum and the paperwork was prepared. The following day, I hand-delivered and filed your request. I pleaded and begged to have the annulment granted immediately and it was."

Delia placed her tear-filled face into her cupped hands. Victoria got up and embraced the sobbing beauty, saying, "Hey, stop. This is a very happy day. You can finally marry the man you love in a beautiful church with your beautiful family."

An overly excited Delia hugged Victoria, thanking her profusely. She approached the Bishop and very innocently asked, "Bishop Pestoni, can I give you a hug?"

The Bishop gleefully responded, "Certainly my child, certainly."

It took a little while for the magnitude of this gift to be digested. Delia wouldn't marry her beloved Danny as someone else's widow because now, in the eyes of the Church, she was never married. Her regretful mistake eradicated by a stroke of Victoria Galliano's pen. She could now wear a beautiful white wedding dress as she had planned all those years ago. Victoria Galliano was becoming the mother Delia Hoffman never knew.

When they left the study and returned to the dining room. Nicky and his wife Sonia were the only two remaining. Inquisitively Delia asked, "Where did Danny and Mr. Galliano go?" Nicky smirked, shaking his head briefly, and responded, "You know my dad. The two of them are having a meeting with Congressman Morano."

Gus, Danny, and Congressman Morano retreated to the sanctuary of his private game room. Gus had informed the Congressman that the young Marine might be interested in a political career. Joe Morano had been a close business associate of Gus Galliano. He had profited extensively from business deals where his influence and authority were needed. In order to secure certain construction permits, newly formed agencies such as the Department of Environmental Conservation had to sometimes be persuaded, motivated, and greased by the Congressman. Joe Morano was unusually persuasive. He knew how to grease and how to be greased. The congressman had a demanding demeanor and a demanding wallet. His friendship was not without a price.

The Congressman knew much about the background of the heroic Marine, but had questions. Morano asked, "So Danny, I know you are a surviving POW, and more importantly you saved my dear friend's son, Nicky, from drowning. According to Gus, you are a well-trained combat soldier and a brilliant businessman. What I don't know is your scholastic background. What exactly is the length of your education?"

Danny squirmed as he shunned talking about himself but responded, "Well Congressman I graduated from the Bronx High School of Science, then I went to Bronx Community College. I soon transferred to Fordham University, where I earned my engineering degree. I loved the classes and teachers at Fordham. I graduated first in my class."

Congressman Morano glanced at Gus, who was studying both of them with great interest. Approvingly, the Congressman bobbed his head and said, "I'm impressed and you're still so young. How old are you, Danny?"

He answered, "I'll be twenty nine on May 17th of this year."

Congressman Morano spent a half an hour explaining the election process to both Gus and Danny. They listened attentively. When his educational symposium about the election process ended he offered Danny his professional advice. Morano's voice had a confident smoothness as he said. "As you can imagine, it's 1976, and the notion of being elected without a connection to one of the big political machines is impossible. Not a chance. So what I recommend is that you become a member of the Democratic Party. Why the Democrat Party, you might ask? It's really simple; we live in a state that votes Democrat all the time. Secondly, and most importantly, I recommend that you get a law degree. If you start out running as an Assemblyman, that's one thing, but if you have aspirations of becoming a Congressman and beyond, a law degree will give you a great advantage. One last question and please don't think I'm being rude, did you ever have your I.Q. tested?"

Danny had a look of reluctance on his face. He let out a deep breath of annoyance and said, "Congressman, I try to be a humble guy. Believe it or not, no one has ever asked me that question but here is your answer. My IQ was tested twice, once in Science, you know high school, and once in the Marines. My score in Science was 162 and in the Marine Corps it was 168."

Morano pivoted to make eye contact with Gus. Gus was pleased at the congressman's sudden reaction. He was grinning; his deep dimples exaggerated with the joyous reaction. Morano remarked, "That's incredible. I mean really incredible. You're in genius territory. I had to ask you that question because not everyone is mentally equipped to do what I'm about to propose. So here is a helpful legal tidbit for you young man. You do not have to go to law school to earn a law degree. All you have to do is pass the bar exam and work for one year with a judge or law firm. From what Gus tells me, your business is thriving, and that may not continue if you take a sabbatical to go to law school. That's a risk you should not be made to take. Give me a week or two and I'll map out a strategy so you can get your law degree in the least amount of time possible."

Gus rose from his chair and clapped his hands in approval. He cried out, "Bravo, thanks Joe. I knew you'd be able to help my boy. Let's go upstairs and get some well-deserved desert."

Soon both Congressman Morano and Bishop Pestoni bid the Galliano family and their guest's farewell. Danny and Delia were anxious to leave so they could share their conversations with the Bishop and the Congressman. Gus was a thorough man; he had more information he had to share with Danny. Once again, he would use the business angle to summon Danny and his son Nicky to his study. He promised the girls they wouldn't be too long.

The boys sat in their usual chairs facing Gus. Gus removed his suit jacket and loosened his tie. His face no longer bore the look of holiday jubilance; something was annoying him like a pesky pimple on the tongue. He rolled up his sleeves as his eyes darted from one boy to the other. Finally he began to speak, "Danny I know you were in Viet Nam when the first one came out but did you ever see the movie The Godfather? There were two of them."

Danny knew that question had a deep hidden analytical meaning behind it as he answered, "Yes, I saw both of them."

Gus firmly pressed his lips as his head slowly rocked up and down, acknowledging his answer. His voice became surprisingly soft and gentle as he said, "That Puzo guy was a genius. He educated all of America on the inner makings of the Mafia. The average American knew squat about the Mob. No one really knew about consiglieres, soldiers or button men. No one really knew anything about the heads of the five families. Well they sure know now. The guy is brilliant. I can see by the blank look on both of your faces you have no idea why I brought this up."

The gentleness in Gus's voice was rapidly transposed to a scolding snarl. Without further preamble he resumed speaking, "Nicky you came to me for guidance because you wanted to prevent Danny from killing that scumbag, Rango."

His eyes were now firmly affixed on Danny Corvo. His breathing became an anxious wheeze as he continued, "I came to see you all the way out on Long Island because I wanted you to stay clean. Please don't bring up all the gooks you killed in Viet Nam. I really am not interested in hearing it, and that story is getting old. Killing people as a Marine in combat is a whole lot different than killing someone as a civilian."

Gus got up from his desk and walked to the bar. He poured himself a shot of brandy and resumed speaking, "Danny you did a masterful job at convincing me that you had to personally kill Rango. You transported me back in time, making me see that when I was your age under the same circumstances I'd have probably done the same thing."

Gus's anger was not subsiding as he turned to his son. "And you, you had to become an accomplice. Don't try to deny it because I know. I didn't set you up in a multi-million dollar business so you could become a petty ass killer of a punk. So here is what I'm going to tell the both of you. Stop the shit! This is no fucking movie about people with cotton balls in their mouth that everyone tries to mimic and imitate; some-one who gets shot five fucking times and lives to tell about it. This is reality. When you play, you must pay. Now, Nicky you go inside and talk to the girls. I'll be finished with him soon."

Deep in his soul, Danny Corvo was stewing with anger that his friend and mentor Gus Galliano would bring up the killing of Rango. He, too, removed his sport jacket and loos-ened his tie. He knew the sermon wasn't over and that he had to listen intently.

Gus refilled his brandy glass and offered Danny a drink, knowing he would refuse. He sat down, resting his elbows on the arms of his chair; his heavy hands folded in front of him. Once again he appeared to be calm. He softly continued, "Danny, Danny, Danny you are a multi-talented young man that I love and admire. I think you know that Victoria and I love you and Delia as if you were our own. You may think forty or fifty is light years away but it's not. This event called life flies by. When you told me why you had to kill Rango, I understood, because as I said I was able to transport myself back in time to when Victoria and I were young. She was so beautiful but I was thirty and she had just turned twenty. Every swinging dick in the Bronx wanted to be with her, but once they knew she was going out with me, it all stopped. They knew who I was and were fearful of my easily lit short fuse. Being Stephano Galliano's son didn't hurt either.

"Of course in the Bronx, especially in those years, there would always be one asshole that would be blinded by a girl's beauty, forcing his suicidal bravado to test you. Such a fool was a guy named Jimmy Roach. I'm no faggot but he was a really good-looking guy, movie star good-looking, but he kept pestering Victoria. I won't bore you with all the details, but I can tell you this; he's not too good looking anymore.

Benny 'the foot' and I grabbed Roach when he least expected it. We drenched his face with acid. Needless to say he gave up pestering Victoria. So, in spite of all my raving and ranting I do understand. I just don't want you and Nicky to get caught doing stupid shit others can easily do."

Gus refreshed his brandy glass for a third time and lit up a cigar. Danny dreaded that this lecture was still in its infancy. He opened a bottle of Pepsi and re-seated himself in front of Gus. His steel blue eyes fixed on Gus Galliano. Gus sat in Nicky's vacant chair and slid it next to Danny. Affectionately he placed his hand on Danny's shoulder. He appeared calmer and once again started to speak, "You know I give you a lot of credit. I know you for just about ten years and you never asked me any questions about my personal life or my business. I know you know that I am not an altar boy and that my business dealings are diversified and go way beyond the parameters of construction and owning a restaurant. You somehow knew to ask me for help in the Caldo matter. The whole neighborhood knew that Caldo's father is a feared hoodlum. So after our meeting with him and his son, it didn't take much of your brain power to figure out that I had control over Caldo. When we started Corvo Construction, I told you we were going to use your name because the Feds look at mine through a magnifying glass. The truth is they are trying to tie me to my father and grandfather; it's never going to happen. What I'm telling you stays between us and you take it to your grave."

Intrigued, Danny moved his chair closer to Gus; he didn't want to miss a syllable. Gus sensed the young Danny's curiosity was refreshed as he continued, "There is a boss of all bosses but contrary to what some may believe it's not me. However I put him there and he is indebted to me. The needle on his compass moves through me. There is not a major decision he makes without my blessing and okay. Now there's something even a brilliant fictional author couldn't fathom. So, you and especially Nicky with my last name, have to stay clean. I spent years of my life laundering and carefully investing my father's fortune so I could be accepted by society. If the FBI could prove that I was directly involved with the Mob, Mafia, Costra Nostra, call it whatever you want, do you think Congressmen would be coming to my home? Do you think they would be willing to work with me? Never happen. Now remember what I told you and then forget what I told you and concentrate on your law degree. By the way, my diabetes is under control to the point that the doctor thinks I can come off the meds."

Danny was relieved. Everything Gus told him sounded too good to be true, but it was. Gus Galliano was the insidious man behind the scenes. In his hands, he held the steering wheel of organized crime in New York, "the invisible Don."

Danny felt honored that this all powerful man would share his innermost secrets with him. But the combat marine was still unraveled that Gus could so easily dismiss his military record as a menial accomplishment. Gus was anxious to return to the dining hall when Danny asked for a few more minutes of his time. He reseated himself and made a hand gesture for Danny to speak.

Danny sat on the edge of his chair to become closer to Gus. He spoke in a raspy whisper saying, "You just told me a ton of personal stuff about yourself. Now I feel compelled to tell you something I have never told anyone." Gus was impatient as he again made a hand gesture for him to start speaking. Danny continued, "When I was in Viet Nam one of the guys and I took a liking to a twelve-year-old boy whose parents were killed by Americans. We fed him and his grandparents who became his custodian when his family got killed. We taught him how to play catch, the basics of boxing and some self-defense moves. Reilly and I really loved this kid, Bao, and were trying to figure out a way to bring him back to the states.

"One night when I was on guard duty I heard a low grade moan coming from the barbed wire barricade. I flicked on the spotlight to survey the area. The light startled a person partially tied up in the barbed wire who was attempting to free himself without being heard or seen. It wouldn't have been a difficult task if it wasn't for the huge pack of explosives attached to his back. I looked through the high-powered scope to get a better look. It was the kid, Bao. I blew a hole through the top of his head. Bao was a civilian and a kid but at that very moment he needed to be killed. I had to protect my fellow Marines—it was that simple. Now I'm sorry Nicky got involved in killing Rango, but it was his decision. I told you this story because you need to know that the killing of Bao really never bothered me. I was disappointed but not tormented. Some people do things that warrant them to lose their life, like Rango and the kid."

The great Gus Galliano was momentarily speechless. He loved Danny Corvo like a son and thought he knew him well. But this story had shown a side of Danny that he never thought existed. The combat marine had a coldness that even Gus Galliano couldn't explain or understand. He finally ended the silence by saying, "Some people have to think about the things they know they have to do before they can do them. People like you and me just do what we have to and never think about it again. It's a gift. I just don't know if it's a gift from God or the Devil. I guess someday we'll find out. Let's go and get some coffee."

At eight o'clock, Danny and Delia departed from the Galliano Estate. Delia pulled out the copy of her annulment papers from her purse. Her fair complexation was infused with a pinkish glow as she excitedly said, "Danny I couldn't believe this. Victoria had the Bishop get the annulment papers signed before the dirt bag died. In the eyes of the Church, that evil union never existed. I'm so happy."

Danny was pleased that she said Rango had died and was not murdered. He then explained the contents of his meeting with Gus and Congressman Morano. It was New Year's Day 1976, and it was time to plan their long awaited wedding.

CHAPTER 21

When Delia Hoffman regained her strength, she resumed working for Victoria Galliano. Danny winterized both homes in the Hamptons and was temporarily living with his parents in the Bronx in preparation for his wedding. The young couple began working on their wedding plans immediately after Bishop Pestoni invented the instant annulment. Rich powerful people can influence the decisions of almost anyone including Holy Mother the Church.

The young couple chose June 26th at Our Lady of Solace Church for their wedding. The reception would be held at the newly built Marina Del Rae in Throggs Neck, both in the Bronx, N.Y.

Danny's widowed mother felt reassured that her youngest son's hopes and dreams were finally being realized. She knew all too well that all the money in the world could not replace her son's endless, aching need to have Delia Hoffman share his life.

Many candidates spun around in his busy head to be his best-man. He chose his brother Joe, brilliantly citing that he knew him longer than anyone else. "Joe has seniority over everyone else," he said jokingly. Delia chose her pragmatic sister Lee to be her bridesmaid.

Danny had saved and invested his money wisely during the lonely years without Delia. No expense was spared to make their day memorable. Unbeknown to Danny Corvo, it was Gus Galliano's construction company that built the elaborate waterfront Marina Del Rae. The Galliano connection saved the young couple over fifteen hundred dollars. There was no limit to Gus Galliano's generosity and thankfulness when it involved the Corvo kid.

Congressman Morano had taken longer than anticipated to furnish Danny with a viable strategy to obtain his law degree. They say good things come to those who wait. Danny was patient. In true Sicilian format he never complained and never asked. Finally, in late February, the Congressman introduced Danny to Professor Timothy M. Bennett. Professor Bennett was a well-regarded professor at Columbia Law School in Manhattan. A retired Supreme Court Justice for Westchester County, he ran the most prestigious law firm in New York City. He agreed to meet with Danny every other Saturday for the next six months to provide him with case histories and other reading materials pertaining to the law. Danny had to read and digest the material, knowing he would be drilled by the Professor every two weeks.

The former Judge was impressed with Corvo's ability to retain material, but moreover his skill at seeking and discovering loopholes in the law. He told Congressman Morano, "Joe, this Corvo kid is a living breathing 'cream of the crop' student. I never met a student of his caliber in my entire career."

Wedding preparation, work, law studies and training could not deter him from keeping in contact with his few friends. On a Saturday in early April, Danny went to see Paulie Nartico and his nine-year-old daughter, Nicole. She didn't remember Danny from his pre-military days. Paulie's mother Teresa always welcomed Danny and insisted she make them lunch. She had recently re-married a local contractor, Phil Bruno, a few years after Paulie's father died. Lunch was an interestingly prepared medley of Northern Italian cuisine. The food was delightfully different to Danny's Sicilian-German palate. Danny was amused listening to young Nicole tell him about the two-eighty-three Chevy motor. She was certainly as they say, "a chip off the old block."

Paulie's private shop was thriving. He moved his family to a luxury apartment building on Williams Bridge Road. The building was predominately occupied by professionals. The reality of how two kids that barely finished high-school could pave a way to live among the elite of the Bronx thrilled his wife Gloria.

When lunch was over Paulie introduced him to a young neighborhood mechanic he had hired. Bobby Bestone was a thinker, very innovative and a skilled thief. Paulie told Danny, "This kid is a piece of work. He was rebuilding motors when he was fourteen. He's now twenty two and can weld, spray and do body work. I have to keep giving him more money, he's that good. The problem is that even with the both of us, there is never enough time. The work just keeps pouring in." Danny laughed and said, "Its 1976, the country is just starting to come out of the recession and you're complaining about being busy. Paulie, smarten up!" Paulie nodded his head indicating the foolishness of his complaint.

Paulie's shop was comparatively small in comparison to the work he scheduled. He had a three bay garage but not enough ceiling height for a lift. Paulie knew a lift would save him many hours of unnecessary back-breaking labor.

Changing a transmission with jacks and tripod stands was doable but not safe or efficient. As the conversation continued, Danny smiled, as a renovation plan became visible. Paulie was always a good and loyal friend to Danny Corvo; doing favors that were sometimes ethically questionable.

Danny grabbed Paulie by the arm and said, "Come here, I want to show you something." They walked into the last bay of the garage. Danny said, "Look up, I can have this roof off in half a day and raise the walls and roof to fourteen feet by the end of the second day. Of course, you'll have to close for two days but if I start on a Sunday I'll be finished by Monday night and you'll only lose one day."

Paulie was worried about everything from the weather to obtaining building permits and finding someone who could install a lift. Danny assured him that his company had a stellar reputation with the building department, but unfortunately he did not have any influence on God or the weather. He told Paulie to stay calm and pray for dry weather.

In two days Corvo Construction secured the necessary permits. The material arrived on Saturday and work began on Sunday as planned. The weather cooperated, and by Monday evening at 4 o'clock the job was complete. Paulie choked on his words as he thanked his friend for all he had done. He asked, "How much do I owe you? I can pay you in cash if that's better for you."

Danny laughed, saying, "You owe me for the material, period. Your mom paid me when she made that fabulous lunch. Save your money and have another kid." Paulie knew there would be no changing his mind. Corvo was Corvo. Two days later three guys showed up at the shop with two lifts. Paulie's undersized shop had just been given a shot of Corvo adrenaline.

As in many young marriages, life was not all sunshine and roses for Paulie and his young attractive wife. Gloria was becoming more and more irritated at the amount of hours Paulie spent away from home. She felt alone and neglected. Paulie tried to reason with her, arguing that he was the sole supporter of the family and that their rent was extraordinarily high. Sometimes she appeared to understand but the loneliness kept her in a constant state of low-grade anger.

Nicole's school was only a few buildings away from her father's garage. She walked there after school and spent time with her father and grandmother. Grandma Nartico always had a tempting snack for her only grandchild. Her step-grandfather, Phil drove Nicole to her home on Williams Bridge Road, allowing his step-son to continue working. The lonesome Gloria usually invited her father-in-law into her apartment. They shared small talk over a cup of expresso.

Phil Bruno's small construction company employed local laborers and carpenters. He had a good reputation and was a personable man. The majority of his work was roofing and siding. He utilized his time wisely and scheduled interior work when the weather became inclement. Unlike Corvo Construction he didn't own heavy equipment and really didn't build anything. He was primarily a roofer, sider and handyman. Phil Bruno's good reputation earned him an abundance of work in his own neighborhood. He was constantly booked and making a great deal of cash. Corvo Construction was sometimes bound by a "time is of the essence" contract. On occasion, Danny would throw his friend's step-father Phil Bruno a bone, sub-contracting his company to expedite the installation of siding.

In April of 1976, Phil Bruno bought a premium track of farmland in up-scale New Canaan Connecticut. He dreamed of building a new home and eventually moving to Connecticut but feared that his wife would never move away from her only son and disrupt his livelihood. Paulie had been earning a living in his mother's garages since he was fifteen years old.

The Corvo-Hoffman wedding date was closing in rapidly on the young, very busy couple. Gus persuaded Danny to buy a house and forego the common error of renting an apartment. He suggested buying a house with good bones and a rental apartment. He stressed the importance of buying in a really good neighborhood, knowing Corvo Construction was flush with talent and could turn a shanty into a castle.

On a clear Sunday afternoon in early May, Danny coaxed Delia into taking a ride. As he crossed Williams Bridge Road, Delia knew they were nearing the house she had lived in with the late Anthony Rango. She was pleased when they drove in the opposite direction about six blocks from where she had lived. Danny stopped in front of a large Colonial in Indian Village. The house was built in the center of three building lots and had a separate garage with a legal apartment on the second floor. The front portico had bold double doors and ornate Italian columns. The entire perimeter of the property was secured by a six foot high wrought-iron fence. The front windows were seven feet in height and handsomely encased by hand-cast stone mantles.

Danny's face bore a devilish grin as he said, "So Mrs. Corvo to be, what you think of this little wigwam?"

Delia sighed saying, "It's unbelievable. It looks like it should be in Washington D.C. or Italy. Let me guess. This house belongs to one of Mr. Galliano's friends, right?"

Danny smiled bobbing his head affirmatively, "Congratulations Mrs. Corvo you hit the nail right smack on the head." he said. Delia was overcome with curiosity and asked, "Do you know him?"

Danny answered, "Sure and so do you."

Dumfounded she repeated his words saying, "I do? I know Mr. Galliano's friend who owns this house?"

Danny's smile was on the cusp of laughter as he said, "Yes you do, you certainly do, and in fact you know him all too well."

Delia's voice reached the threshold of a shout and exclaimed, "Danny, the suspense is killing me; who? Who owns this house?"

Danny exited the car and quickly strutted around to the passenger side, opened the door and took Delia by the hand. As she exited the car, Danny put his arms around her and applied an unexpected kiss. Absorbed by the moment, she smiled and asked, "Can we do that again?"

Danny obliged and finally said, "This house is owned by Mr. and Mrs. Daniello Corvo. This is our home."

Phil Bruno continued to drive Paulie's daughter Nicole home after school. It seemed like the trip was taking longer and longer. Paulie had a good relationship with his step-father, who never criticized him and always offered his help both physically and financially.

Paulie's young beautiful wife continued to complain about her loneliness. Her complaints prompted him to never work on Sunday, fearing that could put her over the edge. Sunday was family day and the girls always chose the place and activity.

On the first Sunday in May, Gloria awakened in high-spirits. She seemed to be her old self, singing in the shower and teasing her daughter. Her newly found happiness accelerated on the trip to Rye Playland often making her husband and daughter laugh. They spoke about the Corvo wedding and agreed to let Nicole stay with her parents in Pelham Bay, not far from the Marina Del Rae wedding venue.

319

That evening, Gloria asked Paulie to get her a car. She complained about not spending enough time with her mother and being alone all day. Paulie countered that although the business was doing well since the renovations and the new lifts, money was still tight. The lifts were not a gift and had to be paid off. He promised her a car as soon as the lifts were paid off in six months. Gloria's happiness withered as she went to bed angry, refusing her husband's advances.

Phil Bruno drove his step-granddaughter home the following day at four fifteen. Nicole asked her mother if she could play with her friend in the apartment across the hall. Gloria told her it was fine but to remember to be home by 6:30 for dinner. When Nicole left, Phil Bruno inquired, "I thought you two always ate at five thirty. Are you planning on Paulie being home by six thirty?"

Gloria laughed as her facial expression changed to instant anger and said bitterly, "He'll never come home that early. It's all about him, his friends and his fucking cars. Phil, I'm sick of his shit and I'm sick of him. I asked him for a car and he told me I have to wait until he pays off his two lifts. I can't even go to see my mother."

Gloria was a beautiful temptress and Phil Bruno was embarrassingly smitten by her. He boldly asked, "So if you know he's not coming home by six thirty, why did you change your dinner schedule?" Gloria got up to use the bathroom. As she walked past Phil, she caressed his face and said, "Maybe I just enjoy your company."

Phil got up from the table. When Gloria returned, he said, "Listen, I enjoy your company, too, but I have to get going. Whenever you need a ride to your mother's, just let me know the day before and if I can swing by, I will. Just remember, we have to keep that between us. If we don't keep it to ourselves, everyone will start getting suspicious about nothing."

Her pre-planned response was immediate as she said softly, "Tomorrow morning at eight thirty, if possible."

Phil exhaled loudly and said, "I'll see what I can do. I can call you from the shop before I leave." Gloria walked him to the door and gave him an ever-so-brief kiss on the lips. When Phil got to his car he looked up and saw Gloria waving to him from the living room window. He returned the wave and drove home.

Phil Bruno was fifty two years old and his step-daughter-in-law was twenty nine. He loved his wife, Teresa, but was caving in to mid-life lust. Phil Bruno fantasized about making love to this beautiful, sultry, young woman. He wasn't sure if anything was really developing between them, but was tempted to find out. Regardless of his work schedule, Phil Bruno was going to figure out a way to drive Gloria the following day.

The following morning Phil Bruno called Gloria and told her to wait in the lobby of her apartment building. He arrived in ten minutes. Gloria was wearing a very short, revealing dress, her hair was down, and her blouse was unbuttoned at the top. She was sexy from head to toe.

She got into the car and thanked Phil for being kind enough to give her a ride. Phil's eyes were affixed on the young beauty's legs. He was swallowing the bait like a hungry fish. His 1976 Cadillac was equipped with a full length bench seat. Gloria slid her body closer and closer to Phil. When they were a few blocks from her mother's house she abruptly asked Phil to pull over. She didn't want her mother to see her getting out of his car. Phil obliged and devilishly said, "Gloria you look really stunning. Are you sure you're going to your mother's house dressed like that?"

Gloria answered, "Dressed like what?"

"Sexy," he answered.

Gloria replied, "I dressed like this for some older mature gentleman I'm trying to impress. Please don't tell anyone, Philly boy."

Phil remarked, "'Philly boy.' What's with that?"

"I'm just having a little fun with you, don't be so serious," she replied.

Before exiting the car, she thanked him for the ride and gave him a brief but welcome kiss on the lips. As she walked away, Phil Bruno studied her every sway. He could feel his blood pumping through his rapidly beating heart as his lustful thoughts heated his brow. Gloria was arousing him in every way.

Paulie had planned a weekend getaway for his family at a Carnival in Pennsylvania the first weekend in June. His plan was to close the shop early on Saturday and leave for Pennsylvania by noon. Nicole was all excited about going on the Carnival rides with her Mom and Dad. But Gloria had selfish ideas that didn't include Paulie or Nicole. She didn't have to work, and had plenty of free time on her hands. If an idle mind is truly the devil's workshop, Gloria was becoming an inescapable inmate.

She wanted out of her marriage. Her parents never thought he was good enough and she suddenly believed it. Phil Bruno was the perfect prey and perfect catch. Their afternoon coffee evolved into wine, and the casual kiss grew into long, touching make-out sessions. Innocently, Nicole prevented the couple's dalliances from becoming a sexual encounter. She was always around and always too close. It was dangerous.

On the Friday evening before their planned trip, Gloria and Paulie drank wine, smoked a little weed and made love. The love making was a diversion, a mere cover-up for her self-absorbed and devious scheme. After a tiresome day of work, drink and sex, Paulie fell asleep. He awakened at three in the morning to urinate. When Paulie returned to bed, Gloria told him she didn't feel well. He told her to try and get some sleep. She waited until he fell asleep and put her fingers down her throat and forced herself to vomit. Startled by the gagging sound of his wife, Paulie woke. She said, "Paulie I think I got some kind of a stomach bug. I feel awful." She hurried into the bathroom and pretended to be vomiting.

The following morning she persuaded Paulie to take Nicole to the Carnival without her. The tickets for the Carnival and the hotel were paid in advance and not refundable. She acted convincingly upset and assured her husband that everything would be fine. Gloria insisted that she could take care of herself and didn't want to ruin Nicole's weekend of fun.

Still over-joyed that Gloria made love to him, he swallowed the bait. He and his daughter left for Pennsylvania Saturday as planned. The unhappy housewife could now lure the smitten Phil Bruno to spend time alone with her. Gloria was becoming a wizard of deceit.

She knew all too well that Phil Bruno worked every Saturday. If the weather was inclement he would move his small crew to an inside job. She kept calling his office until finally at noon, he answered his business phone. Gloria spoke like a lonely little girl, informing him that she was home alone. She invited him to join her for lunch. The sexually inflamed fifty two year old could not resist her salacious invite. He arrived at her apartment at twelve thirty.

He rang her doorbell and she peered through the peep hole to ensure it was indeed Phil. Relieved that is was, she opened the door and let him in. She had just taken a shower and her long dark hair was still wet. Wearing a long mesh bathrobe, she greeted him with a long French kiss. He passionately fondled her body as they made their way to the bedroom. Phil slid his hands into the front opening of her robe and could feel that she was not wearing any under-garments. He became instantly aroused. His desire to have her became intoxicating as he undressed and put on the condom she gave him. They made passionate love.

When they were finished they began to drink wine. Phil's rapid consumption of wine eradicated any inclination of guilt. In less than twenty minutes, Phil was prepared for another round of love-making. Gloria devilishly acquiesced to his desires, moaning in delight at every thrust. When both of them were physically satisfied, reality set in. *Where do we go from here? Do we just keep committing adultery or do we plan a lifetime together.*

CHAPTER 22

The Corvo residence had been freshly painted and was now in move-in condition. Danny and Delia began furnishing their home in early June. Abby was on a cloud walk, discovering her new bedroom had its own bathroom, a luxury enjoyed by few kids her age.

Danny Corvo was the closest to a father Abagail ever knew. She knew he wasn't her biological father but she always felt his fatherly love for her was limitless. All she knew about her biological dad was him being killed in a car accident. Abagail was fourteen and an over-achieving math student. She could never find the courage to ask her mother about their closeness in age. She thought it best not to ask until the time was right.

In a few short weeks her mother's name would change from Hoffman to Corvo. Abagail lusted for her name to be changed to Corvo. Again, the young teen beauty would wait until she felt the time was appropriate.

Their June 26th wedding day was blessed with a perpetual presence of the infinite sun-filled sky. Bishop Pestoni, at the request of Victoria Galliano officiated the Corvo/ Hoffman wedding. The NYPD was present for traffic control. The handsome young couple looked like they were on a Hollywood set. In spite of her hardships, Delia Hoffman had aged beautifully. She had an angelic face, an unmatched deep blueness in her eyes, and a perfectly formed body.

The Church was filled with beautiful red and white roses that, with the exception of God, only Van Gogh could create. It was the same Church where the Corvo twins were baptized. Danny received the sacrament of penance, First Holy Communion, and Confirmation in this ornate venue. In Daniello's mind this day, his wedding day shined above all the rest. This was the day he would be bonded as one with the love of his life for the rest of his life.

Bishop Pestoni had served as Chaplin of the New York City fire department. He was loved and revered by Fire Chiefs from all the boroughs. When their beloved Chaplin officiated over a wedding, fire trucks from the nearby firehouses were dispatched to pay him honor. The presence of the gleaming monster trucks strategically in line added to the glamour of the day for the bride and groom. Horns blew and bells rang, paying homage to the newlyweds. In New York City where there are Firemen there are Policemen. The NYPD on horseback was a stunning and memorable sight. The large crowd of guests and by-standers marveled at the magnificence of the event.

The guests numbered in excess of two hundred people. Gus instructed that his family be seated on the Corvo side of the ballroom. Old habits die hard, and he requested the end corner table. Flanked by discreet bodyguards, Gus Galliano continued his lifelong practice of having his back to the wall and being able to see everyone in the room.

Danny and Delia chose an old classic, "For Once in My Life" for their wedding song. The song had been sung by many popular artists including Dean Martin and Frank Sinatra. It was masterfully redone by Stevie Wonder in the late sixties.

The band was set up in a large alcove in the main ballroom. The lead singer, a young Italian boy from the Fordham section of the Bronx, possessed a powerful voice and was versatile in his song choices. As the guests slowly entered the ballroom, the band entertained them with classical and pop music. When the band stopped playing, the guests comprehended the big moment had finally arrived. The lead singer made a hand gesture to silence the band. The curtains closed around the alcove, allowing the guests to refrain from distraction and focus on Mr. and Mrs. Daniello Covro. The newly-weds held hands as they slowly paced to the center of the ballroom. They were introduced as man and wife for the first time as the applauding guests rose to their feet. These people knew the difficult and turbulent journey the young couple had endured to reach this day.

The lead singer spoke slowly, emphasizing each syllable as he loudly exclaimed, "Distinguished Ladies and Gentleman, Mr. and Mrs. Daniello Corvo will dance their first dance as husband and wife to the great old classic, 'For Once in My Life.'" As the music started everyone acknowledged the tempo was modern, a little faster than any of the old classics. The harmonica was being played masterfully with a beautiful professionalism as the alcove curtain opened.

When the vocalist started to sing the startled bride screamed in childish admiration, "Oh My God, Oh My God it's Stevie Wonder!" Also startled, Danny spun around with rapid curiosity, bowed his head and began grinning. His eyes gleamed with jubilant appreciation as he scanned the room

327

until he found the Galliano family. He pointed his finger at Gus, gesturing his approval and gratitude with a wide-stretched smile. He understood only Gus Galliano could have the connections to arrange for this monumental surprise. The professional photographers became star struck as they snapped the amazing event from every angle.

Frank Derosa craved the opportunity to meet Gus Galliano, the man his mobster brother held in such high regard. He patiently waited until Danny sat at the Galliano table. He hurriedly made his way through the thick crowd of dancers and approached the Galliano table. Danny rose firmly, embracing the Lieutenant and began formal introductions. Gus extended Derosa a handshake as his head pivoted to capture Danny's attention. Gus knew Derosa was harmless as he said, "Danny isn't that the name you used to conceal your identity from my boys?"

Danny blushed and said, "Yes, that's the name I used but I must tell you, if it wasn't for the Lieutenant, I wouldn't have had the skills to save Nicky. He taught me everything I know about swimming and drowning." The table rattled with laughter.

A long visit to the Galliano table was not happening for anyone. Derosa could sense it was time to bid everyone farewell. He forfeited his common sense to curiosity as he asked, "Mr. Galliano, I think you may know my brother, Nick Derosa, from East Harlem." Gus concealed his disappointment as he curtly answered, "I heard the name. He works for a friend of mine." Derosa departed, knowing his inquiry was not worthy of further comment.

As the wedding festivities started to wind down, the newly-weds mingled with their guests. Danny sat with his friend Paulie Nartico and his wife. Paulie had drunk too much and appeared annoyed. Gloria excused herself to use the restroom. Paulie stared at his close friend and mumbled, "Danny, I have no idea what's up her ass. She doesn't have to work, I'm getting her a car next month, way before planned and she's always miserable. If you're still here when she gets back, you'll see that she's loaded. Remember when you told me you didn't want any money for the labor? You laughed and told me to have another kid."

Danny became annoyed at his friend's self-pity and said curtly, "Yeah, I remember."

Paulie lowered his voice to an embarrassed whisper and said, "Well the way things are going with her that physically can't happen. She treats me like I'm a leper. I really don't know why or what to do. Worse than that, she won't talk about it. Something weird is going on and I can't figure it out."

Danny could see Gloria stumbling to keep her balance as she returned to the table. He said, "She's coming back. Hang in there and when I get back from my honeymoon in two weeks, we'll hook up. Stay strong and keep trying to talk to her. You have to keep talking."

When the wedding ceremony ended, Danny and Delia were driven to their new home, where they spent their first night as husband and wife. The following morning, the young couple rode a limo to Kennedy Airport. Their destination was Rome, Italy.

Their honeymoon filled their hungry hearts with romance as the newlyweds tried to make up for lost time. The Corvos embraced everything the Eternal City had to offer. After one week, they flew to Berlin, Germany where they enjoyed basking in the culture that both shared. Their luggage was filled with gifts for their loved ones back in the States.

When the plane landed in New York, they felt like they just left. Good times evaporate rapidly even for the young. The two week honeymoon abroad had consequences for

Danny. Corvo Construction had three sites being developed and two of them were on a strict time schedule. He knew his time would be consumed with work. Business was important, but he couldn't forget the promise made to his friend Paulie Nartico.

After two days of hustling from jobsite to jobsite, Danny was confident that Corporal Rodrigues had everything running on schedule. He was pleased. It was now time to keep his promise to his friend.

Danny arrived at Paulie's garage at ten o'clock on a Wednesday morning. He was greeted by Paulie's new grease monkey, Bobby Bestone. Danny said, "How are you doing? Remember me. I'm Danny Corvo? Is Paulie around?"

Danny's reputation caused the young mechanic to be cautious and respectful. He answered, "Listen, I don't want to be a blabber-mouth but I know you two guys are really close. Paulie is all fucked up. His wife left him over the weekend. She went back home to her Mother's house in Throgg's neck and took Nicole with her. Paulie's been drinking like crazy. He thinks she's fucking around with another guy but can't figure out whom. I know he has a ton of respect for you. I hope you can get through to him and help him out. No one else can."

Danny stared at the kid and finally asked, "Is there anything else I should know?"

Bobby replied, "No, not that I know of right now."

Danny's first stop was the Wall Bar. Paulie was the lone customer, sitting at the end of the bar talking to the owner Mike. Mike looked up at Danny and seemed relieved that he showed up. He said, "Hey Danny, how's married life treating you?"

Danny didn't think it was an appropriate question under the Nartico circumstances. He answered bluntly, "We're good. Thanks."

Danny stood next to Paulie and ordered a glass of club soda with lemon. He leaned over to Paulie and whispered, "Finish your drink and come with me. We have to talk." The partially intoxicated Paulie started to blabber. Danny's large hand encapsulated the back of his slim neck like a vice-grip and he said, "We have to talk now. Get your ass up and come with me." Paulie knew the voice, knew the tone and knew it was time to go.

Danny got into his car and his old friend followed sitting in the passenger seat. He drove a few blocks and parked by a vacant lot. He glared at Paulie appraisingly and said, "You're fucked up at ten thirty in the morning. If you think this is going to get you your wife back. You're quite mistaken and dumb too. Have you been talking to her like I told you to?"

Paulie clenched his fists and began hitting himself in the head like an out of control mental patient. Unable to control himself, he began to sob, muttering "She told me she doesn't love me anymore and wants a divorce. When I asked her if there was someone else she just laughed. I tried to reason with her. I wanted to know if there was any chance of making it right again. I asked her if we could work it out."

Continuing his drunken sobbing, he cried out, "She said, 'Work it out, who do you think you are one of the fucking Beatles? There is no working this out. I'm done with you, your cars and your fucking loser friends.'"

Danny exhaled in disgust and said, "This all happened too fast. Someone had to get inside her head. You have to get yourself together, and I mean fast. Stop the drinking, go back to work and prepare to hire a good lawyer. If you think losing Gloria is bad, wait until you go to court and she gets full custody of Nicole. If you keep drinking and stop working you won't even get visitation rights. The good news is that she just

331

may be depressed, and in time she'll see what she's losing. But you have to straighten out, ok?"

Paulie's dark sad puppy eyes gazed at Danny. He said, "I'm really glad your grandfather introduced me to you. They don't make friends like you. Now suppose she is fucking around with someone. Can you help me kill him?"

Danny laughed in a humorous appreciation of his question but his face became demonic as he snarled, "Absolutely not. We'll kill both of them." Those seven words registered a sobering reality. The heart-broken mechanic was unable to decipher whether the combat marine's comment was a joke or a promise.

Paulie digested his friend's advice with an open mind. He returned to his shop and pulled the motor and transmission from the 1968 Camaro and persuaded himself that giving her the car as soon as possible could soften her depression and reignite her love for him.

With Gloria and Nicole living with Nicole's parents, Paulie lost all desire to return to their Williams Bridge road apartment. Ironically, he ate dinner with his mother and insidious step-father, Phil Bruno. Every night after dinner, he returned to the shop and continued working on her car until his eyes became blurry with fatigue.

A true narcissist, Phil Bruno was able to emancipate himself from the guilt of committing adultery with his daughter-in-law. He cleverly managed to convince Paulie and Teresa that Gloria was simply depressed and had too much free time on her hands.

By mid-July, the 1968 Camaro convertible was restored to show-room condition. Bobby Bestone painted the exterior of the car white and had a new blue interior and dark blue convertible top professionally installed. All the colors she loved. Anxious to see Gloria's reaction, he had the car registered and inspected.

Paulie was obligated to pick up his daughter on the last Saturday in July. It was a clear hot day—a perfect opportunity to put the top down and show off the beauty of the 1968 Camaro. Paulie had Bobby Bestone drive his car and follow him to his in-law's house as he drove the eye-catching '68 Camaro.

When Paulie arrived, Nicole was anxiously waiting in her grandparent's driveway. Her protective grandfather, Lou, held her hand. Paulie parked the Camaro in the empty driveway and exited the car. His father-in-law silently stared at his son-in-law. Nicole let her grandfather's hand go and ran to embrace her father. Paulie hugged his little girl and gave her a prolonged kiss on the forehead. He focused his attention on his father-in-law and said, "Hi is Gloria around?"

Lou answered dryly, "No, she went out."

Paulie replied, "Do you know when she will be back?"

Lou shook his head from side to side. He replied, "Look Paulie, I told my wife and I'm telling you, I'm not getting into the middle of this mess. Gloria is miserable… even when she's here. She blames it all on you and I know you have a very different song to sing, but I'm not getting involved. Please don't interrogate me. My heart isn't so good."

Paulie nodded and told Nicole to give her grandpa a kiss goodbye. He handed his father-in-law an envelope containing the car papers and said, "These are the papers for the Camaro." He then handed Lou the keys saying, "She asked me for a car, so I got her the car she always lusted for. I'll bring Nicole home by ten tomorrow morning as I promised. I won't be late. Have a good night."

Paulie got into his car and told Nicole to sit in the back seat. He asked Bobby to drive. Paulie's brain was circulating with suspicion and he was determined to find out what was happening to his marriage. He vividly remembered his friend Danny Corvo telling him someone got into her head. It was a big ugly question but one that had to be answered. Who and how?

Phil Bruno had started construction of a one story farmhouse on his newly acquired New Canaan Connecticut property. He had convinced his wife Teresa the new home was for weekend getaways filled with romance and relaxation far away from the cacophony of the city. But Phil Bruno also fantasized about sharing the home with his young mistress.

Danny had relinquished some of his duties in Corvo Construction to Corporal Rodrigues by awarding him a small percentage of the business. The young Portuguese Rodrigues was a faithful, loyal, and an ambitious ally of Danny. Corvo Construction was growing rapidly and now employed over forty people. As Rodrigues absorbed more responsibility, Danny realized more free time to study case law with Professor Bennett. Rodrigues was paid handsomely for his extra effort and responsibility.

On the third Sunday of every month, Danny remained home in his private office studying law. He knew the last Saturday of every month would bring grueling law exams by Professor Bennett. He never lost sight of the frightening fact that he was attempting something accomplished by very few.

On those days, Delia took Abby to visit her Aunts and Grandpa Nelson. Danny demanded undisturbed quiet time in order to fully absorb the material. He unplugged the house phones and his private business phone.

At two o'clock in the afternoon, the doorbell rang. Danny peered through the dark sheer curtains and saw it was Paulie Nartico. Guilty about turning his back on a friend in need, he convinced himself it was time for a break and answered the door. Nartico did not look well. He appeared pale and pasty as his skin tone teetered on a shade of gray. But he was sober. The two friends embraced as Danny led his unexpected guest into the kitchen.

Paulie declined his offer for something to eat but accepted a glass of juice. Danny sat down opposite his friend and asked, "So what's going on?" Paulie placed his head in his left hand and started to rub his forehead in circles of frustration. Danny repeated his question, "Come on it can't be that bad, what's going on?"

After a long gulp of juice he said, "Well, Danny, I did it. I broke my ass with the kid Bobby and fixed the sixty eight Camaro that she wanted. Rebuild the motor, new interior, new convertible top, tires you name it I fixed it. I registered the car, paid the insurance and drove it to her parent's house a few weeks ago when I had to pick up Nicole. She wasn't home. I gave the paperwork and the keys to her father. He told me he would give it to her but was not going to get involved.

"Yesterday my friend, Peter, you know him from that Caldo incident, told me she traded it in. He saw the car on the lot at Pape Chevrolet on Tremont Avenue. I swung by there on my way over here, and sure enough it is there." Paulie got up quickly and asked if he could use the bathroom. Danny waited patiently until he returned, knowing there was a lot more to this unpleasant saga.

Paulie reseated himself opposite Danny and resumed speaking, "I called her parent's house and of course she either isn't home or doesn't want to talk to me. The one time she spoke to me, she told me in the most mocking way to talk to her lawyer."

Danny abruptly thrust his opened hand in front of Paulie's troubled face and shouted, "Stop, stop. Did you do what I told you and get a good lawyer?"

Paulie answered, "Yes, I did. I hired Otto Fusco; he's supposed to be really good. Well, he better be because he's not cheap."

Danny went to the refrigerator and took out two beers. He handed one to Paulie and said, "One isn't going to get us stoned and you need to calm down. Please continue."

Paulie gulped his beer and continued, "Fusco isn't going to be able to find out why she traded that car in so I did the next best thing. I asked Phil if he could find out. He still drops Nicole off from school like he did when we lived on Williams Bridge. The kid has nothing to do with what's going on with me and the mother so he still drops her off."

Danny said sarcastically, "Hmmm that's interesting, so what did Phil find out?"

Paulie's voice broke up into a crying mutter and said, "She told him the car was sold because she doesn't want anything in her life that reminds her of me. She traded it in for a used 72 Chevrolet Impala. She probably got ripped off big time."

Paulie was hopelessly in love with his wife. Even the strong-willed Danny Corvo couldn't begin to imagine how he would personally handle his friend's circumstances. With a theatrical calmness he said softly, "Listen you're doing all the right things. You're not using the kid as the pawn in a chess game. Phil and your mom are still feeding and transporting Nicole after school, demonstrating that they are not taking sides. You hired a good lawyer. Be patient. I know her selling the car got you frustrated and disappointed. Just remember people say and do some crazy shit when they're depressed. I wish Delia knew her better. Sometimes girls will tell a friend more than they will tell their own family. Keep working, keep being the good father that you are, and be patient. Most important is that you stay calm."

Paulie thanked Danny for listening and apologized for disturbing him. Danny assured him that he was not disturbing him and would always be available for his friend.

It wasn't one thing that disturbed Danny Corvo. It was everything his friend had told him. It was a lot to swallow. Married life was euphoric for him and a life without Delia was unfathomable. He planned on sharing Paulie's circumstances with her that evening. With an abundance of hopefulness, he prayed her female intuition could provide some insight as how to approach and resolve the colossal Nartico nightmare.

Danny spoke in extensive detail for forty-five minutes before dinner. Delia listened intently to every word of the Nartico malady. Delia mentally put herself in Gloria Nartico's position in an attempt to understand her behavior. She explored all the possibilities that she believed could provoke a wife to become so volatile. "Danny I know this is bothering you big time, and if it bothers you, it bothers me. I'm going to keep twirling it around in my head and when I think I have something that will help I'll tell you. Okay?" she said.

When dinner was over, Danny returned to his law studies. At ten o'clock, Abby, Delia and Danny went upstairs to their respective bedrooms. After making love, Delia slowly turned to her husband and said, "Danny I keep thinking about this Gloria-Paulie fiasco. Does Paulie ever mess around with other women?"

Without preface Danny replied, "I thought about that too and I can honestly say with certainty that he doesn't. Now, before he married Gloria, this guy had a new chick every week; sometimes two. The minute he started dating Gloria he became a monogamous man."

Delia said humorously, "Monogamous, you sound like a lawyer already. Seriously, if he is monogamous, someone got into her head as you suggested earlier. So, she may have some petty reasons for being upset but she doesn't have any real serious reason for being so angry. I mean some of the things she said were awful. I hate to suggest it but I think someone has to follow her every movement and find out what she's doing. This whole thing will never be resolved until he finds out just who got into her head. I hope I'm wrong, but there has to be someone else. I'm not saying she's cheating but she has to be at least listening to someone else. That's the only thing that makes sense."

Danny reached over and gave his wife a goodnight kiss. He said, "Thanks we'll talk again tomorrow. I need to get some sleep. Love you."

Delia softly sighed, "Goodnight. When we talk tomorrow, I have a quick question to ask you. Not a big deal so get some sleep and we can talk tomorrow after dinner. Love you too, Goodnight."

Danny knew Monday's schedule was devoid of free time. It was going to be a long engaging day and being on time for dinner was doubtful. He turned toward her and started playfully rubbing his nose to hers.

In a cute, girlish voice, she exclaimed, "I thought you were tired?"

He answered, "I'm a little tired but not too tired to answer your quick question if there is such a thing."

Delia was accustomed to his sudden sometimes sarcastic wit and asked for a minute to use the bathroom. When she returned to bed Danny had his pillow propped up against the headboard. He said, "Well I'm awake now so what is your question?"

Delia shimmed closer and put her arms around him saying, "Have you ever thought of names for a boy or a girl?"

Danny propped himself up higher, removing any trace of sleepiness. His blue eyes widened with anticipation and asked gleefully, "Should I?"

She prolonged her answer and gave him a passionate kiss. "You better. I'm pregnant. I found out this morning. Imagine being called on a Sunday."

This would be the happiest moment in the life of Danny Corvo. The ultimate joy had arrived. Danny loved kids and the reality of having a child with the woman he cherished captivated his heart and serenaded his soul.

After they resumed kissing and laughing, Danny remarked, "I'm so glad you told me tonight. Boy that didn't take us long."

Dee said, "Yes, it was really fast. If my math is right, I think it happened on the first night of our honeymoon. Uh-oh, I wonder if those fertility pills the doctor put me on had anything to do with it."

Danny's heart rate reached the normal range. There was no sleep in sight as he continued, "As long as I had everything to do with it I'm happy. Listen, tomorrow I have a really long day. Bobby K asked me to meet him for lunch and Nicky wants me to meet him after work. I had a surprise planned for you. Nicky knows this really good dog breeder and we were going to pick out two Doberman pups tomorrow. One for his junkyard and one for us... but that's no longer a good idea."

There was a childish sadness to her tone as she muttered, "Why not. You know how much I always wanted a dog."

He explained, "Dobermans are very protective and if the child is here first the dog will instinctively protect the baby. If the dog is here first he may interpret the baby as an intruder... not a good scenario. Also I know you're going to ask, why a Doberman? The neighborhood is changing. It's still good up here but the lower end is definitely changing. What neighborhoods do you think the dirt bags target to rob? I didn't want to upset you, but there was a break-in two blocks away. They broke the basement window to enter the house. Once in, they had a field day. They stole jewelry, money, you name it. I'm having iron bars installed on our basement windows next week and then I'm going to search around for an alarm system. I'm not going to live in fear. Also, my dear, you are going to get your pistol license. I'm going to have Chris Chan teach you how to shoot."

Delia whispered, "Danny Corvo, I love you so much but you are fucking crazy. You're really going to trust me with a gun?"

The excitement of becoming a father made him restless. He tossed and turned, fluffed and repeatedly flipped his pillow. When fatigue finally overwhelmed his exhausted mind, he fell asleep in the splendor of his wife's slender arms.

CHAPTER 23

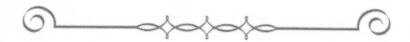

I t was early August. Bobby K had moved to Yonkers but was still employed in the Bronx. He had not seen his childhood friend Danny Corvo since the June 26th wedding. There was a lot of catching up to do.

The overly cautious Corvo entered the Wall Bar through the side entrance. His eyes perused the clientele with the alertness of a sentry. The two friends embraced and sat at the far corner of the bar, a wise tactic he learned from Gus Galliano, to always be aware of his surroundings. Each of them ordered a beer and a sandwich.

Bobby K demonstrated his unique sense of humor was not lost in parenthood. Pointing to the very visible additional inches on his beer-bellied waistline he said jokingly, "Corvo I hate your ass sometimes. Look at you. No beer-belly bursting with muscle and even your teeth are white. I hate your ass."

Danny chuckled with a respectful appreciation of his old friend's humor and said, "Well, some of us have to work really hard but I still love your dumb Irish ass."

The Wall Bar was in the center of the old neighborhood. Bobby explained that he'd moved his family to Yonkers because there were better schools and the neighborhood was safer. The old neighborhood was not as solid as it used to be when they were kids. He told his old friend that if he had his kind of money, he could have moved up where the Corvos lived, among the rich gangsters and businessmen.

Danny was a beaming starburst of pride as he told Bobby that Dee was pregnant. That good news called for another round of beer. Bobby's round Irish face reddened with excitement as he said, "I can't wait to tell Ginny, she's going to be so happy for you two. Do you remember when you and Dee were apart and you came to visit us? You had so much fun playing with our kids that when you left Ginny was crying like a newborn baby after the first smack on the ass. I can remember her saying how much you loved kids. She knew you and Dee were perfect together. She blamed the war and curses it until today. Thank God things worked out. You two belong together. Anyway, that's enough mush-marsh. What else is going on?"

Danny explained in brief detail that he was studying law with an Irish law Professor named Bennett and was planning on taking the bar exam in about six months. Bobby K's facial expression changed from rosy to bright red as he said with amusement, "An Irish law professor? I didn't think there were any. I thought we were all plumbers, cops, fireman and bartenders. That's pretty funny."

The two old friends enjoyed their casual lunch but soon realized time was running out. They agreed to have one more final beer before departing back to work. Two men in their late twenties entered the front entrance of the bar. They were loud and appeared to already have a belly-full of booze.

Bobby K shifted his bar stool closer to Danny and whispered, "See those two? It's scumbags like that who are ruining our neighborhood. Let me tell you what they did. They went over to the Kentucky Fried Chicken place on Tremont Avenue, the one near the car wash. It was late at night and the only person working was the guy who closes. He's an Old Italian guy who speaks broken English. They close at midnight and his job is to clean up and serve any customers that come in between ten and midnight, usually very few.

These two went in there right before midnight and ordered a bucket of fried chicken. The old guy obliged and gave them what they wanted. When the time came to pay they grabbed him by his arms and forced him to his knees. First, they made him make clucking sounds and flap his arms around like a fucking chicken. Then they threw chicken pieces on the floor and told the old man to eat it. When he refused the both of them pushed him onto his belly and mounted him. They wouldn't get off until he started eating the chicken. Scumbags!"

Danny was perplexed but cautious and said, "And you know this happened how?"

Bobby replied, "Do you know the big guy everyone calls "The Moose?"

Danny made a head gesture indicating that he knew of him. Bobby continued," Well, they came here on that very night and bragged about their escapade. Moose told me that when he went to KFC on the following Monday the owner told him what happened. It was the same story. Moose didn't give anyone up but he knew it was them."

Danny stared down at the two punks and asked, "Who are they?"

Bobby answered with great certainty, "The shorter one is a guy named Lockhart. Everyone calls him Junior. The other one, the real big guy is Shady O'Shea. Shady is what everyone calls him. I don't think anyone knows his real first name. In the meantime, the prick has to be Irish or at least part. I'm telling you Danny these are the type of people ruining our neighborhood."

Bobby K glanced at the clock and said, "We have about five minutes left so there's one more story about the two assholes."

Danny nodded saying, "I can't wait."

Bobby continued, "Sometime in July there was this colored kid walking home from Jacobi. He's a college kid and his father got him a summer job in the hospital as a janitor to help pay his tuition. He works the night shift from four thirty in the afternoon until one in the morning. Junior and Shady were driving around, blitzed as usual. Shady carries a phony police badge. They hate colored people, Italians, Puerto Ricans and Jews, so they decided to have some fun with the colored kid. They pulled the car in front of him as he crossed Height Avenue up by Loretta Park. Shady flashed his phony shield and put cuffs on him. The poor kid was scared shitless. He then forced the skinny little colored kid into the back of the car, smashing his head on the drip edge of the roof on the way in.

"They were driving a black four-door Chevy Belair, so I guess the frightened kid thought they were really cops. Once in the car and handcuffed, there wasn't really anything the kid could do. They drove the kid all the way out to the Orchard Beach parking lot. They joked about how the little nigger kid kept begging them to let him go. When they finally let him out of the car, Junior stood in front of the kid telling him he committed the unforgiveable crime of being a Nigger in his neighborhood. Shady smashed him in the head from behind with a beer bottle. The kid went right out. Then for their grand finale they stripped him of all his clothing while he was still unconscious.

"The following morning the Police found him roaming around naked. They picked him up and put a blanket around him and took him to Jacobi to be treated. Could you imagine how the poor father felt? Before you ask, once again their drunken asses bragged about their conquest. This time, my brother Tim was here, and listened to the whole story. You know my brother, Tim—he ain't no bullshitter. Hey, look at the clock. We better get going."

Danny walked past Lockhart and O'Shea, heading for the front exit of the bar. Pestered by the story he stopped and quickly pivoted starring at the two punks. His eyes glittered with rage. He folded his arms as his eyes became affixed on their faces. He was purposefully enticing them to make a comment, an inquiry into what he was looking at. Wisely they turned away from Corvo. Lockhart knew it was the U.S. Marine fighting machine that crippled bikers. Junior Lockhart was only as crazy as he had to be. He knew the both of them could not survive taking on the lethal Corvo.

The two stories had scratched the surface of his lust for street justice. He harbored his instinct, not knowing if the story was fact or boastful fiction. He humored himself recalling Gus Galliano's words of wisdom, "le aquile non cacciano le mosche." The eagle does not hunt flies.

Danny met Nicky Galliano at the Colden Bar at six thirty. He was flush with pride and anxious to tell his close friend that Dee was pregnant. Nicky had a glimpse of a smile on his face but appeared troubled. His usual ear-to-ear grin and protruding dimples were nowhere to be found. He sat on the stool close to Danny and let out a loud sigh as he ordered a beer and a shot of rye. Danny's instinct told him that his friend was troubled. He thought it best to let Nicky speak first.

345

Nicky said, "I'm glad you were able to stop. How are you doing?"

Danny answered, "I'm busy but okay. The big question is how are you doing? You look like you have the weight of the world on your shoulders. What's going on?"

The first shot of rye vanished as Nicky ordered another one. He looked at Danny as his head swung from side to side. There was a scary seriousness in his eyes as he said, "Sonia and I have been trying to have a kid since we were first married. Unfortunately you were in Nam for the wedding but we've been trying to conceive for almost five years. She even took fertility pills but nothing seemed to work. So, I went to the doctor and he told me I should have my sperm tested—so I did."

The only time Danny had seen Nicky Galliano cry was when his twin brother Tommy had been killed in the car accident. The strong-willed Galliano forcefully restrained from crying but his eyes were red and springing tears. He continued, "Danny, it's me. I can't make children. I didn't tell anyone yet, not even Sonia. My Mom and Pop are going to be demolished. They were so hopeful that they would have a grandchild. My father keeps telling me that if it's a boy I should name him Tommy after my brother. God this sucks."

Danny labored to find the words in his arsenal of diction that could console his friend. There weren't any. He knew it was something he and his wife would have to live through. Danny expressed his disappointment and decided the best strategy was to switch gears. He attempted to get Nicky's mind off his personal trouble by switching to their mutual friend. Nicky was genuine. He liked Paulie and felt bad that he was having marital problems. When Danny mentioned having Gloria followed Nicky did not hesitate to offer the services of Detective Ryan.

He seemed calmer, back in control as he said, "Get me the mother's address, and I'll set it up with Ryan. Just remember this would be a side job for Ryan, and you'll have to pay him probably a hundred fifty or so. Are you okay with that?" Danny returned a positive nod. Nicky continued, "People are so stupid. Paulie and Gloria and living high on the hog and have a great little girl so what are they going to do....fuck it all up. I'm not a fucking head doctor but all I know is that kids from a divorced family always have problems. Gloria's a good-looking chick. I hope she's not fucking around. Paulie will lose it."

Nicky's personal problems saddened Danny. He gathered his thoughts and said," I don't know if there is anything today's doctors can do to help you but I'd find the best doctor in the field and go see him. The best in the world is probably right here in Manhattan."

The fingers on Danny's right hand started making small circles on his forehead. He started to rub his eyes as if he were unable to focus. Nicky knew the look. Something was disturbing his friend. Nicky asked, "Okay, so you know I'm fucked up, but what's wrong with you."

Danny responded, "Aside from you and Paulie having problems, there's nothing wrong with me. In fact I was really happy, but now I feel bad telling you what I came here to tell you."

Nicky emitted unexpected laughter and said, "Let me guess, Dee is having a baby."

Danny sighed with relief and replied, "Yes, you got it, Dee is having a baby."

Nicky embraced the closest resemblance of a brother he had and kissed him on the cheek saying, "I'm really happy for you. You gave me a ray of hope. I will definitely find the best doctor in the world. I don't care if I have to fly to fucking China."

Nicky Galliano was a unique kind of guy who possessed an uncanny way of controlling his emotions. He could rotate from hot to cold and from enraged to calm in the blink of an eye. Nicky was Gus Galliano's son, and business matters would always trump personal issues, unless the personal issues were life threating.

The very next day, Nicky called Danny and asked for Gloria's mother's address. Danny explained that he needed a little more time. Both of them agreed that Paulie had to remain ignorant of their plan. The solution was easier than envisioned. During a very mundane conversation, Danny asked Paulie if Gloria was all Italian. When Paulie answered one hundred percent, Danny found his opening. First, he threw a curve ball, asking what part of Italy her parents were from. When Paulie answered Naples, he immediately inquired about her maiden name. Paulie told him Colarusso. A simple browse through the Bronx telephone directory revealed their address and phone number. The plan was now in motion.

Detective Ryan never asked a Galliano the motive behind an assignment. He was paid handsomely for his expert investigative work and his ability to probe and extract information from his faithful colleagues in the New York City Police Department.

A week passed and Ryan had the information Danny sought. It was bizarre and deeply troubling. Ryan had photos of Gloria Nartico and her father-in-law Phil Bruno entering and exiting the Whitestone Motel. The photos revealed the couple kissing in the parking lot of the Motel, both before and after their stay. It was evident that this meeting was not about Phil Bruno giving advice or trying to help his stepson and Gloria reconcile their problems. These encounters were not impromptu. They were insidiously planned meetings driven by adulterated lust.

Nicky paid Ryan and took the envelope. When his got into his car, he reviewed the photos. He kept going through the ten photos over and over like a poker player in disbelief that he possessed a royal flush. He could not believe his eyes. His teeth gritted as he muttered, "The fucking whore bitch is fucking around with her husband's step-father. "

Nicky stopped at the first pay phone and called Danny's home. Dee told him that Danny had gone for one of his long runs but should be home in an hour. Nicky stopped at the Wall Bar to have a drink and settle his nerves. He knew Danny Corvo was going to flip out. This was an unimaginable deed of pure evil.

It was a crisp, clear September Sunday and Nicky intended his visit to the Corvo house to appear social. He stopped at the local German-American bakery and purchased Linzer Tarts that he knew Dee and Abby loved so much. He arrived at two thirty in the afternoon, in time for coffee. Danny came out of the shower and greeted his friend, knowing this was more than a social visit. There was news from Ryan.

After coffee, the two young men retreated to the study. Danny was anxious, asking, "What did Ryan find out?"

Nicky sarcastically laughed and said, "Bro, you better sit down. You're not going to believe this shit."

Danny avoided his instruction and motioned with his hands for Nicky to start speaking. He stood up and threw the envelope on Danny's desk saying, "Look at this shit. She's fucking around with her father-in-law, Paulie's step-father. Walt Disney couldn't make this shit up."

Danny picked up the envelope and sat in his chair. His eyes were seared on the revealing photos, his face expressionless. He concentrated on each photo as if challenged to memorize each one. Over and over he shuffled them between his hands. Rising from his chair he walked to the window facing the rear courtyard. He turned his back, avoiding eye contact with Nicky. He said bluntly, "My first instinct tells me that he has to go. This will ruin Paulie's life, his mother's life, and the kid's life. I don't know where, when or how just yet but this dirt bag has to go, the sooner the better."

Nicky reminded Danny that Gus had ordered them to stay clean. His voice became bold and brash saying, "I know exactly how you feel and you got to know that under my circumstances I'm all for torturing the bastard, but my Pop is right. We have to stay clean. Look at you, getting ready to take the bar exam and become a lawyer. I don't want to throw it in your face, but all of this lawyer shit is happening because the old man loves you the same way he loves me. I know you're studying your ass off but he made it happen. We can't let him down. Think about it Danny, it won't be right. Understand?"

Danny lowered his voice saying sternly, "You understand what you understand and I understand what I want to understand. I'm going to do what I'm going to do. I told you and Gus many times, it isn't a crime if you don't get caught. I promise I won't do anything rash or stupid, but I'm going to do what has to be done. I can't believe that you of all people are questioning my reaction to this guy."

Nicky Galliano was troubled by Danny's comeback to his logic. Did his experience in Viet Nam shroud his ability to reason? Nicky knew all too well that getting Corvo to change his mind was like trying to relocate the stars. Some things in life were indeed impossible. He had to make one more attempt to reason with his friend.

Nicky would now be the one standing before the window facing the rear courtyard. His hands were placed deeply into the front pockets of his pants as his fingers nervously massaged the coins he had. He inhaled deeply, pausing to gather his thoughts to make a closing argument as if he were pleading before a judge. He annunciated his words purposefully slowly, saying, "Okay, bro help me understand what you're thinking. I know how close you and Paulie have been all these years. You have both done a lot for each other. I get it. What I don't understand is why you would risk everything you worked for! Have you forgotten Dee is having a baby? Please listen. I agreed with the Rango thing. That's why I helped you, but this is not even close. What are you going to do, kill everyone who does something you don't like? Think about it, Danny. I hate to break it to you but you're only listening to his side of the story. I'll bet if you spoke to Gloria you'll get a whole different tale."

Danny re-seated himself, resting his feet on the edge of the bold oak desk. He remained unresponsive for a moment as he unbuttoned the top of his shirt. Finally he began to speak. "I don't have to listen to anything Gloria has to say. Ask yourself this question, if Phil Bruno refused to fuck his own daughter-in-law what would have happened? Okay, I'll concede maybe she would have found someone else to fuck but it wouldn't be Paulie's step-father and his mother's newly-acquired husband. That's an altogether different story. If that were the case, we wouldn't be having this conversation. If left alone, Phil Bruno will divorce his wife and probably marry Paulie's wife and take away his daughter! Too many lives will be ruined. Now to answer your question; no, I don't plan on killing everyone. Just the ones, who need it, like Rango."

Nicky Galliano was disappointed. He pleaded his case and was unable to crack the surface of Corvo's stubbornness. He contemplated Danny's words, "This dirt-bag has to go." He didn't have to analyze those words nor did he need to seek

351

interruption from his seasoned father. He knew exactly what Danny meant. Nicky's love for Danny Corvo would cause his personal problems to become distant. Danny offered him a possible solution to his very personal dilemma. Grateful for his words, Nicky could not let his closest and most trust-worthy friend go it alone. He persuaded himself to disobey his father and once again be an accomplice to murder.

CHAPTER 24

Nicky and Danny met at the home of Doberman breeder Max Saltzman. As crime rose in the South Bronx, the need for more trained security dogs at the Galliano salvage yard became a reality. Max was a forty-two-year-old man of formidable statute standing six foot five and weighing over three hundred and fifty pounds. Professional guard dog trainers considered this awkwardly-built man to be the premier dog trainer of New York.

Today would be Nicky Galliano's introduction to his newly purchased fourteen-month-old Dobermans. The two young females had undergone a year of perimeter control and attack-on-command training with the highly regarded Saltzman. The dogs were trained to respond to commands in German and Nicky had to master the six essential commands. Saltzman handed him a neatly printed index card containing the commands, sitz/sit... Bleib/stay... Platz/down... Hier/come... Fass/attack... GibLaut/bark.

The dogs were friendly, almost lovable, in the presence of their trainer, Max Saltzman. The introduction went well but now Nicky had to be tutored on personally handling the dogs in the absence of Saltzman. He would be required to work with his dogs three times a week for six weeks under the Saltzman's guidance. Possession of the dogs could not take place until the training was complete. It was dangerous.

In the front of Saltzman's house, the two men found four young boys engaged in a street fight. Nicky and Danny watched in amusement as two of the boys clumsily wrestled on the sidewalk. When the other two joined forces and started kicking the smaller of the two boys on the ground, it became apparent that this was a lop-sided battle of three against one. Nicky collared the two kickers as Danny pulled the two boys on the ground to their feet. The boys were released and instructed not to move.

Danny asked, "So what's with this three against one shit?"

The badly bruised smaller boy was wild with anger and had to be restrained. He made futile attempts to escape the powerful grasp of Danny Corvo. He shouted, "They told me to go fuck my dead mother. Let me go, I'm going to kill all of them."

Max Saltzman huffed his way to the front of his house and snatched the smaller boy by his shirt. With a heavy German accent he grumbled, "Thomas, what is wrong with you? All you do is fight; can't you get along with anyone?" Max's son, Thomas Saltzman, was eight years old. His mother and older brother had been killed in a car crash less than a year before. The foul comment about his deceased mother had released the hatred stored up inside him.

Danny's physical appearance stifled the aggression of the threesome as he threatened them into an apology. At the same time, Nicky steered Max away from his son, saying, "Thomas didn't do anything wrong. Those three punks told your son to 'go fuck his dead mother.' Give the kid a hug and let it go. If they come around again let one of the dogs bite their asses."

Four weeks of dog training at the Saltzman house passed. During that time Nicky befriended the lonely Thomas Saltzman. He was a sad and angry child, unable to understand the loss of his mother and older brother. Nicky's flamboyant personality proved to be medicinal therapy, a diversion for the youngster. Thomas accompanied Nicky and his wife to Yankee games, Rye Beach and the Galliano family restaurant. Unbeknown to the troubled Nicky Galliano, he too was benefiting from his newly formed friendship.

Every Wednesday, Phil Bruno worked in the city. Danny borrowed an inconspicuous station wagon from his grandfather and drove to Bruno's construction site in New Canaan, Connecticut. The house was framed and the roof shingled to protect the interior of the dwelling. The interior walls were insulated and the plumbing and electrical work had been completed. Phil Bruno proudly pinned the certificates of inspection on the entryway wall. His construction tools were safely locked in an over-sized heavy duty metal toolbox in the back yard of the house.

Mr. Bruno was going to be sent a message. The ex-Marine dowsed the floor with gasoline and ran a fifteen foot fuse line to the exterior of the house. He had a large manila envelope containing a photo of Phil Bruno and Gloria Nartico making out in the parking lot of the Whitestone Motel. The top of the home-made toolbox was flexible, allowing him to pry it up just enough to insert the envelope. He ignited the fuse, giving him two minutes to drive away. Exiting the thruway in Mount Vernon, he drove the station wagon to a self-operated car wash. He power-washed the under-carriage of the car and returned to Grandpa Joe's garage.

At eight o'clock that evening, Phil Bruno received a phone call from the New Canaan police department. He was told that his dream home had been burnt to the ground and they could not rule out arson. Later that night, Nicky Galliano, the master car thief, placed an identical envelope on the front seat of Phil Bruno's work truck. Attached to the photo was a sloppily written note that read, "End it while you can still walk and talk."

Building a second home, keeping a heavy workload in the Bronx and trying to please his young lover frazzled Phil Bruno's nerves. He paid cash for his New Canaan home-site and the building materials. In the absence of a bank loan, he had postponed purchasing insurance. His nerves were rattled as he attempted to find some peace in a night's sleep. There would be no sleep for Phil Bruno until his mind and body surrendered to exhaustion.

Phil and his wife rose early and they drove her Cadillac to the New Canaan home-site. The Police and Fire Department had placed yellow caution tape around the perimeter of the burnt-out structure. There was not a salvageable piece of building material to be found. He knew selling the land would recoup some of his money but in order to do so, the debris would have to be carted away, a very expensive proposition. He held his crying wife and said, "Someone had to torch this house. There is no way it could just go up in flames. I hope they catch the son-of-a-bitch. That's the only way I'll get any money back."

The seldom vocal Teresa became inquisitive and asked, "Didn't you take out insurance on this place?" Phil's face became the pale color of veal as he muttered, "No, it slipped my mind." All the money invested in this project belonged to Phil Bruno. Teresa, the faithful and loving wife, refrained from comment and drove home.

Teresa dropped her husband off at the yard where he stored his work truck. He planned on driving back to New Canaan where he could speak to the police and wench his valuable toolbox into the bed of his truck. The metal toolbox contained Bruno Construction's most expensive tools.

Phil was anxious; his nerves worn thin by the act of arson. He opened the truck door and placed the seemingly insignificant manila envelope on the dashboard. Absentmindedly he drove off without inquiry about the envelope's contents. The early September sun gleamed off the envelope, obstructing a clear view of the road. Phil removed it from the dashboard and impatiently flung it to the front seat. He was back at the job-site by eight thirty and loaded his toolbox into the bed of the truck.

As his eyes perused the burnt-out building, he became nauseous. He sipped his cold coffee and lit a cigarette as he opened the annoying envelope. He viewed the photo and read the harsh note. His hands became sweaty and his chest tightened. His heart throbbed through his chest cavity and he was unable to open the door fast enough to avoid vomiting on himself. He squeezed the steering wheel with both hands, screaming obscenities of fearful frustration.

Guilty and frightful, he forced the incriminating envelope under the truck's rug. The Police informed him that the Fire Marshall had determined that the fire was deliberately ignited by a large amount of gasoline—an act of arson. Phil exonerated himself from suspicion when he informed the Police that he did not have fire insurance.

Phil Bruno knew this fire was in retaliation for his affair with Gloria Nartico. His veil of secrecy had been pierced, but he remained bewildered by whom. He knew two things; one, the spiteful arsonist was elusive and smart. Two, he had to end his adulterous affair with Gloria.

Nicky Galliano praised Danny for his clever murder-free resolution of the Nartico problem. Phil Bruno warned a volatile Gloria Nartico that whoever torched his house and photographed them together also had the power to have them killed. By mid-September, the insidious Gloria manufactured a renewed appreciation of the life her husband provided to her and their daughter. She moved back home even as she secretly loathed Phil Bruno for being a spineless predator who took advantage of her self-induced depression. Hopelessly in love, Paulie accepted his wife's self-diagnosed medical condition as the reason for her recent behavior. He absolved her of any wrong-doing. He loved her too much to search or speculate beyond her proclaimed condition of depression.

Max Saltzman had given his son a young male Doberman as a companion dog. "Rocky" was a well-built Doberman but oversized beyond the accepted standard for the breed. Thomas persuaded his proud German father to train his dog through English commands. At eight months old, Rocky was well-trained but not neutered, a procedure many breeders frowned upon. Thomas was able to walk the fierce-looking Doberman without a leash. When people became intimidated by his presence, Thomas would command the dog to "heel." Rocky would immediately circle the boy and sit at attention on his left side.

The young Thomas named his dog Rocky after the famed movie about an underdog prize fighter. Rocky had no interest in fighting dogs and even tolerated their neighbor's pesky cat. However, the docile, unneutered young male was easily aroused by the presence of a female dog.

The Saltzman's neighbor had a young Collie that was in season. The well-trained Doberman became disobedient when his nostrils inhaled the scent of a female in heat. As Rocky crossed the street in hot pursuit of the female, a Lincoln

Continental Convertible came roaring over the slight incline of the road. Thomas screamed as the driver pushed the car faster. The dog was catapulted through the air as if shot out of a canon. The driver and passenger of the huge Lincoln Continental laughed without remorse as the dog's mangled dead body rolled into the on-coming lane. The menacing car came to a screeching halt, backed up a few feet and steered the car over the dog's lifeless body.

Instantly, the street became flush with inquisitive bystanders as Max Saltzman wrapped his son's dead companion into a towel. The mailman handed the distraught young boy a ripped piece of an envelope that read, 'BX263.' He said, "I'm sorry for what they did. There was no way to stop them but I wrote down the license plate. You should give it to your father."

The loss of his wife and eldest son restrained Max Saltzman from scolding the careless behavior of his only son. Thomas handed his father the paper given to him by the local mailman. Max snatched it abruptly and said, "Was ist das?" Thomas understood, "What is this?"

Nervously Thomas said, "The mailman gave it to me. It's the license plate number of the car that ran over Rocky." Then his temper flared as he grunted, "Those bastards should be put in the electric chair." Thomas's foul language ordinarily would have earned him a slap in the face. Realizing his inappropriate choice of words, he instinctively sheltered his face with raised hands expecting an inevitable slap, but a saddened Max Saltzman soberly controlled his emotions.

Max put his heavy arm around Thomas, holding him close. He spoke in a calm whisper saying, "We live in the city. The dog is supposed to be on a leash. I don't want us to get in trouble for letting the dog roam the streets without any restraint. The authorities will give us a fine and blame us for the dog's death. I don't think we should call anyone."

The young, ill-tempered Thomas disagreed with his pragmatic father but fearfully remained quiet. The broken-hearted youngster found comfort knowing Nicky Galliano was coming in a few days to take his newly-trained Dobermans home. Nicky's generosity cultivated a spirit of trust within the young Thomas. Surely Nicky Galliano would have an opinion that challenged his father's passive logic.

When Nicky came, he embraced the sobbing boy as he cautiously listened to his dramatic account of Rocky's slaughter. Thomas told Nicky that the driver had stopped the car and deliberately ran over the dog for a second time. Nicky seethed with anger as he curtly asked, "Where is your father?" The brooding young boy led him to the kennel where his father was feeding his prized dogs.

Max was pleased to see his affluent, well-paying client. "Nicky, so nice to see you," he said. Nicky's face was stoic as he sourly answered, "Max, send Thomas inside. We have to talk." Max gave an abrupt command with his chunky index finger. A disappointed Thomas begrudgingly shuffled his way into the house.

The large, bulky Max Saltzman knew the Galliano family wielded great power and he became intimidated by Nicky's tone. Without hesitation Nicky asked, "Is it true that someone ran over the kid's dog on purpose?"

Max gave pause to speaking as he searched for a reply. Nicky made a hand gesture that demanded an answer. Max opened his wallet and withdrew the paper containing the license plate number of the car. He handed the crumpled paper to Nicky, as he quickly answered, "I didn't see what happened but that's what Thomas told me. The mailman gave us this paper with the license plate number on it. I didn't report it because the dog did not have a leash, and we were in violation of the city ordinance."

Nicky was a master of facial deception. Disgusted by the master breeder's logic, he cleverly nodded his head implying that he understood his concern as he stuffed the paper in his shirt pocket. His face lost all expression of anger as he soothingly said, "Okay Max, I understand. By the way, I wanted to ask you if my wife and I could take Thomas to game three of the World Series. It's being played on Tuesday night, October nineteenth. We will pick him up and bring him home."

Max was relieved that the canine interrogation had ended. He was all smiles as he briskly answered, "How can I deny him from going to the World Series? Of course he can go. I want you to know that I am appreciative of your kindness. Thank you." Nicky put his two trained Dobermans in the rear seat of his car and drove home to Riverdale.

CHAPTER 25

Young Thomas Saltzman was disappointed watching The Bronx Bombers lose game three of the 1976 World Series 6 - 2 to the Big Red Machine from Cincinnati. Nicky Galliano menacingly ruffled the youngster's hair as he gently sang, "Look what we have for Thursday night. More tickets to watch our loser Yankees. I'll ask your pop if you can come when I take you home." The sudden surprise muted the teary-eyed youngster as he exchanged hugs with Nicky and Sonia Galliano. Unfortunately, the Yankees lost game four as well, 7-2, as the Cincinnati Reds swept the World Series. But a close bond of friendship was formed between the three Yankee fans.

The Nartico-Bruno holiday dinners would prove to be freakishly eerie as Phil and Gloria struggled to conceal their disdain for one another. Phil avoided eye contact with his rabid daughter-in-law as he devoured Teresa's home-made ravioli. Phil Bruno could feel his chest tighten as a smirking Gloria asked, "Any leads on who set the fire?"

Teresa responded, "No, not yet. They're a bunch of Connecticut hicks and don't know their ass from their elbow.

They'll never catch anyone, it's a lost cause. We have to accept it and move on. Right, Honey?"

Phil briefly raised his perspiring brow and said, "I hate to say it but you're probably right." Gloria was pleased; she lusted for Phil Bruno to suffer in every way possible. Losing half of his money was a good start.

Gus Galliano perused the financial section of the New York Times, analyzing the value of his extensive stock portfolio. Printed to the right of the S&P 500 were the names of the law students who had recently passed the New York State Bar Exam. His eyes slowly navigated down the alphabetically listed names until they settled on Daniello J. Corvo, Bronx, New York. Gus felt exalted and called his wife on her private number. Victoria answered, "G and G construction, this is Victoria. How can I help you?" She heard the robust laugh of her jubilant husband as he loudly said, "Danny passed the bar exam on the first try. I just read it in the New York Times. Make sure you tell Dee and call Nicky. Oh, and plan on a celebration dinner. This is big."

Judge Bennett was handsomely paid to list Daniello Corvo's name as a paralegal in his law firm. The firm's subtle alteration of their records validated Corvo's tenure began two years prior to his passing the bar exam. He could now practice law in New York State.

Nicky made travel arrangements to take his wife on vacation to Italy where he planned on sharing his medical misfortune. But before their departure he understood his father had to be the first to know.

Gus's eyes became tear filled as he listened to his son painfully explain his medical dilemma. All his power, political connections, and great wealth could not change or provide a solution to his son's misfortune. He rose from his chair, placing his hands around his son's sullen face. He calmly whispered, "Never believe just one Doctor. They are not infallible. I want you to go on vacation, and when you come home, I'll have the name of the best doctor in New York City. I'll tell your mother when I think the time is right, but of course it will have to be before you come home. Make love to your beautiful wife, eat that great food and drink plenty of wine. It's not the end of the world." He kissed his son farewell. Later, alone in his study, the powerful Gus Galliano wept in quiet solitude.

After speaking to his father, Nicky felt a reassurance of hope. His wise father and his closest ally, Danny Corvo, gave him identical advice. He glowed with hope, believing both of them could not be wrong.

After spending a week in Northern Italy, Nicky and Sonia flew to Catania, Sicily. They spent a week in the Villa of his Grandma Savoca's nephew, his father's first cousin, Roberto. It would be at this romantic Sicilian Villa that his wife would be told of his infertility. Sonia was not a fragile woman but Nicky feared this terrible news could unseat her high-strung temperament.

An emotional Sonia brooded as she digested his every word. Seated on their bed, she drew her knees to her chest and wept. Nicky wrapped her in his sleek, well-developed arms as she burrowed her head to his chest. In a few moments she was composed. She held both of her husband's hands as she soothingly said, "We love each other so it's only natural that we want children. But I love you no matter what. Remember our wedding vows, for better or worse. As long as I have you, there is nothing else in this world I need."

The people operating his salvage yard could not get hired without passing his father's litmus test. They were old school hard-working Italians who respected and sometimes feared the Galliano family. His return to America would be without incident as business continued to profit.

Nicky and Sonia were invited to the Corvo's for dinner. Sonia purchased Linzer tarts and Apple strudel to please Delia and Abby's German-oriented palate. They had purchased a bronze statue of a Doberman for Thomas while in Berlin and stopped at the Saltzman house located five minutes from the Corvo's.

The darkened house was wrapped in yellow caution tape. The bold, hand-carved front door was padlocked. Brightly printed "do not enter" plaques were displayed on every corner of the building. The kennels were empty. All the finely bred Dobermans had been removed from the premises.

The Gallianos had visited the young Thomas and his father a few days before departing for Italy. But while they were gone something extraordinarily freakish had happened. Nicky made his way to the poorly lit front door of the neighbor's house and rang the bell. A short, elderly Italian widow dressed all in black waddled to the front door like a pudgy crow. She answered in broken English. Nicky's ability to speak some Italian and hand signals gave him a clear understanding of what happened to the Saltzmans. Two days after his departure for Italy, Max Saltzman had dropped dead from a massive heart attack at the dinner table. In the absence of relatives in America, the district family court judge ordered Thomas Saltzman relocated to the Mount Loretto Home for Boys on Staten Island. The Police contacted animal control and the dogs were placed in a State-run kennel.

The pleasant dinner at the Corvo's was transformed into a brain-storming strategy. Nicky had his mother Victoria call Bishop Pestoni, who influenced Mount Loretto to release

Thomas Saltzman to the temporary foster care of Nicholas Galliano and his wife. Congressman Morano wielded his power and satisfied the requirements of the family court, obtaining temporary custody. The young counselor, Danny Corvo, obtained the necessary paperwork to probate Max Saltzman's will.

The orphan children at Mount Loretto were notoriously hostile toward new arrivals. Thomas had deep multiple burn marks on his stomach and buttocks from being forcibly held against the hot cast-iron radiators. His left eye was puffed up and his lip was split, impeding his speech.

Nicky and Sonia boarded the ferry to Staten Island. When they arrived at Mount Loretto the administrator, Sister Judith, had them sign the necessary paperwork for Thomas's release. She led them to the cafeteria where breakfast was being served. The Gallianos waited in the hall as the Nun instructed. Sister Judith held the frightened youngster by the hand saying, "Thomas, a very nice man and his wife want to take you out of here. They want you to go home with them."

The young Thomas was untrusting of strangers. When Sister Judith opened the door to the hallway, the Gallianos were in plain sight. The youngster's face glowed as he galloped toward them with open arms. Nicky crouched down to embrace the sobbing, hysterical child. A teary-eyed Sonia fell to her knees to join them. Thomas stammered out a prim salutation before crying out, "I don't have a mommy. I don't have a daddy, not even a brother. I don't have anyone, not even Rocky. I just want to die." All the rigid toughness Nicky Galliano possessed eroded in that single moment. He sternly shook the boy by his narrow shoulders earning his attention. He thrust his face closer bellowing, "You're not alone. You will never be alone. You have me and Sonia. We love you and we'll take care of you." A surprised Sonia raised her eyebrows in delight.

The addition to the Galliano's Riverdale guest house was near completion. The completed guest house was to be great in size. Each of the five bedrooms had a full bath and three had an expansive view of the Hudson River. Gus and Victoria wanted their son and daughter-in-law to live within the confines of their well-protected estate.

Nicky's fondness for the Saltzman boy, added to his chagrin about being unable to father a child. Depressed and irritated, he followed his closest friend's advice and sought the professional guidance and recommendations of a Manhattan specialist. Doctor Sagani's diagnosis was a well-accepted surprise. His recommendation would excite any man with a pulse. "Mr. Galliano, it's all about timing. Your condition is not as severe as you were led to believe, or perhaps may have understood. I want you to make an appointment to come back here with your wife in six weeks. During that time, you must have your wife record her cycle, and most importantly, you must make love to her as often as humanly possible. I believe that in the next year you'll have a little one calling you Daddy," he boastfully said.

The beautiful young Sonia was jubilant, but sworn to secrecy. The anxious couple agreed never to discuss the promising diagnosis of Doctor Sagani until Sonia became pregnant. If she never became pregnant there would be nothing to say.

Saving Nicky Galliano's life led to Danny Corvo becoming a rich young man. The Company's reputation for quality workmanship and schedule adherence created a great demand. Danny's debut into the political arena earned his trusted friend and former Marine Corporal Rodrigues a share of the business. In return, the very capable Rodrigues would be required to replace Danny at the helm. The young attorney could now practice law and enter the political arena. Against all his core beliefs, he took the advice of Congressman Morano and joined the Democrat Party. A congressional district seat was up for grabs in less than two years. Corvo had the money and very rich and powerful backers.

Gus invited Danny to join him for lunch at his Little Italy restaurant, proudly approving his passing of the bar exam. When the feast ended they made their way to the private office on the second floor. Almost immediately, Gus's radiant expression of pride became concern. He removed his suit jacket and placed it on the back of his desk chair. Danny followed his cue, as both men loosened their ties.

Gus's face morphed into a subtle smile as he said, "Danny you're probably the most complicated person I've ever known. You are tough to a fault sometimes, but I admire that quality in a man. I know Nicky confided in you about his medical problem. I can't let on how much it's breaking my heart, so I have to suck it up. At my age a man can only see the brightness of the future through the eyes of his grandchildren. In the absence of grandchildren, a man my age can only see the darkness of the end. That's why I'm glad they decided to take in the Saltzman kid; it will keep their minds occupied.

"Anyway, that's enough of the drama, and not why I asked you to stop by. According to Morano, the Congressional seat coming up for grabs is in the district where you live. We've already discussed all your favorability's but I think it's time for you to get some exposure. The sooner the better."

Gus seated himself as he waited for the newly confirmed attorney's reaction. Danny exhaled, exclaiming, "That's a lot to address and your question is two-fold. I know you appreciate short answers so here it is. First, Thomas is the most lovable little boy you'll ever find, and he's got a huge set of balls. I've learned that you can teach a kid almost anything, but you can't give him courage. He either has it or he doesn't. I think Nicky and Sonia should seriously think about adopting him. I know it's a big decision but that's what I think. Secondly, when I passed the bar exam, I got a call from the Johnny Carson show. They want me to make a guest appearance. How's that for timing?"

Gus sprung out of his chair whisking Danny up into his arms. They embraced and exchanged a traditional Sicilian kiss on the cheek.

They re-seated themselves as Gus's face suddenly became unsmiling and humorless. He sternly said, "All my life I had to pay-off these elected big-wigs to buy protection from them and their magistrates of the public office." His elbow rested on the armchair as his fingers massaged his forehead as if searching for his next words. Abruptly he shoved his laughing face closer to Danny's, grasping him by the wrist, as he cried out, "Imagine the day when we bribe ourselves because we are the 'grandi parrucche' big-wigs!"

Danny was unmoved by Gus's vision of the future. He had become a Galliano by proxy. There were undistinguishable commonalities between Gus and the young Marine. Both men were well educated, financially successful, untrusting, revengeful murderers who sought everything life had to offer. Notwithstanding those similarities, Danny Corvo was adored by the media as a war hero who had survived plunging a hundred feet into the murky, snake-infested waters of Viet Nam and the hellish Hanoi Hilton. He had earned an engineering degree, a pilot license, ran a very profitable business and against all odds passed the bar exam on the first attempt without attending one minute of law school. Gus Galliano owned the most successful excavation enterprise in the tristate area. He invested wisely in the restaurant and hotel business. His wife's orphan fund had raised millions of dollars, earning her a symbolic halo within the hierarchy of the Catholic Church. The magistrates of New York had amassed great sums of money from their association with Gus Galliano and were in his debt.

Danny knew as a politician, he too would become one of the 'quid pro quo' this for that society. He was held in high esteem as the educated, successful war hero of the media, a perfect candidate. Gus Galliano was a man of power and great wealth. He was the only man who had the capacity to direct both the lawful and unlawful power brokers of New York, a perfect sponsor.

CHAPTER 26

A t eleven am on March 11th Delia Corvo was taken by
ambulance to Albert Einstein Hospital. Home alone,
her water had broken, accompanied by severe con-
tractions. Danny was representing a client in the Brooklyn
Criminal Court while Abagail, her sixteen-year-old daughter,
was in school. By three o'clock that afternoon Delia Corvo had
given birth to her third son. The Corvo triplets each weighed
a healthy five pounds. She found the strength to give the
attending nurse her father Nelson's phone number. Delighted
and excited, the dumbfounded grandfather of triplets labored
to find the phone numbers of his family members. He called
the Bennett law office requesting that Mr. Corvo call him.

At four o'clock, a worried and anxious Nelson Hoffman
answered Danny's call. Danny asked, "What's going on, Pop.
Is everything alright?" A nervous Nelson stammered, "Great,
everything is great. Remember at Thanksgiving dinner you
told Dee that you wanted to have at least three sons. Well my
boy, you got 'em." The news tongue-tied the gifted, well-spo-

ken attorney as he became momentarily unresponsive. Breathing heavily, he grunted, "I got them? I got what?"

Nelson snickered as he blurted, "Dee had triplets and they're all boys. Five pounds each and Delia and the babies are all doing fine."

Three days later Delia and her needy triplets were home. Victoria summoned the help of Bishop Pestoni in finding a suitable Nanny to assist the young, very busy mother. Delia chose a middle-aged Italian woman named Rosa La Rocca. She was short and plump but had an angelic face, a perennial smile, and a soft, velvety voice. Danny gave her the guest apartment with the stipulation that in lieu of rent, she would be on call twenty four hours a day.

The Corvos named their first son, Joseph, after his Grandfather and older brother Joe, who was the designated Godfather. They chose Sam for the second boy, honoring his deceased father and twin brother. Nelson Hoffman begged his daughter not to name the third boy Nelson, a name he'd loathed since childhood. Danny thought it was only fair that Delia make the decision to name the last of their boys. Delia glowed with pride as she motioned for her husband to sit beside her. She held his hand and whispered, "I am so grateful for all the blessings we have. I want to name him Gustavo, and I want Nicky and Sonia to be his Godparents."

Danny nodded approvingly saying, "Good idea. Maybe you should be the politician?" She smiled sparingly, not fully understanding the humor in his suggestion.

Gus and Victoria observed closely as their son, Nicky, known for his cold and callous demeanor, suddenly melted in the embrace of Thomas Saltzman. Sonia stared at the boy with glittering admiration saying, "Thomas, you better come here and share some of those hugs with me." He smiled in a coy way, receiving her embrace with open arms. Victoria and Gus became pleased about their son's affection for the orphaned boy. Under the cover of the bold dining table, Gus and Victoria secretly held hands, fully aware that this child might be the closest they would ever come to having a grandchild.

Thomas's ill-fated experience at the Mount Loretto orphanage had fostered a keen appreciation for the Galliano's affection. He had watched his family evaporate before his eyes, yet somehow he could slowly feel the loneliness subside.

The Christening of the Corvo triplets was celebrated in the Pine Tavern Restaurant. The owners were Corvo family friends and they agreed to close the restaurant to the public. Nicky and Sonia introduced Thomas Saltzman to the guests as their Godson. Victoria dressed him in a dandified fashion with a tailor-made Hickey-Freeman dark blue pin-striped suit. The very grateful orphan slowly approached Gus and Victoria. His eyes blinked nervously as he said, "Everyone keeps telling me I'm the best-dressed guy in the place." His eyes became flush with tears as he shimmed his slim body between them. He nervously asked, "Could you please tell me what I should call you? I'm too little to call you Mr. or Mrs. Galliano. I asked Sonia but she told me to ask you."

Victoria glanced at her husband. Gus made a hand gesture insinuating that it was her question to answer. She placed the boy's hands into hers softly saying, "Well, Thomas Gus is Nicky's Pa and I'm his Ma. And since our last name starts with a G, how about you call my husband G-Pa and you can call me G-Ma."

Thomas smiled approvingly saying, "That's great and easy to remember."

Gus's private limo drove the four Galliano's and Thomas to the Riverdale Estate. Nicky and his father retreated to the privacy of the study. Gus, a man of great practical dimension, became concerned that his son's inability to have children had driven him to Thomas –like a small tack to a giant magnet. He soberly and with sincere empathy explained his concerns. Nicky became despondent as he muttered, "I thought you would be proud of me. The only outsider this family ever let in was Danny and that was only because he saved my life. Not trusting anyone is inbred into the fabric of every Galliano, and now Danny has it by his association with us! I tease him that he's more Galliano than Corvo and sadly he agrees. You and mom love him as much as you love me and you know it. I never became envious because Danny and I both feel that we're brothers. I remember when we all thought he was killed in Viet Nam both of you cried as much as you did when Tommy was killed."

Nicky had retreated to the restroom as he mentally rehearsed the words he needed his father to hear. Confident he had chosen the right words he curtly said, "Now let me tell you a little something about this kid. When Thomas was being beaten by those three kids, Danny and I couldn't get over the kid's courage. What a set of balls he had; his face bleeding, kicked in ribs and he still never took a step backwards. He's like a little Danny! I need your blessing, Dad I'm not sending that boy back to any orphanage."

Gus walked to the bar and poured brandy into two long-stemmed glasses. He sat closer to his son and gave him one. His facial expression was blank, unreadable as he said, "All my life I tried to be careful, and that's all I was trying to do, but your answer made me cave emotionally. The point you make is undisputable. Your mother and I love Danny as much as any parent loves a son, so how can I find fault in you and Sonia loving Thomas? Son, I am proud of you and Sonia. You have my blessing and all my support. I just wanted to make sure you thought it through, and I can see that you did. You have a lot of work ahead of you. After Danny probates the will I suggest you sell the house and put the assets into a trust. We have room in the kennel for the dogs so that's not a problem, but you have to promise me one thing."

Reassured, Nicky gazed at his father lovingly saying, "Sure Dad, what is it?"

Gus snapped, "For your mother's sake the kid has to become a Catholic. I suggest you enroll him in Saint Gabriel's where your saintly mother has friends of influence."

Nicky laughed loudly saying, "That's exactly what Sonia said."

As Gus attempted to rise from his chair, Nicky placed his hand on his knee, interrupting his accent. He said, "Dad, can we talk a little longer? I have something to share with you and then I need some advice."

Gus re-settled in the chair and motioned for his son to start speaking. Nicky cleared his throat for clarity. "Well, Dad, the specialist has turned Sonia and me into a pair of bunnies. He gave both of us medication and wants her to monitor her cycle while we do the boom-boom as often as possible. He says it's possible for her to get pregnant. I didn't want to give you and mom false hope but I didn't want the both of you to be depressed either."

Gus Galliano's eyes gathered tears as he inhaled deeply, attempting to compose his emotions. His voice crackled with excitement as he said, "Son, that's the best news I have ever heard. Do you want me to tell your mother or do you want to?"

Nicky softly answered, "You tell her, Dad. Just make sure she understands there are no guarantees."

Gus's face became glum as he nodded indicating that he understood. He asked, "What kind of advice do you need?"

Nicky retrieved the small piece of paper from his wallet containing the license plate number, BX263, and handed it to his father. He said, "That's the number of the car that ran over Thomas's dog. The mailman saw the whole thing and gave it to the kid. His father refused to call the cops because the dog wasn't on a leash and he feared getting into trouble. Danny interrogated the mailman who swore they intentionally killed the dog. After the dog was hit, they stopped the car and ran him over a second time, laughing at every turn of the tires. I could have asked Ryan myself, but I wanted your permission."

Gus glanced at his watch saying sternly, "We have to get back upstairs. When I have the information, the three of us will talk."

Nicky inquired, "The three of us?"

Gus answered sarcastically, "Yes the three of us, the father, the son and your loyal accomplice, The Lawyer."

Detective Ryan retrieved the required information on BX263 through a simple phone call to his colleagues in the 43rd Precinct. The 1970 yellow, Lincoln Continental Convertible was registered to a James Lockhart, residing at 1946 Bronxdale Avenue, apartment 3G.

Gus was remiss in sharing the information with his son. He ordered Ryan to do a background check so he could accurately assess the wild behavior of James Lockhart. Gus was not a man to sentence someone for committing an act that did not affect his family or business, but it was becoming clear that Thomas was going to become his grandson.

The three men met in Gus's well-guarded office above the restaurant. As he read the name Lockhart, Danny's faced became flush as he angrily proclaimed, "I know that asshole, and now I can tell you that his accomplice was a guy named Shady O'Shea."

Gus abruptly interrupted saying, "That's why I have so much faith in Ryan. He's got that O'Shea name in this report." He apologized for his momentary intrusion, gesturing for Danny to continue.

Danny remained livid as he told the account of the Old Italian man at KFC whose dignity was deeply injured by Lockhart and O'Shea. The narrative of the degrading treatment of the black college kid caused Nicky to uncomfortably squirm in his seat.

But Gus was emotionally unmoved by the malady of the elderly KFC employee and the young college kid. They were strangers, and he was not desirous of becoming a heroic vigilante. Still, the insightful father was well-aware that the two angry boys seated before him sought revenge. His face lacked expression. Absolved of emotion he said dryly, "These two deserve to be punished for killing the kid's dog, I'll grant you that. But I'm going to say it again and again and again until both of you understand. There is a lot at stake here and you two have to stay clean. Danny, you're a lawyer for God's sake."

Gus rose and positioned his chair closer to his son as a glimpse of a smile mellowed the tense conversation. His looked at his son as he gently said, "It didn't take long for your mother to grow fond of Thomas. She would probably want the two punks killed, but I think that's too severe for the injustice they committed. I'm going to meet with Tony Pimples and direct him to punish them but not kill them. You two stay out of it. Case closed."

Nicky shared his knowledge of 'Tony Pimples' with the overly inquisitive Corvo. His real name was Anthony Capobianco which in English means white head. In the Bronx, white head translates into pimple, ergo 'Tony Pimples.' A brilliant but ill-tempered medical student, Capobianco was expelled for publicly spitting in his Professor's face and punching his front teeth loose. He possessed a large supply of black market medical supplies and pain killers. The expulsion shamed him, pilfering any chance of rising in society. Instead, he became a soulless diabolical enforcer who savored using medieval methods to punish the enemies of his boss. He cut off and froze the index fingers and thumbs of criminals he killed. He would thaw them before a hit, leaving the prints of a dead man on the murder weapon. The clueless cops searched aimlessly for a suspect that no longer existed.

His father's strategy satisfied Nicky's lust for vengeance. A skeptical Danny remained puzzled about the expertise of Capobianco. His disdain for Lockhart and O'Shea sharply increased, like a metastatic tumor, after they deliberately killed the dog. In a state of choleric anger he asked, "So, what do you think Mr. Pimples will do to them?" Nicky was well-versed on the sardonic expertise of Capobianco. His deep dark eyes glittered with delight as he gleefully answered, "Your guess is as good as mine, but let me tell you a little story. Capobianco drugged the rapist of a twelve-year-old girl, inducing a deep coma. When he awakened, his testicles were gone and his penis was neatly replaced by a catheter. He skillfully cauterized the incisions so the bastard wouldn't bleed to death. Capobianco insists on knowing the circumstances that leads to an assignment. He then carefully calculates the punishment of his target based on the offense committed. I wouldn't want to wake up tomorrow morning being Junior Lockhart!"

After the birth of the triplets, Danny's insistence that his wife own a firearm intensified. He would no longer condone his family being unprotected in his brief intervals of absence. Corvo Construction records listed Delia Corvo as the Secretary. Fictitiously, she had the sole responsibility of depositing large sums of cash into the Company bank. After she was trained by Christopher Chan, a licensed NYS firearm instructor, a full-carry permit was issued in her name.

Junior Lockhart and his accomplice, O'Shea, rarely missed the four a.m. last call for alcohol in the Wall Bar. Capobianco digested every heinous detail of the Lockhart and O'Shea offences. His dutiful assistant purchased the necessary ingredients to execute the punishment, always leaving Capobianco under a veil of presumed innocence.

Tony Capobianco occasionally refused an assignment from a boss but never refused an assignment from the fabled Gus Galliano. Unlike Gus, he was angered by Lockhart and O'Shea's conduct toward the elderly Italian from KFC. His Italian father was a low level janitor who died working three jobs trying to feed a family of nine. From the pronunciation of their last names, Capobianco sensed Lockhart and O'Shea were anti-Italian, an unforgivable sin without possible contrition. He mercilessly devised a punishment that would have them welcome death.

Wally Coleman was an impressively large professional heavyweight sparring partner trained in the art of torture by the only white man he ever trusted—Tony Pimples. No one knew or understood how this confederate bond began. It was rumored that Coleman was being beaten by a group of Hell's Kitchen Irishmen when Capobianco stopped his car and opened fire, causing them to scatter like a panicked flock of frightened pigeons sighting a hawk. A stunned but grateful Coleman jumped into the rear seat of the car, rescued from his own peril. Capobianco's bravado impressed Coleman and a bond of trust was formed.

Dressed in insulated hunting gear, the frigid early morning January air stung only the faces of the lurching Wally

Coleman and Tony Pimples. Their windowless commercial van was parked bumper to bumper with Lockhart's Lincoln, interrupting any attempted departure. Lockhart and O'Shea were the last patrons to leave the Wall Bar, a well-rehearsed habit. With their supporting arms around each other the drunken duo staggered toward the Lincoln like a pair of young lovers laughing at nothing. Lockhart slurred, "Hey Shady, check this asshole out. He parked on my fucking bumper. Go see if any of the doors are open."

The drunken O'Shea gingerly made his way to the front door of the van, blowing warm air into his gloveless hands. As the intentionally unlocked driver's door opened a gleeful Shady cried out, "Bingo, it's open." Lockhart was startled as he listened to the cold engine labor to start. In a voice of jubilant laughter Shady screamed, "The assholes left the keys. Get in; we'll have some fun and burn this bitch."

A scantily-dressed Lockhart made his way to the passenger side of the van. He boldly commanded, "Give me a cigarette and let this cold bitch run its cold like a mother fucker." Unexpectedly both doors of the van opened in perfect harmony as the drunken duo felt the cold steel barrels of 45 caliber revolvers pressing against their unsuspecting heads.

Coleman whispered, "If you speak, we will kill both of you. Put your hands behind your back and put your head on your knees." Raped of their bravado, the two drunks lowered their heads. Instantly Coleman and Pimples plunged the coma inducing needles into their necks. Lockhart and O'Shea slumped over before being moved to the rear of the oversized van.

Capobianco drove the van to an industrial garage owned by a friend. The studious Coleman watched with great anticipation as the Master Capobianco opened his black rounded medical bag. Cautious to a fault, he injected their knees with the most potent pain killer. The wide eyed Coleman observed intently as Capobianco preached, "You can never be too careful. I gave them enough shit to keep them unconscious for ten hours but everyone is different, so I'm giving them a local dose of mega pain killer. Hell, we can amputate their fucking legs and they won't even twinge."

Coleman thought, "Now that would be cool. Strap off their legs to impede the blood flow, then amputate from the knee down and cauterize them; appropriate payback for the shameful abuse of the black college kid."

Coleman understood his place. Whatever fate was in store for the two comatose subjects was Capobianco's call. They dragged the comatose bodies to the rear of the van, shedding them of all clothing. Coleman was instructed to position a rolling metal welder's table at the base of their feet. Both stiffened bodies were pulled to the rear of the van. Their upper torso remained in the van and their four legs were neatly placed on the top of the cold metal table. Coleman grinned as he sensed the infliction of their sentence was near.

Capobianco walked to the side of the van and opened the sliding door. He motioned to Coleman that it was time to load the ten sandbags behind the front seats. Capobianco's freshly lit cigarette dangled from his lips leaving his hands free to wheel the twin acetylene torches closer to his assignment. He and Coleman put on industrial grade respirators. As Capobianco fumbled with the attachment of the respirator he muttered, "Wally, make sure it's on right. This isn't going to smell like no Tennessee barbeque!"

Capobianco lit the torch as he carefully adjusted the flame to reach maximum heat. His eyes blazed with concentration as he slowly inflicted third degree burns to the bottom of their feet. Slowly he passed the intensely heated torch over the shins until the skin became blackened and charred. Stopping at the knees he summoned Coleman to rotate the bodies as he administered the intense heat through the dermis of the skin, assuring it would affect deeper tissue. Capobianco's torture of these men became personal because of the Old Italian. He believed the only thing better than pain for the bullying duo was more pain, as he poured boxes of table salt onto the blackened, blistering skin.

The stench of the burnt skin and tissue seeped into their nasal passages, by-passing the protection of the industrial grade respirators. Hurriedly, they pulled the face down bodies into the van, concealing their naked presence with welder's blankets. The cold January air helped mask the stench of the charred limbs. Coleman, a fierce opponent of smoking tobacco, welcomed the aroma of Capobianco's freshly lit cigarette. The poorly lit van illuminated at every puff of Tony's cigarette. Coleman was in admiration of the frightening blank calmness in his partner's face, as if they had just returned from the cinema. He hoped that one day; he too, would acquire that extreme level of cool professionalism.

Coleman loudly slapped his hands together, gaining him a glance of disapproval from the slightly startled Capobianco. Coleman's hands gestured in a mockingly Italian fashion as he said, "Tony, what kind of an Italian are you? No pepper, no oregano, no basilica and you even burned the meat!" Tony returned a hand wave of indifference and drove to Orchard Beach.

Capobianco cautiously circled the one mile perimeter of the beach parking lot searching for young lovers and patrolling NYPD. A cold weekday night left the lot empty of pesky witnesses. Lockhart and O'Shea were pulled from the van and placed in a pile of leaves at the outskirts of the parking lot. A bag of KFC chicken and Martin Luther King's book, *I Have a Dream*, were placed in their right hands. A dog collar had been attached to Lockhart's neck. The flattened warm sandbags were strategically placed over their nude bodies to prevent hypothermia. The two men drove to the Tremont Avenue diner. Capobianco used the public phone to call a street phone in Brooklyn. He said curtly, "Make the call." The untraceable messenger called the Police and reported the location of the comatose bodies. Capobianco was fearful his subjects would freeze to death. But he was too smart to violate Gus's instructions.

CHAPTER 27

Nicky and Sonia Galliano navigated through the legal roadblocks of the New York State adoption laws. After paying officials and attorneys vast sums of money, Thomas Saltzman became a Galliano. His plea to keep Saltzman as his middle name was granted by his sympathetic adoptive parents.

On January 6, 1978, New York's Italian Americans watched their heroic Marine turned Attorney with great pride as he entered the infamous stage of the Johnny Carson show. His legendary steel blue eyes were highlighted under a canopy of well-trimmed, satiny dark hair. The impossibly good-looking Corvo was dressed in a dark blue Burnello-Cucinelli suit. As pre-rehearsed Danny Corvo seized this widely televised broadcast to announce his candidacy for the United States Congress.

Johnny Carson was an openly vocal admirer of the heroic Marine. The master entertainer spewed out a tirade of political jokes highlighting the many faults of the incumbents. When the audience became subdued, a serious-faced Carson bluntly asked, "So, you are a war hero, successful businessman, a pilot, a lawyer and the father of triplets. Why on God's good earth would you ever want to become a politician?" The audience was hushed by the sincerity of the question as they waited for a response.

Danny nodded his head as his facial expression indicated that he appreciated the concern of his inquiry. He stared at Carson, and then quickly pivoted to the camera as trained. He spoke slowly deliberately annunciating every syllable of his reply saying, "All neighborhoods are made up of three groups of people, the young, the old and those in the middle. I want to work for all of my neighbors and I'll be demanding. I'll demand the young get the best education possible by reducing class size and rewarding our very often unappreciated teachers. The elderly have to be provided with every medical supply and solution possible. This is the United States of America, the greatest country in the history of the world, and I'll demand our seniors get all they need." The Carson audience suddenly rose like helium-filled hot air balloons as they exploded into applause. Johnny and Danny endured the cheering and chanting until the enthusiasm feathered back into silence. Danny raised his clinched fist in appreciation as he somberly continued, "The people in the middle are the vast majority and they need jobs that pay a fair wage. These workers have to see the huge bright light at the end of the tunnel called retirement. No one should have to work until they die."

Gus was pleased listening to his symbolic son, as he cleverly hypnotized the New York electorate. New York's journalist canonized the clever young candidate. Finally, they had a Democrat who spoke directly to the needs and dreams of the people.

Two weeks later a New York Times poll showed the predominately Irish-German district had the novice politician comfortably ahead. The educated Gus Galliano did not have any faith in political polls. While in college he'd studied Joseph Stalin and believed his theory of winning an election was infallible. Stalin said, "The people who cast the votes don't decide an election—it's those who count the votes that do."

Gus instructed his loyal childhood friend Benny Longo to drive a G&G box truck to the Perfection Ballot Box Company in Worcester Massachusetts. The truck's cargo of seasoned, kiln-dried cherry planking would be unloaded and replaced with fully assembled New York State official ballot boxes. These boxes would be stuffed with Corvo ballots and covertly replace boxes in heavily populated Republican precincts of the district. At the close of the election, the ballot boxes were taken to a centralized tallying station. The switched ballot boxes tilted the results for the candidate of choice. The loyal Galliano ally Congressman Morano had been a beneficiary of this illegal maneuver during his re-election bid. In this instance, it no longer mattered who counted the votes.

The Jacobi Hospital emergency staff labored diligently to save the lives of the frozen, near-death Lockhart and O'Shea. The blood flow to Lockhart's extremities was painfully halted, causing the tissue to die. After a week in the intensive care unit, his severely infected right leg was amputated below the right knee. The visible signs of vengeance were grasped in their frost-bitten hands and strangled any desire for revenge. They would live the rest of their lives knowing why but never knowing who.

Danny Corvo campaigned with the robust sturdiness of an undefeatable foe. His eye-pleasing wife and children presented themselves as neighbors of the voters as they accompanied him, shaking hands at supermarkets and local businesses. Two cars patrolled the district seven days a week; their mega-phones blasting praise to the people's candidate, Danny Corvo. The Galliano family made one phone call and the handsome candidate dressed in formal Marine attire occupied every billboard in the district. His opponent was being played like a one-string fiddle. A Congressman Corvo was a necessary ingredient to secretly initiate the Galliano master plan of becoming an American dynasty.

At ten p.m. on November 7, 1978, Danny Corvo, accompanied by his family and close supporters, listened to James Bonner's speech accepting defeat in the Congressional election. The seasoned congressman congratulated the heroic Marine-turned-entrepreneur on his win.

Gus Galliano was pleased but found no reason to celebrate the outcome of an election result he already knew. Danny Corvo had become a son with a different sir-name and the Governorship was now within his reach. A corner stone of the Galliano Dynasty had been neatly set in place–.

Made in the USA
Middletown, DE
13 November 2020